THE WRITER

8/10/02.

Be happy & keep GOD
first in all things.

Adam

THE WRITER

Big Adam

9-BLYT

To order additional copies of this book, contact:
Xlibris Corporation
1-888-7-XLIBRIS
www.Xlibris.com
Orders@Xlibris.com

CONTENTS

For Joe LePage, who made my heart go on...and the guys in
Zeta Eta Theta and the girls in Alpha Alpha Alpha...and my
two best friends, Jason and Michael, who are my treasure in life

CHAPTER ONE

The sun was setting, and the sky flamed bright orange.

His friend Joey was supposed to come by the house for a few minutes this evening and his mother wondered why the house was so silent this time of day, not that it was every day. She was enjoying it as she sat in her rocker next to the window watching for Joey, who would come across the fields in front of their Kansas-style farmhouse from his house, which was just beyond the field.

She watched as the trees outside bent slightly in the gentle breeze, and the soothing rustle they gave off seemed to complement the silence of the house. The TV was off, the scanner was turned down, and her son's stereo was not playing, but if it was she could not hear it. If it were playing, it would be a tune that calms rather than irritates one's nerves.

Her hands were gently folded in her lap as she rocked. She had nothing to do right now but watch for her son's friend to come. She had come home from working at the bookstore in town and was resting. The strain of the forthcoming tourist season was settling in around the area where she and her son lived. Today she encountered the first of a long series of lost and totally clueless tourists who came into the store asking for directions to the Great Smoky Mountains National Park, the Blue Ridge Parkway and the nearest Wal-Mart. So many tourists came in asking for directions she thought of having her son write down how to get to every major tourist attraction in the mountains from the store, making copies of them, and just handing the paper over to whoever was lost. She felt that since her son would add lots of detail of how to get there, they could find it very easily. She knew he'd state what road went where, what you would pass, and what to look for, like houses, signs, and even trees.

There was a movement out in the field. She leaned up closer in her rocker and saw that it was Joey coming to the house. She got up and looked at the clock. It was time for her son's medicine. She went upstairs to his bedroom to make sure he hadn't dozed off. The silence of the house made her think he had but even when he was awake the silence would still prevail.

She came to the top of the stairs and was greeted with darkness. Every room upstairs had the door shut, except for the streak of orange that slipped out from under her son's bedroom door.

"Son," she called out as she reached the top of the stairs, "Joey's coming, and it's time for your medicine."

Nothing.

She knocked on his door and told him again that it was time for his medicine. She went across the hall to the bathroom, switched on the light, opened the cabinet over the sink, and took out the brown bottle of pills. She did not hear the door across the hall ease open.

"Come get your medicine," she said as she turned out the light and turned around.

"AHHH!"

Her heart skipped a beat at the fright she saw. Her son was standing in the doorway to his bedroom, the orange sunlight powerfully beaming behind him from the window in his room, making him the biggest and most terrifying black silhouette she had ever seen. She could tell he was looking at her, but not at her face. He never looked at her face unless it was turned away from him.

"Son you scared me," she said. "Were you asleep?"

He shook his head.

"Well, it's time for your medicine, and Joey's here."

She handed her son the little white pill and the cup of water from the bathroom. One big hand reached out and took the pill. The other took the cup. After he took the pill he returned the cup to her. She took it and tossed it into the trash in the bathroom. She came out and saw that her son was no longer standing in the doorway, but saw a black image going down the stairs. The orange light was blinding to her so she shut his bedroom door and went downstairs after him.

Her son went to the front screen door, looked out, and stepped onto the porch. He could see Joey coming across the field and saw that he had something in his hand as he came closer.

"Hey, what'cha doin'?" he said when he came to the porch. "I brought you your graduation present. It's from me and my mom." His raspy voice was so unique none of his other few friends sounded like he did. It was totally natural. One would think he was a chain smoker or had a bad case of bronchitis.

Joey came up on the porch and handed the present to his friend. He took it and saw that it was a book of poems. He opened it and saw that each poem had a watercolor picture to accompany it. On the inside front cover he recognized Joey's scrawled handwriting.

> *"To The Writer*
> *On his high school graduation.*
> *Your friend Joey"*

He also saw that there was a card inside it. He opened it and read the simple message of congratulations and the familiar signature of his friend. He put it back in the book and held on to it with one of his hands. He looked up at the sky, which was slowly getting darker and later. The orange light was fading.

"I know you don't graduate till tomorrow," Joey said, "so I brought it to you now because I can't come watch you."

His eyes moved into Joey's direction, but he did not look at his face.

"Why?" he asked softly.

"Because I have to go to work. Tomorrow's my first day. I'll be at the ice cream shop in town. That's where Dionne and Lana work, but I have to cover for both of them since they're graduating with you tomorrow."

The Writer nodded, totally understanding of his reason for not being able to attend the ceremony.

"Is that okay?" Joey asked.

He looked at him.

"The present. Do you like it? I just wanted to get you a little something for graduation."

He looked down at it and nodded again. He flipped through the pages and saw the many colors of the pictures in it flutter by under his fingers. He stood still and silent next to Joey, not looking at him, but kept looking at his worn tennis shoes, aging with each step Joey took. Being an athlete in high school can wear hard on shoes, and this pair was his third this year alone.

"Well while I'm here," Joey said, "and since I won't be able to see you walk across that stage tomorrow, can you do something for me?"

The Writer nodded.

"I want to see you in your cap and gown. Can you do that while I'm here, if you don't mind?"

The Writer nodded and motioned for Joey to follow him into the house. They went in, his mother and Joey exchanged a quick greeting, and they headed upstairs for the bedroom. Joey went in and saw the blue cap and gown spread out on the bed. He looked at it and then closed his eyes per The Writer's request as he slipped it on over his other clothes. He took off his cap and replaced it with the cardboard hat, making sure the tassel dangled on the right side and not the left. He poked Joey to open his eyes and look. He saw his friend completely draped in ocean blue from head to foot. A slight breeze caused it to bend and move this way and that.

Joey gave him a solid two thumbs up as he looked at him. The Writer kept his gaze at the floor, letting his friend see him as long as he wanted.

There came a sudden white flash of light.

The Writer and Joey jolted together and saw his mother standing in the doorway with her camera.

"I'm sorry," she said. "I just had to get a picture. Hey, why not one of you two together? It'll be perfect since Joey can't be there tomorrow."

"How'd you know?" her son asked, looking in her direction but not at her face, as usual.

"I overheard. Joey doesn't whisper like you do son."

Joey smiled and put on a pose. He got close to The Writer and wrapped an arm around him. The Writer did the same thing with Joey, and looked in the direction of the camera.

"Okay smile."

Joey did. The Writer didn't.

"I said smile son."

Nothing.

"Son, be happy. You're graduating tomorrow. Aren't you happy over it?"

He nodded. Seeing that she was not going to get as much as a grin out of him, and since the sunlight was so bright it was blinding her, she quickly took two pictures of the boys, thanked them, and went to her room. At about that exact moment the phone rang. The Writer picked up the extension on his desk in a frenzy and heard his mother on the other phone in her bedroom. It was one of her friends from church, so he quickly pressed the 'talk' button on the receiver and put it back on its base.

"Expecting a call?" Joey asked curiously.

He nodded.

"Who?"

"Rusty."

Joey's face turned ashen. He looked at The Writer without a smile or grin. The very mention of Rusty's name made him want to run to the nearest toilet and puke his guts out.

"You're still friends with him?" he asked.

"Why?" The Writer asked.

"Well, I don't know. I guess because . . . well . . . he just doesn't seem your type."

"Have you met him?"

"No but from the stories I've heard he doesn't sound like someone you would hang out with."

The Writer slipped out of the cap and gown and he put his old cap back on. He could tell that Joey had jumped on the anti-Rusty bandwagon along with several others. This included his mother, who had given up on Rusty long ago after another of his infamous broken promises to The Writer sent him to the emergency room with a severe asthma attack, brought on by worry and getting upset. She blamed Rusty for it and had a grudge against him ever since, not only for that, but also for the reputation he had built for himself. He was a wild, rebellious, and highly immature boy about two years older than The Writer.

"Of course that's just me," Joey said. "Well, I better go. Have fun tomorrow. Sorry I can't be there. I wish I could though."

The Writer escorted him to the front door. He opened the screen door and they went out on the porch. The sun was setting farther behind the distant mountains and it was getting darker. The Writer asked Joey if he needed a flashlight to get home.

"No, I can see," he said. "I may see you tomorrow sometime."

The Writer nodded as he looked out at the field where Joey would have to walk to get back to his house. He would stand here on the porch and watch him, just like Mama does when he goes to the mailbox at the end of their gravel driveway. He could feel the sense of a forthcoming temporary goodbye to his friend coming, and he hated to part with him after he came to visit, but he knew he had to get home. In fact he hated saying 'bye' to any of his few friends, because deep down he felt that it could be the last time he ever saw them.

Joey stood still next to The Writer and studied his face. He knew what he was thinking, so he came up to him and wrapped his arms around him. He then hurried down the steps and took off across the grassy field for his house.

The phone rang again. The Writer made a sudden dash for the door but heard his mother answer it first. Please let it be Rusty, he thought as he watched Joey's thin figure get smaller in the distance. Please don't let Mama be hateful to him if it is.

At that moment, he heard her yelling, "STAY AWAY FROM MY SON! DO YOU HEAR ME?! JUST STAY AWAY FROM HIM OR YOU'RE GONNA HAVE ME TO DEAL WITH!"

The phone slammed.

And he waddled away . . . back into the house to see who called.

CHAPTER TWO

"It was that wretched Mrs. Moran from the school," Mama said when her son asked who called. "She was trying to get me to send you to some shrink in Asheville now that school's out."

"Why?"

"She says you still have a 'mental imbalance' that 'impairs your interpersonal skills' and keeps you from doing this and that and I don't know what all she said. I told her to stay away from you and to leave you alone."

He looked at the phone and was thankful that it wasn't Rusty who got the nasty reception from his mother. But he was gravely reminded of that old hag from the high school.

Mrs. Moran was one of the counselors at his high school. Over the last four years, she had tried to get him to go to one psychologist after another because of his behavior. She decreed to him one day that he was "too nice a person" for his age. One day he was summoned out of class to come to the principal's office. As he walked out of class his peers looked and pointed, whispering that he'd finally done something wrong and was gonna get kicked out at long last.

When he got to the office, Mrs. Moran was standing in front of the office door and directed him into her office. Seated at the conference table was a man dressed in a dark three-piece suit with a pen being turned around over and over in his rustic hands over a yellow legal pad and a look of smoldering disgust eating away at his ragged face. The Writer was ordered to sit directly across from him and to listen and do as he was told. As soon as he got his rear end planted in the seat the questions and accusations took full force into his face. The man, Mrs. Moran told him, was a psychologist from some mental health facility in the county and she had him come to talk to him about his behavior. The shrink claimed that his "overly decent and giving behavior" was "highly impractical and out of character for a person of his age." The observations he had from Mrs. Moran suggested that he had done something horrible somewhere in his past and that his behavior was some way of making up for it. She'd seen him loaning pencils, paper, pens, and even his textbooks to whoever needed them for class. When it came Christmastime she saw him giving his friends cards and candy and pencils. She would see him putting cards in his teachers' mailboxes in the faculty office.

He did the same for Halloween, Valentine's Day, and Easter.

On numerous occasions she had seen him helping students who dropped their books, held the door open for somebody, carried things for someone, and looked over term papers for those who needed help with them. All these good acts, among the many others she had seen him doing, made her question his behavior.

Mama was furious when she found out what Mrs. Moran did and ordered her to not ever do it again, and if she thought her son needed therapy she would have to go through her first. Since then Mrs. Moran had tried unsuccessfully to get The Writer to see anymore shrinks. Her attempts were in vain and failed each time, because Mama refused to give any consent for her son to be taken off anywhere.

And now she was still after him even after school had been let out, and on the day before graduation. Mama was getting her fill of that woman and it was running over the rim of her level of intolerance.

"Don't worry about it son," Mama said, drawing the shades in the living room. "If she shows her ugly face around here don't you dare let her in. Call the police to come haul her off. I'm afraid if I see her set foot in my house I'm gonna tear her apart with my bare hands."

Cat fight, The Writer thought. He envisioned his mother pulling Mrs. Moran's curly black hair out of her head, slapping each other, Mrs. Moran swinging her bloated purse at Mama, who in turn shielded herself with her shoe. They were screaming, kicking, calling each other a word that rhymes with 'witch.' Then he saw Mrs. Moran grab a ceramic vase off the mantle, whereas Mama grabbed a poker from the fireplace and swung, shattering the vase in her hand. Mrs. Moran lunged for the poker but she was so heavily built she fell headfirst into the fireplace, ash and dust billowing out all around. She grabbed a handful of ash and slung it in Mama's face. She cried out as the ash stung her eyes. Mrs. Moran oozed out of the fireplace and knocked Mama backward onto the coffee table, breaking the coffee set that Judy, Joey's mother, had given to Mama last Christmas. Mama, her eyes shedding tears of pain and rage, started kicking. She didn't care who or what she hit, but she slammed her foot into Mrs. Moran's mouth and sent her tumbling back against the living room window and onto the floor. Mama got up and started yelling for her son to come help her. She kept calling and calling, but got no answer.

"SON!"

His mind snapped back to the present.

"Are you okay?"

He looked around the darkened living room and saw no sign of a war having took place with his mother and that woman. It all happened in his mind, but it looked so real as he was envisioning it.

"I was telling you to call the police . . . "

" . . . if she comes around here." he said quietly, looking at the living room floor.

"Yes, call the cops and don't let her in. Do you understand?"

He nodded.

"Good. Now I'm going up to my room and getting ready for bed. We've got a big day tomorrow, so don't stay up too late."

He nodded again and watched his mother go up the stairs, saw the gleam of her bedroom lamp go on, then fade out as she shut the door. He turned off all the lights downstairs, went over to the living room window where he could see into the front yard, and pulled up the blind. He pulled his mother's rocker close to the window and sat in it. His mind was in a deep state of thought. He watched the stars twinkle out of the darkened sky one by one and felt the cool breeze of the night breathe in upon him. He kept the phone next to him, hoping Rusty would call and say that he was coming to graduation tomorrow.

He never did.

The Writer awoke to realize that he had dozed off in the rocker. He jerked himself awake and was relieved when he saw that it was still black outside, with the exception of the porch light casting a yellow beam into the yard. He stretched, stood up, and ambled over to the clock on top of the TV. In red digits was 4:32 a.m. early Saturday. He went over to the lamp on Mama's sewing table near the stairs and turned it on to the low beam. Its warm glow lit the living room and was just enough light for him to see his way up the stairs.

He took a shower, changed his clothes, laid out his cap and gown on the bed, and was ready for the big day. The clock in his bedroom read 5:25 a.m. Wandering around aimlessly in his room, he didn't know what to do until time to leave for the high school. He didn't want to go back to sleep, nothing good was on TV this time of morning, and he knew the cable stations were probably still showing their all-night porno flicks, or at least that's what he heard in the halls at school. Mama was still asleep and he was too excited about today to write in his book. He looked out his window and saw that it was still quite dark and the sun wouldn't be up for a little while yet. He put on his waist bag, tied his black coat around his waist since his pants had no pockets in them, made sure his pen was on his necklace, slid a note under Mama's door telling her where he was if she woke up soon, and headed out the door. As soon as he got out on the front porch he looked all around at the vast absence of any life from anywhere. His cats and dogs were asleep under the porch swing, one or two cars were on the distant highway, nothing on the main road that went down in front of his house, and of course no sign of life from Joey's house across the field. The Writer went around to the backyard and looked up at the hill that rose far above the house. At the top of it was a lone elm tree that looked out upon the fields that stretched out all over as far as the eye could see. From this spot, one could gaze upon the Great Smoky Mountains in all their majesty, seeing them stretch forever into the hazy blue mist that hangs over them.

The Writer usually propped himself up against the tree or just sat on the ground under it. Even though his mother would gripe about his clothes getting dirty, he didn't care. He knew the time was well spent up there on the hill, the place where he could think, pray, and talk to God.

He went across the bridge that was built over a small stream that ran out of the mountains. He then went up on the hill through the tall grass. At this time of morning there was no breeze to create the soothing waves that would slink and slither up and down the hillside. He came to the tree, wrapped an arm around it, and gazed out into the early darkness of a new day in its infancy. He looked to the east, where the sun would rise any minute now. Already there were faint beams of light glowing in the distance, signaling that the sun was on its way up to this part of the world.

The anxiety was boiling up inside him now. For four long years he had dreamed of this day, and now it was finally coming into the light of reality. It was like waiting for four whole years for another Christmas to come around. In a little over four hours from now he'd be sitting at the high school football stadium in his cap and gown with the rest of his class. Over the last few years he and his closest friends Annie, Lana, Dionne, Elaine, Nate, and their two special friends, Jackie, who was raised in an orphanage for years, and the one they called "Blade", simply because he loved to collect knives, and would tear out the sales ads from the Sunday newspaper to search out full-page ads for collector's knives, had dreamed of this moment and now it was approaching faster than ever before. He recalled all the times he was persecuted and judged maliciously by his peers for being so "different" from everyone else. To the other students, it was a travesty to be quiet in class, do your homework, stay home on Friday and Saturday nights listening to calm music, reading, writing, thinking, or just nothing. To them, it was either 'do as we do, or die.' They had mocked, spat upon, hit, humiliated, and despised him in several ways over the years. But out of all the ash of this subterfuge of hopelessness and blind faith came someone named Rusty.

Rusty.

The name said it all.

They met in one of their classes together. At The Writer's high school, all four grade levels were sometimes mixed in order to grant all the students the classes they needed in order to graduate. When he was a freshman, one of his classes was like this. There were more freshmen than anyone else. There was a good number of sophomores, some juniors, and a couple of seniors. Rusty was one of the few juniors.

One day the teacher split the class up into four parts. Each group was going to be a study group for a whole week. The Writer just happened to get in the group that had Rusty and a few juniors. Rusty didn't pay much attention to The Writer at first. He was too busy yapping about himself to his friends. The Writer eventually wound up doing the entire work for his group, and had to put down the names of everyone in it. During the time that was assigned to work on it, Rusty spent it making cracks and jokes about things that did not pertain to the lesson. He did, however, critique The Writer's style of handwriting, which severely rivaled his own childish scrawl.

What caused a "friendship" to build between the two was that to The Writer, Rusty was the first one who never ever seemed to make fun of him for being fat and pudgy. True, The Writer was not slim or lean, nor anyone's idea of Mr. Universe. He was round and heavily built, about two inches taller than Rusty. For years he had been made fun of for being so big and round it had destroyed his hope in ever finding someone with whom he could have a true and meaningful friendship with. Rusty was the first one to touch his sensitive heart in a way that was not ugly or hateful, and being sensitive as he was, the slightest friendly gesture from Rusty created a massive reaction in his conscience, and The Writer found himself being drawn more and more to Rusty, merely because he did not persecute him the way others did.

The Writer felt that he had found his first true friend in Rusty, but this of course was before he knew Annie and the rest of his little band of friends that he was so attached to now. All seven of them, plus The Writer, were in the same grade together, and thus went through a lot together all four years of high school.

As time went on, The Writer saw more and more into Rusty's character. He learned that Rusty loved women like crazy, had a knack for hanging out around town all the time in the most unusual spots, such as the volunteer fire department for instance. He loved to do wheelies in fields and pastures, drag race on the highway late at night when it was practically deserted, play his stereo at ear-shattering volumes, so loud it rattled windows whenever he drove past them, and he also hung out with his own bunch of friends, who all acted just alike with each other, rowdy and careless.

The Writer disregarded the other things he'd heard about Rusty, dismissing them as just mere rumors and remnants of high school gossip.

When Mama first saw Rusty from a distance she first noticed the hairdo he had. It was spiked with blonde tips at each end, dyed dark maroon, and there was a slight curl that draped down over his forehead. His hair was also very slick and shiny, with enough mousse and gel to hold the hair of the bride of Frankenstein in place. There were also at least two earrings in each ear and he wore a pair of faded denim jeans and jacket, both that were either torn or shredded open.

The Writer told his mother over and over that he looked past all that and focused only on what was inside Rusty and he wanted her to do the same. She kept saying she'd try to but she usually gave up. It was her fear that Rusty was taking advantage of her son's goodness and she wanted him to be very careful around him.

As far as she was concerned, this was the most bizarre case of "opposites attract" that she'd ever of. It seemed to her that for every good thing her son did for Rusty, he got nothing in return for it.

Rusty promised The Writer he would be at the ceremony today, a promise he'd been making to him for over three years. But The Writer knew that Rusty had yet to keep a single promise to him, and he was hoping that this promise would be the one that he would keep since it meant so much to him. Other promises, like coming to his birthday party each year, going to a movie, or just a simple visit, all remained to be seen. The Writer refused to give up on him. He also wanted to encourage him to start coming to church with him and Mama on Sundays.

After long interludes of thinking back on the past years, all the forms of persecution he'd been through, all the hatred, the resentments, the cruelty, and coming out with a small band of faithful friends, he realized what time of day it was. The sun was slowly inching its way up into the sky, its bright orange beam giving birth to another day. He started to head back for the house when a gust of wind blew out of nowhere. It whipped across his shirt and coat, creating the sensation of freedom to flow through his body.

Is this how graduation feels, he thought as he headed back for the house. Again, the sensation of being set free from the depravity and tyranny of high school seemed to tear through his body, cleansing out the damage and heartache of having to face that place each day for four years. The only things of high school he felt were worth salvaging were his few true friends, which also included Joey, who was three years behind him, the knowledge he had gained from his English teachers who encouraged him to keep working at his talent, and what few harmonious moments he could dwell upon, thought they were few and far between.

He then waddled away . . . to the house to get ready for his graduation.

CHAPTER THREE

Mama told The Writer she would take him to the school in time to get ready with the rest of his class. However he insisted that his friends Nate and Elaine would be by to take him so she wouldn't have to fight the traffic on the little two-lane road that went from town directly to the school. Also, Judy made it clear to Mama that she could ride with her, so everything was set.

Nate and Elaine arrived at his house promptly at nine to pick up The Writer. Both of them were donned in their blue cap and gown, and a big smile on their faces as usual. The Writer had never seen them upset over anything, and if they ever were they did an incredible job of masking it from the rest of the world. Every time Elaine saw The Writer she'd burst out into sheer joy and excitement, calling his name out from wherever she was just to wave to him or send him a smile. And today, the very moment she and Nate pulled into his driveway, she hopped out and ran up onto the porch. She rang the doorbell and until someone answered she played with the cats that were on the porch while Nate petted the dogs.

The Writer answered, and needless to say Elaine threw her arms around him in a huge hug, overjoyed over what today was.

"Ready to go sir? You look great! We have to be there by nine-thirty. Is your mom coming with us?"

"Oh no, I'm riding with a friend," Mama said when she heard Elaine's invitation. "But thanks anyway. You all go on ahead. I'll see you there."

Elaine insisted that they had enough room in Nate's car for both her and her friend but Mama herself insisted that she would be there with her friend, and told them not to be late getting to the school for the processional set-up. Elaine had The Writer sit up front with Nate and they took off for the school.

The ceremony was set to start at ten, but the seniors were requested to be at the gym between nine and nine-thirty for a final count and instructions. Nate and Elaine got The Writer there shortly before nine-thirty and all three of them hurried to their assigned spots in the line of graduates. When told to do so, they would walk out to the stadium seats while the school band played the familiar tune of "Pomp and Circumstance," which you hear at every graduation ceremony across the country each spring as well as on TV and in the movies. They would approach their seats in two lines parallel to each other up the stadium steps, fifty-six per line.

The Writer was glad to see that he would be walking with none other than the one and only Annie Morgan at his side. She was one of his true friends, and since she was Valedictorian, she had a gold vest draped around her shoulders. For as long as The Writer could remember, every Valedictorian of the past years he was here at school with acted snooty around everyone else, simply because they were being accorded the highest honor of any graduate in the class.

But not Annie.

She was her sweet, funny, humble self ever since she found out she was Valedictorian. She didn't even tell The Writer or any of his other friends until just a few days before, because she didn't want them to think she was gonna be acting high and mighty around them, which she never did. Everybody else in the class expected it to be the most popular guy in the school who was gonna get it, but when it was revealed that Annie was gonna be it, everyone laughed, thinking it was a joke. When they learned it wasn't, they became subtle and discriminate against her, claiming it was an insult to let some "geek-faced bookworm" claim the highest honor of the class.

Annie didn't care, and neither did the rest of her friends, about what was being said. They were proud of their friend.

T

There was a joyous atmosphere everywhere. It overshadowed the fact that just the day before, two boys found out that they would not be graduating after all, because they flunked a final exam on the last day of school. The gym was a hustling bustle of noise, from laughter to the annoying redneck yelps that belched out of the mouths of boys who worshiped the rebel flag or spoke in that infamous redneck accent. Words like 'heard' came out as "heerrd," 'no' came out as "naaww," 'so' was "saaawww," and 'pretty' was of course "purty" or "purdee."

Nate and Elaine stayed close to The Writer, watching everyone else go loony and immature. Elaine shook her head in disappointment at what she saw, from guys giving each other the finger as a perverted form of greeting while the girls yapped about their plans for tonight with their boyfriends. Some were explicit in detail while the others were in ragged whispers. Nate just looked around at the floor mostly.

"Well here they are!" a familiar voice screeched. All three turned around to see Annie, Lana, Dionne, and Jackie coming up to them in a little bunch. All of them greeted Elaine, Nate, and The Writer in big hugs, jumping and squealing with excitement over today. Annie came up to The Writer and they exchanged their trademark greeting, which was waving a hand in each other's face. Then all the girls broke into a little circle, their arms around one another as if in a group hug, and started jumping up and down together, going around and around, hollering and whooping it up, so happy. Nate watched with a big smile on his face and The Writer just looked, happy that they were happy.

"This is it! This is it!" Dionne kept saying over and over. She turned to The Writer. "Aren't you excited sir? Are ya huh? Huh? Are ya? C'mon, give me a smile! Here it is the happiest day of our high school years and you look as if you're going to your algebra class. Just one little smile sir please! Here, I'll do it then!" She grabbed hold of his face and with her thumbs tried to raise the corners of his mouth upwards but had no success. Instead she just gave him a hug and held his hands in hers. "I just hope my makeup doesn't melt off my face while we're out there," she said to Annie who was standing next to her. "I heard it's gonna be hot today."

"The only thing for you to do is dip it in bronze," Annie said, adjusting her cap. "I just hope my speech sounds good."

"Did you have The Writer read over it?" Lana asked.

"Yeah, but he said to just read it as I wrote it, because he wanted it to be me up there speaking and not his words coming out of my mouth. He said it should be all mine."

"Now where's that Blade at?" Jackie asked.

"He's always late," Nate said. "He'll be here soon . . . I hope."

At that moment they heard the loud battering of shoes against a waxed wooden gym floor. They looked at one of the main doors and saw Blade come dashing in, half-dressed in his gown and his cap wasn't even on his head.

"Well, make way for the great battalion," Dionne said when she saw him. "What's the matter Blade? Did you forget today was graduation?"

"You're funny you know that," he said as Nate helped him get situated. "My stupid alarm clock didn't go off and I . . . "

"Yeah whatever Blade," Annie said, fanning her face with her speech. "We've heard it all before from you, from the alarm clock to static cling under the sheets."

"And don't forget the urban legend about some guy standing over your bed with an axe in his hand," Lana added.

"And then there's the plunger getting stuck in the toilet," Jackie said laughing.

"And the one where . . . "Elaine started to say.

"Alright!" Blade roared. "Someone help me fix my cap."

"Why? Is it broke?" Annie asked. Everyone else giggled while Blade just rolled his eyes. "I still don't understand what all this fuss is about," she said looking at all the commotion going on around her. "All this hullabaloo over getting some dinky piece of fancy paper with writing on it. I could just make my diploma on my computer at home, then have it for nothing. Gee, I love being a genius."

"Whatever," Blade said in his droll voice. "A sloth is a genius compared to you."

"WHAT?!" Annie shrieked, her jaw gaping wide open.

"You heard me."

"Boy you just wait until the bowling tournament next week! I'm gonna . . . "

At that moment the principal gave the order for all the seniors to get in their places for the procession. After it came a thundering bellow of redneck squeals and howls as well as cheers.

"This is it!" Lana said. "Let's go girls!" All of them grabbed one more quick hug before getting to their places. Jackie and Nate were up near the front, Elaine and Dionne in the middle, and Blade and Lana weren't very far behind The Writer and Annie, who were close behind Jackie and Nate. Annie kept glancing at The Writer and smiled each time. The Writer didn't look at her directly but could feel her eyes on him. His mind was set on just one thing, and that was to get out there, get his diploma, and kiss high school goodbye forever.

They exited in their procession out of the gym doors and into the early June air, which was only cool when a breeze kicked up. Other than that it was rather mild but clear as the eye could see. Some of the graduates were so pumped they found it difficult to keep their mouths shut.

As soon as they reached the gates of the football field, the school band struck up that familiar tune. Some of the kids were still blabbing away like there was no tomorrow. One teacher had his fill of it.

"Alright guys!" he hollered, bringing the procession to a dead halt. "We don't have to do this. We can turn right around and stand in the gym until you all learn to shut your mouths and keep them closed until after the ceremony, and I don't care if we have to stand there until dark if that's what it takes to get you all to shut up. Do I make myself clear?"

"Yes sir," came the ominous reply. Some kids yelled "yeah,"

"sure," or just stood there. The Writer glared at the teacher who told him in math class two years ago that he had no sense or the ability to be a writer, and that it would only lead to a life of poverty and becoming a total failure in life.

I'd just love to prove him wrong, he thought.

"What are you gonna do sir?" one girl hollered from the back. "Give us detention?" Laughter erupted from all over the crowd, and when it died down they proceeded on to the stadium. The audience had fold-up chairs in the freshly cut football field and were positioned to face the home side of the stadium.

As soon as the first couple of students set foot onto the track making their way to their seats the audience stood up. The school band started playing that tune over and over like a broken record. By the time they got to their assigned places the annoying song would be playing over and over in their heads throughout the entire ceremony, which would probably last about two hours or so. It would be followed by a reception in the school cafeteria, but Mama had promised to take The Writer out to lunch at their favorite restaurant which was far away from this small town where all-out rowdiness would set in the moment the last senior got his or her diploma. This was a small community. Nearly all the locals knew a majority of the graduates and there was no doubt that there would be lots of uncontrollable partying rocking the area for the remainder of the day and well into the night.

The Writer was not going out tonight. He was going to stay at home and write in his book, which was his weekly Saturday night routine.

All the seniors finally made it to their places. The music died down. The principal made his way to the podium and motioned for the seniors to sit down. The audience followed the order. The Writer scoured his eyes all across the grand array of spectators, looking for Mama, Judy, and to see if Rusty made good on his promise. He found her sitting at the outer edge of the third row that faced the parking lot. He then recognized Judy sitting next to her. Both of them could clearly see The Writer in the fourth row in the seventeenth seat. He was happy that Judy cared enough to come even though her son had to work.

Then he looked for Rusty.

No sign of him.

His heart sank and he knew it would be a longer ceremony than he thought.

A minister from one of the local churches led the opening prayer. During the prayer The Writer could hear some of the graduates whisper and laugh, talking about how this was just a waste of time. Following this the senior class officers were recognized with applause from the audience. The principal introduced this year's Valedictorian and Annie stood up. The audience responded with cheers and a standing ovation as she went to the podium to give her speech. The Writer and his friends clapped for her and Lana and Dionne were cheering her name over and over. As for the rest of the graduating class, not too many were thrilled to see her up there. They wanted to see the one who was named Salutorian holding the highest honor of the class, not someone who was quiet and hung out with The Writer. She was not on the basketball team, the volleyball team, softball team, track team, homecoming court, nor was she prom queen. She was just Annie, somebody who was shy except when she was around her friends and highly respectful of others.

She made a few opening welcome remarks and proceeded to read her speech. Her original plan was to give credit to The Writer for helping her with it but he insisted that she leave his name out of her portion of the ceremony. As she read it she kept glancing up at him and smiled. The other seniors noticed what she was doing and gave him deep menacing scowls.

When she finished the audience gave her a roaring standing ovation and her friends in the class stood up first cheering. One by one, the other seniors grudgingly got on their feet and clapped. She returned to her seat next to the Salutorian and looked at the audience. Mama and Judy were clapping their hands over their heads and yelling. Then the cheering began to subside and everything quieted down. The Salutorian made her way for the podium and as soon as her name was read by the principal the entire graduating class save The Writer and his friends shot up on their feet and let out the most blistering shatter of screams and howls the county had ever heard in its existence. She stood behind the podium and gazed out at the crowd gone totally berserk. Mama and Judy could not see The Writer since he was swamped under everyone else standing around over him. The principal had to gesture for everyone to settle down so she could give her speech, which was only about a page long. She was one of those popular high school kids who was only considerate and polite when it mattered. She only talked to The Writer when she wanted something but would talk about him behind his back. To her, church was a joke, and she made the crack one day in class that she only went "when she had to."

After another thunderous ovation it was now time to present the diplomas. A row of graduates would come down to the podium and line up. When their name was called they would walk up, shake the superintendent's hand, accept their diploma, move their tassel to the other side, and return to their place until told to take their seats. The school guidance counselor was standing next to a table full of four towers of diplomas in leather-bound cases. No, this was not Mrs. Moran, but the *other* school counselor, the one The Writer and his friends loved, who had encouraged The Writer for years to keep working at his talent and had him enter every writing contest she heard of, and he won either first or second place in all of them.

Whenever a name was called, the audience and fellow graduates all broke out in applause. If the student was a symbol of social idolatry among everyone else the cheers arose to exploding roars of redneck calls, thunderous clapping, and a few standing up. Those who weren't as popular got only ordinary applause.

When it came time for The Writer to accept his diploma, the principal just addressed him as simply 'The Writer.' He went to the stage and could hear Annie and the rest of his friends all cheering for him. Mama and Judy were standing up clapping. The remainder of the spectators just applauded out of habit. Barely a few of the other graduates applauded. The rest just looked on in aggravation.

The superintendent shook his hand, gave him his diploma, and motioned for him to move his tassel to the other side of his cap. The counselor caught him before he got off the stage and had him look at his diploma. She opened it for him and showed him the name that was in the middle written in calligraphic writing.

It read 'The Writer.'

After looking at it for a moment he gave the counselor a slight hug and walked off the stage.

He then waddled away . . . back to his seat.

CHAPTER FOUR

After the principal announced the seniors as the class of the year, they tossed their caps into the air and went totally berserk. The crowd disbanded from their seats and rushed up to the stadium seats to meet the graduates. The Writer was trying to find his cap after somebody behind him yanked it off his head and threw it up. He knelt down all around the seats but got pushed and shoved out of the way by the other graduates. At one point he was knocked down and the other seniors simply stepped over and around him, not offering to help him back up.

Blade yelled for everyone to stop hitting him and he and Nate hurried down from their places to help The Writer. Lana and Dionne heard him yelling and looked up to see The Writer struggling to get up but everyone else kept knocking him back down. He was getting beat around so bad he scrunched up on the concrete and covered his head with his arms. Elaine and Jackie were fighting the other graduates to get to Lana and Dionne. Annie was being surrounded by people congratulating her on being Valedictorian but she kept watching to see where The Writer was. She had to break away from the crowd and go up to look for him. She found two boys stomping on a cap and kicking it around. Realizing whose it was, she interceded. She ran up, pushed one boy back, grabbed the cap, and hurried up to help her friend. The boys called her some five-letter word and gave her the finger.

Blade and Nate made everyone else leave him alone as they helped him up. His chin was scraped and bleeding and his hair was messed up. Dirt was all over his gown. Lana and Dionne bent down to clean him off as best they could. Blade held up his face to see how bad he was cut up. Annie put the tattered cap back on his head. Elaine and Jackie were waving their arms to the audience, summoning his mother and Judy to come up to where they were.

"Where is he?" Mama asked Judy when the other seniors were being greeted by their families down in the field. She looked around at all the kids in blue gowns and caps and not one of them was her son. Judy looked up in the stadium seats and saw Elaine and Jackie waving their arms to them. She pointed Mama's attention to them and she saw who it was. Both of them took off up the steps.

"Oh dear God what happened?" she asked when she saw her son's face. Nate told her what the other kids were doing to him and Blade showed her where he was cut up. Mama took out a wipe from her purse and cleaned the scrape on his chin. Judy took the cap and tried to wipe it off as best she could, then she looked down and saw that The Writer's diploma had been stepped on and kicked all over. She picked it up and cleaned it.

"Some people," Mama said as she kept adjusting The Writer's gown. He kept insisting that he was fine and wasn't hurt too bad. It made him feel embarrassed when his mother made such a fuss over him. "C'mon, we're going out to eat, away from here son. Would you all like to join us?"

All his friends said that their folks had plans with them for the rest of the day and Judy had to run errands before getting to work at the restaurant across town. They all said they'd come by the house soon to visit him. Before they left each one hugged The Writer goodbye, then Judy had them all halt before they got away.

"Everyone, get together right here. I want a picture of you all."

"Oh my gosh!" Dionne said, as if in a frenzy. She ripped open her purse and yanked out her compact. "How does my hair look?"

"Like a wig," Nate said.

"Excuse me Mr. Intelligence Agent but what do you have to show for your head?! Look at that!" She yanked his cap off and exposed his head. "Nothing but black fuzz!"

"A lot less for me to worry about in the mornings," he replied. Pretty soon all eight of them quickly arranged themselves into a happy pose until Annie changed her mind.

"No Lana, get over here. I want over there."

"But Annie . . . "

"Shut up and move. I don't want just half my face in the picture."

"That was the whole point of it," Blade said, standing next to The Writer.

"What!?"

"You heard me!"

"Blade, I swear sometimes you make me so mad, you just . . . "

"Whatever Annie. It's part of my charm."

"Like you have any to spare. A dead skunk has more charm than you have."

Judy lowered her camera as she and Mama started smirking. The Writer just rolled his eyes towards each one whenever they said something to each other. Elaine and Lana started laughing and Jackie just looked away as if she had no idea who these people were.

At last everyone was happy with their places and they all held up their diplomas over their heads. Judy snapped the shutter and thanked them for posing for her. Again they hugged The Writer, his mother, and Judy, and went to find their families.

Rusty didn't show up, he thought as he looked all over the area. Oh well, I won't say anything to Mama. I don't want her fussing at me now about him.

Mama and Judy walked The Writer to the parking lot to make sure nobody else got after him. Already fellow graduates had lost control of themselves and were going crazy yelling, whooping, hollering, and calling out to each other where they were going and with whom. A whole bunch had their vehicles decked out with spray paint, boasting they were part of the class of the year and were headed for the beach or wherever else they were going to. Needless to say nobody asked The Writer to go with them.

"I'll take you all home first so The Writer can change," Judy said as they got in her white convertible. "Then I'm gonna have to run."

"That's fine," Mama said, getting into the backseat. The Writer saw what she was doing and looked perplexed. "That's alright son. You sit up front. I think you deserve it."

"Of course sir," Judy said, scooting the seat back. "Sit up here with me. We'll beat the crowds out of here."

The Writer slipped into the front seat and put on his seat belt. Judy turned the ignition and revved up the engine. "Now watch this my friends," she said. "All these kids think they're tough, don't they Writer?"

He nodded.

"Not around me they aren't!"

She slammed her foot on the gas and tore out of the parking lot in a cloud of dust. The car became a speeding white bullet. Mama was knocked back in the backseat and The Writer grabbed hold of his cap. Mama realized what was happening and started laughing. Judy shot down the main drive and all the other graduates saw what was coming and lunged out of the way. They passed Elaine and Lana who waved and cheered, as did Jackie and Blade, who waved them on. Annie threw her cap after them when they passed her, along with her familiar scream of joy. When Nate and Dionne saw them coming they took off their caps and waved them in the air as they shot past them. Judy would only wave to The Writer's friends and nobody else. The other graduates made mad dashes to get out of her way, falling and tripping over each other. Pretty soon Judy got on the highway and sped down the road back to town, taking her friends home.

Quite literally The Writer left high school behind in a cloud of dust.

As Saturday evening wore on, the scanner at The Writer's house crackled incessantly with reports of drunk drivers, speeding, illegal parking, false ID reports at local taverns, and reckless behavior. The dispatcher gave the dates of birth of the offenders and most of them were either seventeen or eighteen. It made perfect sense to The Writer when the names of the offenders were announced that a huge majority of them were in his graduating class.

He was thankful not to have heard the names of Annie, Lana, Dionne, Nate, Blade, Elaine, or Jackie. The name of the Salutorian was mentioned as being a passenger with one of the speeders on the highways, but not a word about the Valedictorian. Joey was still working at the ice cream shop, and would probably be there until late if the graduates kept coming in.

For The Writer, Saturday nights were filled with nothing but peace and quiet in the house. Usually he just wrote in his notebooks or listened to his stereo while he rocked in his rocker next to the window and nothing more. There would be the sound of a siren wailing in the distance and the scanner would announce what the problem was. Mostly it was drunk driving or speeding, but as the summer tourist season was fast approaching, he could expect to hear more reports of offenses coming in from all over the area. Thus he never went out on a Saturday night unless he had to, and the last time that happened was back in the fall when a slight asthma attack sent him to the emergency room. Other than that, he stayed at the house.

Once he went to his bedroom window and could see the lights from the nearby town in the distance. Out of the specks of white and yellow would appear splotches of red flashing off and on. He knew that there was something wrong, and he grasped the fact that he was perfectly happy at home on Saturday night where it's calm compared to the world going crazy.

Mama put The Writer's diploma on the mantle over the fireplace next to the only trophy he had ever won in his whole life. Of course it was for something he wrote, an essay on school violence when he was in eighth grade, which was also quite possibly his favorite school year of all. That was the year his eighth grade English teacher first made manifest to him his talent to write.

His mother came up to his room and asked if he wanted anything special for supper, and offered to take him out again.

"Isn't it crazy out there right now?" he asked.

"Well, I think we can get in somewhere. I don't wanna call Judy and ask her if there's a place at the restaurant where she's at because she's probably being run ragged. We can stay here if you like."

He nodded and went back to rocking in his chair. He slowly began to doze off, his mind transporting him to a certain place that only he knew about. The images of the real world were slowly deteriorating, but before it was completely banished from his mind, he heard a car rumbling from somewhere. He opened his eyes, leaned up to the window, and looked down. He saw a black Beretta parked next to Mama's truck in the driveway.

"Son, you have company."

He got up and went downstairs, only to be greeted by Annie waving her hand in his face and getting another hug from Dionne and Elaine.

"What brings you here?" he asked quietly.

"We were bored and wanted to come see you," Elaine said. "I brought my game of Monopoly. I thought we could play it if you didn't mind."

He looked at his mother.

"Oh no, I don't mind. Please, help yourselves." She started cleaning off the coffee table and tossing magazines and old newspapers to the side. Dionne and Elaine started setting up the game while Annie talked to Mama.

"Linda, is it okay if the rest of the gang comes over? I mean, we don't wanna go out anywhere tonight being like it is out there, and this being graduation night . . . "

"Why don't I call for a pizza?" Mama suggested. "Nah, I better call for three if Blade and Nate are coming. They love to eat don't they?"

"In that case you better order four," Annie said, taking possession of the bank.

"And we can all chip in for it," Dionne said.

"Oh no. It's my treat, my present to you all. I don't mind a bit. Hey son, why don't you call Joey and ask him to come over?"

"He's at work," The Writer said quickly.

"Oh . . . I'm sorry I forgot," she said, as if she'd just smashed someone's favorite vase.

Pretty soon, the doorbell rang again. Mama went to answer it and Jackie, Lana, and Nate joined the party. Everyone quickly noticed the absence of Blade.

"He's probably trying to think of some lame excuse," Dionne said, examining her nails. "You know, I bet he files his nails with a hunter's knife. Ever notice how worn down they are? And I betcha he'll be late even for his wedding day."

"I betcha he forgets The Writer's present," Annie said, proudly handing out money for the game. Everyone looked up at her with flustered expressions. She quickly covered her mouth when she realized her mistake.

"You freakin' idiot!" Lana screeched, slamming her handful of money down on the table.

"That was supposed to be a surprise big mouth," Jackie said calmly.

"Well excuse me," Annie said, gesturing with her whole body, her hands on her hips. "Is it my fault we left it up to him to bring it with him tonight? Nooooooo. It was YOURS Lana! After all, you're the blonde one here aren't ya? Who else would suggest that we let the clumsiest guy we know handle something as precious as The Writer's graduation gift from us?"

The Writer's eyes had widened up considerably at this point, and he knew that all his friends had been cooking up something for him.

"Annie, dear, I am not the one who bowls with arms that look like the scarecrow's from *The Wizard of Oz*. And when that tournament comes up next week you just wait and see."

"Isn't this fun Writer?" Elaine said to him, sorting out the money Annie was tossing down in front of him. "We're all just one big happy family, nothing but love between us."

Yes, I can see that, he thought as he looked at the money Elaine had arranged for him so neatly.

"You know we could have some music in here or something," Nate suggested. "It's too quiet in here."

"Hey, don't run The Writer off!" Dionne snapped. The Writer handed Nate the remote and he put the TV on the country music video channel. Pretty soon the joyous voices of country giants filled the room.

"Okay," Mama said, coming back in from the kitchen. "I ordered six pizzas for you all, three cokes, and three boxes of bread sticks, or cheese sticks, or whatever they're called. Will that hold you all?"

Before they could answer the doorbell rang again. Mama ran up to answer it and sure enough, it was Blade.

"Everyone, when he comes in here, start laughing," Annie said in a frenzied whisper.

Blade walked into the living room and before he got even within a few inches of the coffee table, everyone broke out in blustering laughter. Lana and Jackie were pointing and Nate made as if he were having a fit on the floor. The Writer just sat and glared at him, drumming his fingers on the table.

"What?" he asked, totally stupefied. "Is there a booger hanging out my nose or something?"

"You have no idea!" Elaine said red-faced.

Pretty soon everyone settled down into the game as they waited for the pizza to arrive. Since it was graduation night it was expected that the delivery boy would be a while getting to the house. The pizza parlor was probably being overrun with graduates not only from this area of the county, but from neighboring schools and counties as well. This afternoon, five other high schools in the area had their commencement exercises, and tonight, four others planned to have theirs. All area police departments had every single officer in their possession on duty, and the area hospitals were ready to handle the results of those graduates who went too wild and crazy tonight.

"YES! I'm cleaning out Annie and her pathetic Miami beach line of condos!" Lana screeched when she rolled the dice and picked up a card off the board.

"Whatever Lana," Annie said drolly. "Just wait until that tournament next week and we'll see whose butt gets kicked."

It was Jackie's turn to roll and she got to collect two-hundred dollars from each player. When she collected it from Blade it left him with just fifty dollars.

"Uh, now look at that Nate!" Blade said in his whiney voice. "I lose all my money to a woman! Isn't that unbelievable?!"

Jackie started laughing. "Hey, when you're hot you're hot!" she said.

"Yes it is unbelievable. Where's the dang pizza boy?!" Annie screeched, looking around the living room. "I'm hungry!"

"Oh get over it you crybaby!" Lana said to Blade.

"Who're you calling a crybaby you blonde fuzz?!"

Lana's mouth dropped open. The insult caused her to turn to The Writer. She pulled him close to her and whispered in his ear.

"See that cleft in Blade's chin? That's what happens when you eat with a Swiss Army knife and not a fork. Just remember that when you have your pen in your hand. You don't wanna look like him."

The Writer looked at Blade, who still had a stupefied look on his darkly tanned, peach colored face. He could clearly see the cleft that ran down the direct middle of his chin. He also saw Blade's deep dark eyes set upon him.

"Writer, do not listen to her. She's all fluff and bluff like her hair."

"Let me tell you something skinny!" Lana said with her finger pointed at him. "Do you know what you can do with that deep loud voice of yours . . . "

The doorbell rang.

"Oh thank God I hope its food!" Annie hollered. Mama grabbed the money from her purse and ran to the door. She opened it and there stood a girl holding six pizza boxes in one arm and a bag of cokes and sticks in the other. Elaine ran up to help her and carried the bags into the living room. The Writer carried the pizzas. That's when the delivery girl got a good look at his face, and that's when her own face turned ashen.

"Okay, is this enough for it?" Mama asked, holding the money in front of the girl's face.

T

"Is *that* your son, lady?" the girl asked rather sickly, pointing to The Writer.

"Yes, THAT is my son, why?"

The girl kept studying him before taking the money. "So he's the one Rusty was talking about huh?"

The moment she heard Rusty's name, Mama waved the money closer in the girl's face, wanting her to leave. "Look, I don't know what Rusty has told you about my son, but would you please take the money and go?!"

"You know your son's crazy don't you? I mean, Rusty says he can't throw a football to save his life much less score with. You really ought to tell your son he can't be going around here spreading his religious hypocrisy with his shirts. They'll put him away for sure."

Mama tore a five dollar bill out of the money she had for the girl and pushed the rest of it in her face. "Just for that, no tip, now beat it!" She then slammed the door in her face and heard the dogs outside barking, chasing her back to her car. Mama looked out the peephole and saw the rear lights of it speeding off down the driveway and out of sight.

"Something wrong Linda?" Elaine asked. Mama brushed her hair back and stuffed the five back in her pocket.

"No, it's just that I can't stand kids who have no manners," she said, helping Annie set out the pizzas on the table Blade and Nate set up in the living room. Everyone stopped in the middle of their game and waited for Nate to say 'grace.' When he was finished, they all charged for the table. Annie snitched a slice off Blade's plate whereas Lana plopped one down on Dionne's. They all came back to the floor and sat around the coffee table, studying their next moves for the game.

"Son, does that delivery girl know who Rusty is?" Mama asked. The Writer looked up towards her and before he could respond, Annie was clearing her throat out.

"Yeah she does," she said, dabbing her mouth with a napkin. "She once dated the nympho, and from what I've heard she had too much."

Everyone looked at her with wide eyes.

"I'm serious. There's this abandoned shack somewhere in the mountains where boys take their dates when they're feeling . . . you know . . . excited, when it's not a banana but the real thing. Know what I'm saying?"

"Annie . . . " Lana whispered, glancing around the room in embarrassment.

"Shhh! You're being rude," she said. "So, like I was saying, this abandoned shack in the mountains. It ain't too hard to find I don't think because so many boys at school talk about how they 'shacked in the shack' over the weekend. When you listen you pick up a few things. Anyway, the story went that he took her up there—her name's Tammy by the way—on Saturday night, and when she came to school on Monday, she would walk with her legs close together."

Jackie dropped her pizza on the table and Dionne covered her face. The Writer flared a glare at his friend, stunned that she was talking about his "friend" this way when nobody was sure of what really goes on.

"Okay Annie dear," Mama said, wiping her brow. "I think you've cleared up a lot of what I was wondering."

"But here's an interesting point," Annie added. "That shack must be somewhere off highway nineteen because this past spring, which was when Rusty took Tammy up there, I saw the most baby rabbits all along that road. Isn't that odd, now I ask you, isn't it? Isn't it? My gosh it's hot in here." She dunked her hand in her drink and splashed it in her face.

"So, where are you all going to college at?" Mama asked, quickly changing the subject. Everybody sighed with relief and was eager to answer Mama.

Lana answered first. "Oh, I'm going to the community college over in Webster. I think I'll drive back and forth everyday. I don't want to stay away from home."

"Yeah, me too," Dionne added, chewing on a stubborn piece of meat on her pizza. "Lana and I got the same schedule so we can help each other."

Blade started to open his mouth.

"SHUT UP!" Dionne declared, pointing at him. "I know what you're about to say. Just keep your lip zipped and nobody gets hurt."

"Annie's up there going off on what this Rusty character does and you're telling ME to keep it zipped up?!" he said, drinking his coke. Dionne raised an eyebrow at him.

"Jackie and I are going to either Western or the community college," Elaine said, wrapping an arm around Jackie. "We wanna be close to our friends."

"What about you Nate?" Mama asked. "Where are you going?"

"Well I'm supposed to start work at the courthouse as a security guard. I think I start Monday. I want to major in criminology, or something like that in school."

"Hey me too!" Lana hollered, slapping high fives with Nate.

"Yeah, he's gonna learn all about freaks like Rusty," Annie said. "I'm going to Western Carolina, and if I don't like it I'm going to transfer to that little community college in Webster. I only have to drive about half an hour to either school. I want to be a teacher, preferably in a Christian school, but my folks can't afford to send me to one."

"Yeah, those are expensive," Mama said. "I would like to send The Writer off to college but none around here want him."

"WHAT?" Lana said.

"You're kidding?" Dionne said.

"No it's true," Mama said. "He wrote to Western, Southwestern, NC State, UNC, Clemson, Guilford, Mars Hill, and a whole bunch of others. All of them wrote back and told him that he was not the type of student they wanted."

"They're crazy!" Dionne said. "If I had known that I wouldn't have accepted Southwestern's invitation."

"Well, it was all over his grades. He can't do algebra, which is a major requirement to be eligible for those big schools, so they didn't want him."

The Writer looked at the table in dismay. Here all his close friends had plans for their future and his was a big ugly blank. He had heard all the other kids in school boast and brag about their getting accepted to Western, UNC, NC State, and all the other universities in North Carolina. It was even more of a wild celebration when they waved their scholarship award letters at each other, telling them how much they won and what it was for. For him it was like everyone he went to school with was now on this giant luxury liner about to depart for areas in the new world of life and he was getting left behind on the dock in the old world, nobody seeming to care about what happened to him in life. He had no idea what to do when August rolled around. There was a reason to get up so early for nine months straight for thirteen years, but now this year, when he woke up early, it would be for no worthy reason. He'd wake up to days devoid of routine and habit. A whole empty world would be there to greet him when he opened his eyes from sleep.

"He doesn't need to go to college," Nate said. "He already knows how to write."

"True," Mama said. "But he still wants to go, don't you son?"

The Writer looked up toward his mother with an empty look. Yes, he still wanted to go, but only to a school that could accept him as he was, not conformed to the ways of the so-called average genius who could think at the rate of five-hundred thoughts a second, get 4.0 on every state test, do scientific levels of math, be a real conversationalist, and be like everyone else. Those schools could care less about morals, he thought. They just want to look good in college books that juniors and seniors get every spring.

It got to be close to eleven o'clock and his friends were getting tired. Lana wound up winning the Monopoly game and was teasing Annie over and over about how she had nothing left. They remembered that tomorrow was Sunday, which also meant church. All of them started getting ready to leave and each one hugged The Writer and his mother, thanking her over and over for the pizza. Pretty soon, the only other car left outside was Blade's.

The last to arrive and the last to leave, The Writer thought as he stood in the doorway. He asked his mother where Blade was.

"He had to go to the bathroom," she said, picking up the empty boxes. "I guess so since he drank a whole bottle of coke by himself. What are you gonna do now son?"

"I may go sit on the swing in the yard for a little bit, then go to bed. You need me to help you?"

"No that's okay. I'll finish cleaning up here. Just lock the door when you come back in."

The Writer walked out into the yard and looked at the distant lights of the town. He could see headlights zooming this way and that at top speed, an occasional blue light flashing, and somewhere in the far distance someone was shooting off firecrackers. It was all signs that another generation had been unleashed into the world to either make a dramatic contribution of change to it or simply nothing.

He saw that his dogs and cats had settled on the porch for the evening and that this day he had so long waited for was finally coming to an end. He sat on the swing under the oak tree next to the driveway to savor the final moments of the day as they passed away with the night. Pretty soon he heard the screen door on the porch slam shut and the crunching of gravel under someone's feet coming closer to the swing. He knew who it was, and he waited for him to come closer.

"What are you doing out here?" Blade's deep voice asked sarcastically. The Writer slowly inched his head around and could make out the silvery outline of Blade standing behind him.

"You going home?" he asked quietly.

"I'm about to. Gotta get ready for church in the morning. I left your present on the coffee table. Did all the girls think I'd forget it?"

The Writer nodded.

"Show's how smart they are," he said.

"You all didn't have to get me anything," The Writer said. "I don't need anything for graduation."

"Ah, but you'll love what we got you sir. The girls insisted and we knew it just fit you when we saw it."

Don't argue with him Writer, he thought. Just take the gift and savor the thought behind it. Just think about who gave it to you . . .

Blade inched his head lower and looked at the expression on The Writer's face. "Is something wrong sir? You look tired."

"I am," he said, slowly turning back around to him. He could see a soft beam of moonlight hitting Blade's forehead and highlighting his eyes. He could tell Blade was looking at him, for a look of deep concern had overtaken his face. "Can you sit and talk for a minute?"

"Sure." He came around and plopped himself down next to The Writer and with a swift kick of his feet, set the swing in motion. "What's up?" He looked at The Writer and saw that he had that far off look in his face and eyes again. They were fixed on the darkness of the night, glaring at whatever was out in the world hidden under blackness.

"Do you remember that Bible I gave you . . . back when we were freshmen?"

"Yep. Still got it. Why?"

"Did it make you happy when I gave it to you?" His voice was faint and trailed off.

"Does this have to do with when that counselor had you analyzed by some head shrinker?"

He nodded.

"Is she still after you?"

He nodded again.

"You should just have her come talk to me if she can't lay off and leave you alone. I'll give her a piece of my mind and I guarantee she'll leave you alone. I don't care how clumsy the girls think I am."

"I just asked you . . . "

"Yes sir it did, and it still does. I use it every Sunday at church. The leather backing on it is losing its shine because of where I hold it during services. You shouldn't be worrying about that sir. You know I love it."

"I just had to make sure. I hope you still do."

"Well, I do sir. It means a lot to me. Nobody else ever gave me a Bible until you did and I don't know why that woman thinks it's a travesty that you did that for me. She's a nutcase, almost as senseless as Annie is." He giggled and The Writer just shook his head. "I'm just kidding," he said. "She's sweet. You all love to pick on me don't you?"

The Writer looked towards him.

"I know you all do. I have no idea where you all come up with these ridiculous insults. You know Annie called me a 'turdbucket' the other day because I wouldn't go with her and the other girls to practice bowling for the tournament next week. I'd rather go with the guys and practice. You think we'll win this year, captain sir?"

The Writer shrugged as he looked at the sky.

"Maybe God will see fit that we win this year. Don't you? We can always ask Him to help us. That's all we can do."

The Writer just sat in silence. Deep down, he was savoring every moment of being with Blade, not wanting him to leave, but he knew good and well that he had to get home and get ready for church tomorrow. He knew Blade was the strongest one of all of them. He told things as they were and didn't dress them up with creative flourishes or embellishments. He told the solid truth and nothing less. That's why he wasn't very appreciated by the other kids at school. They knew that he would tell if something was wrong, especially if he saw them doing it. He wasn't afraid to stand up to or for anything. Even though he was a bit clumsy and klutzy at times he was still loads of fun to pick on, because his defensiveness was reflected in the way he teased back.

"Well sir, I better get on home. Do you need to talk about anything else?"

He shook his head.

"Alright then. Promise me you won't let this bother you anymore, okay?"

He nodded. Blade shook his hand, got in his car, and took off down the road. The Writer looked at his watch and saw that it was almost eleven-thirty. I still have a present to open, he thought.

He then waddled away . . . back to the house to open whatever it was his friends gave him for graduation.

T

CHAPTER FIVE

The Writer awoke early on Sunday. He looked at the clock and saw that he had two hours before church started. He got dressed, made his breakfast, fed the cats and dogs, and went to the phone. He looked at Rusty's number which he kept on a memo sheet in the phone book. He dialed and waited to hear his familiar, oil-soaked voice.

No answer.

He dialed again.

Nothing.

Then he remembered that his folks attend a church where they have an early service, so The Writer took this as the reason why nobody was home this morning.

On the wall next to the clock he displayed the knife set that Blade had got him for his present. It was a set of seven knives and on each one was engraved in gold script a special message from Lana, Dionne, Annie, Jackie, Elaine, Blade, and Nate. Ironically, the knives had a special feature. Each one was also a pen. The back of the set was polished oak wood with a shimmering finish. The knives had a blue marble handle with a rubber grip. This was on the knives in case The Writer should ever want to write with them, but he doubted that he would. Each knife had its own place on the board and aimed downward, the middle one being the biggest, and of course was the one Blade had his message inscribed on. On top of the display, on a small brass plaque, was inscribed in scroll font, simply,

The Pen . . .

and under the knives was another small brass plaque. It read . . .

. . . mightier than the sword

Mama came downstairs in her church dress, went in the kitchen, grabbed a cinnamon roll, a cup of coffee, and came out into the living room where her son was sitting in her rocker looking out the window.

"Did you sleep good last night?"

He nodded.

"I did somewhat. Those sirens woke me up till around two in the morning. I guess all those who graduated went crazy last night partying."

"A whole bunch said they were going skinny dipping," The Writer said.

"Oh my, where?"

"The lake."

Mama wore a look of disgust on her face as she ate her roll. "It's a shame. You'd think young people would thank God for what they have in life now that they've graduated, not go out and get drunk."

After she finished eating she ran back up to the bathroom, grabbed her Bible from her bedroom, came back down, and they headed off for church.

At the church building, visitors and regular members of the congregation were filing in for the Sunday school service. The Writer sat out with the adults in the main hall while Mama took the elementary school kids to one of the classrooms in the back.

The next hour was the worship service portion and the auditorium was filling up close to its capacity. It was mostly visitors from all over the southeast, from South Carolina, Georgia, Alabama, Florida, to as far north as West Virginia, and as far as Nebraska and Indiana. It was just the beginning of the annual summer migration of tourists to the mountains of North Carolina. Between now and the middle of August tourists would descend upon the mountain valleys and resorts like locusts over a field of corn and wheat. Mama could expect to see more customers come into the bookstore in the coming weeks.

The Writer and his mother sat in the third row from the back.

The Writer sat in the spot closest to the wall. He hated being out in the middle of the pew where people could crowd him in. If he had to get up in a hurry because of his asthma and allergies he wouldn't have to step on anyone's foot with his big feet. It also made him feel nervous, like everyone was watching him, from behind and on the sides. Being closely surrounded in a public place totally made him lose focus, and he didn't want to lose focus on whatever the lesson was being presented today. His attention span was on that of a single wavelength, directed to only one subject or person at a time. Anymore than that there a frayed wire erupted somewhere in his mind and no point would ever be made coming from him.

Joey and Judy had to work on Sunday and could not come with The Writer and his mother. His seven friends attended other churches today. Annie, Lana, and Dionne attended one together, Nate and his family went to one, and Blade's family went to another, along with Jackie and Elaine. Since this was the Sunday after graduation, it only seemed fitting that the families of the graduates go to the same church together, especially if they made a long trip to North Carolina to see the ceremony. After the morning service, it was the usual routine for The Writer and his mother— leave the building, go out to eat, go home, rest until time for the evening service, go out to eat again, then go home, and get ready for school. The latter no longer applied to The Writer, as it had for the last thirteen years.

The Writer went to the evening service by himself that night. His mother was too tired to go so she decided to take a nap late in the afternoon. She was still asleep when it came time for the evening service, so he left her a note, telling her where he was, and that he may stop by Joey's house on the way home.

Rather than take the truck, The Writer walked to the church building, which was only a little less than a mile from the house. He had a lot on his mind and this was the perfect opportunity for him to think things out as best he could. The top priority on his mind was Rusty. Where was he for the graduation? Why was there no answer at his house? Was there any truth behind what Annie said about him last night at the house? Only God knows, he thought.

The service was on Philippians 4:8, which taught how to think on things that are true, noble, right, pure, lovely, and admirable, or anything excellent or praiseworthy. All through it The Writer tried to place Rusty in those ideals but didn't know how he could. That was something else to think about as he walked back home.

He also wondered if Joey was true to those ideals. Despite the great gap in their ages, The Writer pondered over what really went through Joey's mind when they were together.

Two boys.

The Writer and Joey.

One eighteen, the other fifteen.

One of them was quiet and the other was loud and outgoing. It was another case of opposites attract, only this one was less afflicted than the one with Rusty. He had let his mind wander so far off that it began to question his friendship with Joey, who had remembered him on his birthday, Christmas, and now graduation. Was Joey too good to be true? he thought. I worry too much.

He turned off onto the driveway, walked up to the front door, and knocked.

"Come in," called Judy.

The Writer went in and saw Judy spread out on the couch watching TV.

"Hey there," she said, getting up. "Grab you a seat and watch TV with me. Joey's still at work. He should be home any minute."

The Writer stood in the doorway and looked around the room. The lamp next to the couch where Judy was lying was turned on and except for the glare of the TV, that was the only light in the house. The Writer welcomed this cozy atmosphere, came on in, shut the door, and walked across the living room, looking at the white carpet. He went and stood behind the lamp, just beyond its beam and watched the opening scenes of a rerun of *The X-Files*.

"This must be the one where someone steals Mulder's identity and they switch bodies. I've seen this before. Do you ever watch *The X-Files*, Writer?"

He shook his head. He had heard of the series numerous times from everyone at school, who would always talk about the episode from the night before on Monday morning. When it first premiered he thought it was a series based on real stories that were unsolved and dealt with the supernatural, like *Unsolved Mysteries*. He was disappointed when he found out that it was all a clever work of fiction, then he went deeper and realized it to be the work of an ingenious writer, one with a head for the supernaturally sci-fi stuff.

Judy saw that he was still standing. She got up and slapped the space next to her on the couch. "C'mon, sit down! You don't have to stand. I won't bite ya, not too hard anyway." She laughed. The Writer gestured that he was fine and that he didn't want to sit down.

"Can I get you something to drink? Water? Tea? Coke? My last bottle of V8?"

He shook his head again.

"Alright then."

The Writer inched around the couch away from the beam of the light. He carefully studied the arrangement of her living room. There was a huge fireplace across from the TV, a love seat next to the front door, a long couch across from it where he was standing, the kitchen off to the side, not open for all to see into, and a dining room set in front of the sliding glass doors that went out onto the deck.

"So how's your mom doin'?" she asked.

"She's okay," came the gentle reply from above her head.

"Tell her I'll get by to see her sometime this week. I've been so busy working downtown at the courthouse in the morning and then working at the restaurant in the evening. Me and her need to plan a shopping trip to Asheville, hit all the malls, spend our money. You know how us women are. Can't live without our shopping malls."

"You just saw her yesterday," The Writer pointed out, getting the impression from Judy that she had not seen his mother in years.

"I know sir, but that was just to see you graduate. I had to get to work the minute I dropped you all off at the house, so I didn't get to talk to her all that I wanted to. You know how women are—they never have enough to talk about."

A light gleamed into the living room from outside.

"That must be Joey," Judy said, getting up to peep out through the curtains. "Yep, it is. One of his friends brought him home. I can't wait until he turns sixteen so he can get his license. Why don't you go out and meet him? I know he'd be glad to see you after today."

He nodded and headed for the door as she held it open for him. "Oh, I'm not running you off," she said. "But if you have to leave so soon . . . "

"I don't want to get home too late," he said. "I just . . . uh . . . wanted to see Joey for a minute."

"Okay, well, I'll see you . . . sometime soon, I hope. Come back anytime alright? You're always welcome."

He nodded and went out, stopped in the doorway, then turned around to her.

"Uh, could you turn off the porch light? I'd just feel better with it off."

"Uh . . . sure. Okay," she said, switching it off. "Make sure Joey doesn't fall out there."

The Writer slowly walked to the steps that were at the end of the porch. He stood up there and watched Joey come walking up the driveway to the steps. When he saw who was up there looking at him he shuddered.

"Man you scared me. Are you leaving?"

No response. Joey came closer and offered to help him down the steps, thinking The Writer couldn't see very well in the dark. From up above the full moon shone a bright silvery gleam upon the earth through the trees near the house. It was just enough for The Writer to see his way around. He came down the steps and stood next to Joey.

"So what's up?" Joey asked. "Boy I worked from ten this morning until about half an hour ago. I'm so tired. I'm ready for bed."

The Writer looked at the gravel in the driveway, then up towards the sky. He kept his hands grasped together on his round tummy, and even with his peripheral vision he could see Joey's eyes fixed on his face. He was trying to formulate in his mind how to ask Joey what he wanted to ask him. Don't stay around here too long, he thought. Joey's tired. He wants to get in the bed. Just say what you want to say to him, get on home, and let him go to bed.

"I just . . . uh . . . wanted to ask you . . . "

"I have something to ask you too," Joey said. "Lana and Dionne were asking me at work when the bowling tournament was. I told them I'd ask 'the bowling king' and tell them tomorrow."

The Writer nodded, looking up into the sky.

"So when is it your majesty?"

He rolled his eyes back to the ground and looked straight ahead at the headlights of a car that was flying fast down the main road past Joey's house. He could see the dust that billowed up from the road behind it. He heard it make a deep thumping noise as it roared past.

"It's uh . . . Thursday night I think," he said.

"Cool. I'll tell our boss to let us have that night off. Maybe we'll win the first place trophy this year."

The Writer's team consisted of Joey, Annie, Lana, Dionne, Blade, Jackie, Elaine, and Nate. It was a nine-member team, dramatically compared to the teams of thirty or forty that usually took home the gold trophy. His team, which he named "The Writer's Pins", usually came in around eighth or ninth place, but that was only due to the scores The Writer got when he bowled. Blade held up the tail end of whatever the scores were for them. This would be the first year Joey bowled on their team.

The Writer looked back up, still away from Joey, trying to figure out the best way to ask him what he wanted. This mention of bowling reminded him of all the times he and Joey had gone together just for fun, and all the times Joey celebrated a victory over him by jumping up and down and screaming "I beat The Writer! I beat The Writer!" When the operator printed out the bowling scores, Joey took the sheet that had his winning score, tore it in half, and gave The Writer the piece with their names down the left side of the scoreboard and he kept the piece that had his score on it. He proudly displayed it on his dresser in his bedroom for all his other friends to see.

Yes, his other friends, who were closer to his age and interests than The Writer was, but could not see what Joey ever saw in somebody like him, an overweight, introverted bastard child who's scared to death that other people in the world make you the towering idol of humiliation and insults.

"Do you need to go?" Joey asked.

"Want me to?"

"No, I was just asking."

Joey looked at his face and could see his eyes begin to sparkle in the moonlight. He came closer to him.

"What's wrong?"

"Nothing."

"You sure?"

He nodded. "I need to go," he said.

Joey came around in front of him with his arms outstretched to him. The Writer turned his head away from him and looked into Judy's rosebushes that grew next to the steps. They were brilliantly illuminated by the moonlight with a silvery outline. No color. Just white silver for a soothing effect.

"Don't I get a hug?" he asked. The Writer did not answer. He began to move away from Joey, but only stepped back a foot. Joey moved closer, kept looking at his face, and put his arm around him. There's something wrong, he thought. Why won't you tell me?

Does he really want a hug or is he just doing it so I won't feel bad? The Writer thought. Yes, I want to hug him, but only if he really means that he wants me to. But I have to ask him. Oh dear Lord I can't tell what's true in life anymore. Why am I so paranoid?

"I just want to ask you . . . uh . . . " The Writer stammered.

"What?"

"If . . . uh . . . you . . . "

Joey looked at him closer. He patted his hand on his shoulder.

"Do you like it when I take you bowling?"

"Yes. If I didn't I wouldn't go with you."

Okay, does he mean that, he thought. Next question.

"Do you like it when I take you places, or when we do things?"

"Yes. Why do you ask?"

Because I think you just go with me so I won't feel bad and because you think you have to so my feelings won't be hurt, he thought. I think you just put up with me when I come around. No, I can't say that. It would make him mad. I wish I knew he was telling me the truth. Maybe he is. How can I tell?

He looked up again at the bushes.

"I was just wondering. Making sure. I know we don't . . . uh . . . I'm not like . . . well . . . we don't do the things you do with your other friends."

"That doesn't matter," Joey said, trying to get a better look at The Writer's face, but he always eluded him by turning it away or by lowering his head, allowing his hat brim to hide his eyes. "I like what we do when we're together."

"It's not much though . . . "

"That's fine with me. I like whatever we do."

He came back around in front of The Writer and stood before him. Again he held out his arms. One hand was in a perfect position where a beam of moonlight fell on it, so The Writer simply slipped his big right hand into Joey's and tightened his grip on it. He closed his eyes, feeling the warm, gentle surge of Joey's bony hand fill his hand, and tried to let the warmth go to his heart. He eventually gave Joey a long hug.

"Can you get home alright?" Joey asked.

The Writer nodded and began backing away, still not looking at Joey's face.

"Call me okay?" Joey said. He stood on the steps watching him slip farther into the dark of the night. He still felt that there was something else bothering him, but he wished he'd just tell him. His shoulder felt cold. He touched it and discovered it was damp where The Writer rested his head during their hug.

The Writer kept backing away.

"Be careful," he said as The Writer turned around and walked forward.

And he waddled away . . . going back to his house.

CHAPTER SIX

The Writer's mind was filled with thoughts, thoughts and images, images that reflected Mr. Graham's sermon on thinking on things that were true and pure and good. What is true, good, and pure to me? What was true? Annie and the rest of the little gang? Probably so. Rusty, how can I tell? Joey, dear Lord I hope so.

WHY AM I SO FREAKIN' PARANOID ABOUT EVERYONE?!

Dear God please get my mind out of this rut. I hate thinking this way, suspicious of everyone, thinking everyone is just putting on a big show to please me when really I am the most disgusting, despicable, loathsome piece of . . . that 's' word everyone called me in school. Am I too fat for others to appreciate? I love to eat. I can't help that. What does Joey think when we're out together and everyone sees this slender guy hanging out with this overweight tub of pudginess? When I sit down my rear fills the seat, my back is widespread, and my chest . . . my chest . . . dear God that made for so many jokes in school. All the boys saw my chest and grabbed for it, yanking and pulling both sides. Some girls thought I was addicted to estrogen, others thought I was undergoing treatment for a sex-change operation. They told me to start wearing a bra. A few asked if I was a mixed gender breed of some sort, as well as being your biggest—they emphasized 'biggest'—mistake in letting me live. Does Joey and the others think like they do and hide it under their "friendship" to me? Or is it true? How can I be sure? God show me in some way that I have nothing to worry about with Joey or the rest of my little band of friends.

It was times like this, walking alone somewhere when it was quiet, that he found himself talking to God openly. He never realized he did it until he thought about it, then stopped, fearing someone somewhere was listening. It was also times like this that his mind began to wander freely around in the vast open spaces of the human conscience. Tonight as he walked home from Joey's house it bumped off of thoughts of Rusty. With that came the looks on Mama's face whenever he mentioned Rusty to her, a look of pain and heartache, for she could remember all the times she'd seen The Writer break down when Rusty never kept a promise, which was every time he made a promise. His mind then hit upon a dim memory from high school as a freshman . . .

He was sitting in the cafeteria, waiting for Nate, Jackie, Elaine, and Blade to come sit with him. Annie, Lana, and Dionne's lunch period had already passed, and they were in class. Joey was not in high school yet, but was still in middle school, and he and The Writer had yet to meet. Neither one knew at this time that they lived so close together for so long.

It was the week of the homecoming game for the school. All the football players were the idols of popularity for the duration of the week. One of the team's biggest and most boisterous fans was none other than Rusty, who just showed up in the cafeteria out of the blue that day to hang out with the team. The yelling, laughter, and irritable Redneck yowls they spewed at each other easily made them candidates for mating calls in the jungles of South Africa.

The Writer kept an eye on Rusty the whole time. Rusty finally saw him and waved. He waved back, happy that he had been seen, but the joy was short-lived. Later in the day there was an ugly rumor circulating around the school about how The Writer couldn't throw a football to save his life. To go along with it, the rumor also said that The Writer's only point of defense was his ability to keep his legs closed, and that he couldn't "score a touchdown" with any girl if he tried. It took him a while to figure out the gross hinting behind it. After that he never ate in the cafeteria ever again, even though his friends tried to make him.

He also didn't know whether or not to believe what Annie had

told him later that week, that it was Rusty who started the vile
rumors.

Dear God please do something to get my mind off Rusty, he
thought over and over.

It usually took about five minutes to briskly walk to his house
from Joey's by way of the main road, but if you cut through the
field that stood between their houses it only took about two minutes. The Writer was quite fearful of snakes and was chilled at the
very thought of stepping on one anywhere in the field, so he walked
next to the road. He never knew how brave Joey was to come across
that field as much as he had and not come upon a coiled reptile
waiting to spring at his bony legs.

The road was rarely traveled at night. Only about two other
families lived down the road past his house. He could see the first
of the night's stars twinkle their way into sight through the branches
that stretched out over the road. Crickets were coming out, fire-
flies began to dance in the open field between the houses, and he
could see the light from the living room at his house, a signal that
Mama was sitting in her rocker with the lamp on, knitting or
crocheting her latest project.

It's so peaceful here Lord, he thought as he walked, trying to
get his mind off the depression circuit. I wish my dad, or rather
Mama's husband, was here to enjoy it, to have seen me graduate
. . . anyway, help me decide on how to set up one of the novels I
hope to start soon. Should I have the main character go off to war
in the Persian Gulf or let him stay here in the states and pray for
those that do go?

He looked up at the stars. A gentle breeze fell upon him from
the night sky.

Okay, he goes off to war, but doesn't fight, he decided as he
kept walking. He'll just encourage others to be strong and coura-
geous, even though Saddam Hussein is the monster he appears to
be.

He continued on his way. His house was getting closer in view
from the road. On up ahead the shadows from the overhanging

tree branches made the road look darker than it really was. Huge bloated masses of black slithered all across the road in all directions, like India ink soaking up tissue paper. The shadows looked as if to be eating up the road. Whenever the wind blew, the shadows would bend and spread this way and that.

But there was something else up there on the road that would not move with the shadows.

The Writer saw it and came closer to it, and saw that it was at the turn off onto the driveway to his own house. It was a big lump in the road, a long, bumpy lump. He slowly inched his way closer, fearing it was a dog someone had mercilessly hit and killed. But it was way too long for a dog and there was no gut-wrenching stench accompanying it. When he found himself standing about two feet from it he could see more clearly what it was.

He was standing right over it now. Whatever it was it was all black. Even if someone were to shine a light on it the thing would be black in color. The moonlight from the clearing in the trees where the driveway was revealed what this black thing was.

He nudged it with one of his big feet. It was soft but sturdy. The thing didn't move at first. He was about to nudge it again when it let out a deep groan and rolled over. The Writer jolted back in fright, as if he had just about stepped on a snake. His heartbeat went into overdrive. He could now see what this thing was.

A human being.

The Writer stood back for a few minutes, allowing his nerves to settle. He looked up and down the road and saw nobody coming or going. He looked out into the field and saw the light in Joey's bedroom upstairs still on, but it quickly went out. He had gone to bed already. He made sure nobody else was around, then stepped back closer to the body.

He knelt down and got close to the face. It was a boy. He had black hair, pale sweaty flesh, whiskers and sideburns all over the face, a goatee, and an odor that reminded him of his mother boiling cabbage in the kitchen. This was enough to tell him that this

guy had not bathed in a long time. He saw that his black t-shirt
was ripped down the front, his leather jacket was covered in red
dirt, his pants were torn open down one of his legs, and his shoes
looked as if they were about to rot off his feet, as if in the last stages
of deterioration. There was a long jagged cut on one of his arms.

The Writer nudged him again and got no response. He felt his
wrist and detected a fast-going pulse.

He looked around again and saw that he was the only one
around this stranger. I can't leave him here, he thought. I just
hope Mama won't bawl me out if I bring him home. Lord, what
shall I do? If I leave him here, he may get run over and get killed,
then I'd never forgive myself. If I bring him home, Mama may fuss
at me till I get rid of him. Maybe I can sneak out later tonight
with a plate of food for him, but what would happen between now
and later tonight? I don't even know how long he's been here.

He thought back at all the times he'd brought home stray
dogs and cats and even rabbits. Mama warned him over and over
that they could be rabid, so she let him feed them and keep them
for one night then call the vet the next morning to come and get
them. Sometimes he brought home animals that were injured.
Mama helped him as best she could with the poor creatures but
always wound up calling the vet anyway.

This was one time she could not call the vet. This wasn't a
dog, a cat, a rabbit, or a ground hog.

This was a human being.

Her first impulse would probably be to call the police, he
thought. God, I hope she doesn't. Please make her understand
that I can't just leave him here like this. He needs help.

He thought it over long and hard as it got to be later than
when he was supposed to be back home. What if this is some
crazed killer who's had too much to drink or too much sniffed up
his nose? What if he's a drug thug selling crack? A horny rapist? A
mentally deranged patient from a madhouse? A good potential
convert?

The last thought stayed in his mind as he began to recall all the lessons he'd heard in Sunday school concerning how to look on the inside of a person and not to judge by what the naked eye saw. It would be so easy to just walk away from this boy and let him see what his lifestyle just got him into. But he also knew that if Jesus were standing here over him, and in some sense He was, He'd want to take care of him and not cast him out into the dark of the night.

I know what I'm doing Lord, he thought as he stooped over the stranger. Help me out here please. I know I can do this. If I don't who will?

Or is it if I don't, who else won't?

He then waddled away . . . carrying the stranger over his shoulder to the house.

CHAPTER SEVEN

When Mama heard the dogs start yelping and carrying on, she went out onto the front porch with her knitting needles in her hands.

"Queenie! Koko! Be quiet!" she said, then looked and saw what was coming up the driveway to the house. The light from the moon made the dark figure that was coming look like something out of Sleepy Hollow, only this apparition had a head.

"Son what did you bring home this . . . oh my Lord." Her mouth dropped open when she saw what was in her son's arms, limbs hanging as if dead. She looked all around, glanced in the screen door, and yanked it open.

"Hurry, bring him in. Put him on the couch. I'll get a wet cloth or something. My heavens he stinks!"

The Writer carried the stranger into the living room. Two of his cats, Blue and Bunny, looked at the stranger and scolded, their fur standing on end, and inched away as he placed him on the couch. Mama hurried into the kitchen, wet a washcloth, and put it on the stranger's sweaty forehead. She then used it to wipe his face. When she took it off his face, she saw that it was caked with black dirt, thick sweat, and a stench that soon perfumed the whole house.

"Son, open all the windows in the house. No, I'll get the ones upstairs and you get those down here. This smell is awful. We have to bathe him before anything else." She went upstairs to open the ones that weren't already open and her son turned on all the fans that were downstairs, including the one over the stove. He also opened all the air fresheners as wide as they would go. He placed all the fans in front of the windows so they could draw out some of the foul odor.

"Golly, this reminds me of the times you had a smelly diaper," Mama said as she came back downstairs. "Like the time I picked you up out of your crib back at the old place where I used to live and I could feel something squishy all up your back. I pulled your shirt up and all this . . . "

Her son was looking towards her, but again, not directly at her face. He did not look too thrilled at her little reminiscing of his infant past.

"Your diaper was overloaded . . . anyway, can you carry him upstairs to the bathroom? This stink is going to make us sick. Smells like the cabbage I cook."

No kidding, more like fresh roadkill, The Writer thought. He pulled the collar of his black t-shirt up over his nose, lifted the stranger, and carried him up the stairs to the bathroom. Mama pinched her nostrils shut as he passed her. She got a glance at the face and saw that he looked pale as death and as if he had just been hatched from some cocoon in those body snatcher movies.

She followed after them.

The Writer got to the bathroom door, flipped the light on with his elbow, and set the stranger down on the toilet. He propped his upper body back against the tank as best he could. He stood back and felt his own shirt soaked in sweat and whatever else this guy had on him.

"You're gonna have to bathe tonight too son," Mama said, standing in the doorway. "Need me to help you?"

He shook his head.

"Are you sure? He looks pretty big . . . "

The Writer stood back and gestured for her to look at his own build, if she wanted to talk big.

"Come on son. I've seen a naked man before. I know I'm the only female who's seen you naked so what are you ashamed of? At least I hope I'm the only female. I BETTER BE!"

"I can bathe him."

"Are you sure?"

He nodded. Mama looked long at him, then at the stranger,

then at her watch. It was close to ten o'clock. She had to be at work at the bookstore by eight in the morning.

"Well, I guess it's alright. You carried him here from . . . where did you find him? You didn't pick him up did you? Now I know you love to bring stray animals home but people . . . I have to put a limit on this somewhere . . . "

"He was lying next to the road. He was hurt so I brought him home. I couldn't leave him there to die. Would you have done the same thing?"

Mama looked at her son again. She could see the dead seriousness in his face and his eyes, those eyes, the eyes that sent chills up her spine when she remembered who he got his eyes from. Even though they were not focused on her she could tell that he could see her, and that he was watching her as she stood in the doorway. For a split second the eerie spirit of her son's father seemed to drift into the room, but quickly went away when she got control of her mind and realized that this was her strong son, not a reincarnate of his natural father.

"Okay son," she said calmly, slowly backing out of the bathroom. "I'll . . . uh . . . be in my room if you need me, okay?"

He nodded. She then reached for the bathroom fan and put it on high, and in the exhaust mode. The soothing rumble of the fan going at top speed created a sense of elation, as if to signal that this incident will pass without injury. She shut the door and let The Writer have at the stranger.

He took a deep breath and started.

Lord help me here.

He went to the tub and turned on the warm water. The tub slowly began to fill up. He thought it best to set him in the tub than try to stand him up in the shower.

He took off the crumbling shoes and the queasy stench of the dirty feet and toes poking out of the rotting socks nearly knocked him against the wall. They were soiled and dingy, caked with grime and black mold. He peeled off the rotting cloth and it fell to the floor in cracking thuds. He saw that his feet were black with dirt and had cuts and bruises all over them, as well as several blisters.

He stood up and slipped the black jacket off. As he dropped it on the floor he heard a clang. In one of the pockets was a silver chain poking out. He took it and placed it on the counter next to the sink. Pretty soon it was joined with brass knuckles, a pocket-knife that made him think of Blade, and ironically, a razor blade, as if to accompany the thought.

Now came the fun part. Taking the shirt off. He lifted it from the bottom and pulled up. There was a loud rip. The sleeves had torn off. He saw that all the sweat buildup under the arms had eaten away the cloth fibers. The Writer slipped off the remains of the sleeves, put them in the trash, and looked at the stranger.

He was bare shouldered, barely tanned, and had hair all over his chest, down to his belly, and had cuts and bruises all over his chest, back, and stomach. His belly was evenly divided in half by a single line of hair that trailed down to his naval. There was a tattoo on his left arm. It was the name "Brute" written in big letters that looked like black cobwebs. Above the name was the image of two eyes peeping out from under a black hood.

He shrugged off these discoveries and continued to undress him. The water in the tub was now at bath level so he shut it off. He stooped down to take off the stranger's pants. He unfastened the jeans, unzipped them, and closed his eyes. He grabbed hold of the top of his jeans, made sure he also had a grasp of the under-pants, and pulled down as fast as he could. Afraid of seeing where the actual stench was coming from on him, he quickly rolled up the jeans and tossed them on top of the other clothes. Now totally naked, the stranger was still asleep, unknowing of what was being done to him. The Writer lifted him up off the toilet seat and placed him in the tub. He slowly laid him back in the tub, making sure his head didn't hit anything. He grabbed a washcloth from the basket on top of the toilet tank, grabbed the soap, and washed him all over as best he could. The smell had gotten so bad since taking the clothes off that The Writer wore a white mask that covered his nose and mouth.

He slept the whole time while being bathed.

The Writer could not help but look at all the cuts that stretched all over his flesh through the hair on his body. Some were healing. Others looked fresh. He saw how big boned and muscular this guy was. He looked to be in his early twenties. His face was sturdily built and the flesh was peachy colored. The Writer also shaved him while he was in the tub. He shaved off the goatee, the sideburns, and the whiskers. Under all that hair was one of the most sleek and shiny faces he'd ever seen. The cheek bones were high, and his flesh was a tad chubby but solid.

The water quickly turned cloudy with dirt. The stench was fading away.

When he was finished with him he lifted him up out of the water and carried him to his bedroom. He laid him out on the bed and tried to dry him off as best he could. Powdering him was out, since the fine dust would cause him to have a mad sneezing fit. He flipped him over on his front side and dried off his back. He then went to his closet to find him something to wear for the night. There was an old nightgown that he had outgrown last year, and The Writer figured, that if it used to fit someone as big as him, it should fit this guy. As he tried to slip it on him, he thought again. This guy was so dowsed in sweat and heat, he may feel better sleeping without a top on, so The Writer put the gown away. He went to his dresser and pulled out a pair of shorts, slipped them on the stranger, and laid him back down on the bed. He stood back and looked at him.

He does not look very comfy, he thought. I've slept here all week and not washed the sheets yet. I'll put him in the guest room where there's a bathroom. Again he picked him up, carried him out into the hallway, and took him to the guest room, which was at the very top of the stairs. He passed his mother's bedroom door and saw that she had already turned out her light and was gone to bed. He opened the guest room and saw that it was dark, but there was enough light from his bedroom for him to see his way to the bed. He laid the stranger down on it then switched on the lamp next to the bed. It was one of those touch lamps, and he had it on the night light beam. A cool breeze came in from the open window on the other side of the room. It would keep the stranger from getting too hot in the night.

The Writer ran back to his room, turned off the light, and came back to the guest room. He thought it best to stay in here with him all night and make sure he didn't do anything. He pulled the rocking chair that was next to the window up to the bed, went over and closed the bedroom door. The room was calm, glowing, and silent.

He then waddled away . . . to sit in the rocker, and drifted off to sleep.

CHAPTER EIGHT

Mama poked her head in the door the next morning and saw her son dozing in the rocker and the stranger still asleep in the bed. She wondered for a minute if she should take the day off and stay home to help The Writer take care of their special guest. But no, she couldn't. Today was the day a famous local author was having a book signing party at the bookstore where she worked, and it was her job to make sure her spot was all set up and ready to go for the endless stream of eager fans and loyal readers.

She looked forward to the day she could arrange her own son's book signing party at her little store.

He can handle him, she thought. He found him. He carried him home. He bathed him. I did nothing . . . no, he can handle him, I hope, I pray. Yes, Linda, your son can handle him. He doesn't always need you around . . . no, that's too cruel to think about. My son's growing up. I have to let him go sometime. He's still my baby, but he's not a baby anymore . . . this will teach him responsibility in the world. Imagine that . . . my baby's bigger than I am. Dear God look after him today while I'm gone.

She hurried down the stairs to the kitchen, fixed herself a cup of black coffee, and grabbed a cinnamon roll. She switched on the TV to listen to *Good Morning America* as she got ready to leave. They were about to give the weather when she heard the dogs barking. A loud horn started beeping. She looked up from digging around in her pocketbook and realized with disgusted horror who had just pulled into her yard. She could recognize the sound of the car.

It was that of Mrs. Moran, for she was the only one in town who drove a late-70's model for which the parts to it were gradually becoming extinct. Anytime she drove it in town she left a thick trail of blue exhaust hanging in the air, clogging the lungs of pedestrians and forcing other motorists to shut off their air conditioners until the wind took the fumes away.

Mama shut off the TV and went into the living room. I told that woman not to come around this house, she thought angrily. She looked out the window and could see the woman coming up the steps to the front door. She went to it but before she could hit the dead bolt, she saw the knob being jerked and jingled. She glanced at the phone.

That woman is just gonna help herself into my house, Mama thought. She won't get too far with that! There was no time to call the cops to come get this weighty tyrant. She would have to handle her herself.

She hastily unlocked the latches and pulled the door open as hard as she could. Mrs. Moran stumbled inside, her pocketbook thrashing around at her knees.

"Yes, *Cheryl*," Mama greeted sarcastically. "What can I *not* do for you today? I'm in a hurry to get to work."

"No you're not," she said, proudly walking into the living room. "You can go to work when I get done here."

"Well it better not take long and it better be good. I can see now that I should have left twenty minutes ago."

"Aw, then you would have missed seeing your son leave," Mrs. Moran said, tilting her head to the side as if she had all the sympathy in the world for Mama.

Leave? Mama wondered. Why would my son want to leave this house with some broad who is total prostitute? She was looking at the way Mrs. Moran was dressed. She wore a yellow blouse that only had the four bottom buttons fastened and the rest showed a small crack of cleavage. Her hair was sprayed stiff to the point of whenever she moved her head, the brown stuff stayed in one solid position. It was curled and fluffed like a clown in a circus act.

"Excuse me but what do you mean 'leave?'" Mama asked. "I don't recall giving you permission to take my son off anywhere."

T

"I don't need your permission when I have an order here from the courts," she declared, waving a paper in the air in front of her face. "Try to overcome the justice system of our country why don't you? I've done an extensive psychological analysis of your son, submitted my report, and have been granted an order by the court to have your son taken to a facility that can thoroughly examine, decipher, and alleviate his deviant behavior at school and in public places."

"And why was I not informed of this little experiment on my son?" Mama asked. "I always thought the parent had the final say about what happens to his or her child. Did you know I can just as well take you to court for doing this? Coming around my house when I asked you repeatedly not to? Analyzing my son and submitting some report without his or even my permission? And now you have the gall to walk in here and demand to take him off to some mental ward just because he's different? What right have you to do that?"

"It's a case of psychological . . . "

"Oh whatever!" Mama interrupted. She grabbed the paper out of Mrs. Moran's hand and began to read over it.

"Go ahead. Read it for yourself. See if whether or not I'm bluffing."

You're the biggest bluff I've ever seen, she thought as she read the order. The order stated that on some date Mrs. Moran filed a psychological report on her son and his so-called "unusual" behavior which involved being extremely silent, bizarre facial expressions, an overwhelming desire to help and assist others, giving little gifts to his friends at Christmas, an exhibition of religious images on his shirts, which was in reference to all of his t-shirts depicting scripture and scenes with Jesus and other Biblical characters, a style of clothing that was "too ludicrous", which was his wearing his coat tied around his waist, his sweat pants legs pulled up to his knees, wearing a waist bag under the coat, and t-shirts each day. The report also included her son being the source of religious conflict in a public school system, whereas some classes would get into a heated discussion the moment someone mentioned The Writer and religion. A final allegation on the report stated that her son displayed "highly irregular conduct and flawed human character" when he gave his friend Blade a Bible for his birthday one year. This accusation made Mama's hands shake with anger and hatred.

"That part about the Bible is most disturbing," Mrs. Moran said. "The public school system cannot tolerate such unusual acts of charity."

"Well what does the public school system of our country allow these days? Knives, guns, student killers? You all let these corrupt undisciplined kids come in off the streets with guns and knives and such. You don't punish them but get after those who have enough sense not to do that because it's what you all call 'unusual' to see a young boy who knows what it is to show kindness and charity to his fellow man. Is that the norm today? Be rebellious and spoiled. Don't be good-hearted to others. Is that it today?"

"Don't talk to me with fairy tale analogies," Mrs. Moran said, stepping closer to her. "We all know your son's just far too good to be true the way he is."

"Oh, and if I let you haul him off, which I WILL NOT let you do, you'll take him off and train him to be a spoiled, rich little brat like so many other kids out there, whose parents never discipline their own kids when something goes wrong and they're at fault but instead, always blame somebody else for what's wrong. Why do parents always think their child is so perfect they can do no wrong out in the world? They look to blame others, but never themselves."

Mrs. Moran looked at her watch, then at the clock on the living room wall. "Your clock's wrong," she said. "I have twenty till eight and your clock says seven-thirty."

"What if my clock is right and yours is wrong?" Mama asked.

"It just is. Mine's always right. Look, will you just sign the consent form on the last page of that order and give it to me so I can take your son off and do what needs to be done with him?"

"No. I will not sign my name to some court order that says my child is a freak just because I raised him like I did and doesn't live up to your senseless ideals."

"Well that must be where you messed up then," she said. She turned and headed for the stairs. Mama flew out in front of her and stood on the third step, towering over Mrs. Moran. The order was getting crushed in her death grip of abhorrence to this creature that was in her house.

"What do you mean I messed up?" Mama demanded. "Are you saying I'm a terrible mother? Well, look at you. If I had a mother who dressed like some cheap hooker I'd be ashamed to go out anywhere."

"Hey, I'm not the mother of some bastard who keeps to himself all the time. Look at Ted Bundy, David Koresh, Ted Kaszinsky, all loners growing up. What do you think your son will become one day if this behavior goes on?"

Where's my knitting needles? Mama thought. I'd love to sew this bitch's hole shut. She was struck silent. This woman had gone too far in exploiting her son's flaws and differences. She was so tempted to draw her foot back and kick it into her mouth, hopefully knocking her out the screen door and into the front yard. Then she'd probably have the police come after her and enforce the order to take The Writer off somewhere.

"Why is my son a bastard?" she asked, keeping her boiling point as low as she could. "Just tell me that. Why is he what you all call, a bastard?"

"Well, isn't he? An accident. A flaw on God's part. You know you could have easily aborted him."

"ARE YOU CALLING MY SON A MISTAKE?!"

"YES I AM LINDA! YOUR SON IS A BIG AND I DO MEAN A BIG MISTAKE! Good Lord Linda he weighs over three hundred pounds. No wonder he's so easily mocked. How could God allow such a being to exist?"

"Because God wanted him to live!" Mama hollered. "If you didn't believe in God you wouldn't say that He made my son. But apparently some part of you does believe in Him. Why can't you be like Him and look past the surface of people, starting with my son?"

"Because I don't think God had it in mind to let your son be as flawed as he is. Just look at the court order. It lists everything about your son that we are going to take care of. He'll be back in about a month if you'll just sign it! Just admit it Linda. God made a mistake with your son. You didn't plan to have him, and he doesn't even need to be here."

Mama turned away and looked down at the steps. The images and scarring pain of the man's heavy arms jerking her onto the ground, tearing her coat and shirt to pieces, yanking her pants off. flahshed through her mind. She could feel the load of his muscular, sweaty body clamping down on her more and more, her pelvic area suffering heavy blows and stings that reached far up into the pit of her stomach. She recalled the man pulling her hair, mashing his fingers into her flesh, smelling the foul stench of his breath. The one grueling feature she could not rid her mind of was his eyes, his deep, hypnotic, possessed eyes that seemed to reach far into the soul and could see the true affairs of the heart and mind. She then felt the joy of holding her first and only child for the first time and thanking God over and over that she survived the ordeal, the premature birth, and letting her child live.

"No Cheryl!" Mama yelled. "The only mistake here is YOU being in my house! My son is NOT a mistake or a flaw on God's part! He made my son the way he is for a reason and if God didn't want my son here then He would've taken him long before I carried him in my womb for eight months."

"I'm just telling you the truth Linda. It hurts doesn't it?"

"Yes, it hurts getting raped and told you can't have anymore children because of it. And it hurts being told that your only child is a mistake! God never makes mistakes! He never has and never will!"

"There's a first time for everything," Mrs. Moran said, stepping up one step on the stairs.

"Why are you doing this?" she asked. "What has my son done that's so terrible to you all at school?"

"It's all in that order Linda. Look, my time's wastin' here with you. Just sign the paper and give me that kid everyone hails as 'The Writer'".

"It's because you people can't see the unique and individual qualities in other people. If you can't see that or aren't willing to then there has to be something missing from your lives. You have to pick apart the lives of those who have what you may never have in life and try to destroy their precious gifts. Taking my son off and altering his mind is going to destroy who he is, how he is, and what he has. To me that's as great a sin as killing someone."

"Listen Linda, I've heard quite enough out of you. Don't start preaching at me because I don't need to hear it!"

"In that case you had better leave this house. You are not taking my son and I am not signing this order and that is that. And I take back what I said earlier, God DOES make mistakes!"

Mrs. Moran's eyes widened at this.

"Yes, God made all things and therefore He created a thing called the mistake. He instilled it in the environment of human nature for us to learn from. He made mistakes for our own good, because He knew we could learn from them. And maybe it was a mistake that I walked home that night instead of calling a cab like my husband asked me to. No, I had to walk instead, because it was a pretty night. If I hadn't, I would not have been blessed with a boy with a talent that gives him the name of 'The Writer.' He has taught me so much he'll never realize it. You call him a flaw. I call him a gift from God. He has a mother, a friend whose mother loves him as much as I do, and he has friends, just a few, but who love him to death and think the world of him. Who are you to say that someone is a flaw who has friends and is loved by others? Who are you to say he has no place on this earth? The Writer has a place, and that is here in the hearts of those who love him."

She opened the court order and looked at the back page. There was the signature of the one who approved the order. The name of the signer caused a shockwave to shoot up her spine.

It was Judy Lowell.

Joey's mother.

Her best friend.

The mother of her son's dear friend.

Her neighbor who worked in the daytime at the courthouse, and at the restaurant across town in the evenings.

Oh God please don't let it be, she prayed in her heart, the pain swelling up in her eyes. Not my best friend, my son's surrogate aunt, please no. God please let this not be her.

Then something in her head clicked. She looked at Judy's signature, studying how unusual it looked.

Then the date.

It was the date of her son's high school graduation. Then she remembered.

Judy was with her that day. She had taken Friday off just so she could go with her to watch The Writer graduate.

She looked even closer at the signature.

The signature was not hers! It was a genuine forgery! Judy never signs her name with a cursive 'J', but with a manuscript 'J', the rest of her first name with a slight slant to the right, the first 'L' in 'Lowell' with skinny loops, not fat ones like this signature had. And Judy always signed her name on the line, not dropping any parts of the letters below the line like this one showed.

And there was no way Mrs. Moran could've known that she and Judy were best friends, almost as close as sisters.

Now I've got her, she thought. *She isn't going to get away with this.*

"SIGN IT!" Mrs. Moran hollered. "And get out of my way so I can go get your son!"

"Lay a hand on my boy and you won't leave this house without a swollen rear, although I couldn't do much more to it now."

Mrs. Moran stepped up another step and was soon face to face with Mama. She grabbed her by the shoulders and began shaking her violently. Mama dropped the order on the floor, tried to shove this woman down the steps but it was no use. Mrs. Moran jerked her up onto the steps and knocked her backward. Mama screamed for her son as loud as she could.

"He ain't gonna do anything. He's a fool just like you are."

Mama lunged up and threw a fist into Mrs. Moran's face. She stumbled backwards and fell down the steps, crashed into the screen door, which opened out and she fell out onto the porch. The screen door was flung open so far out that it came back and slammed into her head as she tried to get up. The dogs, Queenie and Koko, came up to Mrs. Moran and started licking her face all over. The cats ran into the house over her as if she wasn't even there.

"Ah, the story of Jezebel comes to life on my front porch," Mama said as she got up off the stairs, picked up the counterfeit order, and was about to go down to tear it up in front of Mrs. Moran but the noise of the sirens stopped her. She come down the steps and looked out into the front yard. There was a police car with its lights flashing. Two cops, a man and a woman, got out and rushed up into the house. The male cop got Mrs. Moran up, handcuffed her and escorted her out to the car, despite her protests that Mama tried to attack her. The female cop took Mama aside to talk to her. Mama showed her the forged court order and the lady took it.

Both officers said they would check back on her that evening when she got home from work. She thanked them and watched the police car drive off with Mrs. Moran in the back seat still raving like crazy. The officers said they would have a local wrecker come and haul her car off.

Mama walked back into the house and wondered, how did they know she was in trouble? The phone in the living room was out of her reach the whole time Mrs. Moran was there. Someone had to have called them.

A sudden hush fell over the whole house.

She stopped and felt something chilly on her back.

She looked up the stairs.

It stood still for a moment, gazing towards her, but not at her face. It was totally silhouetted in black, but the eyes were gleaming in the morning sun.

She looked at it in thankful wonder.

And it waddled away . . . with the cordless phone in his hand.

T

CHAPTER NINE

Mama called the bookstore and told her assistant that she would be a little late getting there that morning. Her assistant told her not to worry because the local author phoned earlier and said that there would be a slight delay in her getting there as well, so Mama had nothing to fret over.

After she went into her bathroom and had a good cry, she went to thank The Writer for calling the cops, just like she told him to if that woman ever showed up.

He was standing at the top of the stairs when she came out of her bedroom, dry eyed and ready to go on to work. He was looking into the darkened guest room where the stranger was still sleeping. She came out towards him, but as she came nearer, he stepped away.

"Son, I just want to . . . "She held out her arms to hug him, but he backed away, boldly raising his arms up to her as if in defense. She tried again but each time he shielded himself from her. He raised up his hands and turned his whole head away from her. No matter how hard she tried he refused to let her come near him for a hug. When she gently raised a hand to his shoulder he slapped it and glared towards her, but as usual, not at her face. She gasped and wrapped her other hand around the one he struck and watched her son. His face looked sick but he never looked at her in the eye. She could not remember the last time he did, or if he ever had in his whole life for that matter. His head was slowly turning towards his bedroom, his eyes rolling back and forth between his room and the room where the stranger was. There was no smile, no expression.

"Son, don't you ever . . . " she meant to scold him, but when he flashed another glare in her direction, she stopped and thought. He had a reason, a very good reason for not wanting you to touch him. You can't see it now, but he does not want you to hug him. He doesn't want you thanking him either. He's just like some animal but with an overwhelming level of humbleness. This is what Mrs. Moran wanted him cured for.

"Can I just say 'thank you'?"

He slowly blinked and looked away.

"Is that a yes?"

He lowered his head slowly.

This must be his father in him, Mama concluded. She looked at her watch and saw that it was nearly nine-thirty.

"Well, I gotta get to work son. Do you need anything from anywhere?"

He shook his head as he moved farther into the guest room.

"Can you handle . . . uh . . . ?" she kept gesturing with her hand in the direction of the bedroom.

He nodded. He watched her hurry down the stairs, grab her things, and went out the front door, locking it behind her. When he heard her truck drive away out of the yard, he backed into the bedroom, closed the door quietly, and when he heard it click shut . . .

"WHAT DID YOU DO WITH THEM?!"

The Writer whirled around but before he could see where the horrendous voice was coming from, something wrapped its arm around his chest from behind and flung him down onto the bed. The Writer groaned in surprising shock and tried to get up. Before he could, he saw who was in the bedroom with him.

It was none other than his special guest, and he had suddenly come to life.

He flopped himself on top of The Writer, holding his arms down on both sides of his body. The Writer turned his head away, for the face of the stranger was no more than about two inches away from his. His breath was anything but a bed of sweet roses on a gorgeous spring day in the fields of England. The stranger pressed the cranium of his skull down onto the forehead of The Writer.

"Where are they? Tell me . . . WHERE ARE THEY?!" His teeth were clenched so tight he spat on The Writer's face.

"TELL ME BEFORE I KILL YOU!"

The Writer wriggled his hands free from his deadly grasp, pressed them up on his bare shoulders, and gave a heavy shove. He flung the stranger off the bed and he crashed onto the wooden floor with a heavy thud. The Writer ran up to the door and locked it tight to keep his present enemy inside this arena of battle.

He looked at the floor and saw the stranger crawling at him with full force, his shorts sliding off inch by inch. He got up on his knees and reached in vain for The Writer's face. He grabbed hold of his outstretched hands and wrestled him onto the floor, over-powering the strength the stranger was putting into his reaching for the eyes. The stranger then thrust his head into The Writer's stomach and was about to bite him when The Writer latched hold of his shoulders and pushed back onto the floor. The stranger flopped back and rolled over, his shorts now down to his knees. The Writer hurried over to him to pull them back up on him but before he could, the stranger loomed up, this time on his feet, and knocked The Writer back down onto the bed. He rolled over and again the stranger flopped back down on top of him. The Writer slapped his bare back but when it proved useless, he went for the black hair and pulled. The stranger screamed and bellowed in pain. When he let go of The Writer and reached for his head, he felt The Writer shove him off again onto the floor.

Dear Lord what have I done now? The Writer thought as he got back up on his feet. What do I do with this madman?

He got up and saw the stranger on the floor. He had landed on his front side and was about to get up again.

He tried but failed..

The Writer had his big foot pressed on his back and had him pinned down, or as The Writer loved to think of it, he had him *penned* down. His size seventeen shoe stretched clear across his back.

"Get off me!" he hollered. "Get off! That hurts! GET OFF ME!"

He kept slapping the wooden floor with his hands and kicking with his legs. He tried to reach for The Writer's legs but was no use. No matter how hard he tried he could not reach him. The Writer pressed harder and harder, but not with a lot of force. He did not want to hurt him but wanted him to have enough pain that would make him calm down. My pudginess came in handy after all, he thought.

"OW! GET OFF! GET OFF! GET OFF! OH . . . GOD THAT HURTS! PLEASE GET OFF! PLEASE!!! YOU'RE HURTING ME!"

The Writer eased the force on his foot and slowly let it up. When he saw that the stranger was crying in agony, he rolled him over onto his back. The stranger covered his face with his hands as he began to bawl. The Writer watched him, his other foot ready if he had to step on his front side, which he hoped he would not have to do, but later thought it would be too cruel.

I wonder, he thought. Is he more frightened than angry? Let's see . . .

He raised his other foot over him.

"NO!!! OH GOD NO!!! PLEASE DON'T!" he screamed in tears. He held up his quivering hands as he continued to squall like a baby. The Writer slowly pulled his foot away and set it down next to the shaking body of the stranger. He looked down at him in awe and wonder.

I have never seen a man cry like this before, he thought as he watched. Boys don't cry, they bawl. I've never seen it like this before.

He began to kneel next to him as he watched. The stranger slowly sat back up and turned to face The Writer.

As usual, The Writer did not look at his face.

"Hey man, what did you do with them?" he asked again, this time more calmer and more composed, but still in whimpering sobs. The Writer knew what he wanted. Then he remembered.

He had left what he found in the jacket in the bathroom on the counter. Luckily Mama had not found them. If she had she'd made him call the cops to come and get the stranger.

"With what?" The Writer asked.

"Those things I had. Just give them to me so I can leave."

"You're not leaving."

The stranger looked at him in disbelief. He got up on all fours and inched closer to The Writer, who in turn inched away little by little, but in position to get up fast on his feet if he had to.

"Look man. I had a knife, brass knuckles, and something else . . . "

"A razor blade." Oh great Writer, he thought as he covered his mouth. That was very smart, like something Annie Morgan would do! Just keep your mouth shut as always.

"Yeah man. Where are they? Tell me so I can go."

"You're not leaving," he said again, this time more firm.

"I can't stay here! I gotta go! Let me out of here!"

He dashed up for the door but The Writer beat him to it. The stranger drew back to punch him out of his way but he ducked and he slammed his bare fist into the door instead. He let out another wail of pain as he tried to unlock the door to get out. The Writer got back up and tried to push him back towards the bed. The stranger became wild and out of control. He kept jerking and slapping all around, trying to get to the door. The Writer began moving him for the bed as best he could, but the stranger kept trying to shove him back. He kept hollering and yelling, but it was no use. He began to slide down onto the floor. The Writer held onto his hands to keep him from slapping him. The stranger continued to yell as he slipped farther on down. His back was now to The Writer. He wrapped his arms around him and propped him back up on his feet but his legs were too weak to support him. He could feel the stranger's rapid heartbeat through his bare chest. He was getting hot and sweaty again.

He needed to cool off.

"Please let me go! Man just let me go! Don't hurt me anymore please! Just let me out of here. Be cool here man. Let me go."

"We'll go out here," The Writer said, dragging him across the floor to the door. He unlocked it and pulled the stranger out.

"Oh thanks man. You're cool . . . hey . . . where're we going?! WHAT'S THIS?!"

He saw that he was being taken into the bathroom. The Writer flipped on the light, quickly swiped the things he found in the coat down into the trash can next to the toilet so the stranger wouldn't find them and use them on him. He pulled him on in and with one hand, turned on the water in the shower. After that he swung the bathroom door shut, even though it was just them two in the house.

The bathroom was quickly filling up with steam. He had turned on the hot water and not the cold water like he intended. He tried to reach for the cold water knob but felt his arms give way.

"Let me out of here! I've had enough of this crap from you! You're trying to kill me!"

The Writer saw that all the steam had caused the stranger's back to sweat like crazy and he easily slipped out of his hold. The stranger lunged for the door which was not locked. He bolted after the stranger and wrapped his arms around his hot sweaty body and pulled him away.

"MAN! LET ME GO! TURN ME LOOSE! YOU AIN'T GONNA SCREW ME IN HERE! YOU'RE CRAZY!"

The Writer whirled around and slapped him across the face. He fell back against the door and again started to bawl. He held the side of the face where he was hit. The Writer stood back over him.

The stranger threatened to screw him good.

The Writer lunged down on him and pulled him up by the arms. He whirled him around and faced him towards the shower. He forgot it was hot, so he reached for the cold water knob and turned. The stranger's bare back was pressed up against his face and the thick sweat of his body was going into his mouth. The salty taste sent an eerie sensation to run all over his body. He stepped into the shower and pulled him in. The Writer was fully clothed and the shorts on the stranger were slipping down.

He slammed the stranger into the wall. He hollered as the changing temperature of the water showered on his back. The Writer pulled him under the direct stream of the water, which was now becoming warm and not as hot as it was. The stranger whirled around, grabbed The Writer by the shoulders, and slammed him up against the wall. He pressed his bare body against his, buried his face in his neck, but The Writer thrust him off and he fell against the back of the stall. He began to slide down onto the floor as The Writer grabbed hold of the shower head and aimed the water on him. He cried out for him to turn the water off but soon the cries ceased. He gently eased down onto the floor as the water fell all around him. He had fought back so much he became tired. He stopped jerking and fighting and laid there. The Writer stepped out, his clothes soaked, his black hair matted, and his breathing becoming rapid. He opened the bathroom door to let fresh air into his lungs. When his breathing felt normal, he went back into the bathroom, turned off the water, and looked at the stranger, lying on the shower floor, his head and shoulders tilted up against the wall where he slid down.

It had calmed down by now. His breathing was heavy but he was quiet. The Writer knelt down and sat him back up. His head was hanging down and his black hair was flattened down all around his head. He lifted his head up by the chin. Drool and mucus dripped from the nose and mouth. The Writer grabbed a towel from the rack and wiped his face dry. He stroked the hair back on his head and carefully studied the face of this lost, angry, frightened soul.

It was a warm face, one that could easily love and be loved, but his heart and mind would not let him. His heart needed breaking into. His mind needed changing. His soul needed to be touched. The smooth curves and clean peachy flesh of his face, all molded and crafted onto his muscular, strong boned skull, reflected another distinctive creation from the mastery of God's hands.

I will help this boy, The Writer vowed in his heart. He is not leaving this house until I've done that. God help me with this. I really need you for this one.

The Writer scooped him up out of the stall, still wet and na-ked, and carried him like he did when he found him lying out next to the road.

I'll just let him sleep, he thought, and I need to change my clothes.

And he waddled away . . . back to the stranger's bedroom.

CHAPTER TEN

The stranger slept the rest of the day in the bedroom with The Writer always by the side of the bed. He had gotten out of his wet clothes and had them hanging outside on the line to dry. It wasn't until after his fight with the stranger in the shower that he remembered that there was a bathroom right there in the guest bedroom. When he remembered this he slapped himself across the face.

Mama returned home from work later in the afternoon. She threw her things down on the couch in the living room and hurried upstairs. She found her son sitting in the rocker in the bedroom, his eyes upon the sleeping stranger.

"Still keeping watch huh?" she said. "Did he give you any trouble today?"

"Hardly," he said. What she didn't need to know wouldn't hurt her. Had he told her that the stranger tried to attack him in the shower she would freak out beyond belief. Besides, he thought it best not to tell her after what happened to her that morning with Mrs. Moran.

"Well, Judy's taking me out tonight for supper and a movie. She heard about what happened this morning and feels its all her fault. I told her not to worry about it and that she wasn't to blame, but she insisted that we BOTH needed a night out, so we're going tonight. Can you get your own supper, as usual?"

He nodded.

"Good. I shouldn't be out too late. I'm gonna go get ready. She said she'll be by here at five to get me."

When she closed the door The Writer resumed watching over the stranger. A few minutes later he heard voices coming from downstairs. He cracked the door open and saw that it was the two police officers who came that morning to take away Mrs. Moran. They were just checking on Mama like they said they would. Mama spoke to them for a few minutes and they left. He went back to the rocker. Pretty soon he found that he was unable to keep his own head up, and he dozed off soon after Judy came and got Mama.

When The Writer awoke he looked at his neon light watch and saw that it was close to midnight.

I slept the whole evening away!? he thought. Crap! I missed my nightly writing session this evening! Now I'm behind by two days in my journals.

He got up out of his rocker and saw from the moonlight that poured into the room that the stranger was still there, sound asleep. The window was still open and cool air had filled the room, making it the perfect night to drift off into a deep, seductive slumber of sleep. He walked over to the window and looked out. He could see his spot on the hilltop, outlined in the moonlight, and the breeze sending waves through the tall grass all over the slopes.

The perfect night for thinking, he thought as he gazed at his favorite spot. But how can I with our special guest here? What will I do with him? What day is this? Monday or Tuesday? He looked at the date on his watch and saw that Tuesday had arrived just a few minutes ago.

He stepped out of the room to make sure Mama was back home from her night out with Judy. I'll have to ask her all about it in the morning, he thought. Mama deserves a night out now and then. He cracked open her bedroom door and saw her sound asleep in her queen size bed under the window. He pulled the door shut and went back into the bedroom with the stranger. He sat back down in the rocker and began to doze off once again . . .

When he woke up he found that his neck was stiff. He rubbed it and looked at his watch. It was almost four-thirty in the morning. He got up out of the chair and kept rubbing the stiffness out of his neck. He felt now that he could not go back to sleep even if he tried. There was too much in his mind now to keep him from sleeping anymore than he already had. He found sleeping to be a waste of precious time to write and think, and he was a bit irked when he realized how much he had already slept since finding the stranger.

He's slept this long, he'll sleep longer, The Writer thought as he got ready to go out and sit on the hill for a little bit before the full outbreak of daylight. He put on his usual get-up of the waist bag and the black coat tied around his waist. He still donned his black cap that had 'Writer' stitched into it in fading orange thread. He had been wearing it ever since it was given to him as a birthday present from Lucille, the owner of the little grocery store in town at the little plaza, who looked after him after school when he was little while Mama was still at work. She always made him a snack from the meats and bread in the deli section of her little store. From kindergarten till he was in high school that was the routine, and when he was able to drive he still come by after school, found Lucille standing in the doorway with a sandwich in her careworn hands for him, picked it up, and went on home with it.

Now that school seemed to be over for him, he hoped it didn't mean the end of such a long and tender tradition. He would still go by in the afternoons when he could. He had become attached to that little old lady who never failed to make sure The Writer had something to eat everyday after school.

He pulled the door to the guest room shut and crept down the stairs, went to the front door, and as quietly as he could, un-locked it and stepped out onto the porch. The cool air welcomed him and he could see the world shrouded in a thin haze of bluish fog. The sun was not too far off behind the mountains in the dis-tance, but this tone of morning color served as a prelude for the coming day, as if it were nature's way of telling the night creatures that it was time to let the day creatures have the earth until night returned.

He walked around aimlessly on the porch for a few minutes. The dogs were asleep under the swing. Queenie had heard him come out. She wagged her tail at him and then went back to sleep.

Koko slept on dead to the world. At the other end of the porch were the cats, sprawled out in all their glory. The biggest of the cats, Blue, which was indeed a Russian Blue cat, slept in the middle, but the fattest of them all, Sampson, was in a nice plump ball of orange fur next to the wall. One of the mother cats, Jackie, was expecting a litter any day now. Of course they were Blue's.

The Writer considered Blue as the king of the cats, because he was so strong and could kill a snake on his own. That was why Mama wanted Blue with her in her flower garden. Whenever she saw a snake slithering around she backed away and let Blue have at it and have at it he did, tearing and shredding the thing apart before it could attack him. The other cats could kill snakes as well, but not as brutal or alone like Blue could. They had to team up on a single grass snake alone.

Blue was also a loyal cat, as loyal as an animal could be. The Writer felt that cats had a special sixth sense about certain things, and he knew that cats had the power to predict earthquakes. He felt that Blue could sense certain days. On his birthday one year Blue leapt up in the window with a dead bird in his jaws. On Father's Day he presented The Writer with a dead snake, and on Mother's Day, he jumped up in Mama's lap with a dead rat in his mouth as she sat on the porch. The Writer decided years earlier to write a novel about his cats, with Blue as the main character. The first few chapters of it were in a box in his bedroom, along with dozens of other first chapters to more novels.

But for now the cats were in dreamland, and The Writer went around back of the house to go up on the hill.

He thought he was alone.

No sooner after he went out the front door it opened again. An unfamiliar bare foot stepped out onto the porch. The dogs watched in wonder and some of the cats could smell it. Another foot came out and the door shut behind them with a small pop. The animals watched the feet stride across the porch and go down the steps slowly. When they saw the face of whom the feet belonged to they lowered their heads and turned away. Queenie

T

watched as the individual went around the side of the porch towards the back. Blue and Sampson were now awake and watched with big eyes.

The Writer was slowly making his way in the fog across the little bridge that was built over the little stream. He did not suspect anything behind him.

Whoever was behind him now found The Writer and got close to him, but stayed back about four feet. He could see the huge black build of a person ambling his way across the bridge in the early morning fog. He could see that he had his hands clasped together in front of him and that he tied his coat around his waist, thus giving him a more ghostly appearance whenever he walked, because the coat would sway this way and that. He could see that this guy had big feet, and he realized that one of those feet had pressed down on his back the day before.

A board on the bridge squeaked when he set foot on the end of it.

The Writer stopped dead in his tracks.

The stranger froze, not from being out in only his shorts, but not knowing what this big guy was going to do. It was enough being afraid of his feet.

The Writer slowly turned around. The stranger could see his eyes sparkle in the blue gleam of the morning as The Writer's face came around. Nothing more of him could be seen.

Neither one said a word.

The stranger looked longly at him.

The Writer could sense that he was looking at him, but his eyes did not meet his face.

What's he doing here? he thought. I thought I left him asleep.

There was still silence between them.

One of us has to speak, The Writer thought. It won't be me, as usual.

Still nothing.

The stranger still looked at him, his eyes blinking every few seconds. He showed no signs of being cold out here in nothing but the shorts The Writer had put on him.

"What?" The Writer asked suddenly, not realizing that he had spoken first.

"Huh?" the stranger replied.

"What're you doing here?"

"I . . . uh . . . followed you."

I realize that, he thought. What do I do now with him? Talk to him? Yes, Writer, just talk to him. There's nobody here but he and I. We're alone, and will be even more alone when Mama goes to work this morning. I can talk to him, find out all I need to.

The Writer approached him across the bridge. The stranger started inching back when he saw those huge feet coming at him.

"Don't step on me man," he said. "Your feet hurt. They're as big as Godzilla's."

Godzilla, The Writer thought. Interesting . . .

"How do you feel?" he asked.

"Hungry." He rubbed his bare stomach with his hand.

Hungry?! The Writer thought in horror. I totally forgot. Been here since Sunday night and we haven't fed you squat since then! You haven't eaten since . . . oh boy! I gotta get this boy fed. He came closer to him but the stranger backed away with each step he took forward.

"I won't hurt you," he said. "I'm gonna feed you."

"Really? I so hungry I could eat you."

That's the last thing I need in this house, The Writer thought. A sadistic cannibal. He'd tear off my clothes and bite me . . . change your thoughts Writer . . . right now!

"Let's go to the kitchen," he said. He started out in front of the stranger, but coaxed him to walk next to him so he could keep an eye on him. When they came to the porch the animals looked in wonder at them. The Writer paid no attention to them but the stranger had his focus set on each one of them.

"They won't hurt you," The Writer said.

"If you say so," he said.

They came into the darkened kitchen. A soft beam of blue

reached in through the open window, which hit the table and created a soothing sensation of peace and emotion.

"Where's the light?" the stranger asked, clumsily groping his hand all along the wall. When he found it he switched it on.

The Writer slammed his hands on his face and whirled away from the powerful yellow beam that soaked up the room.

"Turn it off."

"Why?"

"I don't want it on."

"Why?"

"I . . . I just don't. Turn it off. I don't like it on right now."

The stranger flipped it back off and looked at The Writer, who turned back around from the wall and made his way for the refrigerator. He opened it and the beam of the light inside the fridge seemed to call forth the stranger. He hurried up to it, shoved The Writer out of the way and went straight for the leftover ham Mama cooked a few days earlier for supper. The stranger tore off the wrapping and sank his teeth into it, water and pieces of meat falling to the floor. With both hands holding it to his mouth he chewed and gnawed at it till the water and fat drippings were smeared all over his face. The Writer watched as he stuffed the last pieces of it into his mouth, dropped the end on the floor, and lunged into the fridge for more.

"I think there's a turkey br . . ."

"WHERE?!?"

But before he could get it for him the stranger had already ripped it out of its sealed plastic and took huge bites out of it. The floor became so slick and slimy from the water of the ham that the stranger began to fall. The Writer caught him but soon they both went down together onto the floor, The Writer holding the stranger by the sides. The stranger cradled the turkey breast to his face as if he were sucking face with some girl. He smooched and spit and chowed on it like a carnivore. The Writer reached a hand into the fridge to find something else for the stranger but before he could the stranger grabbed hold of his hand and yanked it back out.

"NO! IT'S MINE!" he growled loudly as he thrust his hands into the shelves. But his eyes caught hold of something else on the top shelf, where the drinks were.

He grabbed the bottle of apple juice, yanked the lid off, and shoved the opening into his whole mouth. Big bubbles splashed all around inside the bottle and The Writer saw the huge gulps of it go down through his throat. He soon pulled the bottle out of his mouth, fell back against the door, let what was left in his mouth gush out and down his bare chest, and poured the rest of it down over his head. He dropped the bottle on the floor next to him and began panting. His chest, soaked all over, heaved up and down. The Writer was sitting on the floor on the other side of the open door, watching this guy literally make a hog out of himself. He had no idea when he ate last, so he just let him eat all he wanted. He'd figure out some way to tell Mama that half their food was already gone.

"More!" he said. "I WANT MORE!"

The Writer reached again into the fridge but the stranger wrapped an arm around him and yanked him backwards onto the floor. He sat up and saw the stranger on his knees, searching in mad vain for more food. There was a bag of shredded cheese that he dumped into his mouth. A can of coke he opened and gushed out over his head. In a plastic container was the last of Mama's lasagna. He found it and stuffed all of it in his mouth, letting half of it fall to the floor. He kept making gurgling sounds and he grunted over and over. He discovered the tray for eggs. He tore the lid off a fresh box, grabbed two, knocked them together, and slung the insides to his mouth. He did the same for a few more eggs, then went for the box of uncooked bacon. He shoved the raw strips into his mouth without a care in the world. He grabbed the ketchup bottle out of the door and sprayed it into his mouth, as well as the mustard. A half-bottle of French salad dressing he poured into his mouth, then dropped the open bottle on the floor. From the top shelf he found the tea Mama had made just the day before. He grabbed the whole pitcher and splashed it into his face. What didn't come out he poured into his mouth.

The Writer watched in wonder as the juices and drinks he splashed onto the floor made waves that resembled miniature tidal waves, washing upon the floor of food, which to him represented deserted houses, the floor a coastal area, the food crumbs helpless citizens, the light in the fridge the sun, and the stranger a big sea monster causing all the havoc.

This could also be a catastrophic hurricane, he thought. But there's no wind.

Out of nearly anything The Writer could envision a scene for a novel . . .

After the stranger doused himself all over he turned around and slid down onto the floor, his head resting just on the outside of the bottom shelf of food he'd wrecked into. He was panting heavily, out of breath, his whole body was soaked in food remnants. The floor was a total disaster area. Wasted pieces of food and liquids of all kinds reflected in the light from the open fridge. The Writer knew he'd have to get it clean before Mama saw it and got after him.

The Writer crawled back up closer to the stranger. He saw him and lifted his soaking head up out of the muck of food.

"Oh man that was great! Never been better."

The Writer rolled his eyes in disgust. He looked at his watch and saw that it was almost six. Mama would be up at seven, so he had an hour to get the place spic and span for her. He got up and went for the closet behind the table for the mop and paper towels. When he came back he saw the stranger wallowing and squirming around in the mess he'd made. He was slithering around in it on his back and rolling over onto his stomach, moaning the whole time. When he apparently had enough he got up and faced The Writer, who had set the mop and towels down on the floor. He came close to him and placed a hand on his left shoulder. The Writer held his breath in uncertainty as to what he would do now. He shook him a little, then slapped his hand on his shoulder.

"Man, that was great. Thank you. I feel better. Now I'm going back to bed. Come up when you're ready."

He released his hold of him, smirking and giggling, and went back up to the bedroom.

The Writer stood still for a long time, the images of savagery he'd just witnessed played over and over in his mind. He could still see the stranger tearing his way into the food, throwing it, stuffing it, immersing himself in the joy of feasting.

He had never gone one day without food but realized now what it can do to someone who has not eaten for a long time. All manners are dormant and the food groups have no existence. Nutritional value is like a foreign language. The food becomes the number one passion in life for that person. Nothing and no one is going to tear the two apart from each other until the hunger is put to rest.

The Writer also discovered that his appetite was no longer with him after what he'd just seen. He turned around and faced the mess, which didn't look all that much of a hardship to him now. It was there for a reason, a noble and humane reason.

And he waddled away . . . to clean up the stranger's beautiful mess.

CHAPTER ELEVEN

The sky was ablaze with red. The earth was shrouded in a bloody dye of crimson.

When the boy ran up to the football field he could see them still charging after him. He dashed across the track and into the field. The other boys leapt over the fence and still came after him. He ran for the field house, his eyes stinging with sweat, and the sky so red, the clouds looked like cotton soaked with blood. He slammed into the fence, looked back, and saw the black images sprinting across the field, only now there were some racing up from both sides of the track. He shot into the house and slammed the door shut.

He looked around the guys' dressing room and saw that he was the only one there.

But then a door from somewhere on this floor smashed open. Then a door upstairs was busted down. Several pairs of feet were running overhead for the stairs that came down here. The boy ran past the shower stalls and found that the girls' dressing room was locked. He turned around and saw three of the guys standing before him in the red beam of the sun from outside. When they approached him he stumbled and fell backward into the shower stalls. The other boys from outside soon poured into the room, found the boy in the stalls, and then . . .

"Son!"

Darn, The Writer thought, his mind violently jolted back into this reality. I almost had that boy pulverized. Now they'll all just have to wait until I can come back to them and finish the scene . . .

His head began to throb, his eyes refocused to the darkness of his bedroom, and he felt his heart pick up a few beats. Through the curtains, there were fiery beams of orange light radiating from the setting sun into the room. A streak fell across his lap where he sat next to the window in his rocker. It brightly illuminated his hands as they rested on his lap. His class ring became a shimmering jewel in the sunlight, as well as did the name of 'Writer', which was on one side of the ring. The other side bore his graduation year.

His mother called him again. Before he could get up out of his chair to go see what she wanted his bedroom door flung open and there she was.

All she could see was the hideously black figure of her son sitting in front of the window with the curtains drawn. All around him blazed shades of orange light streaking in from the window, which was open, and a breeze caused the curtains to move every few seconds.

"Are you asleep son?"

The head turned towards her, but the eyes didn't.

"Well, I'm going to the market to get a few things for supper since our guest cleaned us out this morning. Can you stay till I get back?"

He nodded.

He sat still for a little while, then he went back to the stranger's bedroom. The last time he checked on him that afternoon he was still asleep, but he didn't know if he still was.

He opened the door.

Still snoozing away.

The Writer went downstairs and was greeted with the whole living room ablaze with the orange evening light. It nearly blinded him.

This is too much for me, he thought and began pulling all the drapes shut. He switched on the light next to Mama's rocker, turned on the air conditioner, and picked up the remote control for the television. It was too hot to write. It had to be cool and dark before his ambition could be aroused . . .

The six o'clock news dominated nearly every major station.

They were giving the weather for the rest of the week. On the station out of Asheville the weatherman reported that it would be clear and sunny all through Saturday. He changed channels and the station out of Chattanooga, Tennessee, reported that a severe thunderstorm could be hitting the mountains by early next week sometime. He switched it and saw blinding flashes of different shows before his eyes with each press of the channel changing button. He came to the sci-fi channel and saw a glorious sight . . .

A big black fat monster, accompanied by a huge caterpillar and a big grayish looking bird of some sort, were about to team up on this three-headed yellow monster which had big wings and two tails. There were other monsters on the scene, but The Writer was only amazed by that big black one.

It was Godzilla.

The Writer got up out of the chair and approached the television. He kept his eyes on his champion monster as it breathed his radioactive breath on the three-headed beast, called Ghidrah. The Writer looked around the room and saw for sure that he was alone. He began to root for Godzilla when he knocked Ghidrah down on the ground. The Writer began jumping and clapping, simulating what Godzilla was doing by throwing fists out in front of him and swinging all around.

"YES! GO GO GO GODZILLA! KILL THAT BIG LUG! STOMP HIM! KICK HIM! TEAR ONE OF HIS HEADS OFF! IT LOOKS JUST LIKE MRS. MORAN . . . BUT NOT AS UGLY!"

Godzilla slammed Ghidrah down onto the ground and began to stomp on all three of his long necks. The other monsters were throwing rocks or kicking at the thing. One monster was chewing on its tails. Another was breathing fire on it. Ghidrah was screaming and bellowing in agony with each stomp Godzilla gave him. The screaming was music to the ears of The Writer.

"YES! THAT'S IT! YOU'VE HAD IT BABY! YOU'RE DEAD! GODZILLA IS KING!"

The Writer raised his arms in triumph for his favorite childhood monster as he jumped around, like some kid who had just won his first bicycle. The monsters on the screen were roaring in victory as Ghidrah lay still, dying or already dead. Godzilla was roaring that he had won another battle with the forces of evil.

"YES! YES! YES! GODZILLA YOU'RE MY HERO! YES! YES! YES!"

He spun around to throw another mock punch into the air and instead whirled right around into his Mama's face, who was already back from the grocery store.

Her eyebrows were raised in wonder at her son, who humbly composed himself, switched off the TV, and turned towards his mother. She stood still looking at him, waiting for an explanation even though she had seen why he was jumping around the living room.

Neither one said a word.

"Did Godzilla win?" she finally asked.

He nodded.

"Good. I'm gonna fix hot dogs for supper. In the meantime cool yourself off." With that she went into the kitchen with her bag of groceries from Lucille's store. "Oh and by the way, Lucille sent you a sandwich. I'll put it in the fridge for you. You might eat it later tonight."

He nodded even though she couldn't hear it. The phone rang and Mama called out to her son that she got it, then a few seconds later, hollered after him.

"It's Annie," she said. "She needs to talk to you."

The Writer picked his cordless phone up in his bedroom and closed the door.

"Hi Sir!" her high-peaked voice screeched. "Was you busy? You weren't? Okay, listen, I have something I want to tell you, but I want to tell you in person so is it okay if I come by your house tonight around nine or so, because I have to help my mom with something first. Okay? Okay, I'll see you tonight at nine! Bye!"

Click.

The Writer looked stupefied. Nice talking to you, he thought. He never got a chance to say a single syllable to the girl. For all he knew, she could have spoken to a hot movie star and not have known it, or some crazed killer or demented stranger . . .

Stranger . . .

Is he still asleep, he wondered. He went out of his room and hurried over to the stranger's bedroom.

He swung the door open.

The stranger leapt up out of the bed and onto his feet. He grabbed the top sheet and was holding it around his waist, looking sheepishly at The Writer.

"What?" the stranger asked.

"What?" The Writer asked back.

"What's the matter? Haven't you seen a naked guy before? It gets hot at night during the summer. Don't you sleep nude?"

He shook his head. He slept in a pair of shorts and a very baggy loose-flowing t-shirt.

The Writer went on into the room, keeping his eyes focused on the window as the stranger put his shorts back on. When he could sense that the stranger was no longer naked, he turned back around.

"Say man, why don't me and you go out tonight and check out the chicks? I saw a bunch of good ones in town the other night. Betcha I can land a hot one for ya."

I'm sure you can, The Writer thought. He shook his head.

"C'mon man! It'll be fun! I bet I can find one with boobs the size of . . ."

BAM!!!

The Writer slammed a hardback book down on the dresser that faced the bed. The last thing he needed to hear was how big a girl's chest was when his was the brunt of jokes in high school. He closed his eyes in painful remembrance of the day when three boys pinned him up into a corner in the hallway and began a contest to see who could reach out and touch a side of his chest. When one boy could reach it he wrapped his whole hand around it and pulled. The pain of it made him sore for days, but he had no idea how to tell anyone of what had happened to him.

"What dude? I was just saying . . ."

The Writer waved his hands up to tell him to hush. He didn't want to hear anymore about that from him.

He decided to change the subject, and mention that Mama was cooking supper. At that precise moment the stranger asked,

"When's supper?"

Annie arrived promptly at nine in her black Beretta. The Writer and Mama had finished eating but due to the stranger's severe lack of table manners, The Writer carried his food up to him where he could gorge it all down. After that he went to sleep again.

That guy sleeps the most, The Writer thought as he went to answer the door.

"Howdy sir!" she shrieked and they waved their hands in each other's face as usual. Mama came out of the kitchen drying her hands. She and Annie exchanged greetings and then she said she was going on up to her room to read and then going to bed. She told The Writer and Annie to sit and talk as long as they wanted.

She left it with her son's own judgment as to whether or not to mention to Annie the presence of a stranger in the house.

Mama went up to the top of the stairs and stopped at the stranger's bedroom door. He had been here since Sunday night and she still had not had a chance to talk to him.

Why not now? she thought. If he's asleep I can talk to him later.

She cracked open the door and saw that he had flopped down on the bed, sound asleep. She saw the plate The Writer took to him with his food on it. She quietly crept in and took it and rather than disturb The Writer and Annie, she kept it in her bedroom until Annie left.

"So what brings you here?" The Writer asked, directing her outside to the swing next to the driveway. "I hope you don't mind sitting out here."

"Nah, it's pretty out tonight anyway," she said. "Okay sir. Guess who I saw today in town?"

He looked towards her.

"I saw Rusty."

His eyes widened up towards her. She jerked back when she saw the fiery whites of his eyes set upon her face. She quickly regained focus on what she was talking about.

"Okay, I saw Rusty today. He came to the ice cream shop while I was talking to Lana and Dionne and your friend Joey. Well, I heard this loud 'vrooom vrooom' outside and I looked. I saw Rusty on a motorcycle."

"A motorcycle," The Writer said. "Must've traded that old truck for it."

"Well, he's got more than just power between his legs, as if he really had any in the first place."

He glared towards her.

"Sorry. Anyway, I'll just give it to you straight. He had a girl with him."

The news stunned him. His mind stopped and his heart skipped a beat. It was like he had just heard of the death of a friend, only the news had yet to settle into firm reality for him.

"A girl?" he asked, making sure he heard her right.

"Yes sir. It wasn't that Tammy freak who delivered the pizza the other night, but another one. She had maroon-dyed curly hair, skinny, and looked like she'd been in a tanning bed for days. And those eyes! Sir, she had the darkest eyes I've ever seen, and I thought yours were scary."

The eyes rolled over towards her.

"Sorry. Anyway, he came into the store. Joey saw him and ran behind the register. Lana and Dionne backed up to the wall. I just stood there, because I wasn't afraid of him."

The Writer listened intently, envisioning it all as best he could.

"He looked at me and he goes, 'Hey darlin'. How're you doin'?' in that piercing tone of voice. That girl just gave me a look, so I gave her one back. He asked Lana if she had change for a twenty. She took it, gave it to Dionne, who then gave it to Joey. Joey opens the drawer and pulls out a ten, a five, and five ones. He gives it all to Rusty, and he says, 'Have you been to see The Writer lately?'

And Rusty says, 'The Writer?! Ha! Naw, I hain't. Ain't got time to. Been busy with my woman here.'"

The Writer looked down at the dirt under the swing, kicking up small puffs with his monster shoes. He could feel his head getting warmer and his stomach churning with anxiety.

Annie went on.

"Then he introduced her to us. He said, 'Everyone, this here is Kelly, my sweetie. She's good with me. Found her walking by the volunteer fire department last week. I was just hangin' out with my buddies and she comes struttin' by. I got her before they did.' And I tell you sir, that girl is total prostitute. She wore a skin tight tank that was cut off below her chest, her shorts were so high up I was afraid to see where they started on her, and she had the most disgusting strut I've ever seen. That butt went from side to side. I'm surprised it didn't hit somebody."

He picked up his pen and held it up in his hand, as if it were the only weapon known to exist on earth.

"I know you can show us with that pen if her rear end is real. You'd just have to give one good stab and all the world will know. Anyway, there's something else about Rusty that I think you should know if you're gonna keep trying to be friends with him."

"What?"

"He had alcohol on his breath."

The Writer slumped back in the swing. Come on Annie, he thought. He can't be this bad. I've never seen him like that.

"Sir I know you don't think so but it's true."

"Annie, did Joey and the girls put you up to this?"

"Up to what?"

"This. Trying to get me to leave Rusty just because he's a little messed up."

"No sir! I'm telling you the truth! Have I ever lied to you about anything?"

"I wouldn't know."

"Well I haven't!" Annie's voice got a bit loud. He had never known Annie or the girls to lie to him about anything. They'd been best friends for years. Why would they start now in deceiving him?

"Listen sir. I've been on one date with this Rusty . . . and that was quite enough. Sir, he only has one thing on his mind on dates . . . ONE THING! That's all he wants. Do you know what that is?"

Yes, he thought, but I don't want to say it.

"Sex. All he wants is sex. He tried it on me and I slapped his filthy face. So what if he dumped me out near Murphy at ten o'clock that night? I'd rather be dumped than screwed by that nympho."

"Murphy?" The Writer asked in shock. "That far away?"

"That's what he does sir. He takes his girls far away from here where he thinks nobody knows them and he does what he wants in some cheap roadside motel."

"You told us the shack on highway nineteen," The Writer boldly pointed out in a weak voice.

"That too. But on first dates he goes toward Murphy, either through Macon County or through the gorge. He took me through that gorge and sir, being with that nympho alone at night is scarier than driving through that canyon in the dark. If he scores what he calls, a 'touchdown' with the girl on that first date, then it's the shack anytime after that."

"And you expect me to believe all this about Rusty?" he asked.

"I don't expect you to believe any of it sir. I'm just telling you what I saw and what I've been through with that guy. Sir, to make a long story short, he's bad news, dangerous, a sadistic nympho monster. He's like some wild animal out stalking the night look-ing for prey, that prey being any girl who doesn't have the audac-ity to just say 'no.' I'm amazed he hasn't gotten anyone pregnant yet. But sir, you were right. Lana, Dionne, and Joey wanted me to talk to you about Rusty because I've known him for a while and was with him at one time. They wanted to come with me but thought it best if I came alone. I know a lot about him that you probably didn't know, and maybe you're better off not knowing.

But I did see him today, and he was with that girl. I would never lie to you about anything like this. Do you understand?"

He nodded.

"Is there something I can do for you?" she asked.

"No. I just never thought he could be like you say he is."

"I know sir. It's hard to believe."

They sat in silence for a long time. Annie looked far off into the distance as did The Writer.

"And something else," Annie said suddenly. "I don't want to tell you what to do about Rusty. I don't know if he's been a great friend to you, I don't know, but from what I've seen and heard so far he doesn't seem to be a true friend to anyone. I've seen you come to school on Monday mornings looking sick and miserable. I'd ask you if something was wrong and you always said 'no' and ran for the bathroom until the first period bell rang. I figured out that you only came to school looking like that following the weekends that Rusty was supposed to spend time with you, and he never did, did he?"

He shook his head, then held up his finger. "Once we went to his house, but I don't think that counts huh?"

"But did you two do anything fun together?"

"Watched cartoons until his mother came home, then he brought me back to the house."

"Okay, that doesn't count then. That sounds dull. If I were him I'd have taken you out to eat, gone to a movie, and done other things like bowling. And since we're on the precious subject of bowling, are you ready for the tournament Thursday night?"

He nodded.

"Good, because the girls and I have been practicing in the mornings before heading to work. Blade and Nate go when they can and I don't know about Joey. Have you gotten to practice any?"

"A little."

"You don't need much practice though. You can always kick

our butts when we go just for fun. I have to get my mom to wash my outfit. Is your mom and Judy making yours again this year?"

He nodded. "Can I ask you something?"

"Sure."

"About Joey . . . do you think he likes me?"

Annie looked in awe at the question, as if The Writer had just slapped her. "Now where in the world did that come from sir?"

"I just want your opinion."

"No sir, I don't think he likes you. I think he loves you. Now why do you ask me such a ridiculous question? Has something been bothering you about him? You know he loves you as much as we do."

"I wonder though. He and I are so . . . different. He's fifteen. I'm eighteen. He's skinny. I'm fat. He's loud. I'm quiet . . . too much is different with us. Sometimes I wonder . . . how he stands me like he does . . . if he sees me coming does he grumble . . . 'Oh here comes that fat Writer guy. I better be nice to him' . . . then puts on a big show when I'm there, or is it real? I know . . . I love him so much it hurts sometimes . . . I love taking him out . . . but does he enjoy it when I do? I don't know . . . he never tells me. But he's been so good to me . . . remembered my birthday, gave me a graduation present . . . "

"See there sir," Annie said. "Only a true friend would do things like that. Has Rusty ever done that for you? No. I know he hasn't. Just think sir, if Joey was pretending to like you, would he come around you or even go out with you? I know I wouldn't if I was pretending. Someone can't be pretending if he does those things. Didn't the eight of us bring you a cake for your birthday last year? We had all our names on it. Didn't we come see you Christmas day? Blade dressed up as Santa. Wasn't Joey in there with us for all that? Yes he was. Why? Because he's your friend and he loves you. Did anyone else at school do that for you? NO! Just us because we're your friends. When we first saw you we knew you were different. You did not act like the other kids. You rarely spoke but you were good to them. All seven of us were hated just like you were, because we were different. We didn't do the things other kids did. You were someone who was just like us and nobody else seemed to appreciate us as much as you."

"Really?" he asked.

"Yes sir. Joey thinks the world of you, just like you do of him. He may not show it, but he loves you."

"I do . . . think a lot of him . . . because he talked to me the first day of his freshman year. He said he was lost . . . I took him to his class . . . he gave me high fives when I passed him in the hall . . . calls me 'punk' sometimes . . . I was so glad a freshman kid liked me so much . . . but I got to wondering if it was real . . . not just a put-on out of pity. So I guess that's why when he hugs me I . . . cling to him so long . . . make him hug me longer than he probably wants to . . . "

Annie held one of his hands. She hoped that what she said would make him think differently about things that she had no idea was on his mind until now.

How long has he been thinking this way about us and Joey, she wondered. Ever since he took up with Rusty? I hope this will make him decide to get rid of him for good, she thought as she got up.

"Well sir, I hate to leave you, but I have to run. Are you gonna be alright?"

He nodded.

"I can stay longer and talk if you want me to."

"No. I'm alright."

The Writer got up and before he could walk her to the car she hugged him. He watched her drive away into the night. He then looked at Joey's house. The light in his bedroom just went off, the sign that he had already gone to bed.

He went and sat in the swing for a long time, thinking over what Annie had told him about Rusty and Joey and everyone else. Bit by bit it took hold of his heart and mind. It was settling into his soul. He had not thought a lot about the bowling tournament this Thursday, and here it was, Tuesday night. He hadn't practiced for it since the weekend before graduation, when he and Joey went to the bowling alley and bowled eight games. As far as he knew, Joey hadn't been back since he took him. The rest of the gang practiced when they found the time. They would just have to do the best they could.

I forgot to mention the stranger being here, he thought. Oh well, she doesn't need to know. Nobody needs to know. It's my business and he's my responsibility. I feel like Miep Gies when she hid Anne Frank and her family and the Van Daans in the attic in Amsterdam. Hey, how about that . . . Anne was a writer too.

You should always forgive your fellow man, even if he wrongs you seventy times seven, The Writer thought, recalling another sermon he'd heard in church. That equals 490 times, but who's counting? It doesn't matter. We all deserve a second chance, so that's what I'll give Rusty. So what if he's a little messed up? He can still be saved. I'll just not look at all the bad things he's done, but focus on his heart. It has to be good somewhere. Maybe if I invite him to join our bowling team Thursday evening he'll see that someone cares. That's it. I'll invite him to join us. He'll have fun.

I'll call him tomorrow and ask him.

That's what I'll do.

Yes. I feel better already. Thanks Annie.

He got up out of the swing and took in a deep breath of the cool night air. He was starting to feel at rest about Joey and Rusty. He knew he could be at peace.

And he waddled away . . . back up to his bedroom.

CHAPTER TWELVE

Tuesday passed away into the night for The Writer, and he spent the night in the rocker in the bedroom with the stranger. It was so dark and desolate up there in the room alone with the stranger that at times the atmosphere beckoned that of a body laid out for viewing at a funeral home. The soft beam of the lamp on the table would enhance such a feeling. The only feature missing from such an allusion was a gentle melancholy score echoing from somewhere in the ceiling.

Again The Writer awoke very early, before dawn in fact.

What's wrong with me? he thought. Why can't I sleep late like everyone else? Oh I forgot. I'm *different*. Fat and different. Quiet and different. Emotionally frail and different . . . STOP IT RIGHT NOW! STOP IT! STOP IT! STOP IT! He was about to smack himself in the face for allowing his mind to seep into the gutter so early in the morning, but thought that the loud pop against his cheek would stir the stranger awake. He got up, tiptoed out, and went down to the living room. He pulled the rocker up to the window, opened the drapes, and let the cool morning air drift into the dank room. He sat in the rocker and let the cool refreshing air of a new day breathe over him.

God is breathing life into this new day, he thought as he rocked contently.

He laid his head back in the rocker and let himself drift off to that special place that only he knew about . . .

This time he would work on setting up another of the many, many, many novels he had planned to write. This one in particular was set over a hundred years ago in a beautiful kingdom, far far away. The king of this land had just been assassinated, and his son

r

has assumed the throne. At age 22, he is the youngest king ever in the 1700 years of the kingdom's existence. However, there are bitter problems with a neighboring rival kingdom. The king of that land was once best friends with the other king. One remains good and the other has turned vicious and cruel.

This needs work, The Writer thought as he saw the good kingdom flourishing with dignity and ethics. The people of it were good hearted and followed the teachings of Christ. When he saw himself standing over it he could see that he had detailed the kingdom so vividly with his words that it seemed to reach far into the horizon where the sun rose and set. I need more people, more character extras. They need to be out on the streets walking around, talking to others, being social, not antisocial like me.

Yes, even I will admit my own disability of being introverted.

The king of that land must be more outgoing, not the stuck-up image of idolatry from the nation of a people of a grand democracy. He will not have cigars, nor will he have a leak problem. His rival might, but not him. He must mix among the people. He must be funny. I don't think a nation today would stand to have a leader with a sense of humor. Well, there's gonna be one in this vision of mine . . . I don't care what our government says . . . worldly politics have no say in my world . . .

If I could bring someone into this place and show them what I have created, what effect would it have on them . . . or me?

I wonder . . .

Later in the afternoon, The Writer found himself letting his mind drift back into the grim realities of this life. He was starting to feel depressed and lost in all things. He began to recall the broken promises Rusty had made to him.

I need to talk to someone about this whole thing with Rusty, he thought, someone who doesn't have a personal stake in it. I need a genuine outlook from someone I can trust. Now who do I know . . . the preacher, Mr. Graham! Of course, who else is more reliable in situations like this! I'll talk to him tonight after services. He can help me clear out my mind about what's going on.

Then he reminded himself . . .

I was supposed to call and invite Rusty to the bowling match tomorrow night. I better do it now.

Luckily his mother was not home yet from the bookstore, so she could not object to whom he was calling. The stranger was up in the bedroom. He had eaten a little that morning, then went back to sleep. It puzzled The Writer how someone like that could sleep so much, but then he guessed that whatever drugs or such he was once on had created this strange series of after-effects on him.

He went into the kitchen to use the phone, where he was sure nobody could hear or see him. Still he looked around in vain before he picked up the receiver.

His stomach began to feel icky and queasy.

His heart began to race hard.

Please let him be there, he thought as he lifted the receiver. Please let him be . . .

His shaky finger punched the seven digits that would either uphold or shoot down his billionth or so attempt at trying to get Rusty to do something with him. They had indeed, gone out once before, but it was when he took him to his house for about an hour. All they did was watch cartoons and look at his cramped bedroom upstairs.

The phone rang once.

His heart pounded even harder.

Another ring.

He started sweating.

"Hello?"

Oh gosh, his mother! he shuddered. What do I say . . .?

"Hello . . .?"

"Uh . . . is Rusty there?" he asked awkwardly.

There was a brief silence.

"Rusty? Is this The Writer?" she asked rather annoyed.

"Yes."

She let out a deep sigh, then said, "Just a minute and I'll see."

He strained to hear. He could pick up the distant sound of a girl laughing, then came a crackling wave of static. In the static he could hear a guy's voice that was cracked and high-pitched, then it disappeared. When it was gone, there was a very faint sound of someone else talking, then a series of whispers, and his mother came back on.

"No he's not. Can I take a message?"

"Uh . . . yes . . . tell him I called . . . and that . . . uh . . . I was wondering if he'd like to come with us to . . . the bowling tournament tomorrow night. Just have him call."

"Well, I'll tell him, but that's all I can do now. I ain't gonna make him call you if he doesn't want to talk to you now you hear?"

"Yes."

The phone slammed.

He calmly replaced the receiver. The nervous wreck he had now become was slowly wearing away little by little. He never knew it would be such a painful strive to make and keep a friend, especially with a mother like Rusty's.

"Who's Rusty?"

He whirled around in fright and slammed his back up against the wall next to the phone.

The stranger stood propped up against the frame of the kitchen doorway. His heavy eyes were set upon The Writer.

I'm caught, he thought. He'll tell Mama.

"He's just . . . uh . . . somebody I know." Boy that was flimsy, he thought.

"I didn't think it was the president," he said, coming into the kitchen. "He's not liberal enough for someone like you."

Compliment or insult? he thought. He turned his head away when he felt the stranger come closer to him.

"I asked you who's Rusty?"

"Just a friend."

"Whatever. I heard you calling for him. You didn't look excited about it. You looked more like some girl who couldn't have an orgasm. Believe me I've seen it a lot."

A sting of humiliation pierced his mind. He closed his eyes. How did this guy know about such things? Maybe I don't want to know . . .

The stranger grabbed one of the chairs from the table and sat on it. He turned to face The Writer, who walked and stood behind him. The stranger saw this and turned his chair around to face him again. The Writer again walked to where he was behind him. The stranger let out a heavy grunt and moved the chair again to face The Writer. Each time though he managed to elude his sight, until the stranger backed his chair up to the wall.

"Now try and hide from me," he said boldly, folding his heavy arms across his bare chest.

The Writer turned his back to him.

"Boy, turn around here and talk to me!" he said loudly. "Let me see your face!"

He turned his body around but kept his head turned away.

"What were you asking me?" The Writer asked nervously. First Rusty's mother and now the stranger was after him. He was starting to feel the first slight touches of regret in bringing this guy into his home.

"Show me your face! I've been here I don't know how long and I haven't gotten a good look at that face!"

"I can't."

"Why not?" he asked, getting up on his feet. "Why can't you? You can't be that ugly."

The Writer lunged for the door. The stranger was faster this time, grabbing hold of his shoulders and holding him up against the wall. The Writer struggled but found it worthless. It was his turn to be pinned by the stranger, who kept trying to position his face to where he could see The Writer's, but he kept moving his head all around and out of his sight. He was squeezing his eyes shut. The cap on his head kept bopping into the forehead of the stranger. He grabbed it and yanked it off. The Writer grappled for it but the stranger held it out of his reach. He threw it across into the living room but The Writer tore loose from the stranger's hands and went after it. The stranger leapt up onto the coffee table and was looming over The Writer.

"Hey, you can't run from me," he said. Looking like a frightened kitten, The Writer made like he saw something behind the stranger. His eyes gave the impression that there was something there. The stranger fell for it and looked behind him. When he did The Writer bolted for the stairs. The stranger turned back around and saw that he had been tricked.

He saw The Writer hurrying up the stairs on all fours like a huge cat.

"Hey, get back here you wild tiger!" the stranger yelled and charged after him, skipping every other step. When The Writer got to the top and was about to stand up the stranger leapt up on top of him. He held The Writer down on the floor but his adrenaline was so fired up he inched his way back up and crawled, with the stranger on his back, all the way into his bedroom. It did not occur to him to crawl into the stranger's bedroom which was just behind him when he was jumped on. The stranger held on as he rode on his back, amazed at how strong this guy was for his size.

As soon as he was in his bedroom he flung the stranger off his back, got up, and locked the door. The stranger got up on his feet and was breathing heavily. He was already dripping sweat off his forehead and bare chest.

The Writer turned around to him but did not look at his face.

"Boy, don't ever try to trick me!" he said, his arms hanging down his sides as if ready to grab him again. "Nobody can trick me and get away with it. Let me see you!"

The Writer dodged him and went for the window. He quickly pulled the curtains shut and turned back around. The stranger was standing on the bed glaring at him.

"Boy, you're making this hard on me!" he said. "Do you know you run just like Godzilla?! A big waddle on all sides! Tell me who that Rusty is, why you can't show your face, and why you always have to have it dark! Tell me!"

He lunged down at him but The Writer moved away, making

the stranger stumble into the wall next to the window. He grabbed the curtains and furiously flung them back apart. The Writer covered his face to shield his eyes from the sudden orange brightness of the evening sun that flooded the room. The stranger saw this and charged up to him, grabbing him again by the shoulders and demanding to know why he couldn't show his face.

"I can't," The Writer said silently. "I never could."

"WHY?"

"Because."

"LET ME SEE YOUR FACE!"

He flung The Writer down on the bed and got on top of him. The Writer kept his face buried under his hands but the stranger was strong enough to peel them off and he held them down with his own hands. The Writer kept moving his face off to the side as best he could but it was no use. His eyes were tightly squeezed shut. The stranger pressed his forehead down onto The Writer's and held it still to where he could finally look at his face. The Writer was afraid to see that sweltering face so close to his. He could feel the stranger breathing and panting down his neck, his sweat dripping onto his own face and mouth. Afraid of a pending asthma attack, he stopped struggling and calmed down, hoping this would be over a lot sooner if he stopped fighting back.

"Okay, I see it. Your face. Not bad. Now let me see your eyes."

Oh no, I have to look at him, he thought fearfully. The stranger let go of his hands and they immediately wrapped themselves back on his face. But the stranger again seized hold of them and angrily tried to peel them back off. He heaved himself down on him with his body and tried to get him to let loose of his face. Nothing seemed to work.

Mama came home from the bookstore and heard a muffled scuffling sound coming from upstairs. She didn't see The Writer around but could see the stranger's bedroom door wide open. She set her things down in the chair next to the door, hurried up the steps and didn't see a sign of either one of them. She then turned in the direction of the noise and found it emerging from The Writer's closed bedroom door.

"Son, what's going on in there?"

"Oh thank God," The Writer said. The stranger got up off of him, panting and out of breath. The Writer told his mother to come on in.

When she did, she saw the stranger sitting on the edge of the bed over The Writer, who was lying on the bed on his back, sweating, gasping, and looking up at the ceiling.

She looked at the scene and almost assumed the greatest atrocity she could think of in human relationships.

"Son, what in the world is . . ."

"Look lady," the stranger cut in. He pulled The Writer up and positioned him towards his mother. "Look at him. What color are his eyes?"

"His eyes?"

"Yeah, look, his eyes. What color are they?" The Writer sat still and let the stranger pose him however he wanted, but his eyes would not set sight on his mother, who was standing in the doorway. She came closer for a better look.

"I don't really know," she said. "I think I saw them one time and that was it. He never looks at me when I talk to him." But she was afraid to look into them and be reminded of the face of his natural father.

The Writer was looking at the wall behind his mother. He could tell she was looking at him.

"What was going on in here before I came in? I heard heavy breathing."

"Oh, that was me," The Writer said before the stranger could open his mouth. "I thought I felt an asthma attack coming on, so he kept me from getting excited while he tried to find my inhaler in my pocket. Didn't you?" He pulled the inhaler out of his coat pocket and showed Mama.

The stranger looked at him in wonder then at his mother, who had her head turned at him and her arms folded.

"Well son, is that how it was? You two weren't up to anything reckless in here, because when I opened the door it looked like you two were . . ."

"That's it lady," the stranger said, putting an arm around The Writer. "I tried to keep him from having that attack he said, whatever it was."

She stood still for a moment in silence, then let her arms down.

We're two-faced liars, The Writer thought.

"Well, if you say so, as long as you're alright. Listen son, Mrs. Graham called me at the bookstore and told me the air conditioner was broken at the church building, so services tonight are in one of the backrooms where there's shade from outside. If you wanna go you can, but in this heat . . . "

"I may go later and just talk to Mr. Graham," he said. "That's all."

"Okay, that's fine. I'll get supper while you're gone."

Mama made The Writer take the truck to the church building. She forbid him to walk in the excruciating heat that had taken a bitter hold of the mountains for early June. She had also forbid him to walk to the mailbox which was at the very entrance to the driveway. She always picked it up when she came back home from work. If there was no mail she would assume that her son had walked in the heat to get it when she said for him not to. Other than that nobody sent them anything. When the weather was cooler she allowed him to go get it, that is, under her watchful eye from the window.

When he got to the building, several church members were headed for their cars in the parking lot. The Writer parked on the other side of the building so nobody would see him and make a fuss over his not being there this evening. When he was certain that everyone was gone, he got out and went for the back door. He met Mrs. Graham just inside in the first classroom, picking up little odds and ends from her preschool kids.

"Well hello sonny," she greeted happily, as usual. "What can I do for you? We missed you at services tonight."

"I just need to see Mr. Graham," he said.

"Oh, he'll be back in a few minutes. Why don't you wait in here? I'll make sure nobody bothers you while you're with him. I'll lock the outer doors and just leave this one open. That way you can leave when you're done and not have to look for a key because I don't think he ever carries one on him. He never has and never does, I don't think. Anyway, can I get you anything while you wait?"

You could bring me peace and quiet, he thought as he inched for the room. Mrs. Graham bid him a good evening and went out the back door, just as she so wordily said she would. The Writer put his keys down on one of the tables and looked around the room. It was gently illuminated with a tranquil shade of orange from the growing dusk outside. He could see the shadow of a branch vibrating on the far wall from the wind. The windows were shut, so The Writer opened them and let the gradual cooling of the day sweep into the room. The black coat that was tied around his waist blew back with the first gust.

He walked away from the window and wandered around aimlessly for a few minutes, waiting for Mr. Graham to return. He peeped out the window and looked to the left. He could see Mrs. Graham walking across the backyard of the church building and making her way to the house. He walked back around the room and observed his surroundings. Up against the wall behind the door was a long table. On it were the remnants of the projects the third and fourth graders had been working on, such as paper scraps, scissors, bottles of paint, and pencils. There was a clock over the bulletin board and a chalkboard on the wall on the left side of the door. On the wall directly across the room from the table, there was nothing. It was totally bare, except for the dancing shadow.

The room was dead silent except for the slight tap of his shoes as he wandered across the aging tile floor. The building was over fifty years old and had undergone numerous renovations through the years. The walls had been painted who knows how many times and the floor colored with years of hardened dirt.

The Writer let out a deep sigh and propped himself up against the table. He looked at his watch and saw that he had last glanced at it just two minutes ago. His mind began to swirl with thoughts and images, which it usually did when he was alone in a quiet place.

The first image was that of Rusty, then it melted into that of the stranger, then Joey, and finally, each of his close friends, one by one, face by face. He began to recall visions of his graduation ceremony just less than a week ago. He could hear the screams and cheers for all the popular kids at that school, while the not-so-popular ones got a drowned decibel level of applause.

He continued to wander around the room, then heard a voice out of nowhere . . .

His own . . .

"What am I going to do? What has happened to me? Graduation, the stranger, Mrs. Moran, Rusty, Joey, my friends, suspicion, worry . . . dear God what is going on? So much in so little time. I can't even begin to think of where to start to think about these things. My mind is so foggy like these mountains you made millions of years ago. Okay, I got it now. I came here to see Mr. Graham about Rusty and what I should do about him. Rusty. Dear God you know him. You know all. Annie says he's a nymphomaniac who only wants to date girls for sex. Does she tell me this because she once dated him and now hates his living guts or is it true? I know Mama is not too fond of him. So what? He's made mistakes. We all have. Mama told that Mrs. Moran the other day that you did create a thing called the mistake. Therefore, in simple terms, you made the mistake, something for us to learn from. So maybe Rusty hasn't kept every single little promise to me. So what if he hasn't taken me out anywhere like he promised, or taught me how to wrestle, or to the block party in Asheville, or to the flea market in Murphy, or to those song and dance marathons they have around here, or to the lake, or having our picnic like he's promised over and over and over, or going with me to that special place I love so much down below Murphy . . . those little things

. . . dear Lord those things I can overlook. Everybody else seems to think that if he can't keep those promises he's not worth having. I always give him another chance to make up for it, and he says he will. I just cannot give up on him. I told Annie why I don't want to lose him, but I don't know if she bought it. Maybe you can show me in some way what I am to do about Rusty. Take him or leave him. I leave that up to you. I know you'll show me in a way you know is best."

He kept looking at the bare wall.

"What am I going to do with the stranger? What can I do? I should have thought of all that before I carried him home Sunday night. I can't just adopt him as my son. That would mean that some boy has a father younger than he is! How silly is that? How would the conception for him have taken . . . oh no! Listen at me! What am I thinking?! Annie's allusions to sex about Rusty has rotted in my mind! But the stranger . . . he's had sex before! Where else could he have learned that thrust of . . . Writer—stop it right now! Stop! Stop! STOP! Stop thinking about that! It's none of my business what he did in the past unless he wants to tell me. I just brought him home because he was lying next to the road and looked as if he were near death. Would you have done the same thing? I suppose so. I just don't know now what to say or do with him now. I know Mama may be getting tired of him being in the house, eating all our food, and keeping me up late. I know she can't take in another son. She has enough to worry about with me and my asthma. She doesn't deserve to have another burden on her heart.

"Now I wonder who raised the stranger. Was it some flophouse spinster or what? Where did he come from? I can never think to ask him. I don't even know his name, or if he even has one! Why can I not remember to ask him? I have to know what is to be done with him. He was a wild man when he first came around, now he's a bit tamer. Did my foot make him afraid of me? Was it the shower? What? What is it about me that has suddenly calmed him down? I would imagine he'd have knocked me off, assaulted

Mama, took our money and valuables, and left us poor by now. But he hasn't. He did, however, make me lie to Mama about what we were doing in the bedroom. When I think about what she saw when she opened the door I guess it did look a little gruesome. I admit I lied. Forgive me, and for whatever else I may have done in your sight that is not right. But I still wonder why Mama has been so understanding and willing to let me keep him in the house this long. Other moms I guess would have already called the cops and forgotten it all by now. I'm just thankful that my mom hasn't done that."

Then he stopped. He took a closer look at what he'd been talking to the whole time. Although his heart and mind was centered upon his conversation with God, he found himself face to face with something that had been with him the whole time.

"I can't believe it," he said, backing away. "I'm talking to a wall. The scary part is I think you're listening."

He hesitated.

"Am I crazy? Some dumb wall has overheard my prayer and talk to God! I've been yapping away at something that does nothing but hold up the roof to this old building! I bet you see a lot of what goes on in here don't you? You see all the little kids come in, listen, learn about Jesus, and you watch them make stuff. How long have you done that? Years I imagine. Doesn't it get boring, watching the same thing for over half a century? It would make me a stark raving lunatic. I'd be foaming blood at the mouth. If you could talk what would you say? Let me guess, you'd say something like, 'I've watched you since you were a toddler, come in here, learn about Jesus, and make things. I saw you on that Sunday morning years ago after you and your mom had a fight. You came in here and wrote all over the table. Your name is still there if you look close enough. I saw you make paper projects, several of which your mom has stored in the attic and only uses them to decorate the house at Christmas and . . . 'How would you know all this?!?! You're just a wall! A brick wall! You have no feelings, can't think, and you can't defend yourself when somebody gets mad and throws things at you, like Scarlett O'Hara did with that ceramic vase in *Gone With the Wind*. Does it hurt when someone drives nails into you so you can be covered up with pictures? If so, you don't fight back do you? Ha! People take you for granted, thinking you walls will always be around to hide what goes on in secret. Well, you know what . . . walls don't last forever. They can fall apart like people, and make manifest to the world what's been going on in their sight. People hide behind others so they won't get caught. They forget to cover that vast area over their heads. God looks down and sees what is really going on. No wall can cover His sight of what happens upon this earth. At this moment He's watching me talk to you. Someday you're gonna come crashing down on the earth and be shattered to pieces. You won't be able to hide any-more of what has gone on in here, or in any room in any house anywhere in the world. People won't be able to hide behind their lifestyles. Their walls will come crashing down someday. All of our walls will crumble to the earth. God will pull them down when we stand before Him on that day of judgment and nothing will be hidden from His sight. You walls will fall. You are weak and vul-nerable and don't know how to fight back when someone contradicts you, so don't think that you can outdo what someone thinks or does!"

As he turned to walk out the door he picked up a green highlighter pen that was on the table. In his frustration with what he'd just gotten himself into an argument with, he hurled the pen at the wall.

It clanged against it and came hurling back. It bopped him on the back of his head, fell to the floor, and rolled away.

He slowly turned around, his eyes flaring angrily as he lunged for the wall and kicked it savagely. He slapped it till his hands turned red and began to feel numb. He backed away from it, panting and sweating. He looked at the table and picked up a glass bottle.

"That didn't hurt ya did it?!" he said loudly. "How does THIS feel?!?!?!"

He threw it and the glass shattered like an exploding fireworks display, each fragment lit in glimmering orange from the setting sun outside.

But there was something else.

The bottle had red paint in it. Red oozed down the wall from its splattered point of impact, as if someone had fired a gun at the wall. The paint went onto the floor and into the grooves between the tiles. An eerie silence took over the room. The Writer went for the door, turned around, and took one last look at the bleeding wall.

Then he waddled away . . . going back to his house.

CHAPTER THIRTEEN

For the first time since his arrival the stranger ate at the dining room table but held the knife and fork as if they were pitchforks when using them on the steaks. He drowned all three steaks in A1 sauce and licked his plate clean of any sauce that remained after he had devoured his meat. After unleashing a huge belch that blew directly into The Writer's face, the stranger made his exit and headed back for the bedroom.

"Son," Mama said, wiping her mouth, "you know he can't stay here for good."

He nodded.

"Has he said anything about where he's from or what?"

"He won't answer," he said. "I know he has to go sometime. He's eating all our food."

"Oh son, I'm not kicking him back out on the street. I'm just saying he probably has a home somewhere or a family. We can at least try to help him get back wherever he came from."

"What if he doesn't?"

"That's what you have to find out son," Mama said, taking her plate and putting it in the sink. "He won't talk to me, but he likes you."

He turned towards her.

"Oh yes son, he likes you. I can tell. He keeps asking me who this Rusty is. Did you say something to him about Rusty?"

He shook his head. The last thing he needed was the stranger and his mother teaming up on him and his intentions with Rusty. He just wanted them and everyone else to leave him alone and let him handle Rusty on his own. Besides, he had put the whole matter in God's hands. It would be up to Him to settle the whole thing once and for all.

Mama began to fill the sink with water for the dishes. While it was filling up she came back to the dining table and picked up more plates. Her son sat still in his chair, as if he were stoned to it. He was looking far off into space. His mind was a huge blank, had been ever since she mentioned Rusty's name.

Mama saw the look on his face and knew he was going into deep thought. Before he could get too deeply into it, she looked at the calendar next to the phone, and remembered something.

"So, how was your talk with Mr. Graham at the church?"

Oh no, he thought. I can't tell her that I got into a fight with a wall. She'd think I was crazy for sure. "I never saw him," he said. "He must've been busy, so I came on back." He studied Mama's face and saw that she believed him. He didn't actually lie to her. True, he never saw him, and he was waiting, but the waiting had escalated into a furious argument with the wall.

"Son, I want to talk to you about this Saturday."

He inched his head towards her.

"Judy came by the store today on her lunch break. We got to talking about this weekend, and she had the greatest idea. This Saturday, instead of watching the morning fashion show on QVC, Judy and I have planned it as our day out together in Asheville. We're gonna hit all the malls and department stores."

He lifted his right eyebrow. He could just see himself trying to keep up with two adult women caught in the mad frenzy of the latest sale JCPenney, Belk, and Sears had going on, not to mention whatever Wal-Mart, K-Mart, Roses, Lowe's, T.J. Maxx, and the other major chains had to promote. He knew the gals would be there at all of them one way or the other. He also knew that when they found Goody's, they'd lose control of themselves and go totally berserk over whatever was marked down by at least 2%. Asheville was the perfect place to lose your mother, your wife, your aunt, your grandmother, or whoever you know who loves to shop, and not care whether or not you got her back. Either way you knew she was happy.

"But do you know what else Saturday is?" she asked. He looked towards her without a clue.

"How could you forget sonny? It's the seventh anniversary of your baptism. Your second birthday. You always take one of your friends out for the day to celebrate it. Remember?"

This coming Saturday . . . my anniversary . . . GOOD GOLLY! he thought as he realized it. What's wrong with me?! How could I forget that day?! The day I was baptized? First I fight with a wall and now this! I must be crazy like Mrs. Moran and the rest of the worldly social critics who think I am.

The reminder slashed his mind open and apart. Whatever he was thinking about prior to that was so long gone now it didn't matter what it was. This was the greatest day in his life and each year to commemorate the event, he spent the day out with one of his friends at that special place he discovered in Murphy. It was a place that made him feel so proud and happy about his strong faith and beliefs and he was willing to share it with others, as long as they were willing to accept it.

Let's see, who could I take this year, he thought as he sat at the table. I took Elaine and Jackie last year, the year before that I took Lana and Dionne, the year before that I took Nate, before that it was Annie and Blade, and the years before that Mama took me there because I couldn't drive and I had no friends then who wanted to go look at it. Who does that leave now to go . . . ? I know Joey may have to work . . .

Aha! he thought as the idea swelled up in his mind. I know who I can take this year. This would be perfect for him. We can do all the things he's promised me this time . . . yes sir, my weekend is planned . . .

What could go wrong, he thought as he headed upstairs to his own bedroom.

On the day of the bowling tournament, all of The Writer's teammates had agreed to meet at his house that afternoon and leave from there at six and be at the bowling alley by seven. It would take about forty-five minutes to get to the bowling alley and to get to their reserved lane. Mama took the afternoon off from work so she could help her son get into the new captain's outfit she and Judy had designed for him. Tonight was also Judy's night off from the restaurant, and she and Joey came over to the house to meet the rest of the team as they arrived. Joey was wearing his outfit, which was simply a silk orange shirt, his name and number sewn in black onto the front upper right corner and on the back, black pants, a black cap, and was sitting in the living room flipping through the *TV Guide* while Judy and Mama were in The Writer's bedroom, helping him get fitted into his outfit.

The stranger was in his bedroom.

The doorbell rang.

"Joey, can you get that please?" Mama called out from upstairs.

He answered it and in came Lana and Dionne in their outfits, which looked just like his. They also had their bowling balls and satchels.

"Okay, where's the bowling king?" Dionne asked first thing. "I wanna get that trophy."

"He's right here," Joey said, spreading his arms out. Dionne frowned at him.

"Get real Joey," Lana said, putting her ball down on the floor. "You know The Writer can whip your butt on the lanes. Let's see, your last score with him was what . . . "

"Lana, don't even . . . " Joey protested, regretting now that he made the smart crack about being the bowling king when he knew good and well that she meant The Writer.

"I remember! 102. And what did The Writer get . . . ? Huh Joey . . . what did he get?"

"Lana shut up," he said in giggles. "It doesn't matter."

"What was it huh? Tell me. Huh? What was it? Huh? Huh? Huh?"

"194."

The sudden reply out of nowhere made the girls jump and Joey stand back. They looked on the stairs and saw their captain, decked out in the outfit Mama and Judy designed for him. The girls' mouths fell open and a smile melted across Joey's pale face.

The Writer stood before them, in a dramatic blend of orange

and black. His shoes were black and had a silk orange lightening bolt shooting across both sides of them, his socks were orange, his silk pants with the orange drawstring dangling were baggy and black so he could move more freely, there was his waist bag with an orange star sewn onto its front, where his black coat was usually tied around him was now something similar but far more catchy— Mama took the look of his coat draped around his upper legs and with a huge piece of black silk, made the outside portion black and the inside of it was a flaming orange silk color, so when he moved or if the cloth was blown upwards the orange would stand out. She designed this to tie around his waist just like his black coat always did. Mama said it would make him look more powerful, especially with the orange. His shirt was of black silk with his name and number sewn in orange in the corner like everyone else's. On the back in silk orange was the name 'Writer' sewn above his number, which was seven. His sleeves stood out the most. The black portion ended just above his elbows and from there, Judy made the sleeves longer by making them orange from the inside of the cloth at the elbow down to just above his wrists. They were loose fitting so he could swing the ball with more force. His cap was cleaned to the point of where the name 'Writer' shined on the front of his cap in orange.

"Oh wow," Lana and Dionne said in unison. Joey was waving his thumbs up all over in the air with a big smile on his face. They had never seen The Writer look this captivating or out of the clothes his mother buys for him from the local flea market, as she says that it's the only place that sells clothes perfect for his big build.

The Writer stood still on the steps, letting his friends get as long a look as they wanted. He came on down and let the girls get a closer look. Joey could only stand and look.

"Linda, how did you make this?" Lana asked as she caressed his sleeves and Dionne the mini-cape.

"Simple. My son loves orange and black, so I thought, why not go as far as I could with both colors, knowing how much time he spends in the dark."

"I know it," The Writer said quietly as he wandered away from the girls. He then began to lift his cap off. "But when you can go as far as making a bandana for the head then you know you've conquered everything from head to toe." Sure enough, as soon as his cap was removed, there appeared a black silken bandana wrapped around his head. On it was an intricate design of an orange sunburst sewn onto the very top of it. The tie-ends of it allowed him to make it as loose or as tight as he wanted it to be, and they hung down the back of his neck to his shoulders. One was black, the other orange. Whenever he moved his head he looked like he had an orange and black ponytail.

"I was gonna make one for Joey but nooooo, he wouldn't wear it," Judy pointed out.

"Mom, I told you I'd look silly wearing it," he said. The Writer whirled his eyes towards him. "But on you man it looks great!" he quickly spit out.

"Oh, I forgot the finishing touch," Mama said, rummaging her hand in her apron pockets. She pulled out an orange string that turned out to be the necklace for an orange pen she bought earlier that day at the store. She hung it around her son's neck and adjusted it.

"Can't be 'The Writer' without the pen can we?" she said.

The doorbell rang again.

"Come in," Mama called out.

Annie, Elaine, and Jackie came hurrying in.

"I thought we were going to be late, but I finally got . . . . . . ohhh-woahhhhhhhhh!" she exclaimed when she saw The Writer and approached him to give their familiar greeting. "Now THAT is a bowling king's garb of royalty," she said, closely examining it with her glasses.

"Cool," Jackie said with a huge smile on her face. "I could never make something like that."

"They should have you and Judy on QVC," Elaine said as she gazed over it.

"Fine. Where's my bowling ball Mama?" The Writer asked.

"It should be up in your room."

"I'll help you look," Joey said and the two went up the stairs
to his room. Elaine, Jackie, Lana, Dionne, and Annie sat on the
couch to wait for Nate and Blade to arrive. Mama and Judy went
into the kitchen. As soon as Annie opened her mouth to talk,
the doorbell rang again. All five looked at each other, totally
clueless.

"Could someone get that?" Mama hollered. All eyes fell on
Annie, along with sly grins.

"Oh sure, make the smart one serve the dunces," she said as
she got up. Lana and Dionne raised their eyebrows in wonder.

She opened the door and there stood Nate. He saw Annie and
immediately looked frustrated.

"Annie, you shouldn't open the door without asking who it is
first," he said.

"Fine then," Annie snapped back and slammed the door on
his face. "Who is it?" she asked.

"Open the door Annie," Nate said. "It's me, Nate."

She opened it and in came Nate in his outfit, shaking his head
at Annie and her wisecracking attitude. He came into the living
room where the other girls were, and was soon joined by Mama
and Judy.

"Well long time no see!" Elaine said when she saw Nate and
ran up to hug him.

"You'll have to excuse Annie, Nate," Lana said. "She just found
out she has the same interior designer as Cher."

Judy and Dionne started chuckling and Annie's mouth gaped
open in astonishment. For some reason, everyone loved to pick on
her and Blade. It was her top priority to find out why sooner or
later.

"Are you sure it's up here Mama?" The Writer asked from the
stairway. Nate turned around and saw his outfit, and gave the
same stunned reaction that everybody else had.

"Yes I'm sure son. Just keep looking." The Writer went back

up the stairs. As soon as she was certain he was back in his room, Mama got everyone's attention.

"Watch . . . 'I can't find it Mama," she said, mimicking how her son would say it any second now. She pointed to the stairs and sure enough, very faintly . . .

"I can't find it Mama."

Everyone broke out in a chuckle. "Just look son. I'm sure it's there."

"'Just look son. I'm sure it's there,'" The Writer said to Joey, mimicking how she just said it and sent Joey into a fury of laughter. "Amazing how she's so sure of everything."

The two boys then opened the closet and looked again. Joey got up on a chair and rummaged around the boxes on the top shelf. He pulled out one big box that was almost falling apart. The Writer saw it and lunged for it. Instead, he grabbed Joey and they fell onto the bed. The box tore out from The Writer's hand and fell to the floor. As soon as it did, a big black object came rolling from out of the shadows of the top shelf. Joey saw it and got up after it. Instead it crashed to the floor and rolled out the bedroom door, hit the stranger's door, and then proceeded down the steps, creating a thunderous thud with each step it hit.

The doorbell had rung just seconds before the ball hit the floor in the bedroom. The door had opened and the first thing Blade saw was the ball coming down the steps headed straight for him. He stumbled in slight panic and fell backwards onto his rear end on the porch. The ball rolled straight to him at full force and came to a dead stop between his legs.

"STRIKE!" Joey hollered from the top of the stairs.

Everyone was finally ready to go. Judy insisted that The Writer drive her convertible since it could hold more people, so Joey, Nate, and Blade took possession of it, piling into the back seat. The Writer kept looking all around him, wondering if Rusty would show up. An inner gut feeling was telling him that he wasn't, and some part of him kept saying that it could happen yet.

Dionne brought Lana in her car, so she said she could haul

Annie as well as Elaine and Jackie. The two mothers insisted on
going in Mama's old truck. Dionne's car also had a sunroof, so it
would be easy to compete with the guys who had absolutely no
top on their car this clear sunny afternoon.

Mama looked up and saw The Writer glancing all around. She
looked where he did then looked at the house.

Something was missing.

"This feels so strange," she said to herself as she looked around.
"Someone's not here . . . strange . . . that stranger! Oh no!" She
had just remembered. They had left the stranger locked up in the
house in his bedroom. Mama was so afraid to leave him alone in the
house for ANY reason. Quickly she called The Writer over to her.

"Son, we're missing someone," she said.

"I know. Rusty hasn't shown up."

Mama's face melted into a sudden scowl. Of all times for him
to be concerned about Rusty when their guest was still in the
house. She had the notion to grab him and shake him severely by
the shoulders until all knowledge of Rusty's existence on this earth
was jangled out of his mind. But he was bigger than her, and it
would seem awkward for her to try anything like that on him.

"Son . . . just . . . forget about that Rusty for a minute please,"
she said in her most fiery tone of whisper so nobody else would
hear her. "Did you invite him?"

He nodded.

"Well, he isn't going to show up. Common sense should tell
you that by now. He's just as bullheaded as his mother is. Now,
what are we going to do about that boy in the house?"

The Writer looked to the upstairs windows and saw the one to
the stranger's wide open. He was probably hearing all the activity
that was going on and knew something was up.

"He'll have to come with us," he said firmly. "He can't stay
here."

"I know, but what about the rest of the gang?" Mama said.
"What do we tell them when we bring out a total stranger we've
been hiding in the bedroom?"

Mama studied the eyes of her son and saw that they were not set on her but looked to the skies above. They beamed the deep blue sea color that was above them and she knew that he was thinking of something to do.

"You explain to them and I'll handle him," he said. In truth he had no idea how they would react when they learned that for the past week, he had been playing nursemaid to a total stranger from off the streets who had apparently done crack, coke, alcohol, sex, and committed offenses like nobody's business. He thought it was quite a milestone for him to get his mother to let him keep him here as long as he had now, because other moms would've kicked him out after the first night or called the cops without talking to him first. But he knew his friends as well as Judy loved his mother, and he felt that anyway she could explain to them about what he was doing here would suffice enough to not make them question him or her about the stranger.

As The Writer went back inside the house he heard his mother say, "Alright now, I have something to tell you, so please listen . . . "

He hurried up the stairs to the stranger's bedroom and opened the door. He saw him sitting on the edge of the bed with his elbows on his knees and his hands at his mouth. He had heard everything that was going on downstairs.

"Where're ya'll going?" he asked bluntly. "Leaving me here huh? Just say you want me to leave and I'll go, okay man? Don't sneak it around me. And why do you look like something out of a Japanimation cartoon?" He was referring to The Writer's outfit.

"I'm not," The Writer said calmly. "You're coming with us."

"WHAT? WHERE?!" he said in astonishment. He leapt up on his feet. "The cops?! Fine! Go ahead! Tell them how I tried to screw you, how I ate all your food, how I made your lives a living . . . "

He stopped when he saw The Writer shaking his head. He sat him back down on the bed.

"We're going bowling with my friends," he said. "I want you to come with us. Can you bowl?"

"What's that?"

"Just pick up a ball and roll it down this alley and hit a bunch of pins. It's not hard. It's fun. You try to knock down as many as you can in two tries. If you knock them all down on the first try, you get a strike."

"So?"

"So you're coming with us. Wanna try it?"

The stranger looked at him for a long time, then at the floor. It would be the first time he'd been no farther than the backyard since he'd been there. He hadn't even worn a shirt on his body since Sunday night when The Writer bathed him. It would be a major transition for him to go with them tonight.

"But your friends? They won't like me. They're probably not like you are, willing to have me around."

Not like me, he thought. Could that mean . . . maybe . . . I guess . . . I don't know. I won't wonder about it.

The Writer explained that his mother was telling them all about him and were going to be made to promise not to tell anyone else about his being here in the house. She hoped they wouldn't turn against her for helping The Writer with the stranger. If so, then he'd have to find a way to go on in life without them.

"Okay I'll go," he said finally. "What do I wear?"

The Writer led him into his bedroom just down the hall. They went to his closet and stepped on the contents of the box that Joey pulled out earlier. The stranger bent down to see what they were. The Writer caught him looking, swooped his arm down, and grabbed the papers out of his hand.

"What're those?" he asked in the same tone when he asked who Rusty was. The Writer quickly tossed them back into the box and kicked it back into the closet on the floor.

"Tell you later," he said as he rummaged through the clothes, then remembered where what he was looking for was at. He shut the door and went over to the dresser. He pulled out an orange and black outfit that looked like the one he was wearing, but not the same design. It was more like the ones Joey and everybody else was wearing. The only difference was that it had 'Writer' and '7' on it in orange. The shirt portion was black and the pants were orange, but all silky and shiny, just like the one The Writer was donning on him.

"This was my outfit last year," he said as he pulled it out and shook it. He then held it up to the stranger's bare body and saw that it should fit him. "Put these on," he said. "You'll be one of us."

The stranger hurriedly put them on and he stood in front of The Writer. "These feel slick inside," he said. "They're cool."

"I always say when it comes to clothes, if it can fit me, then surely it'll fit you," The Writer said, looking at the stranger decked out in lustrous orange and black. The final touch was a black cap, and the only one he had handy was one that had 'Godzilla' sewn on it in green.

"You like Godzilla?" the stranger asked in fascination. "Do ya?"

"Tell you later," The Writer said, gesturing that it was time to go and was standing near the door.

"No really, do ya boy? Because you look, groan, and walk just like him, especially with that coat tail thing dangling around your rear end. I think I'll start calling you Godzilla, Zilla for short. How about that boy? Zilla just fits your size."

"Alright now," The Writer said, looking at his watch. It was already a few minutes past six. "It's time to go."

"Okay but you've got three things to tell me later . . . who this Rusty is, what's in that box and if you like Godzilla. Deal?"

He nodded.

The stranger went out in front of him, and The Writer saw that he was barefoot, then remembered that they rent shoes at the bowling alley anyway, so another problem solved itself right there.

Please don't let the others forbid his going with us, The Writer prayed over and over.

They came to the front door and The Writer opened it for the stranger to go out first so he could lock it from inside. The moment the stranger set foot onto the front porch . . .

"HOORAY! WOO-HOO! YEAH! AW YEAH BABY!
YIPPEE!" It was loudly blended with cheers, applause, and
whistling from everyone out in the cars and from Judy, who was
standing next to the truck waving and raving. Mama could only
smile in the satisfaction that she had done her job and that her son
had done his with superior results in getting the stranger into the
outfit.

The stranger stood stock still, soaking up this sudden tidal
wave of affection that had never been heaped upon him before like
this. He slowly let a smile come over his face.

The Writer heard the accolade, of welcome as he locked the
door.

Mama's done it again, he thought.

He then waddled away . . . to take the stranger and his friends
bowling.

CHAPTER FOURTEEN

Upon their arrival at the bowling alley, they were greeted with the outlandish and bizarre whoops and cries of the other teams that were in the parking lot.

"Look, The Writer's freaks!" someone hollered from across the way.

Nobody paid any attention to it but went on ahead inside to get their lane. All around the main desk were signs blaring the big tournament tonight and that the alley would be closing to the general public promptly at seven. The team in orange and black eased their way through the thick crowd to the desk to sign their names on the register for the judges.

The entire joint was seething with excitement and thrills. People were finishing up their games before they had to leave and other teams were cheering and chanting their names over and over. The lights were being adjusted by maintenance for the big night. They would go from boring white halogen to every dazzling neon color in existence, shooting them all over the alley along with lasers, clear Christmas lights hanging over the lanes, plastic glow-in-the-dark ornaments adorning the ceiling, and there was a huge crystal ball hanging over the direct center of the alley. Inside it was a multicolored collection of bulbs that would cause a sweeping sensation of color change every few minutes over the whole alley.

The total effect would be one of magnificent amazement to the scope of the human mind.

"How many players?" the operator asked. The Writer made a quick count and told her ten, counting the stranger.

"We've put you on lanes thirty-five and thirty-six, the very last ones, since you're the smallest team here playing tonight. You'll have to split up into two groups of five, and we'll add your totals from both lanes. Good luck."

They went down to their assigned lanes in the alley and got glances at the other teams and their colors. Some went as far as neon green, purple, beige, maroon, white, gray, magenta, and even a nauseating blend of green, blue, and yellow. They could not escape the bombardment of raw cussing, bird-flipping, and foul references to kicking the other teams' you-know-what and beating the s-word out of them.

"Okay," the announcer said upon greeting them at their lanes. "First, you all look very sharp tonight, especially your captain. Awesome look sir!" she said.

He nodded to her.

"Anyway, what you need to do first is tell me who brought their own balls to use so we can keep an accurate count of what we have here. Second, put your name on the scoreboard as you want it to appear on the trophy should you win first place tonight. The judges and the operator will monitor who does what on each team in each game. And lastly, tell me your team name and your mascot, if you have one."

"We're 'The Writer's 'Pins'!!!" Joey hollered from the back. Dionne slapped him a high five and the others cheered. The Writer closed his eyes in embarrassment at the name he gave his team when they started in this thing four years ago. He felt he could do better with it, but they all seemed to love it so it stayed.

"And your mascot?" she asked, writing it all down on her clipboard.

The Writer looked lost at her handwriting.

"Uh, it's for the trophy, if you all win," she explained. "If it's one we have available, we mount it onto the top of the first place trophy the moment the winning team scores the highest after the seven games."

The Writer thought for a moment what their mascot could be. If they didn't pick one and they wound up winning, all they'd put on the trophy would be a gold star.

What did the stranger call me the other day? he thought, trying to remember what it was when he scurried up the stairs on all
fours.

Ah yes, he thought. That's perfect . . .

"The tiger," he said.

"That's good," she said, writing it down. "And I don't think I
need to ask what your colors are since they stand out so well on
you all. Okay, that's it. Go get your shoes and your bowling balls
and good luck!"

She went on down to ask the other teams the same things. But
since The Writer's was the smallest with only ten, it would take
her longer to get to everyone because the other teams had anywhere from fifteen players to thirty. All of them had to complete a
total of seven games in order to qualify for first, second, or third
place. There was only one trophy, and at four feet high, it was for
first place. The captains of the second and third place teams only
got plaques, and The Writer had none of these honors, coming in
at either fourth or fifth each year since this tournament started.
He knew this losing streak to the big dog teams had to come to an
end someday.

The Writer was putting into the score machine at their lane
the names of his teammates. When they tried to divide themselves
up, it wound up being five boys on one lane and the five girls on
the other one. Annie assumed control of the score machine for the
girls and The Writer entered the names of the boys playing with
him. When he came to naming the fifth bowler, he knew it was
the stranger and went along with Mama's advice that Rusty was
not going to show.

"Hey, what name do you want in here?" he asked the stranger,
who was putting his shoes on.

"For what?" he asked.

"The scoreboard."

"Oh for scoring," he said brightly. "Girls always called me
Brute because I sounded so beastly while . . ."

"Okay, thank you," The Writer said, not wanting to hear

anymore about the background of his name, which he would call him from now on.

Brute.

The name tattooed on his arm.

"Hey, it don't sound any different than Zilla," he said.

It was now seven o'clock. The doors were shut to the public and the director of the event made a few opening remarks about what was to happen, the rules, the procedure, and that each team would be carefully watched and monitored. The announcer then took hold of the microphone and went through the names of the teams, starting with the team in lanes one and two, then the team in three, four, and five, and so on until she got to lane thirty-five and thirty-six. As each team was called out there erupted a blast of cheers from that team and occasional booing from others. When The Writer's team was called out, it was a series of just a few screams pitted against a massive inundation of boos and wails from the others. Lana waved them off and Dionne stuck her tongue out.

"When I count to three, the captain of each team will go first," the announcer said. "And as soon as the first strike is made by whichever team that makes it, the lights will transform into the cosmic phase." There was another wave of cheers as all the team captains stepped up with a ball in their hands. The Writer had his and the support of his small but loyal team behind him, rooting all the time.

"Ready? One . . . two . . . three . . . GO!"

A smashing boom that sounded like a titanic drum roll filled the whole alley as the balls were sent rolling to their targets. The moment the red 'X' over lane 36 started flashing the lights shot off and went into the cosmic stage. An orange spotlight splashed down on the small screaming team gathered around their silent captain who only wanted to get back to his seat.

"It looks like The Writer's Pins have scored the first strike!" the announcer declared. "Way to go guys!"

The lights went off and all the cosmic and neon lights shot on and wild music descended from the speakers all over the walls.

Laser lights flashed from all corners of the alley. Greens and blues, hot pinks, reds, yellows, and other shades of the color scheme slithered and slid all over the floors and wall. It was like walking into the portals of another world far off in the outer reaches of human comprehension. The surreal blend of every color ever un-veiled by man seeping into another, the smoke billowing up from the alleys whenever a strike was hit, those beams of neon carica-tures stunning the mind immune to the problems and travesties of the real world. Here there was no care left in the world. All the miseries were covered by the darkness and shielded back by the laser lights and flood lamps. No way could the thorny briar of life's grim realities pick its way into this place. There was not a single mind open enough to let it take root.

Joey's turn came up next. Lana and Dionne were whooping and hollering as he got up to bowl. Mama and Judy just sat at the tables behind the bowlers' seats. They wanted to stay as far out of the way as possible. From where they sat they could see everything that went on. Judy clenched hold of Mama's hand as her son swung the ball and scored the second consecutive strike for the game. She jumped up clapping and laughing, then sat back down. Everyone screamed their cheers as he returned to his seat next to The Writer.

The strike streak came to an abrupt end when Blade knocked down only six pins. He could only get two of those for his spare shot. Nate hit nine and got the ten pin on his spare, and by the time it was Annie's turn, everyone stared at her as she got up to bowl.

"Why're ya'll lookin' at me?" she shrieked. "Blade's the one who's the oddball!"

"WHAT?!" he demanded to know. "I'm what?"

"You heard me boy!"

"Girl, I bet you don't even hit a single pin! I root for a gutter ball!"

"Hey, I'm not the one who's bowling with a five pound kiddie ball. Mine's a twelve pounder so poo-poo on you smarty!"

"Annie just bowl," Lana said. "You can bicker with Blade later."

"Yeah, we can't lose that trophy," Dionne added, applying another layer of lipstick to her mouth as it was her turn after Annie's. "I wanna look good for the picture if we win."

"We still have six more games to go," Nate reminded her. "You'll need more than that before it's all over with."

"I bet you're going to major in cosmetology in college aren't ya?" Jackie asked as she got her hands ready to bowl.

"Darn right honey," Dionne said, looking at herself in her mirror.

Annie went up to the lane, inched back, positioned the ball in her hands, moved back again, inched over slightly, adjusted her rear end, then moved over a few inches. She backed up and kept focusing her point of impact on the pins. She would stick out her thumb, move it around, lick her finger and stick it up in the air, reposition her rear every few seconds . . .

"AW COME ON!" Dionne and Lana screamed in unison.

"Shut up!" she shrieked. "Do not rush me. I must make this a perfect strike and I can't do that without getting set up perfectly."

"Look Martha Stewart!" Blade hollered. "This isn't QVC! Just throw the stinkin' ball!"

No change.

"COME ON ANNIE!" the guys screamed in unison except The Writer and Brute, who were sitting at the score table for their lane. Mama and Judy were laughing at Annie, as were Jackie and Elaine.

She was still trying to focus her shot.

"Sir, you're the captain," Lana said to The Writer, almost desperate since the other teams were fast approaching their second game. "Do something! We're gonna lose thanks to Miss Smarty Bloomer Britches up there."

He stood up, motioned for Lana to make way for him, and he silently approached his friend, who had approached him two nights earlier about Rusty. But for the moment Rusty did not matter to him, because this year he did not want to come in fourth or fifth place. He had to break his team's losing streak.

Everyone on the team could only see a huge black beastly image silhouetted by the orange light that was all around them for the moment looming over the skinny and frail image of Annie. Out of it came a hand, then out of that came forth a finger . . . aiming straight for Annie . . .

"YEEEOWWW!"

She dropped the ball with a shattering thud just a few inches from her toes. She whirled around clutching her side and saw the fiery gleam in her captain's eyes.

"WHAT'RE YOU DOING?!?! I HAD IT JUST RIGHT! I COULD'A MADE THAT SHOT! WHY ARE YOU . . . HEY, COME BACK HERE! DON'T YOU DARE WALK AWAY FROM ME WHEN I'M FUSSING AT YOU! GET BACK HERE! HEY, I WILL NOT BE IGNORED WRITER! GET BACK HERE!"

A red 'X' was flashing over their lane.

The team jumped up in a ballyhoo of cheers. Annie returned to her seat red-faced, mixed with frustration and exhilaration at her score.

"Well what can I say?" she was saying wryly. "When you're hot you're . . ."

"Shut up," The Writer said, watching Dionne get up to bowl. She picked up her bright shiny ball, held it up to her face, and adjusted her hair.

"Never go bowling with a girl," Blade said to Nate.

Dionne and Lana each scored a strike, raising the team score by several points.

By the time it came to be Brute's turn to bowl, everyone on the team was very nervous to see how he'd do. He had picked out the heaviest ball in the alley and made his way up to the lane. Nobody said a word as he got ready. He had watched everyone else and studied their moves, their positions, and how they walked up to the lane and just let the ball go.

They make it look so easy, he thought as he held the ball up.

And he held it.

And was still holding it when The Writer came up to see what was wrong.

"What is it?" he asked.

"Zilla, I can't do this," he said weakly. "It's too hard. I won't make it. Can I just watch?"

The Writer put his hands on his shoulders and carefully pulled him back. Had the judges seen just how far over the line Brute was with his ball their team could have been disqualified. The Writer leaned up to him closely.

"I'll help you," he whispered.

"How?"

"Just do as I do," The Writer whispered. He took hold of Brute's arm that had the ball and he wrapped his other arm around his back. He pulled him back a few feet and told him how to stand up, holding the ball in alignment with where you wanted it to go, how to back up, bend, and how to swing, but telling him did no good. All he got was a stupefied look of cluelessness from Brute, so he decided to show him rather than tell him. He got behind Brute and held up his hands and arms with his as if he were going to bowl. His hands had a hold of Brute's wrists. He would step back with The Writer every time he moved. From where everyone else could see, it looked like a tender love moment from a 30's movie, of that of some couple dancing under the stars.

"What are they doing?" Blade asked. "This looks like *The Cutting Edge*." He was apparently trying to tie it in with his love of knives.

"No kidding!" Annie shrieked. "I thought they were rehearsing *Hamlet*, but no long knives to fight with."

"Annie, you are so clueless, you know that?" he said, wiping his brow. "And it was not long knives. They were swords!"

"Could you two please shut up!" Dionne hollered, again filing her nails. "Don't make me hurt you when I bowl again Annie, because I just might accidentally on purpose drop it and have it come rolling into you like that ball did Blade at the house this evening. Now THAT was funny!"

"THAT WAS NOT FUNNY!" Blade roared from his seat, pointing at Dionne.

"It was too!" she screeched back.

"Was not!"

"Was too!"

"Was not!"

"WAS TOO! See, I'm laughing! HA HA HA HA HA HA HA!"

"WAS NOT! It hurt my future kids!"

Nate's jaw dropped and Lana bust out in muffled giggles. Dionne and Annie both stared at him. Jackie dropped her ball as she got up with it to bowl. She was laughing hysterically.

"How dare you talk to us that way in the presence of The Writer!" Annie shrieked. "And I'm amazed that you can still go to the bathroom on the same day you have a major accident with a bowling ball!"

"I did not have an accident," Blade said in laughs. "It is not like I peed on myself. And I am not the one here who is griping about . . ."

"Oh you don't gripe?!" Annie screamed, standing up over Nate to face Blade. Dionne and Lana bust out laughing while Mama and Judy could only gaze with sheepish looks. "Oh well, excuse me then! Pardon Miss Valedictorian of the Year if you don't mind! Shall we perish?! Shall we perish tonight seeing that our sacred rights to gripe are no longer legal in this country just because of your lousy opinions?! Whatever shall we do?! Why don't we just get The Writer over here to . . ."

A cataclysmic thunder erupted from the end of the lane. Everybody forgot what they were arguing about and flung their heads around to see what happened.

The ball had crashed onto the floor at top speed. It shot directly into the center pins, causing them to explode into the air out of their places, into the gutters and out into the lane. The ball slammed into the back of the hole and bounced into its mechanical retriever. It was one clamoring thud after another as Brute made the first strike in his whole life.

The Writer's jaw dropped open as did everyone else on the team who was watching.

"He broke it," Blade gasped in horrific excitement.

Brute turned to face The Writer and asked, "Is that good?"

The Writer motioned for him to look at the team who then blasted into a shattering accolade of screaming cheers. Mama rushed out of her seat and threw her arms around Brute, then stopped herself, realizing what she was doing.

Everybody else was too as they crowded around their new player and expressed their thrill over his triumphant first-ever strike. The lane was going crazy in shooting off sparks from the retrieving system at the end of the lane that indicated that this team had finished up their first game in the tournament and was ready for game number two.

In each game, Brute stunned and amazed everyone on the team, including himself. He had made consecutive strikes and spares over and over without fail. He had even surpassed The Writer in the scores, then pretty soon found himself at the top of everyone on the team, and nobody seemed to object to it. He just got up there and swung the ball the way The Writer showed him and returned to his seat, as if it were nothing.

"Is this all it is Zilla?" he asked The Writer as it came time to start the sixth game. "Just roll the ball?"

He nodded.

"Man, if I'd known that I'd been bowling long ago! This is cool! All these lights and music. Looks like that bar I used to pick up babes at."

The Writer closed his eyes and tried to overlook what was just said. He knew that Brute came from that part of life that he had never set foot into and hoped he would never have to. If he did he had no idea how he'd react to what he saw. His mother had kept him sheltered from all that since he was born. But thanks to an innovation called television, he had picked up enough to get a general idea of what was out there, even though the tube did little to capture the reality of it all. Until he'd met Brute he had never had a taste of what one goes through out there in the real world. High school had a daily dosage of it for him to swallow, but rather than feel it he had only seen it from a safe distance.

Suspense began to mount as the sixth games were coming to a close for the other teams. Several players were getting tired from all the heat and pressure of the smoking alley that they just bowled for the heck of it, not caring what the score was.

Not a dull moment existed for The Writer's team. Everyone continued to tease and cut on each other about this and that, especially Blade and Annie. They would mock and impersonate how each one looked when they bowled. Dionne would get up with her ball and waltz around with it before rolling. Blade meditated on his for a few minutes by "transferring" power from his mind to the ball. The Writer told him not to make the ball any dumber. When he got a strike he pranced up to The Writer and said, "How 'bout that O' mighty Writer?"

"Sit down," he said through clenched teeth.

Nate would get up and throw from between his legs or blindfold himself, turn around seven times with the ball, and then bowl. Once the ball slipped out of his hand and it rolled back to where everyone was sitting. It came to a dead stop between Blade's feet.

Everyone laughed, except Blade, who just turned his lip up, shook his head, and folded his arms across his chest.

The seventh and final game was about to start. A final tally indicated that The Writer's Pins were in second place by a mere 438 points from the Devils, a team that had close to 25 players.

But there was a little problem with the Devils.

Most of their players were men smoking, spitting, and getting drunker as the night wore on. Several of them were swearing and cussing like nobody's business each time they didn't get a strike. Their captain had his whole team look down to The Writer's and they all flipped a birdie at them. They ignored this and went on their own business.

"We can do this," The Writer said to himself over and over, now feeling the tension and agitation of the event. Never before had his little team been this far ahead of everyone else, but thanks to Brute it looked like there would be at least a plaque on the wall to join his one and only trophy for the essay he wrote years earlier.

-BLYT

He bowled his turn and could not hit the nine pin on his spare.

The Devils got a strike.

Joey bowled a spare. Jackie was so nervous she swung the ball before she was ready and it plopped into the gutter. Dionne only hit five pins and three on the spare, whereas the Devils were racking up strikes like crazy.

By now it was Lana's turn on her side. She was sweating all over and looked like she was going to pass out. Annie had tossed a cup of water in her face but it did not good. She slowly got up, picked up her ball, and started shaking when she saw the other teams racking up scores like crazy. She started to stumble as she neared the lane. The Writer ran up to her.

"Sir, I can't do this," she said, almost out of breath. "I can't help us anymore." Her knees had given way and she slipped onto the floor. The Writer got down next to her and propped her back up. Her face was red and she was soaking in sweat. His whole team stopped to watch. He turned to them with a glare in his face.

"Keep bowling!" he yelled. "Don't stop. Keep going!"

Lana was still unable to get up. "Sir, I can't do this. Please don't make me! I can't!"

The Writer got behind her and wrapped his arms around her body. "Listen to me, you're one of the strongest girls I know and you're NOT going to mess this up for us this year! So come on! Get up! Bowl! Just roll the ball I don't care! I'm tired of losing to those bigshots down there!" He started dragging her to the lane and he helped her hold up the ball and she rolled it with what little strength she had left. The ball slowly made its way down to the pins and one by one, all ten of them fell. A red 'X' flashed over the lane and all the girls crowded around Lana and helped her back to the seats. The Writer fell into his and put his head down on his knees. The announcer brought a slide for Lana to use for the remainder of the tournament.

This is it, The Writer thought as he banged his head against the back of his seat. We've lost again. Dear Lord what are we gonna do? Help my little team here. We're not as big and strong as the other teams, but please don't desert us in this moment of decision, no matter what the final score is . . .

"Writer look!"

He felt Elaine's soft hand on his shoulder. He looked to where she was pointing and saw the cops hauling away several players on the Devils team, among them the captain.

"They got in a nasty fight down there," she said. "Somebody threw a beer bottle and smashed it on someone's head."

The announcer came on and said that the players left on the team could still play and were still in first place with The Writer's Pins in second and the Panthers in third.

It was now Brute's turn. The Writer turned and saw that he was not sitting next to him anymore. He stood up and glanced all around the area and didn't see him. He walked around to ask Mama if she'd seen him and then he saw him hiding behind the seats where Nate and Blade were sitting.

"Are they gone Zilla?" he asked.

"Who?"

"The cops?! Are they gone?"

He nodded. Brute loomed back up, grabbed his ball, and scored another strike for them. The Writer sensed something odd in his hiding from the police, but could not think on it now. The tension and excitement of the game was all he could think about. His heart was going faster with each passing second. He sat back down before it set off an asthma attack, which was the last thing they all needed now. Everybody else on the team stood up on their feet to root and holler for each other. The Writer bowled his turn, got a nine, then a spare. Joey did the same thing. Jackie and Elaine each hit nine pins then got a spare. Lana scored a strike, Dionne a seven then a spare, Annie a nine but no spare, Blade scored a perfect split with the pins but could only knock one down. Nate scored an eight then a spare, and Brute continued his winning streak of strikes and spares.

Mama and Judy held hands as the scores on the screen overhead blared the numbers, now climbing up into the three digits for this game, and was in the five-digit format for the whole tournament. The screams from the other teams indicated that they were getting close to the end. Everyone was up on their feet to watch the spectacular drama unfold on the lanes. The snack bar had closed up to let the workers watch, the pool room closed up, and the arcade room was deserted. It was like watching some great battlefield in the Civil War. The smoke further enhanced the allusion.

The tenth and final frame was up. The music stopped and all the lights stopped flashing and settled onto a single tone. Some of the teams saw that they were not going to win so they just gave up. Others were going to the bitter end.

Silence slowly took over as each frame was filled.

The Writer bowled two strikes then a nine. Joey bowled a nine, a spare, and a strike.

Lana bowled a nine but missed it on the second try. Dionne hit four pins, then only hit one the second time. Annie bowled a strike, a nine, and a spare. Nate bowled an eight, a spare, then a strike. Blade bowled a seven, spare, and a strike. Elaine and Jackie each got a strike, a seven, then a spare.

Brute got up, bowled two strikes, then it came to the final hit. He looked up and saw that it was just him and one guy on the Devils team. The whole alley grew silent and watched. A drum roll resounded from somewhere in the back. Everybody had jammed up to the seats behind the bowlers' places. Mama and Judy stood up, holding each other up and had their hands tightly clenched into each other's.

The Writer was frozen to the back of his seat, watching in misery, not knowing of what the outcome would be for his little team. Joey came up behind him and put his hands on his shoulders. The Writer did not question if the gesture was genuine or staged, but looked as Brute got ready to bowl. Dionne held one of his hands. Elaine held the other. Annie and Jackie were with Lana.

The other player inched up to his lane.
All eyes in the building were watching.
Hearts were pounding.
Fingers were crossed.
Hands were clasped in prayer and hope.
The other bowler went first.
Brute shot his down the lane.

The thunderous crash from both sides of the alley resulted in a red 'X' flashing over both lanes.

Then both screens went black.
A hush fell over everyone.

The Writer turned to watch the judges as they wrote down and tallied up the scores. A sheet was handed to the operator, who then handed it to the announcer, who disappeared into a back room. The Writer began to breathe deeply through the slit in his mouth. Brute was still standing at the lane, watching.

Mama and Judy were shaking.

The announcer emerged, carrying the sheet and a gold figurine in her hand. She stood the trophy up on the stand that overlooked the whole alley. Then another man emerged from the backroom where the announcer went into. He handed her a black plate that had gold writing on it. She slid it into the front of the trophy and turned it around. The trophy shined in the dim light of the alley.

The announcer read the sheet again and picked up the microphone.

"Well, by a difference of only 43 points, it was a tight tournament, and one of the most exciting ones I've seen in years."

She looked around the room at both teams.

The paper fell to the floor next to her as she raised the figurine over her head.

"THEIR STREAK IS OVER! 'THE WRITER'S PINS' IS OUR CHAMPION!"

Joey grabbed The Writer, yanked him up on his feet, flung his arms around him, and buried his face in his shoulder. Lana was the first one to break out crying. All the other girls swooped around him screaming and crying, hugging each other. The boys yelled and slapped high fives then wrapped up each other in hugs. Mama and Judy both broke out into a crying frenzy, hugged each other then hurried down to their sons. Everybody else soon broke out into applause as the lights started flashing shades of orange like never before. From somewhere the sound of a tiger was roaring into the speakers all over the alley. The Writer stood stock still, not knowing what to do. His team members hustled around him and pulled him towards the podium for the trophy, which was having a gold tiger holding a gold bowling ball in the air over its head mounted onto the very top of it. Flashes from cameras were all over the place. Screams from total strangers deafened him as he got part way, realized what was going on, and hurried back to the lane. Brute was still standing at the lane, just as lost as he could be in all the ruckus.

He took hold of his hand and led him to the podium with him. If it were not for him and his striking craze this would not have happened. Brute followed without objection, not knowing why. As they approached the announcer's podium the crowd parted back for them, like the Red Sea. The Writer kept looking at the carpeted floor seething with colors and images. He could see tiger stripes and footprints all over the place.

It was over. They had finally won.

All the insults and cutting on each other paid off.

They were happy.

He was happy. His face refused to show it.

And he waddled away . . . to get the trophy.

CHAPTER FIFTEEN

The Writer woke up after eleven the following morning. He went downstairs and looked on the mantle. Sure enough, just as he suspected, his mother had placed the grand bowling trophy in the direct center of the mantle. It was positioned to where the morning sun would hit it first thing in the morning. The fiery reflection of gold beams and its blinding luster lit nearly half the room.

He walked up to it and looked at the gold tiger, on its hind legs, holding up a gold bowling ball with its front paws over its head. Down at the base between two of its pillars was the thin black marble plate that had all of his teammates' names inscribed in gold. He studied each name that he saw. Joey's was first after his own, and he saw his face in his mind, his small, pale face, and he could remember the sensation he felt that night when Joey hugged him outside his house. He recalled slipping his hand into his, and how he felt during it.

He looked at Annie's, Lana's, Dionne's, Nate's, Elaine's, Jackie's, and Blade's names. Upon seeing their names their faces sprung to mind. He could see that look of sheer joy when they were declared the winner no less than twelve hours ago. All of them crying and hugging each other. Had they never won anything like this before? he wondered. I guess not. In high school we were always overlooked for things like the annual talent show, the girls were rejected for cheerleading, the guys were refused for the varsity teams, and nobody wanted me for anything. I got stuck in the classroom, writing this and that, writing for the yearbook, the newspaper, essays, reports. Joey's the different one. He got on all the teams he wanted. Everyone loves him, yet he hangs around us. Does he really want to, or is he just . . . oh no, I'm doing it again,

he thought. He grabbed hold of his forehead and drove his finger-
tips into his flesh, as if trying to crush out these thoughts that
were once again trying to overcome him. He squeezed his eyes
shut and opened them. As they came back into focus he could see
the name of 'Brute' before his eyes. It was the last name on the
plate.

Brute.

The stranger.

Off the streets.

The Writer's mind began to fill up with thoughts of Brute,
from carrying him home that night to seeing him score the winning strike for the team, and it being his first time ever bowling!
He had never known that to have ever happened in his presence
and doubted that he'll ever see it again.

At least I know what his name is, he thought. But it sounds so
. . . so . . . different. Well, they call me 'The Writer'. It doesn't
sound any less unusual. He calls me 'Zilla', for Godzilla I suppose.
Who would've thought that there's somebody else out in the world
who likes the King of the Monsters . . .?

He still had no idea where he came from or if he was being
hunted. When the cops came in last night to haul off members of
the Devils bowling team, Brute hid behind the back seats. Is he a
criminal? An escaped convict? No, it couldn't be. The news and
the scanner would be full of details of an escaped inmate and his
description would be on flyers all over the county. His mother
would tell him over and over not to walk anywhere at night on
account of there being a madman out there.

He's just a little raw, he thought, just like Rusty.

Now his mind filled up with Rusty.

Then tomorrow.

Saturday.

It would be the seventh anniversary of the day he was baptized.

It was also the day Mama and Judy were going out to Asheville
to clean out all the stores.

I have to call Rusty again, he thought. Tell him what tomorrow is, and what I want to do. We can go to that place in Murphy, then to the flea market that's down there, the lake for our picnic, all that he's promised we'd do. We can do it all tomorrow. It'll be a day to remember. I have to keep the spirit of the greatest day in my whole life alive and going. What could possibly go wrong? All I have to do is believe that he won't forget. How can he if I tell him now? He'll have to remember. It'll be fresh in his mind. When I tell him where I want to take him he'll have to not forget. I just know that place will touch his heart and make him think. It did me when I first saw it.

He found himself in the kitchen dialing the number to his house.

After four rings, the machine kicked on.

"Hello. We're not here right now so leave us a message and we'll call you back."

It was his mother's voice. She sounded tired and irritated, but when the high-pitched 'beep' sounded, The Writer simply said,

"Hi..uh . . . Rusty, it's The Writer. Uh . . . tomorrow is the anniversary of my baptism, and I was . . . wanting to take you out somewhere for the day. If you can please call me back later and we can talk about it. Don't forget. Bye."

He had forgotten that everyone in Rusty's house must've gone to work. It was Friday, still a regular day of the work week. In school, Fridays were always a time to celebrate the end of the week and the forthcoming festivities of the weekend. All the kids would avoid listening to the teacher and could only think about what they were going to do on Saturday and Sunday. It usually consisted of wild parties, sleeping, staying out late on Friday and Saturday, going to the movies, the malls in Asheville, and whatever else they considered to be fun.

For The Writer, it was the same thing every weekend. Write and think on Saturday, go to church on Sunday, and get ready for the upcoming school week. Sometimes he and Mama did go to Wal-Mart on Friday or Saturday evenings but all the craziness from the other kids made them go to the stores on Saturday morning or afternoon when they needed to. They only went to Asheville about once a month. When they did, they went to the Asheville Mall, the 24-hour Wal-Mart, Phar-Mor, the bookstore, and Mama had to make her monthly contribution to either JCPenney or T.J. Maxx, but come this Saturday she and Judy would have a shopping frenzy like never before, taking over Goody's, Belk, Hess's, Dillard's, and whatever other leviathan department store their eyes fell upon.

He'd be with Rusty.

He looked out the window and saw the mail carrier putting their mail into the box at the end of the driveway. He wanted so much to walk down there and pick it up but the thermometer on the front porch had the mercury reaching 85 degrees, and not even noon yet.

Perfect asthma attack weather, he thought as he went back upstairs to his bedroom. On his way there he looked in on the stranger, who was still sound asleep. The sensation of their victorious win last night thanks to Brute swept over him again. He could hear the screaming cheers from those who cared enough to and could feel Joey's hands on his shoulders.

It was a night to remember.

He went on into Brute's bedroom, sat in the rocker, and pulled the drapes closed. He still felt he had to be near him, although the need didn't seem to be as strong as before. It was deathly quiet in the house. He began to let his mind take him into that place he had created for himself . . .

Mama came home around six that evening. The Writer was watching the news when she came in and saw that Brute had eaten a late afternoon lunch, consisting of a full loaf of bread and a full jar of peanut butter. The crumbs on the kitchen floor, the torn bread wrapper, and the empty jar on the table told the whole story.

"Son, remember what you were doing this time last week?" she asked when she came into the living room from the kitchen. She sat in her easy chair next to the couch where The Writer was sitting. He looked at his watch and stared out into space.

He could clearly recall last Friday evening.

The orange sky. The night before graduation. Waiting for Joey. The poetry book. The picture in the bedroom. The hug. His reason for not being there at the ceremony. Hoping Rusty would be there to watch.

He nodded.

"Imagine, only a week and so much has happened. I swear son, I think more has happened this week than all summer long, don't you? I mean you graduate, you bring home a stranger and nurse him back to health, you win the bowling tournament, I have to let that wretched Mrs. Moran know who's boss, and you have a fight with a wall at the church building."

He looked towards her. How did she find out about his bitter quarrel with the wall? He hadn't told her about it, afraid that if he did she'd have no idea what was going on with him.

"Relax son," she said, sensing the tension in his eyes. "Mr. Graham came into the bookstore this morning and told me all about it. He said he heard you in there having it out with the wall about everything from Mrs. Moran to Rusty. He thought it was rather impressive that you could compare a wall to that of a human conscience, said he'd make it into a sermon for church in a few weeks."

Oh boy, he thought. My words leaked out. I knew that wall was a flimsy coward, couldn't hold it any longer. Went and confessed to the preacher about it all.

The weather was being shown on the news. The weatherman kept pointing to big blotches of red, yellow, and green on the radar that he said were slowly moving northeast from south Alabama. He said the storms could be in Western North Carolina by late Saturday or sometime Sunday. He was giving the predicted temperatures for Saturday thru next Wednesday.

"Speaking of Saturday," Mama said, changing the subject. "Are you taking anyone out tomorrow for your anniversary?"

He nodded.

"Really? Who?"

"Rusty."

Way to go Writer, he thought. Just blurt out the name of the one guy your mother cannot stand without thinking. Maybe you should just go ahead and blurt out that you took a shower with Brute, or that you lied about what you two were doing in the bedroom that day Mama came in, and whatever else you can't think of thinking before you say it.

"What?" she said, worriedly. "Rusty?"

He was silent. She grabbed the remote from the coffee table and switched the TV off. She then scooted to the edge of her seat.

"Why are you taking Rusty?"

His eyes rolled towards her. Because he's a friend and I want to take him to that spot in Murphy. I know he hasn't been there and maybe it'll do him some good to see it. I wish my thoughts would make themselves verbal.

"Son, why are you taking Rusty?" Her voice was losing sincerity. It was on the border between sweet and loving to totally intolerant of what's despicable in the world, and he knew where Rusty belonged in her frame of diversity.

"Because . . . I . . . want him to see that place . . ."

"Son, let me tell you something about Rusty. Do you know what he is? He is nothing but a spoiled little brat who ain't got a lick of sense in that foolhead of his. He doesn't go to church, can't hold a decent job, plays that music so loud it rattles the window at the bookstore every time he drives by, and he mouths off at Lucille at the store. Do you know what he said to her the other day?"

He shook his head as he continued to look far off.

"You know how stooped over Lucille is. She can't get around like she used to. Well, Rusty went in there and bought three packs of cigarettes and a can of skoal. Lucille came in to open up the register, and the phone rang. She went to answer it and as she walked over to the phone, Rusty told her she could move a lot faster if she'd find someone who'd give her a little and make her legs move faster. Does that not tell you what goes on in that foolhead of his, son?!"

He didn't move. His eyes slowly closed.

"Son, I don't know what to tell you about that boy. You and him do not go well together. I could never see you and him together doing anything as friends. All I see is Rusty making all these big nice fat promises to you that he swears he's gonna keep and he never does. He didn't even come to the bowling tournament last night, not that it surprises me any. I knew he wouldn't. He could've at least watched. Let's see now what else he's so lovingly promised you . . . a trip to that place in Murphy you love so much, a concert, a day at the lake, a picnic, taking you bowling, and God knows what else. And has he kept a single one of those promises . . . NOOO."

"He did take me to his house one day," The Writer said, hoping to change her mind in the least possible ways he could.

"Yeah, for what, two hours? You did nothing but what . . . watched cartoons, waited on him to take a shower, then he brought you back here when his mother came home. I don't think that's much of a fun time together. Do you?"

"I got to be with him."

"Son, that doesn't really sound like two best buddies having a great time together. If he really wanted you with him would he not have taken you out to eat or done something else? He come and got you around three that afternoon and you were back here before five."

"He had to do something else."

"Son, stop making excuses for him!" she said, smacking the arm of her chair. "I know you're trying to defend him and it ain't doing you or him any good. I wasn't gonna say anything and hope and pray that you would find out for yourself but apparently you're not so here it is son . . . I don't like Rusty."

He slowly aimed his eyes at her. His peripheral vision allowed him to see the look of aggravation and bitter frustration that had overtaken his mother's careworn face. Her dark sandy hair looked frazzled here and there and she kept rubbing her fingers on her forehead. He could sense that she either had a bad day at work and was unleashing her anger out on him, which he didn't mind. In fact that was what he wanted to believe was the cause of her sudden quarrel with him. If it was Rusty he did not want to face it. He refused to let his mind even consider the implication.

He vowed to let nothing stop him from trying to take him tomorrow.

Including his own mother.

"Son, I've kept quiet long enough about this. For the last three years . . ."

"Four," he corrected, holding up four fingers.

"What?"

"Four. I've known him four years."

"Three, four, I don't care how many years it is you've wasted your time, money, energy, and talent on him. I know that story you wrote that won first place at the local art show this year was about Rusty. You think I can't tell? That story about a loving friendship between two boys has never happened between you two. You and Joey maybe but not that Rusty character. I cannot see any love between you two. You may love him but he doesn't have the heart to love you in return. What has he done for you, son, that makes him so high and mighty to you?"

"He just . . . uh . . ." His mind went blank.

"See there son, you can't even mention one decent little thing he's done for you. I bet you could mention a thousand little things about Joey or even Annie, Lana, Dionne, Blade, Jackie, Elaine, and Nate when you can't even think of one for Rusty."

"He was good to me."

"When?"

"In school. When so many other kids were hateful he wasn't."

"So a few minutes of mere goodness makes him your hero huh? I know high school was a nightmare for you. I wish I could have put you in a Christian school somewhere but I couldn't afford it. But if I had you wouldn't have met Joey or any of the others in your little gang. We wouldn't have known that for years Joey and Judy were our neighbors had you not been going to that school. But you found just eight true friends in that dreaded place that you can be thankful for and Rusty IS NOT one of them. Can you get that in your head son?! RUSTY IS NO GOOD FOR YOU! Son, you deserve better than him! You don't deserve each other! You never did! You deserve so much more than some rowdy immature brat who has no respect for anyone but himself and cares only about getting some girl and dipping skoal, cruising around town at night in that dirty rebel truck, and . . . oh God I don't know what all he gets into. I'd hate to even hear about some of the other things he's done, his nasty habit of picking up girls and taking them to that shack on highway 19, those wild flings I hear kids on the street brag about, how he does it and where and when, that rumor last year about him picking up prostitutes at some 24 hour store and finding the nearest, cheapest motel . . . son, it's filthy, and I can't bear seeing you with someone like that."

He lowered his head.

"I don't want to tell you what to do son. You have to do that yourself. I know I'll have to let you go someday and I think I'll start now by letting you make your own decision about Rusty and tomorrow. If I had my way I'd bust your butt wide open if I saw you taking him with you tomorrow. I would forbid you to ever see him again or even talk to him because he is doing absolutely nothing good for you and he's making you miserable and ashamed of who you are. I can see it in your face son. Even though you won't ever look at me I can see when he's hurt you and got you so upset. How many times have I seen you sit in that rocker, looking out the window, watching for hours for him to come take you out? It's the same thing every time son. He tells you all week he'll be by here to take you out. You're happy about it all week you look as if you're about to bust apart. And finally when Saturday morning comes you sit there waiting, waiting, waiting, for what . . . nothing. That's what Rusty is son . . . nothing. He never comes. You sit there from seven in the morning till after ten at night, watching that empty road. And he never comes. You call the house. He says he's on his way. You call again. His mother smarts off that he's gone somewhere and it turns out it isn't even here. You wait until after dark and you finally give up, run up to your room crying, and never come out until time for church on Sunday."

She paused and saw The Writer's eyes looking out the window. The sun was going down, and the orange tint of the day was coloring the earth little by little. It was getting close to his peak time of the day for thought and creativity.

"And son, I'm so afraid the same thing's gonna happen to you tomorrow, on the anniversary of the greatest day of your life. I don't want to see it ruined or you devastated because of Rusty."

"I won't," he said. "I'll be going after him instead."

"I know but still, something could happen. He'll think of some lame excuse to not go with you. I just don't want to see you get hurt. And I still don't know what it is about him that makes you want to keep him in your life. Is just a few minutes of being good to you worth salvaging for the years of deception and lies and broken promises he's done to you? Your birthday comes and goes and Rusty never calls or comes by here when the others do, but on his birthday and on Christmas you go running to his house with a present, and in no way does he show his appreciation, if he has any, for it. Son, just think about this please. Don't let the greatest day of your life become a disaster for you. You can stop it if you just take someone other than Rusty. Take Joey or Annie or Blade or someone . . . I don't care! Anybody besides that Rusty. I can't bear to see you a mess on your anniversary. Please just think about it. Will you at least do that for me son? If nothing else, please just think it over, and I hope and pray to God that you'll finally see what we've seen for years."

The Writer stood up and straightened out his coat that was tied around his waist. The evening sun was beaming into his face and he was shielding it with his hand.

"Where you going?" Mama asked.

"My room."

"Aren't you hungry? I can make supper if you are."

She was suddenly sounding very sincere and almost apologetic for what she just said to him. The hatred had drained from her face and eyes and the look of deep abiding love and frail emotion was back. Her duty and role in life as a mother had just been carried out. But with it comes the reality of the inevitable that the child must one day be allowed to break free and go out into the world, thinking and doing for himself. The mother had lead the child as far as she could into the sea of life, and now before them lay the eternal vastness of life's trials, tribulations, and rewards. She would have to watch her child go out alone and fend for himself, for her time on earth would not be eternal. She could only watch, and hope that she had done her job as best she could, with what she had.

He hurried up to his room without answering her.

"Son, if you want I can . . . "she started to say, more calmly and more gentle than ever before. She got up and went to the stairs to try to catch her son's attention.

He had already slammed his bedroom door shut on her.

". . . order something for you." she said faintly. She held onto her face, sat back down in the chair, then lowered her head to her knees.

The Writer saw Brute sitting on the edge of his bed. He was about to storm back out but decided not to. How could Mama do this to me, he thought. She doesn't know Rusty well enough to judge him like that. He can't be like she says he is. Nobody could be. Rusty's just a little raw. He could not bear being around Mama after one of her few and extremely far between lectures at him. Instead he came on into the room, drew the curtains shut, and sat in his rocker. Brute kept his eyes on him the whole time.

"Is this Rusty the reason why you never smile Zilla?" he asked suddenly.

The Writer held up a hand to him, gesturing to leave him alone. Apparently Mama had raised her voice so loud she woke him up.

"I've never seen you smile or even laugh. I never knew your mom had to yell at you."

"She wasn't yelling," he said, keeping his face turned from Brute.

"Well if it's louder than some girl screaming 'it's too much' then it's yelling. I know yelling when I hear it."

Don't tell me about it, The Writer thought. I'm trying to think. Don't mess my mind up now.

"Now tell me who this Rusty is Zilla. You promised you'd tell me later so here it is. Tell me."

He shook his head. The subject of Rusty was not favorable with him at this time.

"Well then tell me what these are!" He got up and opened the closet. The box of papers that Joey had pulled out the night before while looking for the bowling ball came piling out onto the floor. Brute knelt down to pick up a pile.

"Let's see here now, this one's called *The Great Deception*, this one is *The Dead Silence*, and what's this about, *The Seventh Day?* And this one, *The Dance at LaGardia?*"

"Put them back!" The Writer said. He got up and came over to Brute. He raised his hands to swipe them but Brute was quicker. He held them up over his head just out of The Writer's reach.

"Give them here! They're mine! You can't read them! PUT THEM BACK!"

"Wait now Zilla, let me see what these in here are," he said, bending over to pull out more piles of papers. The Writer flung himself on his bare back and caused him to fall onto the bed. Brute rolled over on top of him.

"Alright you wild tiger cat!" he said, holding his hands down onto the bed. "Now I've got you where I want you! Tell me who Rusty is and what those papers are! I ain't gonna get off until you tell me!"

The Writer turned his face away from Brute's, which was just a mere inch away from his. He could tell he had not washed or anything since last night. He hoped he'd get tired of holding him down and get up, but he didn't. Instead he could feel Brute pressing his whole body down on him harder and harder. He was slowly stretching his arms out farther and farther as he held him down and began pressing his forehead down against his harder and harder. He squeezed his eyes shut.

"Hurts doesn't it?" Brute hissed. "Now you know how I felt when you put your Godzilla foot on my back." He lifted his head off The Writer's and lowered it down next to the side of his face. He could feel his heavy breathing on his neck, then the tingling sensation on his ear as he whispered menacingly to him. The hot flesh of Brute's bare shoulder rubbed up onto his lips. He could taste the salty sweat that oozed its way into his mouth.

"Just tell me who Rusty is and what's in the box, and nobody gets hurt."

"Okay, I'll . . . tell you," he sputtered out. Brute rolled off and The Writer felt a sudden surge of renewed strength come over him when Brute got up. He lay on the bed for a few minutes to let his breathing return to normal. This guy is a total nympho, he thought. He sat up and Brute was standing over him. The Writer picked up a few papers and put them on the bed.

"This first," he said weakly. Brute nodded and sat on the bed next to him. The Writer spread out stapled packets of handwritten pages of notebook paper all over the bed. Brute pulled out more and more and pretty soon the whole bed was covered.

"These are the beginnings of novels I plan to write," The Writer said. "None of them are finished."

"Can I read this one?" he asked, picking up the thickest packet he could reach. It was entitled *The Great Deception*. The Writer yanked it out of his hand and tossed it back onto the bed. "Hey Zilla, you said you'd tell me."

"No. I just don't want anyone to read them."

"Why?"

"Because you may . . . uh . . ."

"I may what?"

"Laugh at me."

"Why would I laugh at you Zilla? Have I since I been here?

No. I haven't. Is that why you keep these hidden, so nobody can read them and laugh at you?"

He nodded. "What I write won't be pleasing to other people. They won't like it I know."

"How do you know?"

"They don't like me."

"Who doesn't like you?"

"Everyone."

"Hey I like you Zilla. You're different. If I hated you I'd left long ago. You amaze me you know, how you act, talk, that look in your face. Nobody else I've met does what you do."

"Don't be polite, just . . ."

"Just what?!"

"Let me think okay . . . I've had a fight with Mama and I need to get away."

"Where?"

My you're nosy, he thought as he got up off the bed and went back to his rocker. Don't feel sorry for me Brute. You don't know what's going on. It doesn't concern you. He went to his rocker, pulled it up to the window, and sat down. Brute went over, pulled up another chair, and sat on the other side of the window facing him. The Writer turned his face away.

"I thought you were going somewhere Zilla?" he asked. "Why're you still here?"

How do I explain, he thought. How do I tell a perfect stranger . . . well, I guess he isn't a total stranger anymore, about how I think, what I see when I do, where I put myself . . .?

Could I show him? Has it ever been done before? Writers achieve it in their own ways, so I'll do it my own way. Others may think it's crazy, but hey, that's what they think.

Not what I think.

The Writer motioned for Brute to hand him a stack of the papers off the bed. He handed him about seven fat packs put together. He took them and picked up the one that was on top. It was entitled *The Great Deception*.

"This one's the most spectacular thus far," he said softly. "A huge palace in a faraway land, a sweet, youthful, but clumsy king, a corrupt rival kingdom, and a friendship that's anything but sweet."

"Like you and this Rusty?" Brute said. The Writer glared towards him, then let the thought of saying something to him pass. He picked up another packet.

"This one's *The Scarlet Dawn*. When a boy goes missing for several hours and can't remember where he was, clues begin to turn up, revealing a terrible secret about the football team. All he can remember is that the sky was a bright flaming red when he was . . . " He looked towards Brute, whose eyes were deathly fixed on his face. He continued with the stack.

"This one's *The Seventh Day*. It has a powerful storm that wrecks half the state of Florida. This one's *The Dead Silence*, about a deaf-mute with a burned face. There's an earthquake in it. In this one, *Long Forgotten*, a young man spends his life helping others and teaching about Jesus. He doesn't know that he'll die at an early age thanks to an old friend's hatred. *The Tragedy* is about a mental breakdown and the victim being tormented mercilessly . . ."

Brute took the papers out of his lap and dropped them on the floor. The Writer looked out into space, wondering what he was up to. He could see that the sun was getting lower behind the mountains. A breeze was causing the curtains to sway inward. It was blowing right over Brute's bare back.

"Show me," he said.

"What?"

"What you write. I want to see how you do it. I can't write. I know you can. Show me how it's done. I want the one everyone calls 'The Writer' to show me."

The Writer lowered his head and began to twiddle his thumbs. If I show him, will he laugh at me? I can't tell him how, I have to show it to him. He has to see it. Looking at words is not like seeing them. Seeing has a greater effect than being looked at. He shall see what my words have created.

The Writer stood up and parted the curtains even wider. The

gleam of orange spilled into the room. The breeze was greater now, bringing relief from the scalding heat of the day. The rest of the room was dark. He came up and let one side of his face in the evening light, the rest in shadows. His eyes were set upon Brute, but not on his face. Brute was looking up into his eyes. There seemed to be an eerie silence fall all over this world. Nothing else existed but The Writer and Brute. The Writer stretched out his hands and took Brute's hands into his. Brute felt the soft pudginess of his flesh and tightened his grip on the hands. His heartbeat became more and more rapid and he felt a tingling sensation kindle in the pit of his stomach.

Their hands glowed in the orange light.

"Here's how I do it," he said in a whisper. "This only happens when I'm alone or upset or if Mama's attitude isn't very pretty like it is today. My mind takes on a life of its own, going on what I think about, and what all I envision."

Brute kept his gaze on him. He had the hands of The Writer in his, was looking at his face, and was experiencing the most alluring sensation of ecstasy he had ever felt in his whole life. His whole body felt weak and faint to him. Only a writer, he thought, could have such an amazing effect on another person.

"Close your eyes," The Writer said in a deep breath. "Just listen."

Brute closed his eyes. The effect of the light from outside soon wore off. He began to feel darkness all around him. It was cool and soothing. He could hear The Writer breathing, then his voice came back into the air.

"Just listen . . . and keep breathing. Let your mind wander. Don't think. Just picture what I told you . . . the kingdom . . . the sky . . . the people . . . another time . . . another place . . . not in this world."

The Writer closed his own eyes and sat back down in his rocker, still attached to Brute.

The breeze from outside fell over on them. He slowly rocked back and forth, the warmth and tender feel of Brute's hands in his seeping into his soul and heart.

Total blackness.

All was silent.

He saw himself in the dark. Brute was with him.

Alone.

He felt dizzy, and could feel Brute clinging tighter to him. He was dizzy as well.

They were on their way . . . they were going . . .

And he waddled away . . . taking Brute with him into the dark . . .

CHAPTER SIXTEEN

"Where am I?" Brute asked. He reached out into the darkness and felt nothing but cold. "What have you done?"

Nothing.

"Zilla, this isn't funny! I can't see anything."

"Don't you trust me?" came a familiar voice out of the cold darkness. It sounded like The Writer's voice, low and soft, but this time it was louder and sharper. "I told you I'd show you what I do."

"Then show me! Zilla, this is making me crazy! I can't see and it's cold here."

"Does it not feel better than where we were a few minutes ago?"

"Well . . . yeah."

"Now, just stand still and look in front of you."

"Which way? I can't see where the front is."

"Just stand there. I will show you first thing what I have written over the years, and you'll see what my words look like in my eyes."

Brute stood still, afraid of what would happen next. From out of the dark came a loud thunder, then a sudden gust of cool wind. Brute nearly fell down but found that a mysterious force was holding him up. There was something behind him in the dark holding him up. Then the thunder took on the sound of a voice.

"Brute, do you think I'm a good writer?"

"Is that you Zilla?" Brute was looking up into the dark, not knowing what was up there hidden from his sight.

"Yes. Do you think I am?"

"You have to be."

"Very well then. Look before you, and we shall see what kind of writer I am . . ."

Brute looked directly in front of him and out of the darkness came something truly spectacular . . .

The wall of dark began to peel away in the sky above him. The blackness looked as if it had turned to cloudy water and was being blown away. An orange light shot out of it, knocking him down. He held his hands over his eyes and saw the light eat away the black. As it did, he looked at the ground.

He saw grass in the brightest color of green he had ever seen. It seemed to spring up out of the dark. He got back to his feet and saw the orange light highlight features one by one. He saw trees, animals, a stunning blue waterfall, mountains, eagles, a tiger come out of the dark up to him and started purring. Then another gust of wind tore out of the air and made the remaining darkness become a wall of hideous black clouds on either side of Brute in the far distance. He looked up into the sky and saw that the clouds reached up as if far past the heavens of this place. Then they parted and faded into the air, like blood washed away by water. One final crash of thunder and there came out of the last of the darkness a whole new world.

Brute rubbed his eyes and looked down into the valley of this place.

He saw a magnificent palace of shimmering colors, an ocean, towers, fields of flowers, trees of every form known to man, a sky beaming blue and orange, people running all over the place. Some wore odd looking costumes, like long white robes, golden armor plates, modern clothes, silk outfits of bizarre colors, and so on. Brute rubbed his eyes again and looked farther into the distance and still saw images springing out of nowhere. Somewhere out there was another palace, a huge lake, canyons, huge gold statues of tigers and butterflies, cats, birds, eagles, and one that looked like a big mutant lizard of some sort.

Brute turned around to look for The Writer and found him propped up next to a nearby tree, looking at Brute with his pen between his teeth.

"So, what do you think?" he asked, coming up to him.

Brute looked again in amazement. His mouth was wide open and he kept pointing at all he saw, and it still wasn't finished. Behind him there was more coming into existence. He saw vast endless fields of grass, towns, kingdoms, more people, more animals, more water, more of nearly everything.

"Man, Zilla . . . you . . . made all this?" he finally said. An eagle came to perch on his bare shoulder. He tried to knock it off but it stayed there.

"It won't hurt you," The Writer said. "I won't let it."

"How?"

"Because I created it. I wrote him therefore he exists. The same for everything you see here. What you see, I created with a pen. Somewhere in my life, I wrote about this and that, and it exists for me only in my own little world. If it's on paper somewhere in that real world we just left, it's for real here. It can be seen, felt, experienced, not just read. This is my world, where anything I want to happen does. I can create what I want, when I want, however I want, and nobody can tell me what to do here. My pen is my weapon. I do with it as I please. See its power my friend!" He aimed the pen into the air and out of it shot a golden beam of orange accompanied by gold sparkles. The beam went up into the air, then exploded as if it were fireworks, created an orange cloud, and out of it fell drops of shimmering orange rain.

"You love orange don't you?" Brute said, holding his arms out as it fell on and all around him.

"You can drink it," The Writer said. He opened his mouth and cocked his head back. Brute did the same thing.

"Man this is good!" he said. "What is it?"

"I just gave the rain a tasty flavor with color. I can make it blue if you like, or red, or pink, or green, whatever. You say the word, and it's yours."

"No, leave it like this. I love how it feels. I think I'll take a bath in this rain!"

The Writer aimed his pen at him, closed his eyes, and out of the fiery beam came a dazzling array of golden sparkles that swirled

all around Brute's legs. It got wider and wider then gathered into
the shape of a huge swimming pool. One final flash radiated out of
it and it became full of orange water from the sky. Brute then felt
himself fall into it. The Writer watched him swim to the bottom
of it and come back up. Brute hollered how great it felt. He saw
The Writer standing on the edge of it watching him. Brute made
a big splash at him but saw something he didn't count on.

The water he meant to splash onto The Writer did not achieve
its purpose. The Writer held up his hand to the pending wall of
water that came for him. He reshaped it in midair, gave it the look
of a huge hand, and turned it around to face Brute. He then touched
it and the water shot directly into Brute, knocking him back under
the water. He reemerged and got near The Writer.

"Man, don't kill me! I was having a little fun."

"So was I," The Writer said, examining his pen. "And another
thing, here you can breathe and talk under the water. You can't
drown here unless you're a character I have created and I can kill
you or bring you back to life when I want."

"Really?"

"Characters are a writer's own creation. They come into existence however the writer wants them to, and the writer can kill
them or get rid of them however he or she pleases, and bring them
back however they please. How they can die is up to the writer. I'll
show you a few ways of my own later."

Brute looked down at the water that shimmered and shined
like nothing he'd ever seen.

"I can talk under here?" he asked. "If you say so. Get in here
with me and show me. Prove it."

"Oh I'll prove it to you Brute," he said. He backed up away
from the pool, closed his eyes, held on to his pen, and then jumped
about thirty feet into the air. Brute watched in amazement as The
Writer did a somersault in midair over him, appeared to do a
backflip, then in a twisted ring came shooting down into the water next to him, the splash so big it brought him down under to
The Writer. He found him walking on the bottom of the pool, just

as if he were walking on land. Brute put his feet down on the
bottom and saw that he could do the same thing. The Writer came
up to him with his pen, writing words in the water.

"So, what do you want to discuss?" he said. His voice was as
clear as if he were out of water. No bubbles came out, and he was
breathing.

"You amaze me Zilla! You really do! Can any writer do this?"

"Different writers have different worlds," he said. "This just
happens to be mine. Here, I want to show you more."

"Let me get out of . . . " Brute started to say, but before he
could finish he found himself standing on a brown path of dirt.
On either side of him was a field of wildflowers, growing at the
rate of an inch a second. They got about as high as two feet then
stopped. They were all bending towards him, their color getting
brighter and brighter. He looked around and saw that there were
clouds in the far distance that seemed to be lower than where he
was. A cool breeze breathed over him. He realized that he was dry
all over, even to his shorts, which was all he was wearing from the
real world. He looked around and saw The Writer floating, on his
back, past him at shoulder level in the air, happily munching on a
sucker he had made for himself. Out of midair he handed Brute
one.

"Come. Let us go over here."

"And just what is over here Zilla?" he asked. "I can't wait to see
whatever it is."

The Writer lowered himself down onto the ground and walked
with Brute to the edge of the field. Brute sucked and munched on
the sucker as if he were starved to death. As soon as he finished it
the stick vanished in front of his eyes.

"No litter here," The Writer said. "All trash here is made to
vanish, something that cannot be done in the real world."

As they came closer to the edge of the field, Brute could see in
the distance huge rocky mountains that seemed to reach for miles
high above the clouds. He could see eagles, hawks, and bigger
birds flying all around. Far beyond the mountains he could see a

shimmering blue lake that seemed to spread out forever past the horizon. The colors he saw were so bright, they beamed their radiance. Every shade of red, blue, green, yellow, orange, pink, and every other color one could think of was here, in some form or fashion. No painter or artist or color consultant would dare to match or even top the prismatic luster of this place. Only the words of The Writer could have achieved what he was seeing here. He looked up and saw that the sky was the deepest, brightest shade of blue he had ever seen. It was so bright it seemed to light up this whole world without the aid of a sun. He looked all around and saw that there was no sun in the sky. How could this place be so brightly lit without a sun, he wondered. I must ask Zilla later, unless he tells me before I can ask.

They were nearing the edge of the field. Brute soon realized that they were on top of a mountain this whole time. The Writer led him up onto the cleft of a rock that perched out over the great valleys below. He went out onto the very tip of it and looked down at all he had spent years writing to create. There was a lake beneath him, crystal clear blue, almost like a sprawling diamond. In it the dolphins and fish were swimming around in merriment. On its shore were animals of all types. Tigers and lions roamed around together. Bears and deer were sharing food The Writer had created for them. He didn't dare let them kill each other here. Cats and dogs were romping around together in the fields near the lake, and on the hills that reached up from the lake were big butterflies flapping their wings to cool off a tiger that was spread out in the grass. The characters he had created were walking around, some in pairs, some alone, others in groups, pointing and looking at different things.

And he saw all that he had created, and he said, "This is good."

He turned around to Brute and motioned for him to come forward.

"You won't fall," he said. "We're gonna do something I know you've never done before."

"What's that?"

"Swim."

"I've swam before Zilla," Brute said, looking down at the lake. "And won't we mess up your beautiful lake if we dive into it from here? I mean scare away the animals."

"Yes, we are going to swim, but not down there."

"Then where?"

The Writer pointed to the sky and how blue it was. There was a billowing wind that carried the birds in waves and droves all over the world. The wind swooped down onto them, causing The Writer's black coat to blow back behind him. Brute still had no idea what was going on.

"Stand here," he said. He held his hand out to Brute and pulled him close. "Now just do what I do." He stretched his arms out into the air. Brute did the same thing. They stepped forward together, then fell over the edge.

It was a breezy free fall. Brute could see the lake below come zooming at him faster and faster. The wind was so cool it made his eyes water. He looked over at The Writer and could see that he was enjoying whatever it was he had them doing. The wind didn't even blow the black cap off his head.

"ZILLA, WHAT IS THIS?!?!" he screamed. Suddenly, as if he were about to plunge into the lake, he felt a strong force pull him up into the air. He saw the world drop out of sight in a blur and saw nothing but blue. He felt The Writer let loose of him and before he knew it, he found himself "swimming" in the blue sky over the world. He saw The Writer next to him, stroking his arms and pulling himself in the air. He'd turn and dive down, then back up. Brute did the same thing, then they just floated around as if in water, looking down at everything.

"What's that Zilla?" Brute asked, pointing at a small array of buildings in the distance.

"Part of a kingdom called Dalraida," he said. "It's in *The Great Deception*."

"Why Dalraida?"

"I don't know. It just sounds pretty for a kingdom. It comes under the threat of war from its cruel rival kingdom, which I've rightfully named Satania. Shall we visit it?"

"Can we? I wanna see just how bad you've made it."

"But first, let's drop in on Dalraida. I'll show you the king of the land."

The Writer and Brute drifted in the air and after passing through a few improvised clouds, they were approaching the palace of the kingdom. It was a massive leviathan of rich thick marble that had veins of prismatic color running all through it. Seven tall towers that poked up out of it seemed to scrape the sky. The tallest of these towers was on the second story of the palace, the very center of the entire structure. There was an open balcony in the direct center of it. This was where The Writer and Brute came to land.

"In here is where the king does his business. Don't worry. I've made him clumsy and very friendly. His name is King Luke II."

"Why the 2nd?" Brute asked, admiring all the luscious detail The Writer had written for the palace.

"You'll have to read the book when I finish it to get the whole story," he said. "I don't dare reveal it here before you can read it and experience it for yourself."

At that moment a door slammed shut and in came a young man with short brown hair, darkly tanned flesh, wearing nothing but long shorts and a towel draped around him. Brute looked at The Writer.

"When I left off working on the story I had him in the palace's royal pool waiting for his friends to arrive. Before I had them arrive I left him in the pool, but since we're here I've had him come here to us. This is the king out of his royal garb."

The Writer stepped out in front of him and raised his hand to him. The king looked up, his face twitched, and he came closer to him.

"Writer sir, how long are you gonna keep me in that pool? I'm getting waterlogged waiting for Larisa and Joshua to show up."

"As soon as I get back to writing on the story. Until then,

here's someone from the real world, who may read all about you in the future. Brute, this is King Luke II."

The king held out a hand to Brute, who held his out, and The Writer saw someone of the real world shaking hands with a fictitious character, something that could only happen in The Writer's world.

"How are you?" Brute asked.

"I'm fine, but I'm waiting to see what this guy here's gonna have me do next in his little story. So far he's had me in a huge parade, had my father assassinated, and . . ."

"SHHH!!!" The Writer hissed with his finger over his mouth. Brute didn't hear him but the king did. "Don't give the story away! Let him and the rest of the future readers find out for themselves."

The king went to The Writer, fell on his knees, and grabbed hold of his black coat. "Oh forgive me O great and mighty writer, who is far more superior over me and what all I rule here in this kingdom you so lovingly created for me. Please don't delete or throw me out. I bow down to your gold pen O master."

Brute looked at The Writer in wonder, not knowing what to think.

"I also made him very pathetic," The Writer said. The king kept groping around at his feet, then got up on his knees and wrapped his arms around his waist.

"Yes I am very pathetic O master writer. I love you for creating me and for giving me life in your world and for making me the king over this kingdom. Please don't write me out!"

"If I did that then the whole novel is messed up. You're the heart of it and I can't get rid of you. Now go back and wait for me to finish the story. You're gonna be in the spectacular climax I have planned."

The king got up and adjusted The Writer's pen. He headed back where he came from and disappeared.

"This won't be in the novel," The Writer said to Brute. "He won't even remember this when I get back to writing the rest of the story."

"Does every writer do this?"

"Like I said, there are different writers who do different things, and this is what I do with what I write. Do you still want to see Satania?"

"I guess not. I think I'll wait to read what happens. If I saw it will it spoil everything?"

"Maybe. Yes, it would, because Satania is near the end and when you saw what was happening you'd lose interest in wanting to read it. The same applies to all my other novels I'm working on. If I show you too much the plot is given away. A writer's work is top secret until he releases it to the real world. But I can show you some highlights of what I can do with my pen."

The Writer led Brute to the end of the hall where the king disappeared. He took him out of the room and they went down a dark hallway, then down a flight of steps. They were milky white and had an illustrious shine to them. They were reflecting the light from outside, which meant that there had to be an open door or window somewhere down here. The Writer led Brute on down into what appeared to be the foyer for the palace. One of the main entrance doors was half open. He pushed it all the way out and they stood on the front steps to the palace. There was a cleaning lady right outside dusting off the benches where she had set out plants. She saw The Writer and bade him good day. He returned the gesture. He then led Brute on down the steps and into the main yard of the palace. There were people, or rather characters, all over the place, socializing, visiting, buying, selling, eating, doing whatever. It looked like a closeout sale at some overstocked flea market.

"They're all waiting for me to write what they're to do next," The Writer said. "Until then I let them wander around."

"So where are we going now?" Brute asked, looking all around him. "I know what. Can you show me how you made all this?"

The Writer turned around to him. He still did not look at his face but aimed his sight close enough to it. His face wore a look of resonant emotion, as if he were calm and at ease. Brute noticed that The Writer did not have those dark circles under his eyes like he did in the real world, his mouth wasn't turned down at the ends, his eyes looked brighter and not as dark and sinister that he had now grown accustomed to, and he appeared to have more color. He looked all around again and noticed the sharp colors of this world.

I wonder what he's had Rusty do here, he thought. Has he brought him to this place? Does Rusty have some part here? Will he get mad if I ask . . . ?

"Come this way," The Writer said, leading Brute out of the palace courtyard. "I'll show you a few more novel scenes, how this all came into being, how I can kill characters, and more."

And he waddled away . . . leading Brute deeper into his world.

CHAPTER SEVENTEEN

"Now what are we doing?" Brute asked in wide-eyed wonder. The Writer had led him up onto another mountain that appeared to be hundreds of miles away from the first mountain they were on. He looked down to see what his feet were standing on. The mountaintop was really a mighty leviathan of blue rock that did not scrape or cut his feet. It was like standing on a fluff of silk fuzz. He looked far off into the distance and could see more vast images of the world that he had not yet seen.

"This is how it was created," The Writer said. "You will be shown what made all that you have seen thus far, and hopefully, someday, what the rest of the real world will read about and can picture it for themselves in their own way." He cast his pen over the world and it faded into pitch blackness. Brute then felt the darkness take over him as well, and he could only watch and see what his writer friend would show next.

His voice came out of the darkness.

"In the beginning, there was nothing. No characters, no stories, no places. It was a bleak, barren landscape devoid of any life, real or unreal.

"Then it came out of the heavens of the real world. Envision it as a fluffy ball of soft orange fire, lighting up the divine path it found itself taking in the darkened skies, going through clouds, searching for the perfect soul upon the face of the earth in which to take root, to plant its seed of creativity and talent, which was indeed, from God."

As The Writer spoke, Brute could see the images he was referring to take place before his eyes.

"When it found the individual God directed it to, it took root in his heart and mind, and began to flourish. But I won't waste my words and my tongue telling you. Look and watch how it happened . . ."

He cast his pen out into the darkness. The orange beam of fire began to boil over with sparks and flickering. The Writer began to explain that all it needed was watering from the real world.

"Because of how I was treated out in the real world, I retreated to places alone, and would think ever so deeply about what was happening to me. I'd watch other people, places, saw what went on in the real world. Then when I was alone, all that I had thought of and had seen was recorded in my memory, and I would play it back over and over, and wonder what would happen if this or that happened instead. I'd rebuild and retell it in my own words. But soon I realized that I was tying myself down to things that were factual. I could be as spontaneous in detail as I wanted. It was my mind and I could do as I pleased with it, so I began to create what I wanted to see in life, what I wanted to feel, see, touch, believe. When I began to write my first story ever, well . . . this happened . . ."

He aimed his pen out in the darkness for the ball of fire. A gold beam had shot out of his pen and into the ball. It broke apart and out of it blasted a huge bolt of gold light up into the dark sky, if the sky was up there in the blackness. As soon as it hit the sky it shattered apart even more, as if a colossal case of fireworks had been sent up into the air to explode on target. The flares and falling sparks of it shot out in all directions in every color possible. They fell on all points of the darkness. A whole bunch gathered together on what Brute presumed to be the ground. As they began to take the form of a human being, The Writer's voice again echoed out of the dark.

"When I was four, Mama took me to a river in Cherokee, a town close to where we live. There was a pipe that stretched out from one bank to the other. Over this river was a chairlift ride up to the top of a mountain. It went directly over the pipe."

Brute could see the river, the pipe, the banks, and the chairlift begin to come into sight for him.

"Mama showed me the river and I kept looking at the chairlift. I began to envision a girl riding it. She was my first character ever, a little girl about four years old with brown curly hair, a pink dress, and a simple rag doll. She was alone in the chairlift. My second character was a man on the pipe about to jump into the river for a swim. Before he could jump in, he saw the little girl's doll slip out of her hand and fall into the river. I then saw the man jump into the river after it. He found the doll, then found the little girl, and gave the doll back to her."

As The Writer spoke, Brute could see the short and simple story unfold before his eyes. "That was because I saw something in the real world and just envisioned what I wanted to see happen. At just four years old, that was my first story. See, the girl and the man are still here. I saw that they were alone in my world, so I went all out with more. I figured, if I could do that with what I saw, then I could go for the whole Titanic, not just the flimsy lifeboats. Why buy a measly package of sliced ham when you can grab the whole pig?"

"So you saw and wrote more huh?" Brute asked.

"Correct my friend!" The Writer declared. "I saw more . . . and what I saw I wrote, and it came into being here. Look for yourself . . ."

Then all the heavens of this world tore apart. The sky opened up to unleash a cascading golden wave of fiery orange. It spilled out into the world and washed all over as far as Brute could see. As its mighty waves tore the darkness away it left behind images of places, people, things going on, and incredible scenes. Brute could see that some were violent while others were sweet and tender. The Writer's voice again was heard as the world was being created.

"Let the waters of ultimate creation reveal what The Writer has done!" he said boldly. "The pen shall be mightier than the sword, for the pen shall tear down, rebuild, and create, thus the sword only kills and sheds blood. The pen can do that and more in the hands of its master."

He aimed his pen into the world and out of its shot the beam

of gold. It splattered into the center of all that was there and everything began to appear just as it looked the moment Brute set foot
into this awesome place. One scene from a story followed another,
and as each one came into full view, The Writer told Brute what it
was . . .

"For *The Seventh Day*, see the seven couples fight and argue
over their childish errors in life, and the mighty storm that will
overtake their flaws and judgments." Brute could see the couples
and in the sky overhead there was a chilling appearance of black
clouds looming over them and the small town in which The Writer
had chosen the story to unfold in. The Writer did this with the
rest of the stories he introduced Brute to, all of them he had started
work on, had envisioned, planned out, and would write to bring
into full existence for all the real world to see, or at least those in it
who were willing to read it.

"For *The Scarlet Dawn*, there's the little boy running for his
life across a deserted football field. The sky is red and somebody is
after him. What happens to him he will not remember. For *The
Dead Silence*, that boy is a deaf-mute, facially burned at the hands
of his cruel owner. Wounded creatures will eventually turn against
their attackers, and an earthquake will, quite literally, settle all
things. I shall bring down the horrendous rule and debauchery of
the vain Saddam Hussein in *The Seventh Year*, which is something
of course that can only happen here in this world. That will also be
my message of warning to the rest of the world of things to come.
For *The Tragedy*, we shall experience the agony and suffering of a
mental breakdown and the horror of being stalked by a killer. When
I write *Long Forgotten*, you'll see what it's like when other people
take you for granted for all that you do, then they in turn will
regret it. That explains those scenes of war in the Persian Gulf that
you see, because my character goes there to spread God's word to
the soldiers robbed of their faith. Look at all those tigers out in
that field down there, playing around and acting like little kittens.
They stand guard to a kingdom not like the one in *The Great
Deception*, but for another kingdom in *A Wretch Like Me*, about a

lone traveler who finds a place of wanting and belonging in an intolerant world. Ever been held hostage inside a house by a bunch of corrupt teens who have hidden away drugs and pot? You will when you see what I've done with *The Incident at Jonah's House*. For a little slice of the real world, a family brought back together in a small southern town after a mother drowns her two little boys in a lake. When you read *Union*, I hope to make you cry. Remember my cat Blue at the house? Well, he rules over his own little kingdom of furry funny felines and other animals as *Blue, King of the Cats*, who has all the loyalty in the world for his owner, whom I shall make physically weak. You'll have to read it and see what I mean. And for all the crappy and hateful teachers in the world, and I've had my share of those ugly hags, they get what they deserve when I put my pen to work on a story that will make you wanna strangle your own hateful teachers."

"And what is that called may I ask?" Brute said.

"That's one that is not titled yet. I have several that aren't, so do not despair. They will have a name. As for my ideas, you seen enough?"

"Man I've seen more here than I'll see in my whole life," he said, gazing at all the scenes that had just played before his eyes. He looked up and saw that The Writer had been standing over him the whole time. They were still on top of the blue rocky mountain and he could see all that The Writer had created. The novels he would write and his stories, as he saw them, would be what readers would read, and he would give them the freedom to envision what he wrote the way they wanted to.

"When you leave here," The Writer said, "you will remember all this the way you want to, not the way I have it created. There is more to show you. What would you like to see now?"

"Man I don't know," he said, getting up. "But could you give me a shirt or something to wear? I feel weird being here without a top on."

The Writer aimed his pen, closed his eyes, and a beam shot forth. It shattered into Brute and he found himself wearing an orange muscle shirt which was thin, cool, and loose-fitting on him.

"When we leave here that won't be on you," he said. "It'll be left here, but anyway, have you ever rode on the back of an eagle?"

"No, but my guess is that we're about to huh?"

The Writer waved his pen into the air and there appeared out of the blue yonder of the skies a huge bald eagle, about 100 feet long with an incredible wingspan of nearly 120 feet . . . each. It flew straight for where The Writer and Brute were standing. He grabbed hold of Brute's hand and when the eagle came to the mountain and was about to turn to avoid hitting it, they jumped down onto its back and climbed up to the back of its neck. Its feathers were shiny and soft. Whenever Brute pressed his foot down it went deep into the feathers, but still helped him get up to the neck. He laid down and watched as the eagle swooped up and down in the sky, going through clouds and letting him see more of what was here. The eagle soared miles high over a huge empty canyon that stretched for miles on land. She dipped down into it every few minutes. When she came out they were over a huge jungle, which was on the shore of a massive body of water that was the cleanest, clearest color of crystal blue Brute had ever seen. He could see for miles down into it, all the caves, the fish, the whales, dolphins, and even the smallest of the goldfish.

"Man this is so cool!" Brute hollered. "I wish I were a writer now! I could do anything I wanted to whenever I wanted."

"That's the freedom of being a writer . . . there are no rules when you use the pen to create what YOU want to see and hear and everything else I said earlier. Now you see why I spend so much time to myself. I'm here in this place."

At that precise moment the eagle began a slow nosedive for the water below. The water came closer and got bigger, more clearer, and still closer.

"Get ready for this!" The Writer hollered. "A flight under water!"

"Oh no!" Brute yelled, clinging tighter to the feathers. The water was now rolling under the eagle so close they could reach down and touch it. An abrupt splash down suddenly made everything blue and light. The eagle continued to fly as if she were in midair, but she was under the ocean The Writer had created. Brute found that he could still breathe and talk as if on land. The Writer would not let him drown here. He was a part of reality, something The Writer had no authority over.

The fish that swam past them came by for a greeting. They extended a fin and Brute shook them. Dolphins appeared and nodded to them. The Writer gestured for Brute to get on the back of one. Without question he did so, and before he knew it, the dolphin took off for the surface and Brute found himself riding the back of it as it leapt up out of the water, back down, and up again. It was just like riding a bull in a rodeo. Every time the dolphin crashed up into the surface Brute would extend his arms out and look up into the sky with his eyes closed. Once the dolphin leapt up about thirty feet off the surface of the ocean, did a triple flip in midair, then came back down. It brought Brute back to the eagle and dropped him off. He saw The Writer and fell on top of him.

"Man I love you! If you were a woman I'd kiss you!"

"We can arrange that," The Writer said, taking hold of his pen and about to close his eyes.

"NO!" Brute grabbed hold of his hand and forehead. "Please don't. It's just the thought of . . . well . . . I love ya like you are. Now what else are we gonna see?"

The Writer got the idea and was glad Brute dropped the suggestion. He looked off to the far left and pointed to the distance in the water. Brute looked up and saw something long and gray swimming out of the shadows.

"He's miles away yet," The Writer said, "but he'll soon be here."

"What will?"

"Just something big I created, for sheer enjoyment. If I were to experience it in real life it would kill me. Here I can easily get away from it or make it go away when I want to."

"Well what is it?" Brute asked, getting impatient.

"Look."

He turned his head and screamed, falling back onto The Writer as he looked up over his head.

An enormous black open mouth about 75 feet in diameter was about two feet behind the eagle, its teeth looming over Brute and The Writer and under the eagle. Each one looked to be about 15 feet long and the sharp ends flickered in the light from the surface. The mouth seemed to go forever into its stomach. The end could not be seen.

"Oh my god you've made Jaws!" Brute screamed, getting behind The Writer for shelter. "Look at those teeth!"

"I know! No cavities!" The Writer said. "Isn't he big?"

"Big?! Man he's bigger than anything! Did he have to be so scary?"

"Don't tell me you're scared of a fictitious character?" The Writer said. "That's got to be a first in the annals of literary ideals."

"Man the way you write you could make a druggie afraid to go to the bathroom! You could have an octopus waiting for him in the toilet for all I know!"

"Not a bad idea," The Writer said, closing his eyes. Soon, a giant octopus was seen swimming past them after a haggard man in dirty clothes. It was his assumption that the octopus had pulled him down into the sewers.

"Okay, I'll send him away." The Writer aimed his pen at the gaping hole that was after them. It slammed shut and the beast vanished beneath them. Brute let out a deep sigh of relief and fell back onto the back of the eagle, letting the coolness of the water envelope his whole body. He took a swig of it and found it to be quite tasty. Sure beats city water, he thought as he happily drank away. He looked up at his tour guide and saw that he was holding his forehead, his eyes were closed, and he looked sick.

"What's wrong?"

"We've come too far," he said. "I didn't want to come here and worry about this."

"What?"

The Writer pointed straight ahead. Brute looked and to his renewed horror saw what looked like an enormous wall of black

and gray clouds spewing up out of the ocean floor. It looked more
like a pack of ink opened under water. The clouds were thick and
hateful, as if waiting for them to never be seen again. It reminded
Brute of the pictures he'd seen of Mt. St. Helens when she blew
her top, only this eruption was underwater.

The eagle steered away from the wall that seemed to reach for
miles ahead on their right. A huge black cloud seemed to loom at
them as they passed it. Brute looked up and saw that it appeared to
have an arm that had reached for them. It had stretched out over their
path flight. He also saw that it was getting darker and darker.

"Zilla what is this? It's giving me the freaks!"

The Writer looked up at what was ahead. This side of the
ocean would be clear for a few more minutes, then it would all be
blackened. He knew what was causing this sudden onslaught in
their trip here, but was afraid to tell Brute. It was something all
writers felt at some point in their lives, and in their hearts. It's
what caused their bad days, their tempers, and their
disillusionment.

"This is doubt, fear, and worry," The Writer said bluntly. "It's
caused by the battering a writer takes from the real world. He puts
it away to where he can't think of it, but when he goes too far in
thinking, his mind eventually winds up here, and it takes a while
to get back to the beautiful side of things." He held up his pen
and tried to use it but it only flickered out. The gold beam died
down and ashes of doubt were covering up the inscription of the
message from Joey. The Writer looked up in disgrace. An omen?
Or just a mere literary technicality? Does such a precept even exist?

"Can't you do anything Zilla?!" Brute hollered. "This is making
me freak out! You writers are weird you know that!"

Tell me about it, he thought. Maybe Mama should've let Mrs.
Moran commit me anyway. I'd be out of her life and Joey's and
Judy's and . . . oh no, now my thoughts have turned ugly. I'll be
getting ugly in a few minutes.

"Let's go up to the surface," he said. The eagle soared for the
top of the ocean and as soon as she broke the surface, the true

colors of doubt and worry had overtaken everything that was in sight. The color was deathly pale, sickly, and queasily pallid. Brute saw that the ocean was now gray and dark, the sky was cloudy and severely overcast. He looked down at where they came up and saw a smoking inferno billowing up out of the water. The clouds of it had made a huge, frightening pillar of smoke and dust that was at least 15 miles wide and in diameter. It made him think of the movies he'd seen where an atom bomb drops and makes a giant mushroom cloud in the sky. It groaned and creaked, reaching forever up into the heavens of this very different dimension of the world that just a few minutes ago was the most ravishing creation a human could ever create for others. Now it only sent them running back for the real griminess of the real world.

The eagle took them through the haziness to a forbidden landscape and dropped them off. The sky here was solid black in the far distance and there was a fire somewhere in the other direction, emitting a golden gleam that was barely enough to see by. The rocks were sharp and pointy, the surface dry and cracking. Brute kicked a stone and saw it vaporize into a small cloud of dust. The air was thick and muggy and there was the stench of cooked cabbage mixed with the smell of a cow pasture. Brute saw The Writer holding his forehead and the eagle disappearing into the hideous blackness of the far distance.

"Now where are we?" Brute asked.

"WHAT?!" came the sharp and angry reply. Brute jumped back and saw that The Writer's face had lost that gentle gleam in it. It was now smeared with ash, the eyes were almost popped with dark circles under the eyes, which were red as blood. His mouth was turned down like never before and he was breathing harder to the point of grunting.

He had never known someone like The Writer to get angry.

"I asked you where we were. Zilla, are you okay?"

"HOW THE CRAP SHOULD I KNOW WHERE WE ARE?! GOLLY YOU EXPECT ME TO HAVE CONTROL OVER EVERY LITTLE BLAMED THING THAT HAPPENS HERE?! JUST

SHUT UP AND LEAVE ME ALONE! GO SOMEWHERE
WHERE I CAN'T SEE YOU! GO ON! GET AWAY FROM ME!
WHEN I FEEL BETTER I'LL COME TO YOU! FOR NOW
JUST STAY AWAY FROM ME! PLEASE!"

Brute's mouth fell open when he heard the painful and mali-
cious tone in The Writer's voice, which used to be the most gentle
and fragile sound he had ever heard. Now it was full of hatred and
hostility. His entire mood had changed. This was not the same
caring creature he had met in the real world. It had become the
most rabid of all he'd seen. He could only stand back and watch as
The Writer verbally stabbed him. He walked back into a huge
boulder and sat down next to it. He had no idea what to think
now of The Writer or where they were at now. For a moment he
longed to go back where he came from, but he had to get out of
here first, and only The Writer had that power to do so.

He had to have made all this somehow, Brute thought as he
studied his dreary surroundings. What could he have seen or felt
in real life for this to be here? He looked up at the sky and saw that
it was seething with black clouds. In the distance he saw what
looked like red cyclones dipping down from the black sky. They
were ripping apart open spaces of nothing down in the valleys.

Just a moment ago I loved this guy, he thought. I wanted so
much to hug him in a death grip for bringing me here, but now I
don't know. These writers are so crazy. I can't figure them out
much less this one. I'll just sit here and wait. Maybe something
will happen.

He peeped around the corner and saw The Writer rubbing his
face.

He leaned further around and saw him begin walking for a
small mound not too far off on the mountainside. He was kicking
stones into midair and swinging his arms. Brute could hear him
grumbling loudly about something

He thought he heard Rusty's name.

And he watched as he waddled away . . . into the dark of this
place.

CHAPTER EIGHTEEN

"Oh get out of my way!" he said as he kicked the stone down the mountainside. It didn't make a crash sound for about ten seconds. It had landed somewhere under the layers of smoke, ash, and dust that surrounded the lower areas of the mountain. In the far distance he could see a red beam glowing from out of the blackness of the sky. It would fade and dwindle, then reappear every few seconds. He picked up his pen to make it go away but all it did was sputter and dribble crusty flakes of gold.

The Writer came to the end of the crooked path and sat down on a rock. He whacked his head with his bare hands over and over, making it sore and red. A wind began to kick up. As it did there came faint screams and wails, as if it were a person out there somewhere crying for help. The Writer looked up into the darkness and tears began to fall from his inflamed eyes. Soon the screams took the shape of words. He could hear "bastard," "idiot," "freak," "craphead," "crapface," "retard," "failure," "fathead," "fatso," "fatbutted crapper," "Satan," "Billy Boobs," "transie," "barrel butt," "faggot," and other terms that he had no idea existed in the vocabulary of demoralized teens, adults who never learned respect, and teachers who relished in making him the weirdo of their classes. The wind blew gusts of dust all around him. He could see some of the gusts of dust take the ghostly form of fingers pointing at him from the sky. Disparaging laughter came out of the wailing wind, a sinister reminder of how he was mocked and humiliated in high school. He looked down and saw some of these small drifts evolve into rejection slips from various publishers. Some were yellow, some were white, and others were pink. They evolved into the shape of business cards, half-pages, full-pages, and mere strips. They gathered at his feet and attached themselves to them. He kicked them up into the air and they fluttered all around, eventually coming back.

The wind now took on full fledged sentences, screaming things at him like, "Writers are crazy. They should be put away." "Only geniuses can be writers, not fat kooks like you!" "You couldn't write to save your life!" "YOU WRITE WHAT I TELL YOU TO AND YOU THINK WHAT I WANT YOU TO!" "You're getting a 'D' in this class because I don't like your opinion." "You're a sick disgrace to every writer out there!" "Fat slobs can't write!" "You'll never make it as a writer! You'll wind up in a nuthouse for being one." "There are better writers than you, so just give up!" "GIVE UP YOU FAT JESUS FREAK!" "You're killing trees!" "GIVE UP! GIVE UP! GIVE UP!"

"Only hell could be worse than this," he said, thinking about all the negative feedback he had acquired from his high school years.

The Writer fell backwards off the rock and looked up into the sky. It was getting blacker and blacker. He rubbed his eyes despite the excruciating burning sensation that had now conquered them, making them shed water like crazy. He looked back out into the darkness where the red glare was beaming off and on and out of the skies above it came forth another sound. It was that of a cruel heartless laugh. It was deep, strangled, and dry. With each laugh a cold splatter of water came out of the sky. The Writer then saw that it wasn't water, but spit. It only came out with every belch of laughter and guffaw the wind carried his way. Soon his clothes were soaked with the saliva from whatever was out there mocking him, trying to make him give up. The wind was now laced with a powerful stench, an odor unlike anything else. There was something rotten out there, so strong it made his stomach queasy and he looked in vain all around him for a toilet but none could be found. He couldn't create one because his mind and his pen were both clogged with this negativity. What he needed he could not get. His mind was far too overpowered by the nasty discouragement that had for so long built up in his memory. He had gone back too far in this world, unable to go on and let the past go. There was something here that he was holding on to, something he would not release from his possession. Whatever it was it was of the real world, and it had taken a tyrannical clutch of his world.

Something gooey and wet smacked his face. Then it hit his stomach, legs, and his eyes. He rubbed it off and saw that it was black, thick, moist, and had a sour aroma of grass. He smelled it and realized that huge splotches of freshly chewed skoal, wet and drippy with thick spit were bombarding him. It was flying out of the skies like hail, smashing onto the rocks all around him. He stumbled backwards and leaned over the other side of the rock where he was sitting. He looked down and saw nothing but an eternal drop down to the vast unknown below the mountain.

He opened his mouth to throw up but nothing came out. He tried to make himself throw up but only succeeded in choking himself. The chewed wads of skoal were piling up all around him. With each smack it splattered and dribbled all over.

He could not think now. His mind was a total blank. His head was cringing in pain and everything was getting blacker. Pretty soon he would not be able to see to get away from here. He would be trapped in this state of mind for he didn't know how long, and as long as he was he'd be a walking mass of melancholy, sadness, and internal anger.

"Hey Zilla, get up!"

He opened his eyes and saw Brute standing over him. He was shaking him by the shoulders and could see piles of skoal fly in midair past him. He could feel his huge bony hands lift him up out of the muck of skoal that had gathered all around his body as he lay there.

"Zilla, tell me now, who is this Rusty?"

The Writer's eyes flared up more than ever before when he said the name. He smacked Brute in the face, shot up to his feet, and vomited a shocking blow of thick black ooze into the wind. Brute saw it and lunged for The Writer again. He fell with him onto the rocky path and he grabbed both sides of his stained face.

He was squirming and moaning to be let loose from him. Brute watched in horror as The Writer's face turned a souring yellow, the whites of his eyes were yellowing, and he began to drool.

"Zilla, tell me . . . WHO IS RUSTY?!"

The sky in the horizon blasted into a rage of thunder and green lightning. Brute looked up and saw that the sky was now tearing open to reveal a sinister shade of red. It began to slither its way higher into the sky and was shaping itself into the image of a person. Brute could only see a vague outline, then he could hear someone breathing. It was more of a heaving sound that went up and down. Then came a woman gasping for air. She began to scream, and then a man's voice was grunting and growling. The woman was now sighing deeper and deeper as the sounds of the man got louder and louder. Then it went in the form of a rhythm, over and over. Brute looked again at the image and it had now dissipated. The redness was slinking away into the blackness.

"Zilla, is Rusty doing this to you? IS HE MAKING YOU BE LIKE THIS?" He was yelling at him. It was the only means he could think of to get into him.

The sky rumbled again. The Writer sat up, covered his face with his hands, then let them down. His face was a mess of sweat, blood, tears, and drool. Someone had pierced that portion of his mind that was hiding the true nature of this part of the world. Nobody else was bold enough to come out at him and say it.

Yes, Rusty was causing all this. Together with the pain and hatred of the real world, along with the endless string of broken promises and rumors related to Rusty, it had all piled up here and was making his world a total wreck. Brute would not stand for it.

"Zilla, I don't know who this Rusty is, BUT GET RID OF HIM! NOW!"

The Writer looked towards him with his messed up face. He had his pen in his shaky hands, afraid to open it.

"I . . . I can't."

"WHY NOT!"

"I have to help him. This was his part of my world. If I can only . . . sort it out . . . plot it . . . overcome what the real world has done to me . . . I thought he could . . . help me do it."

When Brute heard this he grabbed him by the shoulders and began to shake and jerk him violently. The Writer's pen fell out of his hand and he closed his eyes. The jolting jerks that Brute was putting him through made his muscles snap and pop, his head was slung all around. He mumbled and sputtered sounds that Brute paid no attention to. He then slung him down onto the ground, stood over him, grabbed his shirt collar, and yanked him back up. He slapped his face several times and held his body up to his. The Writer was streaming tears and shaking all over, from his head to his knees. His arms felt limp and only dangled lifelessly at his sides. Brute pulled him over to the rock where he was sitting and stood him up against it. He grabbed hold of both sides of his wet face and made him face him, but he could not make his eyeballs meet his.

"LISTEN TO ME! YOU ARE THE WRITER! GET RID OF ALL THIS! LET IT ALL GO! FORGET WHAT HAPPENED TO YOU IN LIFE! FORGET ALL THOSE IDIOTS WHO ARE MAKING YOUR LIFE A LIVING HELL! AND FORGET THAT RUSTY! YOU OWE HIM NOTHING! HE'S PART OF THE REAL WORLD! LOOK WHAT HE'S DOING TO YOU! HE'S MAKING YOU A MESS, RUINING YOUR WORLD AND KEEPING YOU FROM GOING ON!"

The Writer looked out at the grim ugliness that was settling over everything. He pointed out to an area where there was once a valley he had created for all the inspirations he felt Rusty had given him, but even they seemed as dreary as the rest of this side of his world. Brute saw him pointing out into it and slapped his hand.

"ZILLA I DON'T CARE WHAT YOU HAD OUT THERE FOR RUSTY! GET RID OF IT! NOW! ALL OF IT! IF YOU DON'T IT WILL TAKE OVER YOUR WHOLE WORLD AND YOUR LIFE! YOU CAN'T WRITE THINKING ABOUT ALL THE WORLD HAS DONE TO YOU! JUST GET RID OF IT!

YOU ARE THE WRITER! YOU CANNOT LET THE REAL
WORLD OVERPOWER YOU! DON'T LET THE WORLD
CONTROL YOU! NOW GET RID OF ALL THIS! RUSTY
TOO! ALL OF IT!"

The Writer looked back towards him.

"Now! Do it! Here, take the pen and GET RID OF ALL THIS!
If you don't Zilla, you'll die! All this will kill you! Rusty could kill
you IF YOU LET HIM!"

In tears and with shaky hands, he opened his pen back up and
aimed it out into the dark. Nothing happened at first. He looked
back at Brute, who got right behind him and grabbed his shoulders again.

"You are The Writer! You have the power to create and destroy, give life and kill, give and take away. The real world can fall
to its knees at you! The writer is mightier than the real world.
Now KILL ALL THAT OUT THERE! NOW!"

At that moment he felt a sensation of powerful strength fill his
body. It overtook his arms, legs, and hands. It made him stiffen up
and jolt out of Brute's grasp. His eyes cleared up and his heart shot
into full throttle. The shaking stopped and the sweat, drool, skoal,
and tears blew away into the wind. He closed his eyes, envisioned
this portion of the world gone first. When he did, he saw a ravishing site. He saw events that he felt were soon to come in real life.
He saw two boys having a picnic at a lake. He saw someone getting
up before a crowd to accept an award of some sort. When he did,
the crowd jumped to its feet in screaming applause. He could see
people dancing, fireworks exploding in the air, a family reunited.
There were friends hugging each other just because they were happy
to be together. After this he opened his eyes and was met with the
sinister look of what he had stored from memories of the real world.
He could only enjoy those beautiful sites once this smutty place
was gone.

He raised his pen, closed his eyes, and envisioned how he
wanted to see this all gone. If he wrote it he would tear up the
sheet or burn it. It had to be totally obliterated from his world in

the most spectacular and most devastating way he could think of. Then he saw how it should be destroyed. He aimed his pen out into the darkness of the clouds, and out of it shot a gold beam of orange. It went up into the clouds and gathered into a ball. The Writer and Brute moved back.

The world became dead silent.

The wind stopped blowing.

In the far distance was rumbling thunder. It came closer and got louder and louder.

The Writer stood on top of the rock, aimed his pen at the orange ball, and spoke.

"Let me see . . . a blast like no man has ever seen in his existence . . ."

The ball blasted apart and sent huge billowing circular waves of orange clouds shooting in all directions. The light was so bright it lit up the valleys far below. Brute looked down and saw thousands of people running everywhere. They were screaming and pointing to the orange mushroom cloud that was reaching up higher and higher into the sky. The Writer aimed his pen for the valleys.

"See all those weak characters? I don't need them anymore! They are the products of what the real world has spawned within me. Watch how I destroy their existence in my world!"

Brute looked and watched in horrified wonder as thousands of seemingly "innocent" characters began to flee and run in sheer desperation for their "lives." A huge mountain came crashing down onto a small village. A black twister was sucking up people and houses. There was a monstrous black tidal wave emerging from out of the distance and it came smashing its merciless way into the area. People were screaming as it carried them away, made buildings shatter apart from its sheer force, and completely covered up mountains. In another section there was a hurricane blowing. He could see people getting knocked into the wind and carried away into the skies. He saw a mother and a baby in its stroller. The stroller was knocked out of her hands and the baby was seen getting sucked up into the skies. The mother was screaming her lungs out and a house came out of nowhere, slammed into her, and they were pulled up into the sky. A couple in a small town were holding hands trying to dodge all the havoc but then The Writer summoned a huge portion of a brick wall to come down. It fell on the woman, tearing her loose from the man, who then turned around to see a bolt of lightning burn the ground out from under him. He saw hundreds of more people running everywhere in the streets. The Writer aimed his pen and ordered that the ground be ripped open and it was so. The road broke wide open and people were falling into it, screaming for mercy, which would not be granted. Families were split apart forever, parents saw their children falling into it, and they could not fight the powerful monster cyclone The Writer sent in to finish wiping this out.

Brute looked up at The Writer, who was having a ball destroying everything that had plagued his mind, images of those in the real world who had tried to tear him up. He was screaming for this to happen and that to happen. He wanted to see oceans torn from their depths, meteors falling everywhere, people screaming till they could not scream anymore. By now he was just shooting powerful beams of death from his own hands. It went down and wiped out whatever he wanted to see gone. There were explosions everywhere of all colors. Tall buildings collapsed onto hundreds of fleeing people. He created a huge dust storm in the shape of a giant snake that slithered across the valley and devoured anybody in its way. His pen was shooting gold beams everywhere. He was turning around at random, pointing and shooting, killing, bringing death to all that threatened him and his talent.

There was now so much awesome destruction going on Brute didn't know what looked the most amazing. It was also quite noisy. All the wind, the people screaming, the explosions, the twisters, storms, all of it was putting a strain on his ears. The Writer saw him covering his ears and decided it was time to dispose of everything once and for all. He raised his pen again, closed his eyes, and ordered everything here be taken away forever. That's when a twister

BIG ADAM

of golden orange emerged out of the sky and came down, touching the valleys, pulling up everything once and for all. It was about 100 miles wide and pulled up huge areas of land, whole mountains, cities, people, everything. It widened up and got bigger and bigger, wider and wider. Pretty soon it was so close to The Writer and Brute they could touch it. It widened up to where they found themselves standing in the very eye of it. All around them swirled what The Writer had created from the hatred of the real world and could not make into something worth saving. This was everything the real world and what Rusty had filled his mind with, everything he felt that was inspired by them. It was all going up into the skies without a trace. Brute watched it and came up to The Writer, pointing to the golden light that was at the very top of the leviathan twister. They watched it and when the twister had picked up everything, it lifted back up into the sky and exploded, causing thousands of small fireballs to fall to the earth. They were of every color imaginable except black and gray. The skies overhead were glowing orange and the blackness was dying away.

Thinking he was finished, The Writer lowered his hands and watched the vast openness he had just made for himself to do as he pleased with. It would be beautiful and full of more awesome wonders for his readers, if any, to read about and picture for themselves. He no longer felt the melancholy that had prevailed here just a few minutes earlier.

"Zilla, what's that down there?" Brute was pointing to someone walking around, untouched, still living. "Didn't I say everything?!"

He's the inspiration I got from Rusty, the model character, The Writer thought. He survived. Some part of me still wants Rusty here. But I can't. If Brute says he's making me miserable, I have to get rid of him. How do I do that? Maybe if Brute sees this he'll drop the whole thing.

The Writer raised his arm straight up and ordered a huge cloud to be created. The pen emitted a gold dust that made the cloud. He sent it into the sky and spoke.

"Now go and do as I say. Destroy that flawed image, and never come back unto me again!"

The cloud descended over the valley and began shooting lightning bolts at the character, which just dodged and escaped every blow. When The Writer saw this he went into a rage of lost patience.

"NO! THIS CAN'T HAPPEN TO ME!" he screamed. He grabbed Brute and they flew into the valley at top speed. He dropped Brute into a barren spot where he could watch what would happen next. The Writer landed in a cloud of orange dust about 30 feet away from the character. It stood there with an evil grin on its face, watching its creator.

At that moment a huge fireball of orange came over The Writer, followed by clouds that seemed to lift him up into the air. His arms were outstretched and his whole body became solid black. A giant mushroom cloud was created as he appeared to get bigger and bigger and blacker. Brute fell over backwards watching The Writer go through a hideous transformation unlike any other he had ever seen. He saw his image go higher than the clouds and then it got wider.

The head got bigger.

A tail shot out from his rear end.

His arms got thicker and looked more muscular.

Stripes of orange and black took over his flesh.

His legs became longer and looked heavier.

The cap he wore was still on his head, only it was hundreds of times larger than before. He still had the same eyes, but the rest of the face was transformed into that of a huge beast, a meat eater, a monster.

He had become a colossal tiger monster, over 200 feet high, and was sitting up, watching the character start running for its life. He got up on his hind legs, opened his mouth, and out came a fiery blast of orange fire. It hit directly in front of the character, who then raced for the shelter of a nearby forest. The Writer, as a tiger, lunged up into the air and pounced right behind it. He smashed his jaws shut about two feet behind the character. He then got back on his hind feet and breathed fire on the whole forest, setting it ablaze. The character was seen scurrying up the mountain where The Writer and Brute were standing earlier. The Writer roared and swiped his paws at the character, his claws outstretched, hoping to pierce him apart, or at least knock him into the fire below. The character climbed as fast as it could, throwing rocks at The Writer and kicking at him. The Writer looked down at Brute, then at the character, which looked up at him.

Brute saw the horror of it as The Writer slammed his jaws shut on the character, which was screaming in pain as The Writer clenched him tighter in his teeth. Blood was dripping down onto the ground and he pulled the character into his mouth and began chewing. Brute turned away and buried his face in his hands. Even though it looked literary, it was still horrifying to see or even read about. He did not see The Writer spit its remains out into the fire. All he felt was a cool breeze come over him and he looked out into the empty fields. The skies were becoming brighter, as if a new day were being born after a storm that had raged all night long. He saw The Writer, now back in his original appearance, walking up to him, dusting his hands off.

"That was good," he said in his usual tone of voice, the tone Brute had become accustomed to. "Let all this settle down and we can go back to that beautiful part of my world."

The Writer summoned the eagle to come for them and it appeared in the sky. It circled over them once and came to a gentle landing.

Brute looked at it with a huge smile on his face. He was never so happy to see a big bird. He was about to ask The Writer if he felt better now that he had gotten rid of the real world's ugliness but was afraid he's start thinking about it all again. He decided not to say anything about what he had just helped him get rid of. He hoped he'd forget all about it like he wanted him to.

"There's another thing I want to show you," The Writer said. "It's big and strong and some think of it as a king."

"Another king?" Brute asked. "We already met one."

"But I think you'll like this one even more."

With that Brute hurried up onto the back of the eagle. He was now anxious to see what The Writer had created that they did not get to see in the other part of this world.

The Writer took one last look at what was here that should've been here in the first place. It was beginning a new life of its own. Beauty was taking over. The real world had lost its battle in trying to control his heart and mind. Even Rusty's spirit was gone from this world . . . but not the real world.

It was still there . . . waiting for The Writer to return to it.

And he waddled away . . . to join Brute on the eagle and go back to where they started from.

CHAPTER NINETEEN

The eagle came to a perfect landing next to the lake that was under the cliff where The Writer and Brute took off to "swim in the sky". As soon as he got off the eagle's back Brute found himself surrounded by dozens of playful tigers that came running up to him. Several held their paws up to him in friendly greeting. Others purred around him.

"Their creator has trained them well," The Writer said, sending the eagle back to its nest which was miles away. "Over here is what I wanted to show you." He led Brute up the hill away from the lake and across an open field. Butterflies had taken possession of it, for they fluttered everywhere in droves. Several came to rest on Brute's shoulders. "I take it you love butterflies," he said.

"Indeed. Look over there on that mountain slope." He pointed and Brute saw a thick dark cloud coming up over the ridge. It looked like a thick haze but was really thousands of butterflies descending upon the valley. Pretty soon the cloud was making its way for where they were standing. Brute saw that it looked no more than about four feet off the ground and about 30 feet high coming straight for him. It was so thick of the little critters he could not see through the wall that appeared to be chasing him and he started to run. He fell down and rolled over. Thousands of little wings gave off a cool breeze as they fluttered over him without a care. None of them seemed to notice that he was lying there. He saw the varied mixture of colors of the butterflies and he stuck his hand up into the cloud that blew over him. It was like sticking your hand up to the face of a fan on the 'high' mode. When the last butterfly went over him he got back up. The cloud was settling onto a patch of flowers next to the lake in the distance.

"Cool," he said, getting back to his feet and following after The Writer, wondering what he'd see next. They went into a dark forest of tall evergreens, mixed with redwoods and pine firs. Again, only in this world could such a forest exist.

"In here, the colors of autumn can be seen anytime," The Writer said. He aimed his pen up and out came the beam. It sprinkled into the mass of limbs and branches overhead. The leaves evolved into rich golden shades of yellow, orange, red, pink, brown, and gold. Even the evergreens came under the spell. "Imagine how the Great Smokies would look if I could do this to them in reality."

They came to a stop on top of a black mound of what appeared to be a huge flat rock poking out from a wall of bushes. It was round and very rough. Little ridges of various formations seemed to be etched out of it. The Writer sat down on a little raise on the rock and Brute sat next to him. He looked in front of him at the forest and saw the trees going back to their original green color. Further beyond it was the fields they had just walked through. It still had its rich greenness but looked as though it were becoming blurred with fog or haze.

"I think it's about time to go back," The Writer said, rubbing his forehead.

"Why? We haven't seen everything," Brute said.

"You can't see everything in a writer's world in one journey," he said. "It takes several. He's always creating something new for you to read about and to see. What we've seen here is just a small sampling. Right now I'm losing my drive to think on this place. That's why it all looks so muggy now, but this one thing I have to show you may make you happy."

At that moment they were going up into the air. Brute saw the trees and the ground around the rock suddenly drop out of sight. He was getting a full scale view of the rest of the world as he was taken up higher and higher on the rock. The air was crisp and cool. Everything below was like the work of the great Thomas Kinkade, only it was real enough to touch here and not just to

spend hours gazing at. They came to a stop and Brute got up
to get a better look at the world below and far out into the
horizon.

"Man this is cool," he said. "We're higher than where that
eagle picked us up from."

"Oh, you like the view?" The Writer asked.

"Yeah man, why? Is this not what you wanted to show me?"

"Well, it can be an added bonus. I really wanted to show you
the answer to a question you've been asking me."

"Okay, what is it?"

"You kept asking me if I liked Godzilla, right?"

"Yep."

The Writer motioned for him to look behind him. Brute followed the gesture and turned to see what was there. He looked up
and fell onto his rear, his eyes and mouth as wide as they could be.

He was no more than about ten feet away from a huge black
face with big yellow eyes looking at him.

"Brute, meet my imaginary pet, the king of the monsters, the
one and only . . . Godzilla."

The great beast lifted his other arm up and with one gigantic
white claw, waved to Brute, emitting deep grunts. Brute took a
better look at where he was sitting. He saw The Writer propped
up against Godzilla's thumb. He looked all around his back and
saw the rest of his hand, the fingers, and the claws aimed up. This
whole time he was sitting in the palm of his favorite monster and
never knew it.

"Zilla..uh . . . I mean . . . you . . . Writer," he stammered,
trying to get the words out. "You mean . . . you . . . uh . . . like
. . . God . . . Godzilla too?"

"Ever since I was six or seven years old. I was afraid you'd laugh
at me if I told you."

Brute kept his eyes on the face of the monster. He got back up
and slowly approached him. "Can I pet him?" he asked sheepishly.
The Writer nodded and Brute began running his tiny hand over a
portion of Godzilla's black nose. The beast responded with a

soothing growl and nodded his head. Brute nearly lost his balance and stumbled back into the palm of Godzilla's hand.

"You . . . you know . . . I..uh . . . watched you beat that three headed monster in that movie. You were great."

There was a deafening roar from the monster upon hearing this. The Writer covered his ears and fell, rolling down next to where Brute was. The hand trembled and hundreds of birds took to the sky from all directions. When the roar was completed, The Writer stood up and shook his finger at the monster. He nodded and began walking across the valley. Brute saw that they were being taken someplace else and looked down. He could see the monster's huge feet crashing their way to wherever he was going.

"Hey Zilla."

The monster came to an abrupt stop and looked down at Brute, as did The Writer.

"I was talking to your master," he said, looking up into the face of Godzilla. The monster took the hint and proceeded on his way. He got The Writer's attention and was pointing down at the ground far below. "See how big your feet are?! They look just like his!"

The Writer nodded sarcastically and sat down with his feet dangling off the side of the hand next to Brute. He showed him where the beast was taking them to and saw that they were headed straight for the mountain where the eagle picked them up earlier. It was just as big and blue as it was when they last saw it. The monster set them down just below the very top of it.

"Nice to meet you Godzilla!" Brute yelled, waving to the monster. Godzilla waved back, turned around, and went past the mountain, headed for the lake that was behind it. He gradually walked into it and then slipped under the surface.

Both boys turned to look at the world. There was a bright sunbeam of orange coming out of the sky in the far distance straight ahead. With it came a voice that sounded like Mama.

"Sonny. Son, where are you?"

"What's that?" Brute asked, looking around for the source of it.

"My mother," The Writer said. "She's calling me. It's time to go back."

"You can hear your mother calling?" he asked.

"That's how it is when you let your mind drift. Someone has to call you back over and over and that's what Mama is doing now. That light means that we'll be back in the real world as soon as it gets so bright we can't see. All this will fade away till I come back to work on it. Let's go up here and watch it go."

The Writer led Brute up to the highest point of the mountain. They looked down into the world and saw the golden light overtaking portions of it, the fields, kingdoms, valleys, houses, settings, fields, everything. As they neared the top Brute grabbed The Writer's arm.

"Look," he said, pointing at all that was down there. "Look at all you've created."

The Writer took a long look at it and saw that it was more stunning than ever before. The light was granting one final look for now before it went away.

"Look at your world Zilla. Don't you think others would like to come here, and see what I saw here?"

The Writer looked towards him. He knew exactly what Brute meant, referring to the stacks of paper from that box in his bedroom. He wanted others to see this, but only when they read his works would that happen.

He took Brute up to the top of the mountain and they got one final look as the light continued to overtake everything. Everything was golden as the rays of the light hit it. The voice of his mother was heard in the wind, getting louder and louder. It was time to go back and face life, to dwell on the positive, and forget the negative.

A strong wind came upon them. The shirt The Writer made for Brute disappeared. The Writer's coat was being blown back as he stood by Brute's side. His eyes were closing. The light was getting brighter to the point of blinding.

Brute closed his eyes. They were going back. He grabbed hold of The Writer's hand.

The Writer could feel the sensation of the wind, his mother's voice, and the light overpower his mind.

The world vanished into pitch black.

And he waddled away . . . with Brute, back into the real world.

CHAPTER TWENTY

Mama came up to the top of the stairs and looked at her son's bedroom door. It was shut and as far as she could tell, there was no light inside the bedroom. She gave her eyes a final wipe from her tears after talking to her son. She hoped he hadn't gone to bed already without any supper. He did not answer her when she called him. She saw that Brute was not in the guest room, so she assumed they were in the bedroom together.

Just as she was about to turn the handle to take a look the door swung open. She jumped back and saw Brute standing in the doorway and The Writer was turning his lamp on. Both boys looked sweaty and were out of breath.

"Is everything alright?" she asked. "I called and called and got no answer."

Brute came on out of the bedroom, put his hands on her shoulders, and said in deep gasps, "Your son is amazing!" He went past her and headed for his room. She looked as if she'd just seen a headless chicken when he said that to her. Amazing? How? In what way? I'll just ask my son.

Mama stepped in her son's bedroom and saw him pulling the curtains shut. It was now pitch black outside and his head was soaked with sweat. On the floor she saw that both chairs had been turned over and the rug under the window had two of its corners rolled up. The Writer was at his dresser with the fan blowing straight into his face. His eyes were closed and the hair on his forehead was matted with sweat. His face looked flushed and his heart was racing as fast as it could.

"Son are you okay?" Mama asked, coming up to him. She felt his forehead to see if he had a fever. He didn't, but her hand came back wet and sticky.

"What time is it?" he asked.

"Almost nine," Mama said. "I must've dozed off after our discussion, because when I looked out the window it was getting dark outside."

She looked at her son. The color was slowly returning to his face and the sweat was slacking away. She stroked his hair back and kept feeling his forehead.

"Do you have a headache?"

He shook his head.

"Are you hungry?"

"A little. I guess everything's closed now huh?"

"No, but being Friday night I guess everything's crowded. What do you want to eat?"

The Writer opened his eyes and looked down at his watch. It was five minutes to nine. We were gone for nearly four hours, he thought as he rubbed his hands over his face. How come I feel so cool? I'm not hot. My head's not hurting. I feel so . . . so . . . strong. I could drive to Florida tonight if I wanted. What's come over me?

It was as if he'd just woke up from a deep coma that lasted for years. He refocused his eyes and saw that everything in his bedroom looked brighter and sharper. The lamp on his dresser next to the fan put a warm white glow on his face. In his chest he could feel an eerie sense of burgeoning strength and power. He was breathing steadily and kept looking around his bedroom.

Mama just looked at him. She waved her hand in front of his face and got his eyes to look almost at hers but not quite. She put her hands on his shoulders and positioned him in front of her.

"Son, are you okay? Did something happen in here, because Brute said you were 'amazing.' What did you two do?"

His eyes took on that deep dark look of inner fear and wonder. They widened up and he slipped out of her gentle hold.

"I'm fine Mama," he said. "I . . . I just showed Brute something. That's all. I'm hungry. Can I eat?"

"Oh son I'm sorry," she said almost apologetically, ushering him for the door. "Go on down to the kitchen. Do you want me to call and order pizza? If you don't I can run to Wendy's or McDonald's or Burger King and get you something. Do you want me to?"

Why the sudden royal treatment, he wondered. I can get my supper. You don't need to drive into town and fight those tourists who can't read a map in their own language. When the Fourth of July rolls around here we are staying here in the house, or at least I am. He went on down into the kitchen and headed straight for the fridge. His mother came in behind him and started giving him a guided tour of what was inside. He saw the sandwich Mama had brought him from Lucille. He took it out along with a can of Hawaiian Punch and went for the counter. Mama saw what he had and told him to eat more if he wanted.

"I want you in bed early tonight if you're going out tomorrow," she said. "You're still going aren't you? Judy and I are leaving for Asheville promptly at nine. We'll only get to see an hour of the morning fashion show on QVC before we leave."

The Writer nodded his head.

Mama turned to go back up to her room but stopped in the doorway.

"Oh by the way son, have you decided who you're taking tomorrow?"

He raised his head and looked out into space. Oh no, not again, he thought. I can't stand her preaching at me again if I tell her.

"Never mind son," she said. "You have all night to think it over. You can decide by tomorrow." She then left him to eat.

Oh I know who I'm taking tomorrow, he thought as he looked down at his pen, then he looked up, dead ahead . . .

Only God Himself can keep me from taking him . . .

The Writer awoke the following morning to see the day outside his bedroom window bleak and miserably gray. The sky was hidden behind a thick blanket of fog and haze and it was cooler than usual. He couldn't even see the top of the mountains in the distance. It was tempting him to crawl back under the covers and go back to sleep, and he would have if he hadn't been baptized on this day seven years ago. He was determined to keep tradition going.

He got out of his night clothes, showered, and put on his usual outfit. This time he wore a tan t-shirt with a picture of folded hands in prayer and a piece of rope tied around the wrists. Under it was the scripture that said, *"Forgive them, for they know not what they do."* He put on his black sweat pants, his black waist bag, and tied his black coat around his waist. He went to see if Mama was up and sure enough she was in the living room on the couch. Judy was in the chair next to it. Both were eating breakfast and watching the first hour of the Saturday morning edition of the A.M. Fashion Show on QVC. The only light that was on besides the blare from the TV screen was the lamp on the stand in the corner between the couch and the chair. It was a warm comforting glow to complement the atmosphere of such a gray morning.

"When we go to Belk's I want to get an outfit just like that," Judy said, hastily writing down the description of the outfit the host was showing. "It'll be the perfect addition for my summer wardrobe."

The Writer walked in and stood next to the chair where Judy was sitting. She felt his presence looming over her so she decided to humor him. "Linda, why does it feel so literary in here all of a sudden? My pen's hot." She looked up at The Writer and started laughing. "Oh, good morning sir. Happy Anniversary!"

"You remembered?" The Writer asked, rather astonished.

"Well of course. Joey had it written all over the kitchen calendar in red letters and he sent you a card. He left early to get to the shop and have it ready for the day." She dug around in her pocketbook and pulled out a blue envelope. In Joey's all-too-familiar scrawl was simply 'The Writer' written on the outside of it.

"And when we get to the mall we're gonna get you a present," Mama said, lifting her cup of coffee to her lips. She took a sip and then looked at her son. "Oh, you're all ready to go I see. Did you decide who you're taking?"

Fib to her Writer, he thought. Don't make her fuss at you on this day of days, and in front of Judy. Tell her you're taking Blade or Nate, but no, they're at work. Elaine works at the nursing home. Jackie has to baby-sit on Saturdays. Lana and Dionne work with Joey at the shop, and Annie's busy today helping someone design their living room.

That only leaves you-know-who.

"Rusty."

Both Mama and Judy spit their coffee out in midair upon hearing the name. There was a faint mist hanging in the air over the coffee table and the droplets of it were snowing down onto the waxed surface. The Writer watched as they scrambled to hand each other a napkin to wipe their mouths and faces.

"You're taking who?" Mama asked, as if she needed to hear it again. "But I thought you decided . . ."

"Rusty?" Judy asked. "You're not serious, are you?"

He nodded.

"Oh son, please think this over, really deeply. I mean, son, are you absolutely sure he won't do anything to hurt you this time?"

He nodded again.

"Really? Because I've just got this sick feeling that something's gonna happen once you get to his house. I don't know what but it's just a sick feeling. I had it all night after I went to bed."

"You've got a premonition," Judy said. "I get those all the time, of course I'm usually wrong though. The only time I don't get them is when Joey goes out with The Writer somewhere. I never have to worry when my boy goes out with yours. Never." She looked at The Writer and stood up to him, and placed her hands on his shoulders. "Sir, please, for your mother's sake, and for mine and Joey's, are you sure about what you're doing? It's just that none of us want to see you get hurt, and today being your anniversary."

"I know what I'm doing," he said. "Nothing can go wrong today. I've left it in God's hands."

"Well I can't argue with God," Mama said, getting up off the couch. "Son, you're eighteen now. I can't always tell you what to do. You're old enough to make your own decisions and I can't keep you from doing or even force you into doing something. All I ask is that you be careful today, please. And if something happens and you feel that you can't go on, come on back home. We're not leaving for Asheville until nine. If you're not back here by then, we're going on, and we're gonna assume that you're okay. Is that alright?"

He nodded. He took the card from Judy, grabbed his keys, and headed for the door. As he opened it he heard Mama and Judy following him out onto the porch.

"Uh son, the truck may need gas so you may want to fill it up somewhere before you head down to Rusty's," Mama said, standing behind the railing on the porch next to the steps. He nodded back to her. Judy looked up at the sky and saw how dreary it looked.

"Looks like it may storm today," she said to Mama. "At least we'll be inside if it does."

An omen, Mama thought. Could God be saying something with the sky? Every year my son's gone out for this day and it's never been cloudy or foggy. It's always been warm, clear, and pretty until this year. Why?

Judy held her hand as they watched The Writer go down the steps. Mama clutched her hand as tight as she could and turned to her friend. " I can feel it Judy. Rusty's gonna pull some cruel stunt on my son and he doesn't know it. What can I do?"

"Let God handle this like The Writer said," Judy told her in her firmest voice. "Linda I don't want him taking Rusty any more than you do but like you said, he's eighteen and has to make his own decisions. But if it'll make you feel better we won't leave for Asheville until ten. How does that sound? That way if something should happen and he comes back we'll be here. It's 8:20 now. This will give him time to get to his house. Is that alright Linda?"

She nodded. At least we can pray that God will watch over my son, and bring him home if something should happen, she thought.

With heavy hearts they looked at the dull sky, then at The Writer, who was heading for Mama's truck with his keys dangling at his knees.

And he waddled away . . . into the fog, to go to Rusty's house.

CHAPTER TWENTY-ONE

The Writer drove to Rusty's house with his mind brewing with everything they could do today if the sky decided it would clear up. He had mental pictures of him and Rusty going to that place in Murphy, the market, the lake, the picnic, and all the other little things he'd been planning on for days. He had felt this way ever since last night when he and Brute came out of his world, his mind refreshed and revitalized with all the doom and gloom this world had given him over the years now long gone. Gone with it were the past errs and flaws of Rusty. He saw today as a new beginning for both of them, and he hoped Rusty would feel the same way once he saw the majesty of the place The Writer wanted to take him to.

He parked the truck in the driveway below the house, which sat on the side of a hill and had big long flat rocks made into steps that lead up to the front porch and wooden steps that lead up to the backdoor on the side of the house. He got out and saw the red motorcycle Annie talked about leaning up against the bottom of the hill. It had room for two people and was heavily adorned with all the grotesque apparel one could find, from a woman barely dressed to a snake with its tongue lashing out at the admirer.

Oh good he's here, he thought as he shut the door of the truck and started walking for the wooden steps. He could see that his mother had already left for work and his father was gone somewhere. He could feel the microscopic droplets of moisture in the air on his skin as he walked, the gravel under his feet crunching with each step. He then felt his foot kick something round and green. He picked it up and saw that it was an empty skoal can. He tossed it into the trash can next to the bottom of the steps and he heard a loud clang. He looked inside and saw that the skoal can had hit what appeared to be dozens of empty brown bottles. Please let it be just root beer, The Writer thought as he picked one up to get a closer look. He was wrong. There was a gold label wrapped around the neck of each bottle, boasting the name of the brand. Nervously he dropped it back into the can and it broke into several big pieces.

Please don't let it be, he prayed as he stepped away from the can. Just his father, at least, but please don't let it be Rusty. God please don't . . .

With uneasiness slithering around inside his stomach, he started up the steps to the back door. When he got to it he paused for a minute, took a deep breath, and knocked on the screen door three times.

Nothing.

He knocked again, only louder, thinking he was still asleep.

Still nothing.

He looked all around him and couldn't see anybody else around, due in part to the fog. He pulled back the screen door and slowly turned the wooden door handle, hoping it was unlocked.

It was.

He slipped on in and quietly pushed it shut till it barely clicked. He looked all around the room and saw that he was in the kitchen. It smelled of old food and dirty dishes, which were piled up in the sink. It was very dark, the foggy light from outside dimmed by the branches from the trees on the hillside behind the house. He could see that no light was on anywhere, not even in the living room, which was straight ahead of him.

This is too eerie Writer, he thought. This house looks as if it is holding some dark sinister secret that it doesn't want you to see or find out. Quiet empty houses tend to have something to hide.

He walked across the floor of the kitchen, holding his keys in one hand and had a hold of his pen with the other. With each step he took his big feet made a muffled squeak on the floor. He looked to his left and saw the sink full of dishes, the faucet dripping every few seconds, and the window above the sink showing nothing but dullness from outside. To his right was the kitchen table, spread over with mail, magazines, newspapers, and the typical salt and pepper shakers and napkin holder. The fridge kicked into a rumbling purr as he passed it, stepping out into the hallway.

The living room was lit by what little light came from outside. There was nobody in there. He turned and slowly started down the hall, which gradually ascended into a flight of stairs that sneaked up into the darkness of the upper reaches of the house. They came to an abrupt stop at a small hallway. Rusty's bedroom was the last door on the left.

Maybe he's still asleep, he thought. It is rather early.

Then he heard something.

He looked down at his feet and saw that he had stepped on something that looked like plastic. It was lying just outside the bathroom. He picked it up and looked at it. Whatever was inside it had been torn out. He wanted to get a better look so he stepped into the bathroom and switched the light on.

His eyes widened.

It was a condom wrapper.

The label to it was still inside.

He dropped it into the sink and saw even more.

On top of the toilet tank was a blue box marked 'contraceptives'. Lying next to it was a sheet of foil that held little white objects that looked like tiny missiles. He could see that four of these things had been torn out. On the counter around the sink he saw a tube of spermicide and a fresh box of condoms. He gasped at the sight and quickly slammed the switch light to 'off'. His heart began to race, his breathing heavier, his hands cold and clammy. He could feel the sweat begin to ooze out of his skin on his lower back and on his forehead.

He proceeded on to Rusty's bedroom. As he got closer he heard something else.

Someone breathing. Each time it was deeper and a tad longer.

It got louder as he slowly approached the bedroom door, which was barely open a crack. He could see a thin white ray of light reaching out into the hallway. His mind was totally blank. Nothing came to mind as he got closer and closer to the door. The sounds from the bedroom were luring him, calling him, bringing him forth closer and closer. His eyes were big, wide, and empty, gleaming in the ray of light from the bedroom. His stomach began to make gurgling noises, his hands feeling clammier than before. His flesh felt weak, useless, dead.

He got to the door.

There was a rustling of some sort, then something hit a wall. Someone inside said "Ouch!" Then another one said, "Sorry."

The Writer slowly let his right hand wrap around the door handle, then he let it slip off. He raised his left hand up onto the door and with a powerful shove pushed it open till it slammed into the wall behind it. It sent forth a huge breeze across the room, blowing papers off the night stand and bending back the curtains.

He saw someone in the bed roll off of someone else, then disappear under the sheets. He heard a girl scream from under the sheets and then Rusty appeared out of them, his hair all bunched up and pointy, the blonde touches warped and deformed out of place, his face flushed, sweaty, breathing hard, his bare chest heaving up and down.

He looked at The Writer standing in the doorway. His breathing was constant with short intervals.

"Man, what are you doing here?" he asked. "You scared us to death."

The girl raised her head up from under the sheets, looked at The Writer, and pointed at him.

"Rust, who the freak is that?!" she screamed. "Get him out of here! How dare you barge in here on us like this! Get out! I ought to call the police!"

The Writer's eyes were cast over what was in the bedroom. What he saw told the whole story. Her shirt was lying crumpled up at the foot of the bed, along with her pants, bra, and shoes. His shirt was thrown across the room towards the window, his pants lying in front of the shelf next to the bed, and his underpants and socks at the foot of the bed. There was a wrenching foul odor hanging in the air. It resembled that of urine and rotting feces. On the floor lay another opened packet. A few feet away lay something else. It was tan, looked rubbery, and had something thick and white oozing out of it. It looked like milk in the middle of its souring process.

He figured out what it was and stepped back into the door, his breathing becoming more and more rapid. Dear God this can't be, he thought. It can't be. Not Rusty. It can't be true. Please let me be dreaming. Let me wake up and let it be a clear and beautiful Saturday for my anniversary. Please God wake me up now if this is a dream!

"I told you to get out!" the girl screamed. Rusty gestured for her to be quiet.

"Writer, this here is Kelly, my woman. Six touchdowns already on her, somethin' I know you can never do. Kelly, you haven't met The Writer have ya?" Rusty asked. "They call him 'The Writer' because he thinks he can write."

"Well what's he doing here?!" she demanded. "I want him out of here, NOW!"

"Do . . . do you know what today is?" The Writer asked shakily. "Did you get my message?"

"Lemme see . . . uh . . . yep . . . think I did get your message 'bout today bein' yer anniversary or somethin' like that huh? I forgot. Sorry. I had somethin' else to do anyways, and you're lookin' at it."

The Writer felt his stomach go flat. His head was feeling hotter and hotter and he couldn't stand what was going on. He asked him why he didn't call him back.

"Aw come on Writer, I got better things to do than be a wastin' muh time with some bloated bough butted bastard freak who can't throw a football. Why would I waste muh time with you when I could be with muh honey here? Why don't you go on and do yourself or somethin'? Make yourself useful for a change, or wind up like that drunk I hit near your house when was it . . . last

Sunday night? Whenever it was, some retard was a swingin' his business around in the road so I let him have a taste of muh old truck. Got him out of the way. I may've killed him I don't know. Don't really care either. I thought it was you seein' how big that caboose of yours is."

Brute, The Writer thought. You tried to run over Brute! That was you Joey and I heard that night at his house, and you thought it was *me* you were going to hit! Oh God what kind of monster is this guy?! What did I ever see in him?! God get me out of here! I can't stand him anymore! He's everything Mama and Annie and Joey and everybody else tried to tell me he was. I was too bullheaded to listen or believe it. Oh God do something to me now! I'm so stupid!

That was the truth. This was truth about Rusty. It was all in front of his very eyes. No way was this a dream. God had shown him the bitter truth about Rusty. It was no longer open to debate between him or anyone else. This is who the real Rusty is. This was not the same guy who had a touch of goodness for a few minutes about three years earlier. This was the real person, the true colors, the true essence of this corrupt soul that The Writer tried to show love to but only got trash in return. It's impossible to be friends with trash.

"Rusty, get up and do something to that fat kid or I'm gonna handle him myself!" Kelly screamed.

The Writer pulled himself away from the door and caught sight of a large cardboard box next to the door. In it was a mess of pictures and letters. He got a closer look and saw that it was all the letters and cards he'd sent to Rusty over the years, telling him how much he wanted to be his friend and how much he meant to him. He also saw the football that he'd given him for his birthday one year sitting on top of the letters. The Writer had paid plenty to get it for Rusty. Now it was just tossed aside with the rest of the pieces of his life he'd been willing to share with Rusty. He had thrown The Writer away, disposed of him out of his life.

So he would do the same with Rusty. Right now. This very

moment. He was out of his world and now he would be kicked out of his whole life for good.

He picked up the football and placed his fingers on the white ridge on top of it. He drew his arm back, and started to aim.

"Man, what're you doin?!" Rusty hollered, leaning forward.

"Put that down!" Kelly screamed.

It was too late.

The Writer had already aimed and released it from his hand. In the most beautiful football pass Rusty had ever seen as it glided across the room, its form perfectly level and straight, not a single wobble in it, and crashed into the shelf that was over the bed. The football knocked off several collector's items Rusty had up there, such as gold trading cards, pictures, collectable coke bottles, and even his trophy for playing little league football in elementary school years ago. It toppled and fell right onto Kelly's back, making her scream. Rusty was shielding his face from the falling objects but he could not stop the football from falling into his groin area. As soon as it did he let out a painful moan and fell over in Kelly's lap. The football had shattered a bottle full of coke and it had rained down on her, getting in her hair and on the bed.

The Writer whirled around, kicked the door back against the wall, and stormed out into the hallway. As soon as he saw he was no longer in the bedroom he began to run out of the hall, down the stairs, through the kitchen, swung the door open, and out onto the back porch where he came in. He grabbed hold of the railing and tried to control his breathing. The wheezing was starting up in his chest and if he didn't keep it down it would start clogging his throat and breathing tubes. He felt his coat pockets for his inhaler and saw that it was not there. It had fallen out somewhere, in the house he suspected during his flight to get out of there. I'm not ever going back in there, he thought. He began to go down the steps, but paused at the top step. He shook the dust off his feet and then proceeded down in a mad haste. His eyes were starting to burn with tears. His stomach and intestinal organs were going to fail on him at any moment. That ball of vomit was building in his throat. As soon as he heard his feet start crunching the gravel he hurried for the truck, got in, and turned the key in the ignition. His hands were so cold and clammy they slipped off the key several times before he could turn it. He was shaking all over, about to lose everything. He backed up, threw the shift into 'D', floored the gas pedal, and screamed his tires as he headed for the house.

Red lights and stop signs meant nothing as he flew past them. He had a death grip on the wheel, sweat oozing out from under his hands, his eyes unable to stop the gushing tears. The needle on the speedometer was approaching the fifty mark steadily. He didn't care if he got pulled over and got his first ticket ever for speeding. He had a reason but knew the cops wouldn't buy it. But if they knew whose son he was then maybe they'd be sweet and kind to him about it.

I doubt it, he thought.

The clock in the truck read 9:20. Mama and Judy are already gone, he thought. Joey's at work with the girls. The boys are all at work. Oh God my anniversary this year sucks! Why today dear Lord? WHY TODAY?! Why did you do this to me now?!

Before he knew it he was on the road that went to his house. He shot into his driveway and sped for the front of the house. He could see Mama and Judy coming out onto the porch. Judy grabbed Mama's arm and pulled her back. The Writer brought the truck to a screeching halt near the spot where it was earlier, opened the door, and fell out onto the ground. As soon as his face hit the earth he started puking and choking.

Mama and Judy rushed down to his side. Each one helped him up on his feet. But he cut loose from them, slid on the gravel, but grabbed hold of the truck door. He started slapping and kicking it with his hands and feet, screaming over and over "why, why, why?" Mama put her hands up to her mouth in horror at how her son was acting. She had never seen him this violent or upset in his whole life. Judy tried to calm him down but he knocked her away.

"GOD WHY WHY WHY?!" He kept screaming those words over and over. He kicked up clouds of dirt and gravel and then stumbled away from the truck. Seeing where he was he then made a mad dash up the porch steps, ran into the house, and up the stairs for the bathroom. He flew in, slammed the door shut, and flung his face down into the toilet and started puking like crazy. His hands hugged the bowl and he tightened his hold of it more and more. When he felt he was finished he got up and stood with his back to the wall. He was covered in sweat, vomit, dirt, and drool. It had splashed up into his face and hair and was dripping all over the floor. He had his eyes closed, the scene in Rusty's bedroom vivid in every detail possible. His words were stuck in his ears, like a broken record, saying everything over and over. He started to feel a total breakdown come over him. He banged his head against the wall a few times, then opened his eyes.

He saw someone in front of him. He had black hair, a chubby face, a t-shirt, sweat pants, a coat, and a pen around his neck. He stepped up closer to the person, who also did the same thing. He blinked. It blinked. He got closer and he hit something. The sink counter. He looked up and saw he was face to face with this other guy who also had vomit all over his face and hair, was crying, had red eyes, and a crushed spirit.

It was The Writer.

He had just met himself in the mirror face to face, eye to eye.

"They tried to tell you," he said to the mirror. "But no, you wouldn't listen. You thought you could handle anybody like that. You didn't want to believe those things. You thought they were crazy, but you're the one who's crazy for letting this crap go on for four years. It's all your fault you fat lazy bastard. You just messed up your whole freaking life for that dirtbag. Mrs. Moran was right. You deserve to be put away someplace where you can't mess up your life or anyone else's. You should be committed, because you are crazy, a crazy writer, a crazy no-good backstabbing lowlife bastard who can't even face the truth when he hears it oh STOP IT! STOP IT! STOP THIS!" He began to slam his head up against the wall so hard he left dents in the wallpaper. Feeling his stomach acting up again he looked at the toilet. It looked so far away from where he stood in the bathroom. He reached for it but couldn't grab it. He forced himself away from the mirror and looked at the toilet.

And he sluggishly waddled away . . . to the toilet to throw up again.

CHAPTER TWENTY-TWO

Mama and Judy went into the bathroom and they saw The Writer scrunched on the floor on his knees, hugging the bowl, his face in the toilet, choking and spitting. Mama had Judy hand her a towel from the rack behind the door and she got on the floor next to her son. She put her hands on his shoulders and slowly pulled him back off the toilet bowl.

"Son," she said gently, "what happened? Tell me. Do you need to go to the hospital?"

He leaned up and fell against the wall. His face was splattered with brown and yellow splotches of vomit. It was dripping from his hair and was all over his shirt. Globs of it still oozed from his mouth. It dribbled down the picture of the praying hands on his shirt.

"Oh Mama, please don't say anything," he said in breaking sobs. "Please don't say 'I told you so.' I don't need to hear it. Please don't say anything Mama. Please, please. Don't say it!" He slammed his hand on the rim of the toilet bowl.

"Oh I won't," she said, wiping his face with the towel. "Just tell me what happened. Can you do that for me son? Just tell me. I promise I won't get mad at whatever you say"

"You want me to go downstairs Linda?" Judy asked. "Because I can . . ."

"No, stay," The Writer said, holding his hand up to her. "Don't go." Judy nodded and sat on the floor next to Mama. They looked at his ghastly appearance and waited for him to calm down to the point of where he could talk. But he was so upset he kept gasping and sobbing that Judy got him a cup of water from the sink. Mama was afraid he'd have an asthma attack if he didn't calm down.

"Son, did Rusty do something to you?"

He shook his head.

"Did he say something?" Judy asked. He nodded his head at that. "What was it?"

"Told me I was a bastard freak, that he had better things to do today than be with me . . . everything. Everything you all said he was. I . . . I caught him in bed with some . . . girl. It was so . . . so nasty . . . what I saw . . . and smelled . . . it was all over . . . that room . . ."

"Okay son, that's enough," Mama said, wrapping her arm around him. "Don't say anymore."

"But today's my anniversary! Of all days for this to happen why now? Why on the greatest day of my life? This is the worst year ever for it! What am I gonna do now?"

Mama looked at the floor, her mind totally blank for a moment, then it hit her. She looked up at Judy and gestured for her to come out into the hall with her. Mama whispered to him that they'd be back in a minute.

When they disappeared down the hall he lowered his head back down. His head was throbbing, his stomach empty, and his flesh still clammy. He looked in the toilet and saw the gunk he had vomited still floating around. He flushed it and watched the mess swirl around and gurgle its way down the hole. The water spit back up tiny slivers of the stuff. Too weak to flush it again he fell back against the wall. All you had to do was believe them, he thought. You could've spared yourself all this misery years ago. They're not kidding when they say the truth hurts.

He closed his eyes and began to feel the spell of sleep falling upon him. It would be so easy to sleep now. The sky outside was still white and hazy. The house was dull with no lights on except in the bathroom. His mother and Judy had planned to go to Asheville today and now he didn't know if they'd still go now after what happened this morning. If they went on he'd be alone today, the seventh anniversary of the day he was baptized.

He could recall how Mr. Graham's rough, bony hands felt

against his back, dipping him down under the water, and raising him up. He remembered opening his eyes and seeing Mama burst into tears. His heart and mind felt a renewed sense of strength and power for life after he came out of the water. It was the greatest feeling he'd ever felt in his whole life. He vowed right then and there to keep the spirit of that day going every year till the day he died.

So far he had succeeded, until this morning, he thought.

Then he opened his eyes now to this moment in time. He saw his bedroom across the hall with the white light pouring in. But there was something else coming into the bathroom. He saw the muscular hairy legs coming at him, then the white shorts, then felt someone sitting next to him on the floor. He closed his eyes and turned away. He didn't care who it was. It could be a burglar for all he knew. The incident this morning had crushed his sense of care for anything in the world. A portion of his heart had been destroyed. No material thing in this world could ever replenish what was lost this morning.

God had indeed, kept him from taking Rusty out today.

"Hey Zilla," a familiar voice said.

"What?" he said weakly, keeping his face turned away. He realized who was in the bathroom with him. Then the voice came again.

"Uh . . . do you still wanna go today?"

"I don't know," he said, tears coming again. "I don't care now. There's nobody to take now. This whole day is crushed for me."

There was a long pause. Brute kept looking at his face and saw the hurt that had taken a cruel hold of it. It had crushed all hope of joy in life out of it and left behind a scar of melancholy.

"Well Zilla, I . . . uh . . . I'll go with you."

"Huh?" The Writer looked towards him.

"I said I'll go with ya. I wanna see this place you take your other friends to see."

The Writer looked up at his bedroom. He could see two shadows moving on the wall next to the doorway. No doubt it was

Mama and Judy, listening, hoping something would happen. After a few minutes Judy poked her head around the corner, then Mama's head poked in under Judy's. Pretty soon she went back in.

"Son, do you feel like going on today?" Mama asked.

He shrugged.

"Well, Brute wants you to take him," she said, kneeling on the floor in front of him. "Don't let this morning ruin everything for you. It's all over now. I'm sure Brute wants to be with you today anyway, don't you?"

"Of course."

The Writer closed his eyes.

"I'll let you take my car, the convertible," Judy offered. "You'll love driving that baby through those fields."

"Hey that's a great idea!" Mama said. "See there son, you get to drive her car down there to that place. We can take the truck with us to Asheville."

"I can still go?" he asked in broken whispers. "It's kinda late isn't it?"

"Don't worry about the time son," she said. "I want you to go."

The Writer wiped his eyes and looked near her face. "Okay," he whispered. "We'll go."

"That's my boy," she said, helping him up. "Go change your clothes now and put these in the tub to soak. Judy, will you help him? Brute, come with me."

Judy went with The Writer into his room to help him change out of his messed up clothes and Mama took Brute with her into her room. She shut the door and led Brute over to the closet. When she slid back one of the doors, Brute saw the most beautifully arranged collection of men's clothing he'd ever seen. He saw sweaters, shirts, pants, shoes, dress shirts, slacks, a policeman's suit, and several belts. But why were they in her closet?

"You know I have more clothes than Wal-Mart will ever hope to have," she said, rummaging through them. She told Brute to come closer and have a look. "All these clothes belonged to my husband. He's dead now, but I could never make myself give his clothes to the people from Goodwill. I like to have them here. They still have his smell, and when I want to feel him here I just look at a few of his things. But I know they can still serve a purpose. Is there something here that you would like to wear today?"

Brute got a closer look at what was in the closet. There were so many choices for just this one day thing. "Did he have any white muscle shirts?" he asked.

Mama opened the third drawer in her dresser and showed him the collection of muscle shirts he used to wear. She pulled one out and sampled it on him. It was almost a perfect fit. He then showed her one of the button-up shirts in the closet. She took it out and sampled it on him. It was also a perfect fit.

"I just want to wear that over the muscle shirt. Is that okay?"

"Sure." She handed him the muscle shirt and he put it on, followed by the other shirt, which was blue. He left it unbuttoned and rolled up the sleeves, just like The Writer did with his pants legs. He told her he'd keep the shorts on. Mama stood back to admire how he looked.

"I always thought you were close to my husband's size," she said. "Now you need some shoes and socks. Here, try these on." He slipped on the socks she gave him followed by a pair of tennis shoes her husband used to wear. She had kept everything of his in clean fresh condition over the years. Everything was a perfect fit on him. He was ready to go. When they were finished they went downstairs and she had him wait at the bottom for her son to come out.

"I appreciate you going with him today," she said, picking up her shopping list for the mall off the coffee table. "Today means so much to him."

"No problem," he said. "I love these clothes."

"You like them?" Mama asked. "Then you can have them. I don't think my husband would mind. At least they'll be worn and used again. Please, by all means, take them." She then looked up the stairs and saw her son coming down, completely done over by

Judy. He still had the black coat and waist bag, but he wore a white t-shirt with scripture on it this time. He wore black shorts and had his hair combed back. It was easy to see even if it was hidden under his cap.

Brute watched as he came down the steps to him slowly. His face was clean, his eyes were losing their redness, and his color was returning. He could also see that The Writer was admiring how he looked, fully dressed in an attractive summertime outfit. The Writer brushed past him, grabbed his keys, and headed for the front door. Brute followed close behind him. Mama and Judy were chasing after them as they headed out onto the porch. They were surprisingly greeted with a gorgeous sight. The fog and haze had broken up considerably and the sun was shining down upon the earth, highlighting every color that existed. The lush greenness of the fields on both sides of the driveway, the leaves on the trees, the grass, the rolling hills in the distance, everything looked as if it had been reborn. It was warm and the wind was blowing. The sky was turning bluer and bluer with each breath of wind that took the fog away.

"Just a second sir," Judy said after she got her eyeful of the weather. She handed The Writer her set of keys for the convertible, and he gave Mama his set for the truck. Judy also had something else for him. "You know what, I never did give you your graduation present."

"Don't worry about it," he said.

"No sir. Here, this is yours. Don't open it till you get way down the road, okay? Promise me you won't peek at it until then."

"Okay," he said, taking the envelope she handed him and stuffing it in his coat pocket. He and Brute made their way for the car and got in. Judy ran to it and started tossing stuff out of the backseat such as Joey's workout clothes that he had forgotten to put in the laundry and some of her things. Mama just stood by, watching her son about to embark on his annual trip to that special place in Murphy.

The Writer turned the ignition and grabbed hold of the gear shift.

"Okay boys," Mama said. "Be careful and have a good time. Don't get in a hurry son and just enjoy yourself, okay? Oh and son, here's your card from Joey. You forgot to open it this morning. Here you go."

He nodded as he took it.

"In the meantime, while you're gone, your mom and I will be cleaning out the malls in Asheville, won't we Linda?"

"Oh yeah," she said bluntly. Judy backed away from her car as The Writer began to back it up, turn, and head down the driveway for the main road. She got next to Mama who had her hands folded. Pretty soon both of them were waving as the car got further away.

"I just hope God watches over them today," she said.

"He's looking down on them right now Linda," Judy said. "C'mon, let's hit the road for Asheville!"

And sure enough, from overhead one could see the car come down the driveway leaving a golden trail of billowing dust hanging in the air behind it. The car then hit the main road, passed Joey's house, and before long it had hit the main highway that would lead them out of town and onto the four-lane. Brute was seen with his arm resting on the seat behind The Writer.

No matter how far they were going today, they were being watched over.

And He would see The Writer waddle away . . . all day long with Brute at his side.

CHAPTER TWENTY-THREE

"Just where is this place Zilla?" Brute asked, seeing the fleeting trees and houses pass them as The Writer drove on the four-lane, which was commonly mistaken to be an interstate.

"It's in Murphy, just over an hour and a half from here," he said in his usual tone of voice, which Brute could not hear one single syllable of. It was either because of that or because the car top was down, or maybe even both.

"Where Zilla? Speak up. Talk loud like me."

"It's in . . ."

"LOUDER!"

The Writer took a deep breath and raised his head.

"IT'S IN MURPHY, JUST OVER AN HOUR AND A HALF FROM HERE."

"There you go man! Wasn't hard was it?"

He shook his head. Yes, it was, he thought. It hurts my throat to talk loud. That's why I use my pen so much. That way people can see what you said over and over and not have to ask you to repeat it verbally. He looked down and saw Brute fumbling with the radio. He was expecting him to put it on some heavy metal rap station that would blow his eardrums to smithereens. Then he'd have a headache for the rest of the day and have to stop at some roadside gas station to buy Tylenol, boxes of it.

"You know Zilla," he said, looking up at him. "I love Rage Against the Machine, but do you know what I also love?"

He shook his head, keeping his eyes on the road. I'm afraid to guess, he thought. But I'll survive no matter what it is.

"Promise me you won't laugh if I tell you?"

He nodded. If you say you like opera or the classics of Beethoven and Mozart, then I may start wondering, he thought.

"I love country, you know, Tim McGraw, Lorrie Morgan, Reba McEntire, Tracy Byrd, Faith Hill, all those cowboy and cowgirl singers. How 'bout you Zilla? What do ya think of those Dixie Chicks?!"

This guy loves country! he thought. Please tell me he's kidding! That's what I was raised on. Mama had the country station going on the radio all the time. She'd put me to sleep with tunes by Reba and Tammy Wynette and Loretta Lynn. I love country! Dear God what else does this guy love? He leaned towards Brute to where he was sure he could hear him. He raised his voice and said, "I was raised on country music."

"Really?" he said. "In that case, the next song that comes up, if you and I both know it, we sing it together. Okay Zilla?"

Oh golly. I can't sing. Me and my big mouth, that is something I never thought I'd think of myself as having. The Writer leaned back into his regular driving position and watched as they came closer to the first exit that went to his high school. He saw it and began to inch over into the next lane. Luckily there was nobody over there so he got over and pushed the gas pedal. The car revved up and shot past the exit in a blur. When he was sure he was past it he got back into the other lane as Brute continued to look for a country station.

Ironically, it was also the same exit that went to Rusty's house.

"Try 99.9. That's all country all the . . ."

He was drowned out by a familiar tune by Dixie Chicks. Brute eagerly began to crank up the volume and started singing their song about a cowboy. He looked over and saw that The Writer was not singing.

"Hey man, do you know this one? Yea, you do. Don't try to hide it from me Zilla. I know you know this one. C'mon. Sing with me. Here we go, one, two, three . . ."

And together in close unison with the radio, they strained the lyrics in their strongest voice possible. Brute was much louder than The Writer, who could not bear to be seen singing with anyone much less by himself. Every time the line that said 'take me away, closer to you,' came up, Brute would point both fingers at The Writer, who would just close his eyes in embarrassment. One of the last things I wanna be in life is a singing cowboy, he thought. Maybe someday I'll meet a real-life cowboy who can teach me how to ride a horse.

He drove with the radio blaring more country tunes as the four-lane winded down into a two-lane road, cutting around sharp mountain curves and turns. Brute looked out his side and saw that they were driving on the side of a hill with a steep drop down into a ravine crawling with kudzu. He could also see a river with huge rapids coming into sight. The Writer knew he was about to get caught in a slight traffic jam. It was here in the gorge where a rafting company was built and was enjoying summer business.

When they got deeper into the gorge, which was jam-packed with rafters and trucks hauling rafts all over the area, The Writer got an eerie sensation. They were so close to the area that Annie described was where Rusty took his girlfriends on dates. Traffic on the road came to a standstill for a few minutes as rafters were seen running all over the place, catching rides on trucks, meeting their friends, or just coming out of the river from a ride. The Writer kept his patience, waiting for the truck in front to move on. Brute just looked around at all the people, several in nothing more than trunks and swimsuits.

A motorcycle was heard somewhere behind them.

Finally traffic started to move again. The truck drove on up the road in front for a few more miles before turning off. After it did The Writer sped up, keeping his speedometer at the speed limit of thirty-five. They came around several bends that were near the river, which was full of rafters having a wet and wild time. Brute stretched over the side of the door, raised his arms up in the air, and let out a bellowing wail at the ones he saw. A few waved back while others just gave annoyed looks. The Writer rolled his eyes towards him, then kept his gaze on the road.

Brute could not help but notice all the little roads that branched out suddenly from the main road they were on and reached far back into the wooded areas. He saw dozens of little houses, a church building on the left that was so tiny it looked as if it belonged to a small family, a post office, small fields, bridges, all the signs of simple mountain life. Everything he was seeing had a lavish coat of color on them from the sun and the cloudless blue sky.

I think I've seen a place that looked almost as beautiful as this, he thought. But where?

The two-lane road went around a curve and it suddenly burst out into a four-lane again, which stretched far into the vast horizon of the valley it went through. Brute saw the sign that said 'Welcome to Andrews' and saw no need to ask The Writer what town they were coming to next. He looked at the mountains in the distance on either side of the fields. He saw where a forest fire had torched a whole mountainside some years earlier and had left the skeletal remains of the trees. There was a tiny airport in the field to his right and on his left was nothing but tall grasslands bending in the wind. All these minor attractions raised his curiosity about The Writer. He could tell he loved places that were devoid of large masses of people, had a thing for quietness, and he was the first person he'd ever met close to his age that did not find joy in going somewhere that was full of booze, women, needles, and fights.

The Writer was different from everyone else he'd ever met in his entire life. What did he have that none of his other friends had? He'd have to find out . . .

He felt the floor beneath him begin to rumble. He looked straight ahead and saw that the broken line in the middle of the road was shooting past them faster than ever before. He could feel the wind get stronger, and everything they were passing was almost a blur. He looked at The Writer. He kept flashing a glance into the rearview mirror every few seconds and was pressing the gas pedal harder and harder. Brute began to turn around to see what was behind them.

"NO DON'T!" The Writer yelled, grabbing hold of his shoulder with his right hand. He sped up a bit faster.

"Why? You bein' tailed?"

"I don't know," he said, almost panicked. "But that motor-cycle has been behind us ever since we left town. I saw it sneaking up behind us back at the gorge."

"That far back?!" Brute said in amazement. "That was almost an hour ago. Pull over and let's take 'em down whoever it is."

"No. Maybe they'll pass us or something." The Writer kept his eyes on the road and in the mirror. He could see about fifty feet behind the motorcycle trailing after them. Whoever was on it wore a red helmet with a black shield over the face. It was hard to tell if somebody else was on it. It was steadily kept in the dead center of the road and whoever was on it didn't seem to be in a big hurry.

The needle inched up to 85. The Writer was afraid a cop would loom into sight at any moment and present him with his very first speeding ticket ever, and of all days to be on his anniversary. But he had not seen a cop for the last fifty miles or so. The road was not being traveled a whole lot today for some reason. He looked over in the opposite lanes and would see a car pass every few minutes. Where was everyone on such a gorgeous day as today? Not that it mattered, but he just wondered. He would enjoy it while it lasted. But how could he with that motorcycle that seemed to be following them?

"Ever drove this fast before?" Brute asked, holding his arms up in the air, his outer shirt blowing back behind him. "This could be fun."

"No, and it's not fun," The Writer said. "This is too weird. That bike has been behind us too long to just be a coincidence. Why doesn't it just pass us?"

"Hey calm down man! Don't get your nerves in a tizzy. Look, just pull over and see what they do."

"What?"

"Just pull over up here. If they wanna fight we can take them."

"Brute no. I don't wanna fight anybody. I just want to get away from whoever that is back there."

Brute looked at him. "Do you know how to fight? Or wrestle?"

He shook his head.

"Man I gotta teach you this stuff. One day you might need it. You can watch me if they come up here to fight."

When the needle was nearing the 95 mark he pressed the brake and started slowing down, but would not pull off to the side. He kept looking in his mirror and sure enough the bike was now about 25 feet behind them. He could tell that there was two people on it. Whoever was on the back had long hair blowing in the wind from under the helmet.

He finally pulled over, his heart racing, and his nerves quaking. He and Brute looked in the mirror.

The bike was now about 30 feet behind them, and it too, came to a rest on the side of the road.

"Oh no," The Writer said, "they stopped. I'm taking off!"

"No man!" Brute said, grabbing hold of his arm. "Just wait."

The Writer let out a deep sigh of aggravation.

"Brute I don't wanna get in a big brothel here in the middle of nowhere. I just wanna take you to that place down here, not get in a fight with some crazed Mad Max lunatic who chases people."

"Now that movie rules! Ever seen *Braveheart*? Mel Gibson is the man Zilla!"

"Some boy at school took me to his house one night to watch it. I passed out during the battle scenes."

"You're kidding? A big strong guy like you passing out in some movie? I don't believe it Zilla."

"I'm not strong," he said, watching the blackish image in the mirror and recalling the brutal scenes where men got their heads cleaved off, legs slashed to pieces, faces sliced wide open, eyeballs falling out, brains flying all over the place. He also recalled being with that boy who took him to his house that night, how he tried to make The Writer conform to his ways of life. Once he called him asking what size pants he wore. Sensing oncoming humiliation, The Writer asked him why he wanted to know.

"Because I'm gonna get you a pair of blue jeans to wear."

"Why?"

"Because I hate sweat pants, and I'm tired of seeing you wear them everyday at school."

"Why should I wear them? I like wearing sweats."

"I don't care Writer. I hate sweat pants and it just irks me to see you wearing them all the time. Everybody wears blue jeans at school but you. You're the only one who doesn't."

Hoping to make him hush, The Writer tried to think of an allusion he could use. He thought of one and tried it out.

"Blue jeans just bother me. I don't have to wear something like that. Did Jesus wear things like that when He was here on earth? He wore simple clothes that weren't fancy or expensive."

"Yea, but He dressed up like everybody else did around Him."

He hung up on him. The most popular guy in school had tried to upgrade the lifestyle of the least popular guy several times, from his taste in movies to the clothes he wore. His thing was "everybody likes this but you" or "everybody does this but you." It was as if you didn't do what the rest of society considered to be the "in" thing then you were a nefarious atrocity to your generation.

"What do we do?" The Writer asked, looking in the mirror. He could see that whoever was on the bike was conversing with whoever was on there with him, or even her for that matter. The current position of the sun made their appearance a ghastly image of blackness against the gorgeous backdrop of the day. It was as if death had come to call in the most hideously fearful way it knew of for The Writer.

"I'm ready for 'em," Brute said, devilishly wringing his hands together. "I can take them down single-handedly."

The Writer did not feel that this was the time for a lesson in human morals. He kept his hands on the wheel and his eyes on the mirror. It was slowly getting hotter as the sun made its way for the center of the sky. He knew that Judy knew what she was doing when she insisted he wear a white shirt today.

"Oh no!" he said, jerking upwards. "They're getting off the bike!"

Brute looked in his mirror and saw the mysterious riders hopping off and stealthily walking for the car, their arms hanging at their sides, like the alien in *The Day the Earth Stood Still*, only these creeps didn't look as if to bring a message of peace from beyond the stars. The Writer saw that the one who was driving the bike was walking up on his left towards his side of the car, and his female companion was walking up on his right to Brute's side.

Neither one would look back unless it was through the mirror.

Oh God what do we do? The Writer prayed. Brute wants to fight and what do I do? Pray that you turn these freaks around?

Then they stopped.

The Writer and Brute held their breath, watching.

About 15 feet back, the one who was driving had stopped dead in his tracks and kept leaning upwards and off to the sides, as if trying to get a better look at who was in the car. His female companion did the same, pointed at one of them, then stomped her foot on the gravel. The driver slowly backed up, then gestured for his mate to get back on. They both hurried back onto the bike, revved it up, and drove across the two-lane, across the grassy median of the four-lane, then shot onto the opposite two-lane in front of a truck that was blowing its horn. The female gave it the finger as both she and her partner sped back up the road out of sight.

Both boys let out a deep sigh of relief. Oh thank you God, The Writer thought over and over. A million times thank you.

"Darn. I thought I was gonna get a workout today," Brute said, now looking back behind to make sure the bike was clearly gone. After he did he looked at The Writer, who was staring dead ahead and had his hands frozen on the wheel, shaking like crazy.

"What's wrong man?" he asked. "They're gone now. Let's go."

He was taking long deep breaths as he sat there, watching the empty road that lay before them. Sweat was falling off his forehead and he had his hands quivering on the wheel, almost as if he were freezing in this 75-degree heat. He didn't look at Brute, who gently nudged and shook him.

"Just a minute," he said. "I'll be alright."

"Man were you that scared? Do you know who it was?"

"That's just it. I don't know who it was, or what they wanted.

They just looked so scary. Maybe they had the wrong car or something I don't know."

Brute scooted closer to him and waved a hand in front of his face. He never blinked. He then tickled him, and still got no results. When he wrapped an arm around him The Writer blinked and finally looked behind. He then turned back around, regained normal breathing, and stopped shaking when he saw that Brute had laid his other hand on his right one that was on the wheel. It had a firm hold and got tighter and tighter. With his other hand The Writer lifted Brute's off his and told him he was alright.

"I hope so because I'm hungry. Didn't eat breakfast."

The Writer remembered that he hadn't either. He had just took off for Rusty's house without any thought to eating. No wonder he was throwing up so much. He looked at his watch and saw that it was close to noon, almost lunchtime.

"We'll stop in Murphy, get something, and take it to the lake. We can have our picnic there."

"A lake? Picnic? Is that what you wanted to show me Zilla?! A dark body of water with picnic tables?" The Writer couldn't tell if Brute was being serious or just plain sarcastic.

"It's on the same road that goes to the place I'm taking you to. Is that okay?"

"Sure man. Whatever. You're driving. I'm just waiting to see what you're gonna show me." He scooted back to his side of the car, then looked back at The Writer. He was still looking behind him and had his hands on the wheel. Brute grabbed hold of his knee. He jolted and saw who had a hold of him.

"Listen Zilla," he said. "You don't have to be afraid of anything. I'm with you today. Nothing's gonna hurt you."

Those words made his heart leap and grow warm. He looked down at the hairy arm that had its hand grasping his knee. His eyes followed the limb up to the shoulder, and Brute, thinking The Writer was actually going to look at him eye-to-eye now, lucked out, because The Writer's eyes went only as far as his shoulder. He let his knee go and The Writer took off the brake. But before he put the thing back into 'drive', he rolled his eyes to his right. He could see Brute looking at him with a deep tenderness in his face. He had never seen it there before. Why did he look at him like that? Worry? Care? Wonder? Love? What was it? Why? Why did he want to spend his day with a rounded pudgy fellow who loves to write? He hoped to discover the answers. Today was his anniversary. He had left this day up to God so ANYTHING could happen to them.

He knew everything happened for a reason, and God always knows what He's doing when you put Him in control.

The Writer shifted back into 'drive' and they took off for the rest of their day together. Murphy was only a few more miles up the road, then the lake, and after that was the special place he was taking Brute to. What it was could not be found on just any map of North Carolina, but is a public tourist attraction that not many have seen or even heard of. The local people know about it and treasure it greatly. It was the place that had touched the life of The Writer and hoped in some way would do the same for Brute. So far it had touched the lives of his other friends.

Why do I feel this way? The Writer thought now as soon as he got back on the road. I feel so . . . so . . . strong, so spirited. I don't feel any effects from this morning, except being hungry. I've never felt this way in so long. Nothing it seems can hurt me. Is it Brute? No, can't be. My heart is going so strong right now. I feel a sensation come over me every few minutes. I can't describe it. No words can describe this feeling. It's like an intense, burning emotion, swelling from the depths of my soul. Whatever it is I love it. It started when Brute told me . . . ahh, that's what it is.

He had found the nature of his emotion. He looked to the sky and thought, has heaven ever known such happiness to exist in the heart of someone on this earth?

He then drove on to Murphy, with God watching over them from above at this moment, anxious to watch him waddle away . . . all over that special place he was taking Brute to see.

CHAPTER TWENTY-FOUR

"There's Taco Bell!" Brute hollered the moment The Writer drove around the curve that presented the outskirts of the small town of Murphy. "Let's eat there! I'm starved!"

"We're taking it to the lake for our picnic," The Writer said as he got into the turn-off lane to shoot across the two-lane that had traffic coming in the opposite direction. He got across and up into the parking lot. He looked at his watch and saw that it was almost twelve-thirty. The dining room didn't look too crowded so he decided to go in and order.

"What do you want?" he asked Brute, unhooking his pen and opening his left hand to write in the palm.

"What are you doing?" he asked, looking at how he had the pen positioned to write with.

"I'm gonna write what you want, and what I want, and then just let the cashier read my palm. They can't hear me when I speak my order anyway."

"A palm reading?" Brute said sarcastically. "Really? Listen to me O great and mighty writer of writers, you're gonna tell the cashier what we want without the aid of your all-powerful pen. C'mon, let's go. I'm hungry."

"But I . . . " The Writer protested but Brute had already leapt up out of the car and was up on the sidewalk, waiting for him to get out. He reluctantly got out with his palm bare. They went in and Brute shoved The Writer in front of him.

"Now I want ten soft tacos and a large coke. You got that Zilla?"

"How many?!?!" The Writer asked in a loud whisper. "You want . . . "

"Ten Zilla, ten, you know, five plus five, the number of fingers you have, the number of fist knuckles you're gonna get in that face of yours if you raise your pen to write anything."

The Writer closed his eyes in frustration at Brute. I know you're hungry, he thought, but don't let it get to your head like it did that morning in the kitchen when you cleaned out the fridge. "I will tell the girl what we want," he said. "But I'll do it in my own way."

It was his turn to order.

"Can I take your order sir?" she asked. The Writer did not look at her but kept his gaze on the green digital numbers on the register screen. Normally at this point he just laid down a piece of paper or held up his palm that had his order written out on it. But not today. Today it was all to be done verbally. He knew Brute was standing close enough to watch him.

"I . . . I . . . uh . . . want . . ."

"Yes?" the lady said, noticing his stammering.

"I . . . uh . . . the number ten . . . all . . . soft . . . and a . . . large . . . uh . . . um . . . sweet tea . . . with . . . uh . . . ice."

"Is that all for you sir?"

He cleared his throat. Very plainly, calmly, and in the tone of voice Brute taught him when they were singing, he placed Brute's order.

"And he wants ten soft tacos with a large coke."

The lady flashed her eyes at him as did a few other customers in line behind them. Brute just looked around and nodded to them.

"Is . . . uh . . . that gonna be all for you?" the lady asked, smirking. The Writer nodded. He gave her the money, handed him the receipt with their order number on it, and they waited at the front of their line for their food.

"Was that okay?" he whispered to Brute.

"Just dandy Zilla. Just dandy."

After they got their food in two huge bags they went back out to the car. Brute set his bag of tacos in the middle of the seat between them, hopped over the door, and flopped down. The Writer got in and had Brute hold the tray of drinks.

"Now on to the lake," The Writer said as he turned the key in the ignition.

"No I refuse," Brute said. He got a death glare from The Writer, although it was not eye to eye. "Just kidding Zilla. Let's go."

About twenty minutes later, The Writer made a sharp turn-off from the four-lane and was driving down a winding two-lane road with tall looming trees on either side. "The lake is on down here," he said. Brute just looked at all the pretty fields and houses that whizzed past them. It was like a miniature version of what he saw coming down on the four-lane in the middle of the open valleys a short while back. The Writer made another sharp turn-off from the road and was now on a dirt road. Off to his left was the huge river that eventually became the lake he was talking about. The road widened up into a huge parking lot and he parked at the top of the hill that looked down onto the lake and the picnic tables all over the shore, shaded by tall trees.

"Well, this is it," he said, getting out of the car. "Let's get that table next to the water fountain." He and Brute carried the food down the steps and went for the table. A few birds were on it picking up crumbs but flew away when Brute set his bag of tacos down. The Writer set his down and looked around. There was a family of three at a table clear across the shore, but other than that it was deserted and quiet. Exactly how I love it, he thought as he looked up at the trees which provided a natural roof with all the overhanging branches and limbs. A few rays of sunlight beamed through them, creating golden spotlights on the forest floor.

The Writer said grace even though Brute didn't hear him. He had already tore into his tacos and was wolfing them down in huge gulps. The Writer opened one of his, folded the paper back, and put a pack of mild sauce on his. He lifted it to his mouth and took a single bite, then noticed Brute's curious expression.

"Is that how you eat a taco?" he asked in bewilderment. "One bite at a time?" The Writer nodded and wiped his mouth with a napkin. "Oh no man. Not me. Here's how I do it. Huge bites. Open your mouth all the way and stick it in. Get all messy. Eating a taco doesn't have to look pretty. It should be fun, with lots of fire hot sauce."

The Writer took another bite then saw Brute come over and sit next to him. He had already downed three of his tacos. "No, like this Zilla." He took hold of his hand and pulled the taco forward in his hand. "Now take a big bite, with your mouth open all the way. No, wider, wider, wider Zilla! All the way! Godzilla has a big mouth. Does he eat with a napkin? No!" The Writer opened his mouth as wide as he could and took out a huge bite. Brute inspected it and nodded. He then reached for the hot sauce. The Writer held up his hand in refusal.

"No Zilla, just try it. You might like it."

"No Brute. Don't. It's too hot for me." But The Writer's protests did no good. Brute had already poured it all over the last bite of his taco. He then held it up to his mouth.

"Here eat it," he said. "Just try it for me. I wanna see how you like it."

"No Brute," he said, inching away from him. "You eat it."

"No Zilla, you're gonna eat it. Try something new for once in your life!"

The Writer's eyes flared up at him again.

"Don't give me that look Zilla. It may work on retarded freaks like that Rusty character but not on me. Here, try it!"

He set the taco down, grabbed The Writer by the collar of his shirt and yanked him towards him. The Writer tried to wriggle away but he just wound up lying down on the bench with his head in Brute's lap. He held his head in place with one hand and held the taco up over him with the other. The Writer saw it and tried to get away but was no match for Brute's strength. He held his mouth open and rammed the taco into it, then let him go. The Writer shot up and chewed two times. He could feel the sauce spill out in his mouth, burning, as if it were scalding his jaws wide open. His face tightened up and his eyes started overflowing. He leapt up and over to the water fountain. It was one of those that you had to step on the pedal to get the water to come up. He stepped on it and sure enough a single thick arc of clean cool water shot up into his face. He opened his mouth and let it douse the "flames" the sauce had produced. Brute sat at the table laughing. The Writer came back with his face dripping wet, but his mouth cooled out.

After they had finished they went on to that special place. The Writer told Brute it was just a few minutes away now. They passed more walls of trees on both sides of the road which had a lot of curves and turns. The road came to a split at the base of a mountain and he took the left turn. The road now evened out to be straight with one curve every few minutes. They were coming to a clearing.

"Okay here it is!" The Writer said as he started braking. Brute leaned up in his seat and watched it come closer into view. One final curve and there it was.

A turn-off spot went under a huge concrete archway painted white with the name of the park in huge letters reading *The Fields of Light*. They went under it and Brute beheld an amazing sight on his right.

A whole mountainside had The Ten Commandments on it in huge white concrete letters on the grass, with plastic figures of goats all around it. The image itself was made to look as if it were written on slabs of stone, just as Moses had it when God wrote them on Mount Sinai. There was a white border on all sides of the display, in the shape of tablets. Up the middle between the commandments was a flight of steps that went up to the top of the mountain to a huge 25 foot high Bible that had a verse from the book of Matthew painted onto an open page of it. People were going up inside it to the top to look off from it. Others were steadily making their way up the steps, of which there were over 300.

To his left Brute saw a small chapel on the other hillside, more steps that went up to the top of the hill hidden away under trees, a bandstand, and a baptismal pool. There was a gospel theater, a replica of the tomb where Jesus was laid after the crucifixion, a replica of Calvary in the eerie image of a skull, with three crosses perched on top of it. At the head of the valley between the mountains of this theme park was the gift shop and snack bar. Off to the side of it was a small pond with ducks. People were strewn all over the place, in patches, some off to themselves, others just taking in the beauty of it all.

The Writer parked the car at the foot of the Ten Commandment Mountain. They got out and The Writer saw Brute with his head turning every which way, trying to see what was where and how big it was.

"Where would you like to go first?" The Writer asked.

"I . . . I don't know," he said, still looking around. "There's so much here."

"You have to see this one thing." The Writer gestured for Brute to follow him. They went across the parking lot, across the main drive, and up to the other hillside. Brute saw the steps that curved up to the top of the mountain and went around a bunch of trees that hid its ending. They looked painful to walk up at this time of day, but there were a few people on it who didn't seem to have any problem coming down, but going up was a strain. The Writer was already making his way up. Off to both sides of the steps was a slab with scripture on it. Each slab had been dedicated by various church groups all over the country, from as far away as Idaho to as close as Tennessee. The Writer had read each one the last five times he'd come, but decided to let them go for now.

"What I want to show you is just halfway up here," he said. "It's off to the side and in the trees. If you believe in miracles it'll mean a lot more once you see it." They proceeded on up the steps. Every few minutes The Writer would stop to catch his breath and not let his asthma overcome him. Brute stopped next to him and wiped his forehead. It was slowly getting hotter and hotter.

"Zilla, how come you can't go out in the day at home but you can here?"

"This morning Mama forgot I had asthma," he said, going up

one step at a time. "If she had remembered she'd told me to stay off the steps here, but she's forgotten that I have asthma the last five times I've come here." He stepped off the steps and onto a small beaten path that reached straight into the woods. Brute followed and found himself face to face with something tall, looming, and black, a chilling contrast to the green that surrounded him.

It was the rotting remains of a huge tree trunk that was struck by lightening over 60 years earlier. Its branches reached out into the neighboring trees as if crying for a life line, but was totally ignored. The top of it had broken off years earlier, its insides were in the mid stages of deterioration, and the cutting slash the bolt of lightening made in it was still evident in its side. Its burned strip was torn into the side of the trunk, which now looked to be ripped apart thanks to the elements.

There was a sign next to it that gave details about the tree. In short it told about a man who was walking here on the mountain asking for a sign from God about what to do to spread His word. At that moment a bolt of lightening came down and gutted the side of the tree he was standing next to when he offered his prayer. The man realized the beauty of the place he was at and vowed to make it a place for all people to come visit to learn more about God and His son Jesus. Thus the theme park was born.

Brute got closer to the tree and raised his hand to touch the burned out portion of it. It was rough looking yet felt cool and smooth. He looked up at the other trees that towered over it and tried to picture the lightening bolt shooting down through the other branches to torch this one open. He found it hard to believe that he was standing on the spot where an act of God had been performed. It was a tingly feeling once he thought about it, about the divine being that so many people in his life had tried to beat into his skull had actually touched the very ground he was on. He looked back at The Writer who was staring at the tree, overwhelmed by its story as usual.

"You . . . you mean . . . God touched this tree . . . with lightening?" he asked. The Writer nodded.

"Do you believe in God?" The Writer asked. Brute slowly came away from the tree and stood next to him, still looking at it.

"I . . . uh . . . I'd always heard of Him," he said, still amazed by what he was seeing. "But I never really thought much of Him . . . until . . ."

". . . now?" The Writer said, finishing his thought for him. Brute turned to him and slowly nodded. This tree was proof that there was a divine being that possessed all knowledge of all things. This was also the only spot in the whole park that The Writer greatly emphasized to Brute. Following this they went up the hill to the prayer spot. The Writer showed Brute the place he found where nobody could see you pray, which was behind the slab that stood over the spot. It had a set of steps up into the back of it and you could sit on the floor and nobody could see you unless they walked up around it, which some rarely did.

There was a recreation of the tomb where Jesus was laid after the crucifixion, a replica of Calvary with three crosses on top of the rocky structure, a baptismal pool, and a small chapel on one of the hillsides. There wasn't much one could do with these exhibits but look at them and absorb the significance of each one. Each one had its own series of slabs telling what church donated it to the park, what the exhibit signified, and where you could find the story behind it in the Bible.

The Writer and Brute browsed around in the gift shop for a few minutes. Brute's eye was caught by one of those souvenir penny machines that pressed out an image of the park on a flattened penny. The Writer took two shiny ones out of his bag, slipped them in the slot with fifty cents, and watched the machine press the image on the penny. The shinier the penny the better it looked. He gave one to Brute and kept the other one. After that they went into the snack shop adjacent to the gift shop, got a drink, and went out onto the patio to sit.

"What do you think?" The Writer asked, drinking his sweetened iced tea.

"Cool," he said, tossing ice cubes up in the air and catching them in his mouth. "I never knew such a place existed."

"Not many know about it. It's hidden away here in the mountains. There also aren't that many who care to see a place as pretty as this."

After they drank their drinks they headed back to the car. Brute asked if they could drive up to the top of Ten Commandment Mountain.

"You mean you don't wanna walk up there?" The Writer asked. "It's only 350 steps or so up to the top."

"In this 85 degree heat!" Brute yelled. "Zilla, I would like to get up there without becoming a baked tater on a grassy hillside. Just drive up there."

The Writer turned the car around and headed up the shaded mountain road that went up to the top of the mountain exhibit. Once up there he drove past it without a care in the world.

"Uh excuse me Zilla, but I do believe you passed that thing we were gonna look at."

"I want to show you the world's biggest cross up here first," he said, winding around a bumpy road. He came to a small clearing and up on the sloping rise was a series of flag poles with a flag of every country in the world. The Writer parked the car in the small gravel area next to some benches and they walked up to it. Brute stood still and asked where the thing was. The Writer explained that he was standing in it, and that the best way to see the cross was from an airplane.

"And where would I get an airplane Mr. Writer? Just walk into town and ask the first guy I stumble into?"

"I was just making a point Brute," he said.

"I know Zilla. Just kidding. You don't kid very well do you? Why is that?"

The Writer looked away at the far off mountains, covered in a misty blue haze. "I . . . uh . . . never could take a joke. High school kids can be cruel, even teachers."

"How?"

"I did the school newspaper and wrote about what went on at the high school for the newspaper in town. I was told of an upcoming holiday for which students didn't have to come to school. I put it in my article and I didn't go to school that day. When I went back the next day, I was fussed and cussed at by my homeroom teacher, who yelled that because I skipped the day before, he had to assign work for the class. When I was there I told them what I needed done for the paper, and they did it, some of the time. Other times I was stuck writing their articles for them and they took all the credit and hype. But anyway, the class and the teacher told me it was just a joke and they wanted to see if I'd fall for it, which I did. I lost a whole day of school, missed homework assignments, and got behind in other things. Those who believed me when I wrote it also skipped that day. Joey, Annie, Jackie, Lana, Dionne, Elaine, Blade, and Nate all skipped, and all of them were mocked with me for falling for it. We were asked how stupid could we get in our lives, do we just believe anything we see or hear, and if we all had some sort of mental retardation. Mama threatened to go down to the school and get after my teacher for what he did, but I told her not to and to just let it go."

Brute looked at him with deep apprehension in his face. He wondered if it was true, but remembered that The Writer had not told him anything that was a lie, so this had to be just as true as he was.

"You didn't fight back?"

"Nope. I never did fight back."

"Why?"

"Afraid. I knew I'd get in trouble if I hit someone for any reason, either by an adult or God would in some way create a punishment for me to endure."

"So basically you let people push you around?"

He nodded. Yes, it was true. It was no good hiding it. For years he had let other people walk all over him, use him, take advantage of him and his thoughtfulness. There was the time this one boy, saying he was a friend to The Writer when he was anything but, told him his birthday was the next day so The Writer gave him a spare copy he had of the movie *Forrest Gump* along with a card and a package of chewing gum. Later he learned that the boy was just using him to see how far he'd go with his trait of giving to others. His birthday wasn't for months yet.

And there was the time some boy came to The Writer asking him to help him write an essay in order to be eligible to go to some elite political school in the state's capital. The Writer told him to just write out what he wanted the essay to say and that he'd set it up for him to go by. Instead, he wound up writing a rough draft for the boy to follow, thinking he was going to rewrite it to fit his style. In fact that's what he told the boy to do before he even started work on it.

The Writer took the draft to the boy's house one day. The boy came out onto the porch, snatched it out of his hand, and disappeared back in the house. No thank you or any sign of appreciation. That was the last The Writer ever saw or heard of the boy until two weeks later when Mama called him into the kitchen to look at the front page of the local newspaper.

There was a full-color picture of the boy wearing a suit standing next to the region's congressman on the steps of the state capital building. The headline boasted that a local student was the recipient of a renewable $5000 scholarship to *any* university of his choice in the country because of an essay he wrote that dealt with social and community issues in America today. The boy was quoted as saying "I just wrote what I believed and felt. I expressed myself fully and just told what I think should be done about these problems in society today." There was even a quote from the governor, stating that he was proud of the way the boy "made his points direct and clear and that his use of English mechanics and expression of ideals reflects the type of student he wants all young people to become in order to succeed in the real world." The entire essay was even printed next to the article and The Writer clearly recognized it as his own. Every sentence and every word he used was there, and that boy took all the credit for it.

The Writer never said a word to anyone about it, for he feared that nobody would believe him. He just let it go, upset and horrified at how he had been taken advantage of. He never heard from the boy again, and he didn't care if he ever did.

It was The Writer's idea that no matter how bad other people treated him in this life, anything he did to them would look wimpy compared to what God had in store for them one day, so he let Him handle it all in His own way.

"You need to learn to fight," Brute said, wandering around, looking up at all the flags blowing and flapping in the wind. "You may need to fight someone for your life one day, and being a gentle lamb will not save you." He then started back for the car. "C'mon Zilla," he said, "let's go to that lookout point you passed coming up here."

And with that The Writer waddled away . . . back to the car to show Brute one final exhibit.

CHAPTER TWENTY-FIVE

The Writer drove back down the road to the Bible that stood on top of Ten Commandment Mountain. They got out and Brute hurried up inside to get to the top of it. The Writer lagged behind, being careful not to fall down the steep flight of stairs that were inside the huge structure.

"They need to clean out this place," he said as he came to the top. "There's cans and food wrappers all over those steps." He saw Brute standing at the front of the top looking off into the distance. Far below was everything they had just walked around and seen. The bushes that were neatly trimmed near the gift shop was actually shaped into a phrase that said *Jesus Died For Our Sins.* You could see the mountains as far away as those in Tennessee, with the blue haze gently shrouded all over them. The prayer spot was hidden away under the trees on the other mountain as was the tree. Down below was the car, all to itself at the base of the mountain. Other vehicles were parked near the gift shop or next to the road that came up Ten Commandment Mountain.

"Where does that road go to?" Brute asked, pointing to one that snaked its way up the hill behind the gift shop.

"I don't know," The Writer said.

"You don't know?! Man, you're The Writer! You're supposed to know all! Writers are supposed to be geniuses! And you know a lot, but you can't tell me where that road goes to!"

"I'm not that smart Brute," he said, looking down at the steps that came up the mountain from the parking lot. "I'm just a writer."

"Just a writer? Man, I don't think so. You can bowl a killer game."

"Hey I'm not the one who caused us to win. It was you."

"But who's the captain of the team?"

The Writer didn't answer, but instead asked him if he was ready to head back home.

"No I am not ready to go back home. I am waiting for you to tell me who the captain of the bowling team is."

The Writer turned away and looked up at the flag that was waving overhead. It was the state flag of North Carolina. It was swooping so low he could almost catch the end of it. He raised his hand for it but another hand swiped it out of his reach. It belonged to Brute who was trying to get in his face.

"Answer me Writer! Who's the captain of the bowling team that won? Huh? Who is it? Tell me!"

The Writer backed away and went up to the front of the overlook. "Look at those mountains. Aren't they pretty?"

"Why are you so modest man?" Brute asked impatiently. "Can't even tell me who the captain is? Well, I'll ask you this way, who took me home with him that night from off the road? Who carried me? Who fed me from the fridge? Who made me behave with their big Godzilla foot? Who taught me how to bowl? Who did I dream about the other night when I was in your room? I dreamt I was in some bizarre world that was so cool I didn't want to leave. I dreamed that I saw you do all these amazing things like paint with words, become a monster tiger, swim in the sky, fly on an eagle's back under an ocean, and we were in some ugly place full of smoke and chewed tobacco. Then I dreamt that I was shaking you and you were puking this black gunk all over the place. Who brought me here today to this awesome place, a place I've never seen before? Who huh? WHO?"

The Writer had closed his eyes from the first question and never heard a single word after that from Brute. He had closed his mind on the voice that he was hearing and imagined himself seven years ago at the church building in the baptistry, coming out of the water, and seeing the warm and careworn face of his preacher.

The image blacked out when he felt something grab his shoulder.

"WHO ZILLA? WHO DID ALL THAT?"

"All what?"

"Everything I was just shooting off about! Who has been so good to me that they bring me to this cool place in the mountains?!"

I can't say 'me', he thought. I'd be boasting, bragging, sounding just like that boy in school who could not shut up about going to some nationally famous university somewhere in the south. Please don't build me up into something I'm not, Brute. Nobody is as good as all that. Only Jesus can be that good, even better, the best of us all. I'm a pathetic wretch compared to Him.

"Let's go," he said, going back down the steps. Brute took off after him. As soon as The Writer set foot on the solid foundation of the exhibit Brute grabbed him by the shoulders and slung him up against the wall.

"Look Zilla, just tell me who did all that for me and we can go. Just say it and I'll turn you loose."

"Okay, It was all me! Me! Me! Me! ME! Now can we go?"

"If you like."

As soon as The Writer headed out of the main entrance, he asked Brute what he thought of the place.

"It was cool Zilla. I liked it."

"You sure?"

"Yes Zilla. You think I'm lying to you? You think everyone lies to you?"

"So many have."

"No, you mean Rusty has always lied to you. Yes, I have told some wild fibs to all the girls I get but I have not lied to you Zilla. I swear I haven't. I'm afraid to. You've given me nothing to lie about."

Is that a lie I wonder, he thought as he got back on the two lane that brought them here. I am so paranoid it's not even funny. He rounded the same curves he took to get here and was making his way back for the four-lane. The clock on the dashboard read that it was now just past one-thirty. They'd be back home by three or so if nothing happened. No doubt his mother and Judy were still in Asheville cleaning out all the department stores. They'd probably have the living room full of goodies that made them squeal when they saw it on the display stand, and then see what a dud it really was compared to the decor of their houses. But until then he and Brute would have the whole place to themselves. Maybe we can watch a movie or something, he thought. I could order a pizza and have it delivered, then we could . . .

"Zilla look!"

The Writer slammed on his brakes and the car came to a screeching halt in the middle of the road. He looked around to see what Brute had hollered about.

"Did I scare you?"

The Writer's eyes flared up like never before. He whirled his head around towards him and was huffing and puffing, his shoulders and chest heaving up and down in rhythm. His eyes were wide with the whites of them as bright as eggshells. His hands looked as if they were about to choke the steering wheel and the veins in his wrists had made their way to the surface of his skin.

"Getting mad Zilla?" Brute asked. "I've never seen you get mad. You mad enough to hit me? C'mon, give me your best shot. I can take it. I'm strong like you. I can handle anything. Hit me. Slam me the way Rusty slammed you this morning with what he did. Make me cry."

The Writer swung his head back to look at the road. Luckily nobody was coming either way. It was just them out on the road in the middle of a field next to a deserted fruit stand. If a car had been in either lane when Brute pulled his little stunt then Judy would have a hissy fit when she saw her car coming home all banged and beat up. She'd scream at Mama, get her taloned fingered hands on The Writer, then squall over the car. Then she'd forbid Joey to ever have anything else to do with him or Mama.

As he lifted his right hand to readjust the rearview mirror Brute's hand came to rest on it. It wrapped itself all over it and peeled it off the wheel.

"Make a fist Zilla," he said. The Writer did, and Brute compared it to his. They were about the same size. "We can do something with this," he said, rubbing his fingers all over it.

"Brute, don't ever pull that stunt on me . . ."

"You know Zilla, I bet that if you ever got mad enough you'd fight anybody wouldn't you? You'd be a lean mean beast of a fighting machine, able to tear up anyone who got in your way. I bet nobody would dare mess with you once they got a snoot full of this." He was pointing to his fist.

"I don't fight," he said. "It's not . . ."

"Whatever Zilla. I'm gonna show you how to fight, and you're gonna like it too. Now let's go on wherever it is we're going to next."

"We're just going home."

"Uh, like a rat's behind we are! Zilla, look at the clock. Does it not read in plain English one-thirty two?"

He nodded.

"Okay. That means we have time to do more stuff. What else is around here besides that lake? Any stores? Joints? Hangouts? What?"

"I don't know. We gotta get home. I told Mama we'd be back . . ." Brute got up close to his face and had the burning urge to grab him by the throat and pull him closer. Instead he grabbed a vengeful hold of his head and craned it towards him, but he could not crane the eyeballs to meet his.

"I asked you what else was down here Zilla, not if you were ready to go home. Look around you, broad daylight, and you wanting to go home so soon. Why? What's so important that you have to get back home to?"

The Writer jerked his head away from Brute's hold. His cap slid down over his eyes and as he readjusted it, he looked up in the rearview mirror and saw a car coming up behind them in the distance. He quickly turned off and dove into the cracked parking lot of the fruit stand, which was really a mess of graying boards rotting apart and fencing that was aged with rusting antiquity. The tables and displays that once held fresh colorful batches of fruit were now falling apart.

A sign of the times passing away with this generation, The Writer thought as he looked at it.

"Did you not like that place Brute?" he asked, looking down the road.

"Yes I loved it. Why? Did you think I'd say it was the most retarded place on earth where Jesus freaks hang out? Well, did ya?"

"I just asked."

"Well, I was just asking you if there were other places down here we can go to, but nooooooo, you're in too big a hurry to get back home, and you won't tell me why. Fine Zilla, be that way. I thought we were friends, buddies, old pals. I thought I could tell you anything, no matter how foolish it sounded. But since you're gonna be stuck up all of a sudden and won't talk to me then I'm getting out."

Brute meant it. He leapt up out of the car and started walking away. He never once looked back at The Writer. Oh God now what have I done, he thought. Why can't I just let things run smoothly? Please bring him back to me God, please bring him back. No wait, I'll go get him. He then got out of the car and started walking after him, fast. I just know nobody else will feed him or give him a place to rest his head at night . . . oh golly this isn't the time to start thinking lyrical about things!

"And if those guys on the motorcycle ever catch up to you, you're on your own Zilla," he hollered over his shoulder, unaware that The Writer was after him. "I ain't gonna be there to protect you. They catch you, good luck. I'll be long gone."

He looked down and saw his shadow on the fading pavement followed by another shadow that was much bigger than his. He knew who was after him. The billowing coattail was a dead give-away as was the cap on the head. When he stopped the shadow stopped. He waved in the air. It waved. He held out his arms and walked like a monster. The shadow did the same thing. He backed up. The shadow backed up further behind him. He turned around.

The shadow didn't.

He was just a few feet away from The Writer.

"Aha, can't live without me can ya?" Brute said. "Where we going, and if you say home, you're gonna get a snout full of these knuckles up your nose."

The Writer carefully studied the tightened fist that was in his face, again. Oh boy, this guy knows how to get a point across, he thought. Why can't I ever do that? Just give him what he wants Writer, he thought. Of course you can't give him *everything* he wants . . .

"Well . . . uh . . . there's a little flea market up on the four lane next to . . ."

"Let's go." Brute went back and jumped into the car. The Writer got back in and they took off up the road.

The flea market was not very crowded on this Saturday, but was easy to get around in. It was cool and shady and abuzz with potential buyers and sellers negotiating prices. One lady was trying to convince a dealer to let her have a hooked rug for twenty dollars. Another lady had a screaming baby in one arm and bags of items in her other. One man sold stained glass pictures and frames, another had a massive collection of worn out paperbacks. People came by, looked, and went on their way. Some of the women picked up the romance novels, tossed out a few dollars, and went to the next seller.

The Writer picked up a dilapidated copy of the novel *To Kill a Mockingbird*. Its cover was torn in the front and looked as if it had been tossed into the washing machine. Its pages were bright yellow and the text was smudged. He could still see enough of Harper Lee's beautiful words to envision for himself how he saw Jem, Jean Louise, Dill, Atticus, and of course, Boo Radley.

"You like that book?" Brute asked coming up next to him. "Had to read it in school. Got no further than the part where some kid finds cooties in their hair. I was told there was a rape in it but I could never find it, so I never finished it."

The Writer put it down and looked at the other books. Most of them were in the same condition as this one was, old and ragged and falling apart. The seller had stuck tiny white stickers on each book with her price written in pencil. *To Kill a Mockingbird* could be bought for fifty cents, *Gone With the Wind* for thirty-five, the Hardy Boys series for a quarter each, several of John Steinbeck's great works were there for seventy-five cents, and there was a copy of the World Almanac from 1964 for forty cents. He wondered if the authors ever dreamed that one day their works would become second-hand goods being cheaply sold at some roadside flea market. One of the books he saw was once a Nobel Prize winner for Literature, sold here for a measly thirty-five cents.

He closed his eyes and pictured his books on the table being sold tattered and abused for just a few coins. He found a marked up copy of *The Scarlet Dawn* lying on top of a heap of books. Another one he wrote called *A Wretch Like Me* had its golden orange embossment worn down and its pages falling out. When he found half of his novel called *The Seventh Day* on the ground under the table he opened his eyes. It was a grim outlook for his future, that one day people may indeed flock to the stores to get his books, if they were good of course, read them, and when they were finished, toss them aside.

When he saw a Bible selling for a quarter he turned away. It was a sad scene for him, that every writer whose works were here on this table in the blazing heat struggled through years of sweat and blood just to get their words published, only to wind up here.

"Know what Zilla," Brute said. "Someday, people will come by here and ask for your books."

"Maybe," he said quietly. "I don't know."

"At least the poor people can buy them here. Imagine, an old lady with nothing but a quarter to her name and finding her favorite book here after years of searching for it. The price on the book—twenty-five cents. She can have it for almost nothing." Brute then felt around in his shorts pockets and pulled out a dirty quarter that was so dark you could barely see George Washington's head. He waved it around in The Writer's face. "See Zilla, that's all I have on me. A quarter to my name. I can buy this book here." He picked one up and proudly read off the fading title.

Breast-feeding Made Easy.

He quickly shoved it back down into the slot where he found
it and sheepishly looked all around him. A few people at the next
display sniggered, a woman across the walkway made a face, and a
man next to his truck which had his goods for sale in the back of it
shook his head at Brute. The Writer looked off into space. I do not
know this guy, he thought. But I don't wanna lie.

"Look, if you guys aren't gonna buy anything then please move
on," the saleslady behind the table said. "Other people wanna
look too you know."

"Just a minute lady," Brute said, leaning into her face. "Do
you know who you're talking to here?" He pointed to The Writer.

"No I don't and I don't care. Just move it!"

"He is not an 'it' for your information. He just happens to be
The Writer, and he can write anything that will blow your mind
away, and he won't have much to blow away in your case." He
picked up one of the cheap Bibles that The Writer was looking at,
slapped it down near her hand and walked off. The Writer had
already wandered a few feet away to avoid embarrassment.

"You didn't need to do that Brute," he said when he caught
up to him. "We weren't buying anything."

"But she was rude to you Zilla," Brute said. "She didn't have
to get snotty about it. Do you always let other people talk to you
that way? Wait, don't tell me. You do."

"I have my own way of handling it," he said, stopping at another display that had second-hand ornaments and ceramic sculp-
tures. He picked one up and saw that it was chipped in the corner.
He then went on inside the building and found a stunning array
of glass and ceramic designs shimmering before him. There were
so many it was hard to decide where to look first.

"Did I ever tell you about this really weird but cool dream I
had the other day Zilla?" Brute said, examining a sculpture of an
eagle. "You were in it. Both of us were. I saw you standing on some
mountaintop screaming and crying into the smoke that was all
around you. But before that you had told me something about
how the people in 'the real life' who were mean to you suffer for it

in 'your world' through these characters you say you create with your pen."

The Writer held his gaze at the colored glass sculpture of a dragon on the shelf in front of him as Brute recalled details of his dream to him. Yes, he remembered. He could recall the same events of going into his world and seeing all the amazing things he had written about, but never shared with others. It wasn't a dream for me Brute, he thought. It was real. I just guided you there by telling you about it as we dozed off. Nothing more.

A lady was standing next to them as Brute told him what he remembered seeing and all the things he did with his pen, the shooting of orange beams, the orange rain, the eagle in the water, swimming in the sky, the ride on the dolphin, and the other things that went on. She backed away from them and hurried out the entrance. "Those guys are talking gibberish!" she said to someone just outside. "Flying dolphins and eagles underwater!"

"Don't tell that to anybody else Brute," he said quietly. "They may not understand. People don't always appreciate what a writer thinks or sees. They think they're crazy."

"Really huh?"

"Yes really." The Writer turned and headed back out to the main walkway. As soon as he set foot on the cemented walk he heard giggling behind him. He stopped in his tracks and slowly turned around. He could hear remarks about his size, and his coat around his waist. Someone cracked about his being so big he needed a garage door to get into a house. The woman who was inside next to them was saying over and over, "That's him. That's the crazy one!"

Deja vu, he thought. High school jokes galore once again. Maybe if I look at them they'll shut up.

He turned around and saw that some boy was sneaking up behind him on his hands and knees. The boy saw his big feet whirl around in his face and quickly fell back onto his rear, then went backwards like a crab away from him. The Writer clutched his pen and focused his eyes on the small group of about four people who had assembled to look at him via the woman's ravings. When they saw his face and the dead glare in his eyes the smiles on their faces melted away. One man blinked so many times his eyes spilled over and one woman turned and walked away.

The Writer took one step forward. He unhooked his pen and before he could ask the crowd what they wanted, they quickly disbanded in all directions. He then put it back in its cap and turned around to see Brute behind him, clapping.

"Fear this, The Writer!" he said, pointing at him. One woman who was standing nearby heard Brute, looked at who he was pointing to, and hurried up to him with her hands grasping each other at her chest. She was smiling and full of excitement.

"Excuse me sir, but aren't you the one who wrote the weekly high school column for a newspaper this past year?"

He nodded.

"Ah! I thought you were! My son goes to the same high school as you did. I swear sir, he would never tell me a thing that went on there until I read your weekly column, especially about report card time. He had been hiding them from me until I showed him your article. I think you did a terrific job writing for the paper. I hate to see you leave. Where you going to school at?"

His mind became a total blank. Nowhere, he thought. Nobody wants me.

"I . . . uh . . . haven't decided yet," he said shyly. "I'm still trying to decide what to do."

"Well, I'll tell you what to do son, just keep writing. I wish I could do what you do. My son says you're a religious freak but I know better. I'd rather have religious freaks than all these wild-streaked kids running around here. I just wanted to say that I enjoyed your articles, and to say good luck to you."

He nodded to her and she walked past him with a big smile on her face. He turned and saw her grab the arm of the boy who was sneaking up behind him a bit earlier. She was leading him away to her car in the parking lot, fussing at him about how she saw what he was about to do to The Writer. He now recognized him as one of the sophomore kids from the high school. Her son, he thought. I never would've guessed.

Brute came back up to him and they walked down to one of the smaller booths. On the table The Writer spotted a blanket of many colors neatly folded in a warm beam of sunlight. He picked it up and saw that it was in near perfect condition. It looked, felt, and smelled perfect for a summer day. He had to have it. He'd figure out why later, but he pictured it as being the perfect accessory for the couch in the living room. Mama could use it in the winter when watching TV at night.

"How much?" he asked the lady who was sitting in a fold-up chair reading the latest John Grisham thriller. She looked up at him and eagerly got up, her book falling out of her lap onto the gravel under her chair.

"Oh my yes young man, this blanket is perfect for cold winter nights," she said upon looking at it. "It's five dollars."

The Writer opened his waist bag and pulled out his wallet. He handed her the money as she folded it back up and stuffed it in a blue Wal-Mart bag. She thanked him, gave him the bag, and wished him a nice afternoon. He nodded back and went to find Brute. He was standing in front of a small concession stand that wasn't doing much business this time of day.

"What did you buy?" he asked, peering into the bag. "A blanket! Cool! We can have a picnic now! I want three cheeseburgers and two foot long hot dogs and a coke."

The Writer's eyes widened up at this. They had just ate about two hours or so ago. No way could he be this hungry again. Was it humanly possible?

"Brute, you just ate."

"Uh yeah Zilla, like two hours ago. We walked all over that place and inside that Bible and we've walked here and now I'm hungry again. Feed me. Aren't you hungry too?"

"Oh okay, I guess I could use a little snack." He went up to the window, placed their order, and was given a ticket by the cashier with their order number on it. He and Brute sat down at one of the nearby tables until their number was called.

"Where to now Zilla?"

The Writer looked up at the blue sky. Am I having fun Lord? Yes, I am. I don't want it to end. I've never felt this happy in my life with anyone, besides my other friends, but Brute, Lord, he's so different from the rest. What is it about him that is? I can't show I'm happy. I want to, but how? I don't know how. I leave the rest of this day in your hands God, this day, this anniversary of the day I was baptized. Only you know what else can happen to us before this day passes away . . .

"There's a little road up ahead that goes to another lake. We may go there," The Writer said.

"Cool. Is it quiet?"

He nodded. "And it's bigger," he added.

"Cool. Like I say, bigger is better." Brute then looked up and down The Writer's build and grabbed hold of his upper arm. "And you, Zilla, are my biggest friend ever, next to Godzilla of course. That's why I call you that. You're both big and strong. You can take out anybody. How'd you get so big?"

"Mama's a great cook," he said. "But I'm not that strong. Don't make me feel like I am."

"I can't lie to you Zilla," he said, lying his head down on his folded arms on the table, looking at him. "Anybody who can carry me to their house . . ."

"Number seventy-seven!"

The Writer looked at his ticket stub and saw that it was their order. He got up to get their food and when he opened his wallet to pay for it, he saw that he just had enough for the food and the gas to fill Judy's car. We *will* have to go home from the lake, he thought. We can't do anymore today.

He got their food in two huge bags and carried the cokes in one arm. He motioned to Brute that he was ready to go. He got up from the table, grabbed the bag with the blanket in it, and followed The Writer a few feet behind him, watching his Godzilla walk.

He then waddled away . . . towards the car, ready to go for their second picnic today.

CHAPTER TWENTY-SIX

Once at the lake Brute saw that it was much bigger than the one they were at earlier. Here, there were sailboats and skiers out in the water. There was a huge island out in the middle and near the spot where The Writer parked the car, he could see the dam that held all this water.

"Now this is a lake Zilla," he said. "Looks like the one I saw in my dream."

Only Godzilla doesn't live in this lake, The Writer thought as he carried the bags of food and the blanket to a shady spot under a tree. He spread the blanket out and sorted out the food. He built a small mountain out of Brute's food and put it at his end of the blanket along with the coke. He just ordered a hot dog and a coke. He was still full from their trip to Taco Bell.

This time Brute didn't choke food down The Writer's throat. He ate everything he ordered and left nothing to spare or waste.

"Are you gonna eat the rest of that hot dog?" he asked The Writer, who immediately rammed the last bite into his mouth, chewed, and swallowed it. He then nodded.

"Let's walk," Brute said, leaping up onto his feet. "I wanna see where that path goes to." He was pointing to the gravel walkway that bordered the edge of the lake and had wooden fencing on the side facing the lake. The Writer dreaded the thought of getting up after eating. But he knew that if he laid down or kept absolutely still, he'd drift off to sleep for hours while his food digested. If he slept now it would be dark when he woke up, and he knew he'd better dress up his excuse as best he could for his mother if he got home late. He forced himself up on his feet and stumbled down to where Brute was standing on the path.

"Shouldn't I put the stuff in the car . . . ?" The Writer asked, but Brute told him to just leave it and that nobody should bother it. Taking his word for it he went with him down the path. They stopped at a small peninsula that stretched out into the water. A portion of the path also cut down to it, so The Writer and Brute walked to the very tip of it. There was a tree and a bench under it facing out to the water.

"You love the quiet stuff don't you Zilla?" Brute asked as they came to the bench. "You're not a loud person are you?"

He shook his head as he went to the very edge where the water lapped up on the shore. My, how long did it take you to figure that out, he thought. He looked down at the water and saw his wavy reflection in the clear water. Under the surface he saw small fishes swimming to and fro, waiting for someone to feed them. He saw something shiny on his reflection shimmer in the sunlight. It came from his chest area. He looked closer and saw that it was the lapel pin of a gold eagle that Joey had given him this past Christmas. The eagle was carrying a small banner in its taloned feet. On the banner was a verse number from the Book of Isaiah that talked about those who hoped in the Lord would be strong and not grow weary and would be like soaring on wings of eagles. He had found it on his desk at the beginning of the only class he and Joey had together.

"Want me to open it now?" he asked Joey.

"Yeah. Look at it."

The Writer carefully peeled off the red wrapping paper that had a green bow on it. He set it off and opened the little white box. On a black plastic panel on top of a small pile of cotton balls was the lapel pin shining at him. He took it out and looked at it closer.

"Is that okay?" Joey asked.

The Writer looked at it more and more and felt his heart become warm and frail. Why, he thought. I don't deserve this. I don't know what to think. This has never happened to me before. He held it in his hand for the longest time, looking at it, and thinking about the person who gave it to him, who was standing just a few feet away next to his own desk.

"Do you like it?" he asked in his unique tone of voice. The Writer looked up towards him and nodded. He put it on right then and there, so deeply touched by the thought behind it and the faithful symbolism behind the present.

That night he called Joey to thank him for it, and asked him why he got it for him.

"You're a good friend to me," he said simply.

He had worn it on his shirts everyday since he got it. Every time he looked at it he was reminded of Joey and his kindness.

Kindness that is genuine or acted, he wondered. It's so easy to spend two dollars on something for someone just to make them think . . . stop it Writer! Stop this right now! Don't think that about Joey! You know he's your true friend and that he's not putting on a big act! Stop it! Stop it! STOP IT!

"Looking at yourself huh?" Brute said, coming up next to him. He looked down and saw his reflection next to The Writer's. "I look fat," he said. "My belly sticks out all over, like the blob. No girl would want me looking like that. How 'bout you Zilla? Got a girl anywhere?"

He immediately shook his head and started walking back up to the main path. Brute followed after him.

"Aw come on now, you must. I bet all the girls go nuts over you."

Again he shook his head furiously.

"Do you want a girl?"

He shook his head even harder.

"Why?"

"Because . . . I don't . . . don't . . . want . . . one. That's all."

"So you've never had a girlfriend then have you?"

He shook his head again.

"Then you need lessons my friend, on how to get a girl. No girl wants a guy who writes down everything and won't talk. Here let me show you Zilla." He had The Writer sit down on the far end of the bench away from the tree. Brute got up and went to the other side of the tree where The Writer couldn't see all of him. He stuck his head around it and gave The Writer instructions. "Now listen Zilla. Pretend I'm a woman. Just watch what I do and respond to me as if I really were a woman. Here we go."

This should be fun, he thought as he waited for Brute to go into action. Odd but fun.

"Okay now. The first thing you do, Zilla, is whistle. Now, when I come up to this side of the tree, whistle loud at me. Make me feel pretty."

"But I can't whistle," he said.

"WHAT?!"

"I never could. I just can't."

Brute came and sat on the bench next to him. "What do you mean you can't whistle?! Just do this." He put his middle and index fingers in both ends of his mouth and let out the loudest piecing whistle The Writer had ever heard. He covered his ears and squeezed his eyes shut.

"Now you try it Zilla. Just take those two fingers and put them in your mouth."

The Writer reluctantly did as he was told. He grabbed hold of Brute's fingers and was about to stick them in his mouth.

"Not my fingers Zilla! Yours!"

The Writer put his in and looked towards Brute.

"Now breathe in hard. Make sure you're not drooling or spitting."

The Writer exhaled all the air he could and took in a deep breath through his mouth. He got nothing but dry air in his lungs. Brute told him to try again and nothing happened.

"Here, like this." Brute scooted close to him, yanked his fingers out of his mouth, and instead jammed his inside it. He had him close his lips as best he could. "Now don't bite me with those big monster teeth. Blow in hard." The Writer tried it again and nothing happened. Brute adjusted his fingers and had him try once more. The Writer then emitted the loudest squeal Brute had ever heard in his life. His face tightened up and he yanked his fingers out of The Writer's mouth. The Writer sat still looking at the jarred expression on Brute's face.

"Is that okay?" he asked.

"Just dandy Zilla, just dandy." He was holding his hands over his ears and rolling his eyes around. "If something ever happens to you, they can easily find you with that siren of yours. Now, for lesson number two. Professor Brute's crash course in courting a woman." He got up off the bench and went back behind the tree.

This is so ridiculous, The Writer thought. I can't imagine anything sillier than this, except maybe if this was Blade trying to teach me all this stuff. He'd be a blast to see teaching. He'd use a sword as a pointer.

"Now look Zilla, when I come up to this tree, give me a whistle so I'll know I'm being noticed. After that, I'll come over to you, sit next to you, and start talking like a woman."

"Brute this is scary," The Writer said. "I can't . . ."

"Sure you can Zilla. You need to try new things in life. Someday you're gonna meet a woman and not know how to act unless I show ya."

"I don't need any woman Brute."

"Whatever Zilla. Just watch and learn." He went back about five feet from the tree and told The Writer to whistle at him. Reluctantly he did, not quite as loud as before.

Then Brute went into his act. He heard the whistle and looked all around. Blinking his eyes at The Writer, he put on a heavy strut and went to the other side of the tree, peeping around it at The Writer, who just sat and watched, raising one eyebrow in sheer wonder and embarrassment. What if someone saw what we were doing, he wondered. They'd have the loony wagon after us in no time. Maybe if I just play along with this then it'll be over a lot faster and he'll stop pestering me with his lessons of life.

Brute flashed quick glances up to the path and clear across the lake. He then came out from behind the tree on his tip toes, his hands on his hips, swinging them back and forth as far as he could.

An insult to bimbos all over the country, The Writer thought as he watched Brute.

Brute came and sat down at the other end of the bench. He made like he was fixing his hair in the back and patted the sweat off his neck. He then tried to cross his legs but could never remain sitting upright. He placed both hands on one knee and looked all around him shyly, wiggling his rear end. The Writer could do nothing but sit and watch, curious to see just what he'd do next. Brute turned and acted as if he'd just seen The Writer sitting there for the first time. His eyes widened up and he let out a deep squeal of excitement at the sight of seeing 'a man' sitting next to him. He looked behind him and then leaned all the way over to The Writer.

"HI!!!" It was in the loudest and shrillest feminist tone The Writer had ever heard in his life. Not to mention the most humiliating.

Then the unexpected happened.

"WAH HA HA HA HA HA HA HAAAAAAAHHHHH!!!!!!!!!"

Brute leaned back and resumed normalcy when he saw what The Writer was doing. It was something he had never seen or heard him do before until now. He didn't know what to do or how to react. This was an event as rare as seeing Halley's Comet soar across the night sky, or seeing some blimp full of helium exploding over a city. All one could do was watch in helpless wonder.

Brute got down in front of The Writer for a closer look at what was happening. He still couldn't believe what he'd made him do.

He was laughing.

His face was turning red, tears were swelling in his eyes, and he could not keep his face covered. His hysterical laughter soon began to sound like strong convulsions. He was holding his head back, unable to keep his squeals and noisy ravings inside. He tried pointing at Brute but it did no good. He needed both hands to keep his face covered.

"I can't believe it," Brute said to himself. "He's laughing, isn't he? I've never seen him laugh. I've never seen ANYONE laugh like this before. Zilla, are you laughing? Oh my gosh are you really laughing?"

It got even louder and The Writer slumped down onto the bench, hiding his face in the inner elbow of his arm and slapping the seat of the bench with his other hand. He started letting out snorts and grunts like crazy. His whole upper body was quivering and shaking.

"I can't believe this!" Brute said, forgetting all about the lesson he was teaching. "I've achieved a miracle! I made The Writer laugh! He's laughing! Zilla, you're laughing. No, you're getting hysterical! C'mon! Keep laughing! This is so cool to watch!"

After a few minutes the laughter subsided and The Writer sat back up, rubbing his face from the tears that had run down all over it and belching out the final gasps of laughter that were still in his system. His face felt sore and beaten, as if it had been run through a meat grinder. His cheeks hurt when he tried to let them resume their natural position. His throat began to feel hoarse and his heart was at full throttle.

"Oh golly Brute," he finally said after calming himself. "That felt good. That was so funny!"

"What?"

"You silly! Trying to be a woman. That was funny!"

He then got up on his feet and stretched. Brute was still in awe at him.

"Don't you ever laugh Zilla?"

"I haven't laughed like that since . . . since . . . it's been a long time. I can't remember." He started walking back up to the main path and Brute followed. All signs that he had just pitched a laughing fit had suddenly vanished and the lost look of desolation and rejection quickly reclaimed possession of his face.

"Zilla, do you know what I was doing?"

"Trying to look like a drag queen?" he said.

"No. I was showing you how to get a girl to like you."

"Brute, I don't want a girl."

"Why not?"

"Because."

"Why? Tell me Zilla. Every girl wants a guy, and I bet you'll have them crawling all over you when they read what you write. Trust me man, a woman wants a guy who will talk to her and not be a scared little runt like you."

The Writer whirled around to him. You calling me scared?! he thought. I'm not scared of any girl! I'm just scared of becoming what Rusty is . . . a sadistic, shrewd, horny, oversexed beast with an I.Q. of sixty-nine! Of course I can't tell you that. You've probably done it many times.

"Yes Zilla, I called you scared!" Brute said, waving a finger at him. "You're never too old to be scared of anything. You may be the biggest thing I've ever seen but you can still be frightened. Look at me . . . big and strong, and yet you still scared the crap out of me when I saw your foot over me."

"How old are you?" The Writer asked, now that he was on the subject of being old.

"Me? Why do you ask?"

"Well, I'm eighteen."

"And I'm twenty-two, old enough to drink and do all that other crazy stuff out there. Believe me Zilla, that is not for you. Do not turn out like I did, a big mean high school dropout who knew no better than to get high and get laid."

Okay, now his past is coming out, The Writer thought eagerly. Everything Mama and I wanted to know about him is coming out now. Maybe if I keep at him he'll tell me more.

"A dropout?" he asked weakly.

"Yes Zilla, a dropout. Is that so terrible to you? You think I'm a terrible person now that you know I didn't get to walk like you did, in some fancy blue robe carrying some dinky piece of paper that parents go nuts over? Is that what you think huh?! Is it?! Huh?!" His voice was getting louder and more violent. I've provoked him now, The Writer thought. I've tangled with some bitter part of his life that he wants nobody to know about.

"I'm sorry Brute. I didn't mean . . ."

"I know what you meant Zilla. You think I'm gonna spill my guts out to you about everything aren't you, so you can go blab to your mommy about how rotten a jerk I am for not turning out the way you did. Not all of us can become great geniuses in society like you Zilla."

"I'm not a genius Brute. Just a writer."

"BEING A WRITER TAKES GENIUS!" Brute hollered, grabbing him by the shoulders. "I can't write! I can't read well and I can't do anything like you can! It takes genius to do anything in life like you can! You're a genius compared to me Zilla! I'll never be what you or the rest of your friends are in life! But of course I never spent my whole life in a dark room talking to some guy named God or whatever He is and avoiding the real world. At least I KNOW HOW to talk to people!"

The Writer stopped in his tracks. He's bashing God now, he thought. Where did this sudden shift in his attitude come from? All I asked him was how old he was and he blew it all out of proportion. He looked all around him and saw that nobody else was out here but he and Brute. They were alone as far as he could tell. He turned around and headed back for the car.

"Just a minute you!" Brute grabbed him by the arm and yanked him back. "Where are you going Zilla? Trying to sneak off from me?"

"No, I'm going to the car."

"You'll go when I tell you to! Don't ever think of walking away from me! Look at me when I talk to you! Golly Zilla why can't you look at me when I talk to you? What are you so scared of? What has this Rusty done to you? He's made you a paranoid freak who can't even talk! What is it with you letting everyone else walk all over you?!"

The Writer drew back and threw a powerful punch in Brute's face. He jerked his head back and fell backwards onto the gravel. The Writer saw what he had done and turned off the path for the trees up on the hill. He was sorry for saying too much to Brute. Had he kept his mouth shut then none of what just happened would've took place. He was afraid of what Brute would do now. Run away? Attack him? What? He didn't know. He just wanted to get out of his grip and away from anybody who may have heard him and were watching.

As soon as he got up into the small patch of trees he heard Brute's rugged voice.

"Zilla, get back here! You're gonna fight like a man now!"

Oh God get me out of this, he prayed as he looked around gropingly for something to horde this beast away with. I'm sorry I carried him home, I'm sorry for being good to him, for showing him what I do, and for bringing him here to this place. I'm sorry God. I should've left him lying out there on the road that night. Now he's gonna kill me.

The Writer clambered his burly self over a bunch of tree roots that were sticking up out of the ground and came upon a small clearing with trees and bushes on all sides of it. He was standing at the very edge of the clearing when he looked behind him and saw Brute standing just a few feet away from him, his arms and hands outstretched and his face fired with burning monstrosity. He saw The Writer helplessly standing at the edge of the clearing, his hands grasped together at his chest, looking like a frightened kitten cornered by a pack of rabid wolves.

Brute lunged first. He knocked The Writer backwards and they fell down into the middle of the clearing. The Writer hurriedly got up but Brute was faster. He jumped up on his back but was easily thrown off when The Writer leaned forward and flung himself upwards. Brute crashed into a cloud of dust and rolled over on his back. He looked up and saw a familiar horror coming down on him. The Writer had one of his feet looming over his chest and it was coming down fast.

"Oh no you don't Zilla!" Brute said and grabbed hold of it. He tried to twist the shoe off but was unable to. The Writer kept yanking it every which way until Brute just simply shoved it out of his face. He was able to move The Writer a few feet back and got back up himself. He saw him standing face to face with him and was waving his clawed hands at him.

"Fists Zilla!" he yelled. "Make fists and try to hit me!"

He did and one fist slammed into Brute's mouth. He backed away and Brute approached him, stopped, looked at what The Writer might do next, and swung. He missed by barely an inch when The Writer jerked his head back. The Writer went for another punch but missed when Brute bent down, grabbed hold of his waist, and caused The Writer to fall down on his side. The Writer saw everything in front of him suddenly loom out of focus and he felt the soft dirt of the earth cushioning him as Brute got on top of him and tried to beat him around the face. The Writer was slamming hits and slaps on his back and went for his hair. Brute grabbed his hands and slung them back away from him as he tried to make The Writer angrier and more provoked. He did not see his legs come bending upwards and curl their way under him. Brute felt a sudden heave in his stomach and felt himself flying off The Writer and crashing into a small bank under a huge tree. He looked and saw that The Writer had shoved him off with both of his big feet. He was now up again and standing over Brute, his legs outstretched, and his arms ready for more. His coattail made him look as if he had a tail that was swishing madly from side to side like a big cat, or even a tiger.

The Writer let out a heavy grunt and Brute returned the call and went back to face him. The Writer swung even more punches but Brute managed to dodge every one of them. But when he started kicking Brute saw that he was in danger of having this guy's gargantuan feet burying themselves in his groin so he grabbed one of his legs, felt The Writer slapping and popping him on the back, and even though he meant to only make him fall to the ground again, he got something more.

He heaved forward just as The Writer was about to jerk away but he lost his balance along with The Writer, who was about to fall on top of him. Brute's heave prevailed in strength when he found himself doing a mighty backflip with The Writer on top of him. When they crashed together another cloud of dust billowed up all around them that began to hold beautiful golden rays of afternoon light from the sun which was peering down through the branches far overhead.

Both Brute and The Writer got up together and The Writer found Brute with his arms tightly wrapped around his back and his head buried in his chest, trying to pull him forward.

This guy's big, Brute thought as he tried to pull him down again.

The Writer was trying to pry his hands off of him but was not successful. Brute kept turning him around and around until he felt a tapping on his shoulder. Brute turned to see what it was but instead saw a huge hand come flying out of nowhere backslapping his face, knocking him off The Writer. He looked up and saw The Writer come crashing down on top of him and throwing him over to the side. Brute tried to get up again but then saw something else come flying into his face. It was long and black. He realized that it wasn't a tail but The Writer's coattail about to slap him down, which it did.

The Writer stumbled to the bushes and tore off a small limb with leaves on it. He come up to Brute waving it all over the place and began slapping him with it. Leaves began flying everywhere as Brute tried to shield his face. He grabbed hold of it and tore it out of his hand. He got up and tried to stuff it down The Writer's shirt but he grabbed it and broke it in half, throwing the pieces back at Brute. The Writer charged at him again but Brute held up his hands and with one strong shove knocked him back onto the ground. He then approached him but The Writer tripped him and caused him to fall. He got up and got down on his back, trying to pull back one of his legs. Brute heaved up and made him roll off. He then grabbed him and slung him around. He got up on his back and tried to act as if he was going to choke him but The Writer simply backed up as hard as he could into a tree and mashed Brute between them both. Brute hollered and fell to the ground. He began to crawl away but stopped when he saw one of The Writer's big feet plant itself in front of his face. He then tried to crawl back the other way but found it to be useless when he rolled over onto his back and saw The Writer standing over him with his legs on either side of Brute. His arms were hanging down and he was sweating something awful.

"Okay Zilla," Brute said, out of breath. "That's enough. I . . . I can't take anymore. You're too strong to take down."

The Writer looked up and slowly ambled away from Brute, breathing deeply. He just had to be alone for a minute. This was the first time he'd even been in a "fight" with anybody. How it felt was too overwhelming to be defined by any words of the English language, or any language for that matter. It was as if some part of his life had budded out after years of waiting for the right watering source. It just happened to come today.

He closed his eyes as they began to water with tears. He propped himself up against a tree. Then he heard the heavy thudding of footsteps coming close to him. A voice was saying 'Zilla, Zilla' over and over.

One big arm came up around him and another wrapped itself around his stomach. Then there was someone's head pressed up against his and he was being pulled tighter and tighter all over.

"You okay Zilla?!" Brute asked feverishly. "Did I hurt you? If I did I'm sorry. You're not gonna die on me are ya?"

The Writer wiped his face and looked around him. It was just him and Brute here in this patch of trees. He felt like he had been given a rejuvenating boost of newfound strength, like he felt after he took Brute into his world just the night before.

Was it just last night? he thought. It seems like it was so long ago . . .

"I'm fine."

"Are you sure? I didn't hurt you did I?"

He shook his head. Brute rested his head on The Writer's shoulder for a minute and turned him loose. The Writer quickly stumbled away, dusted his clothes off, and looked towards the path.

And he waddled away . . . back to the path, with Brute following him.

CHAPTER TWENTY-SEVEN

The Writer went back to their picnic spot and started to gather up everything. But the spread out blanket looked so tempting and soothing. A mid-afternoon sunbeam was radiating down upon it and had made it feel warm and drowsily appealing.

Maybe if I lay down for a minute I'll feel better, he thought as he crawled onto it and stretched out on his side facing towards the lake. There was still nobody else nearby. The only other people in sight were either on sailboats or water skis. None of them seemed to notice that The Writer and Brute were in the midst of their presence.

About a minute later Brute appeared and came to the spot. He saw The Writer looking far off into space at the lake and laid down next to him, blocking his view.

You're in my sight, The Writer thought. But I'm too tired to lift you out of my way.

Brute laid his head down on the blanket and looked into the face of The Writer. This was the first time he'd been able to get a good look at it, but the eyes would not give him their attention. He could clearly see his reflection in them but he knew The Writer was not looking at him. He waved his hands in front of the face and made like he was going to slap him but nothing worked. The Writer showed no visible signs of life, no blinking, no twitch of any kind, except for the breathing. Other than that it was like lying next to a dead body.

"Zilla, hello Zilla," Brute said, waving at him. "Anybody home? This is your friend Brute calling. Wake up. Calling the King of the Monsters. You're needed to fight Ghidrah the three-headed monster here in the forest."

"I already did," The Writer said, moving over onto his back. "I just fought a monster named Brute."

"You know Zilla, someday I wanna see you take down this Rusty character. Betcha he won't hurt you again once he gets a mouthful of your Godzilla moves."

"Brute he won't . . . " The Writer started to say.

"You know I bet that if he ever saw you up against him, he'll be so shocked at seeing you fight he won't know what to do. Then you can clobber the crap out of him and whoever that snitchy little slut is he's shacking up with."

The Writer began to see the images take shape in his mind. He saw himself giving Rusty a swift kick in the groin and tossing Kelly around by grabbing her hair, making her scream and holler like a swine in the slaughterhouse. Then he saw Rusty trying to punch him in the face but instead felt another powerful blow to his body, this time in the pit of his stomach. Rusty drew back holding his belly while Kelly grabbed something long and heavy, lifted it up over The Writer's head, and with one mighty swing . . .

"Oh no," The Writer said, covering his face with his hands. It was too vivid to not be real. He was letting his imagination run wild with him. Why would Rusty and Kelly want to do that to him? He'd done nothing to them but let them know he was angry and upset. It certainly didn't warrant a severe counterattack such as the one he was envisioning . . . did it?

He didn't know.

"What?" Brute asked. "Something wrong Zilla?"

He shook his head and removed his hands. The image was gone and replaced with what he saw before him, the tree limbs overhead. He didn't want Brute to know what he had just pictured in his mind.

"Zilla, tell me all about you."

The Writer rolled his eyes towards Brute. Had he heard him right? He wanted to hear *everything* about himself, or just the important stuff?

"Me?"

"Yes you Zilla. I want to know what makes you . . . you. Zilla, you are the most amazing guy I've ever known. There can't be anyone else like you in the whole world. There can't be. You just fascinate me with who you are."

Buttering me up with sweet layers of warm flattery won't work, The Writer thought. What's so fascinating about a grossly over-weight boy who loves to write and loves to bowl? Anybody can do those things. Why should I be the epitome of fascinating wonder for Brute?

"And just what is so fascinating about me?" he asked. "Name one thing about me that fascinates you so much."

Brute reached over and picked up the pen that was resting on The Writer's chest. It was still attached to his necklace even after their fight. He held it up in front of The Writer's face, making sure he could see it.

"See this Zilla? You wear your pen. I never see anyone else do that. In my dream you did some pretty cool stuff with this. It shot out beams, made people, made all these places, built a huge castle or something, and even destroyed a whole city."

"So what you saw that thing do in some dream is fascinating? What dreams aren't?"

"No, listen. I hear people gripe about not finding a pen when they need it, and they don't think to wear one like you."

"So you're saying I'm unique huh? Everybody's unique Brute. You are. I am. Mama and Judy, Joey, Annie, Lana, Jackie, Dionne, Nate, Elaine, and Blade . . . all unique. It's been like that for centuries."

"But I want to know how you got to be this way. Just tell me Zilla, and I'll shut up about it."

"So you can make fun of me?" The Writer asked. "I've had enough of that in high school."

"Why did they make fun of you?"

"I was different." He kept looking up at the trees. He could tell Brute was eyeing him. It was as if he were being interrogated in a dark room laced with smoke and one overhead lamp.

"That's what I want to know. What made you so different from everyone else? What made them laugh at you? What makes people like Rusty take you for a stoolpigeon? That's what I want to know Zilla! Just tell me all about you."

You mean brag don't you, he thought. I can't brag. I'm not going to lie here and say I did this and I did that. I refuse to sound like that star athlete at school who was the symbol of social and sporty idolatry, the one everyone compared everyone else to. I will not do that. But if I tell him all about me, he'll have to tell me all about him. That's it! A small compromise should do the trick. Then I'll know all I need to about Brute and where he came from.

"Okay Brute," he said. "I'll tell you. But first, you have to promise me that you'll tell me all about you. Agree?"

"Sure man. Start telling."

The Writer sat up and got to his feet.

"Can't you sit and tell me?" Brute asked.

"No. I do better standing up. If I sit I'll go to sleep."

He walked around behind Brute and was about to open his mouth to begin talking, but he saw Brute scooting around on his rear end to face him. The Writer then walked around him again, but Brute still scooted around to look at him. A third time got the same results. No matter where The Writer stood to avoid seeing Brute's face, Brute was turning around on his butt to look at him.

"Zilla, what are you doing? My butt's getting tired from all this turning."

"I can talk better when I'm not being looked at."

"Well I feel weird listening to someone behind me talking. But if it makes you feel better then go ahead. I won't say anymore. But Zilla, even this makes you different from everyone else."

Brute resumed his position and sat with his legs crossed, picking apart a fallen stick. The Writer walked around aimlessly in one spot for a few minutes, trying to think of how and where to begin.

"Now how should I start this?" he said to himself.

"How about at the beginning?" Brute suggested. "Usually helps."

The Writer thought about it and realized that he would indeed begin at the beginning. He could easily lead up to this moment in life and hopefully make Brute see what made him so "fascinating," if there was anything fascinating about his life.

"Okay Brute, here it is. All about me, as best I can tell it. But it would sound better on paper."

"Zilla, there isn't time to write a 50,000 page life history of yourself right now. Just tell me about you. I'm listening. Now start."

The Writer stood next to a tree and faced deep into space. He saw Brute sitting on the blanket with his back to him. And he opened his mouth to speak . . .

"I was born in October, nineteen years ago this year. From what Mama tells me, she was raped one night while walking home from a grocery store on the corner near where she used to live. The man who raped her got her pregnant . . . with me. She was told over and over by doctors to abort me because they did not think I'd survive if I was born and in the birthing process I could kill Mama. But she refused to have me killed. I was born a month premature, which was a shock to the doctors and nurses because I weighed nine pounds at birth, and they said my eyes looked demonic and possessed as soon as they pulled me out of her.

"And for my real father, he got killed, by Mama's husband. He was a police officer, and when he heard of what happened to his wife he went after her attacker. They got in a fight. The rapist shot her husband, but before he went down, he shot and killed the rapist. A few hours later, her husband died from the gunshot wound. His dying words to his fellow officers were to take care of his wife and any children she had, if any. So I never met my real father or the man who would've been my father. When word got around that Mama was going to have her rapist's baby, they called her a whore, a slut, a bitch, and a bastard carrier. It got so bad she sold the house she was living in and moved away to where we live now, far from everyone who despised her decision to have me. She said it would've been murder if she let the doctors abort me, and she wanted to take care of me.

"But you know how far and how long gossip can spread and exist. Gossip only dies when another form of it is born someplace else. When I was five years old she put me in school. I was nearly five feet tall in kindergarten. My teachers thought I'd failed the upper grades and got demoted back to kindergarten. All the kids made fun of me for being so big and fat. They loved to see me get into trouble. They'd steal things from other kids and plant them on me, tattle on me for things I didn't do, and ask me if my mother was a cow or a pig. One year a teacher locked me in the closet after some kid said I spilled brown paint all over the seat of his pants. The teacher made me give the boy my pants and made me wear his. She said I deserved to look like a baby who didn't know any better. She put me in front of the class, tore off my overalls, and gave them to the boy. She took his pants that were messed up and put them on me, and then locked me in the supply closet for the rest of the afternoon. When I went home Mama asked if I had an accident. I said no, and told her what the teacher did to me. She got mad and had her fired the next week. But that's just one sampling of the hatred I put up with. That lasted all the way to middle school. In all those years I realized that wherever I went, people were gonna look, point, and laugh. I knew I wasn't going to be welcome in anyone's social bracket. I was never invited to parties or got asked to play games. The P.E. coach in every grade level loved to humiliate me. If I ever got the lowest or highest score of a certain athletic ruse he would make sure everyone in the class knew how terrible I did. Once I could only do eighteen sit-ups in one minute. When I told him what it was he boldly announced it in his loudest voice to the rest of the class, who all laughed at me for being so slow and fat. He always made sure someone got me out first whenever we played kickball or volleyball or whatever sport. Any foul-up there was in any game he made sure I would make that error and get out. At one point he said if I wasn't as fat as a bloated hippo I could probably do something right in life. Other teachers said the same thing to me. Some of them knew about the nature of my birth and used it to exploit me. One year the teacher

wrote the term 'bastard' on the blackboard and asked the class if
they knew what it meant. None of them did. She told me to stand
up and said that I was a bastard, a child whose parents are not
married to each other. So from then on out kids would refer to me
as 'the fat bastard.' I was always addressed as 'bastard' until I entered
high school.

"So it dawned on me that nobody out there wanted to be my
friend or even liked me. I learned to stay away from people and do
things alone. I would find a quiet spot and read a book or just
wander around by myself. I usually played on the swings while
the other kids played with each other. I would ask if I could play
and they all would say 'no' and walk off. So I was left all alone most
of the time. It hit me that nobody wanted me around for anything.
I began to feel useless and ashamed of who I was. Teachers and
kids, as well as some others, all refused to have me around or made
others stay away from me. I don't know what was so bad about me.
I did nothing wrong. I always did my school work, did as I was
told, and almost always got good grades. Some teachers tried to
fail me but realized that if they did, they would probably get
stuck with me again the next year, so they passed me, I presume
just to get rid of me.

"The writing thing came when I was young. I was so amazed
by pens and pencils I started collecting them. I would write letters
of the alphabet all over papers, notebooks, and even the walls of
the house, which made Mama quite unhappy. It was always words
and not pictures. The teachers read stories to us all the time and I
began to think up stories of my own, just to pass the time because
there was nothing else for me to do. Nobody wanted me around,
so I thought up different places and people. It was animals at first.
I love animals, cats especially, I guess because that's all I was raised
with, cats and dogs. I'd have the animals do amazing things like
save a young girl from drowning or have them find someone missing. I changed the animals to people when I got older. I even wrote
some of those stories down, but later trashed them when all my
teachers told me I did nothing worthwhile with my time and had

no talent or ability to do anything. I was told I'd be the biggest failure in life because they presumed I knew nothing to do anything in life. So I never thought of myself as a writer when I was young. I thought that nothing I wrote was good or worth keeping. I just wrote because it was something to pass the time. I learned to just watch others and keep my mouth shut. Nobody wanted to listen to me if I ever had anything to say and I was always told to shut up about anything, that I had nothing important to say or was worth listening to. I learned a lot about other people just by being quiet and watching. I would retreat into my own little world where things happened the way I wanted them to. I would think up different stories and characters and write them down. I always felt safer there and I knew that nobody could ever hurt me there. That was heaven to me, and it still is. All the hate and anger against me gave me no reason to smile or laugh because nothing good ever happened to me. There was nothing to make me happy. No friends to play with or visit and nobody telling me what I was doing right in life rather than what I was doing wrong. I never could smile easily. Looking upset and sad all the time wasn't hard to do after a while. The look wore itself into my face naturally. I would wake up every morning and know that there was nothing out in the world to smile or be happy about. I could expect to be hated and abused left and right each day I stepped out into the world. It was the same thing everyday. Nothing to be happy about.

"When I got baptized, seven years ago today to be exact, the hatred got worse. I was called a Jesus freak and the biggest mistake God had ever created. I was deemed an accident because I was the result of a rape and wasn't supposed to be alive. All my shirts have a religious scene or saying on them. Some people in town admired them. Others despised them. Other kids said if I wore those shirts to school I could get kicked out, but two of them got kicked out instead for possession of marijuana on school property. Mama was the one who introduced me to religion and God and taught me all about Jesus and other Biblical characters. It was so amazing to me to learn what mighty powers God has and I read the Bible with great interest. I was taught the importance of getting baptized. I realized that God was the most important part of life because He created all things and is in control. He cares about us and that always helped me when I was young, knowing that He was always there if I needed Him. But the other kids and teachers didn't understand why I was so religious. They all said I was going to be a preacher and was always watching and judging them. One day some boy sneezed in class and when I didn't say 'bless you,' he turned to the class and said that he must be going to hell because 'that religious guy didn't say bless you.' I did my best to ignore him but it did no good. He and a bunch of others asked me if they were going to heaven or hell when they died. I told them I didn't have that power. But nothing about me seemed to please anybody."

He stopped. Brute looked up from the broken pieces of sticks and spoke into the air. "Well, go on Zilla. I'm still listening."

"In eighth grade I wrote a poem about all the abuse and hatred I had endured over the years. The teacher read it and approached me one day in class. I thought I was gonna get a tongue-lashing from her about how atrocious a sight I must be to her but instead she asked me if I had given any consideration to being a writer. I told her no, then she said that I was the only student she ever had who understood the English language and all the mechanics and techniques of writing papers and essays. She said that even though I wrote papers that were about four or five pages long compared to the two-page papers other students turned in to her, I had a thing for writing that none of her other students had. She said the content of my papers were so real and so vivid to her that she entered one of my papers in a local writing contest, something about school violence. It won a first place trophy, and that's the only trophy I'd ever won until that bowling tournament the other night. She even called Mama in for a special conference to talk about my writing ability, and it was decided that I needed to be in an advanced English course in high school. Mama told her that she knew I was always in my bedroom writing, but she never knew what I wrote. The teacher submitted the request to the high school and I got placed in the advanced course for the next four years. At the awards ceremony at the end of my middle school years, that teacher gave me a special certificate addressed to simply 'The Writer.' Under it she had written 'Author! Author!' in one of the blanks that tell what the award is for. She gave me a copy of her favorite book from her high school years and she wrote in it why she loved it so. Word of the special award made it to the newspapers and I was listed as simply 'The Writer.' My picture was also in the papers. People in town would recognize me with Mama and say 'Look, it's The Writer. Congratulations.' But others would look at me with a heavy scowl, that I was just being a big religious show-off. But the name of 'The Writer' stuck with me. That was how everyone came to know me as, so the name stuck. I've been called that ever since, and I love it."

"So do I," Brute said. "I love your name. Zilla is just a nickname for you though. But keep going. You've got me interested now."

I don't think I've ever talked this much in my whole life, he thought. And in one day. This is quite a feat for me.

"I still kept to myself as I entered high school. Still nobody wanted to be my friend. The upperclassmen saw my shirts and immediately began slamming me with insults, so I knew I could forget trying to get to know any of them. They wanted nothing to do with me. Then I met Annie, Lana, Dionne, Jackie, Elaine, Nate, and Blade. They were all freshmen from different schools. I was in the cafeteria one day my freshman year and Annie came up and asked if she could sit with me. Naturally I was alone, so I said she could. We didn't talk at first, then Lana come by, saw that our table was mostly bare, and sat. Nate and Blade came next, and finally Dionne. They all got to talking and finally started talking to me. I told them my name. They thought it was the most awesome thing they'd ever heard. Later I learned that I had classes with all of them throughout the day. We got to know each other better and started talking. Then we just started hanging out together more and more. We formed an 'us against the world' bond between us, because they all came from private schools, and they saw my shirts and said that I was the only one who seemed to be 'like them' in some way. None of them were popular, but were made fun of because they always hung around me. Blade is the most mischievous one of us because he loves knives and sometimes got caught with a pocketknife on him. I don't think 'Blade' is his real name, but that's just how we came to know him, just like with my name. Nate's black you know, and he got his share of the abuse from other kids. Is it any wonder he wants to become a law enforcement officer of some sort? Dionne looks part Chinese or Japanese or whatever, and she was called an 'illegal alien freak' and I don't know what else because of how she looks. Some threatened to deport her back to her country, but she learned to ignore them. They were all bluff. Jackie was passed around from one foster family to another growing up, but now she has finally found the perfect family I believe, because she's been with them for the last five years. Elaine was home-schooled up until ninth grade when she was sent to public school. It took her a while to get adjusted, but once she came to us she opened up a lot. Annie was the smartest one of us. She wore glasses and never did anything with her hair but let it hang around her face. She always studies and yet always finds time for her friends, namely us. Her high-pitched voice made others laugh at her, but she loves decorating houses. Lana was hit upon by all the guys because she's blonde and pretty, but she wanted nothing to do with them. She was an adopted child also and got passed around from family to family. She wants to go into law and I think she said one of her adopted fathers sexually assaulted her when she was younger, so she wants nothing more than a friendship with boys, but she just sticks around Blade, Nate, and me. I guess because she knows that we won't hurt her, and that we won't hurt each other in our little circle. So all seven of us learned to depend and trust each other, because we knew we would not fit in with anybody else at that school. Those were my first true friends ever. They helped me through all the pain I put up with, like the time that wretched Mrs. Moran sent me to a psychiatrist for giving Blade a Bible for his birthday one year. She told me I was being 'too nice' and 'too giving' for my own good and that I had a mental problem. My nature she said, was totally out of character and highly irregular, and that I needed psychiatric help for how I was. But that is too sad to talk about."

"Yes it is. She's the nutcase, not you Zilla. Go on."

The Writer quickly wrapped things up when he felt he was rambling. He just spit out how one teacher made the class pull a cruel joke on him, the hateful algebra teacher, about the other forms of abuse that came his way, and then ended with graduation. He did not want to relive his high school years anymore than he had to.

They were gone. That's what mattered.

"Now do you know me a little better Brute?" he asked.

Brute hesitated. He rubbed his hands over his face and looked up at the sky. The sunlight was now beginning to peer in from the sides and not as much from straight above, meaning that the afternoon was slipping away.

"Well, you told me a little more than what I expected from someone like you who never wants to talk," he said. "But I want to know why you love sunsets and sunrises so much."

"Sunsets?" The Writer asked. "Why?"

"Why do you like them so much? It's that and sunrises that you love so much. You seem to open up a little more during those times of the day than any other. Why?"

"It's just that the sun isn't so bright at those times. Whenever I see that orange gleam in the sky in the mornings, I know God is at work creating another day for us to see, and when I see the orange of the evening, I know that the world is starting to calm itself down to rest for the night, and that's the time I write. Even though the light may be gone, I know God is still there, watching over us through the darkness. Does that answer your question?"

Brute nodded. "But you didn't tell me how you met Joey."

"Joey?" The Writer asked.

"Yes Joey, you know, your best friend, the one at the bowling thingamajig the other night who kept cheering for you. Really Zilla, how could you not mention your best friend?"

"He's not my best friend. He's just . . . "

"Just what Zilla? I know you're his best friend. I can tell."

"How? He doesn't think that much of me. I know I'm not his best friend."

"You don't know that Zilla. You could be."

"I'm eighteen, he's fifteen. There's no way I could be. He has his own friends and he has more in common with them than he ever will with me. I don't deserve to be anyone's best friend, not the way I am."

Brute turned to him with an irate glare in his eyes. The Writer jumped back when he saw his fixed pupils set upon him as he leaned up against the tree. He closed his eyes so he wouldn't have to see them, but he could still sense their gaze upon him. Even through the closed eyelids he could still see them.

"You don't like yourself do you Zilla?" he asked sternly. "I can tell you don't. You hate how you are. You hate being fat and quiet and maybe even being a writer."

His eyes opened at this remark. Me hate being a writer?! Never! I've never thought of such a thing! I love being a writer! How can you say I hate being that?!

"Do you hate yourself Zilla?"

The Writer looked away into space. How do I answer this? he thought. Do I hate myself? Do I like how God made me? So maybe I'm not thin, maybe I'm not a star athlete like Joey is, maybe I'm not the idol of popularity in society. This is how God made me. I should accept it. Yes, I like how He made me. He made me big and quiet and the way I am for a reason. I do like myself. Why should I worry about what others think? This is how God made me and that's that.

"No, I don't hate myself."

"Really Zilla? Well, you know what?"

He shook his head.

"I think you're pretty cool myself . . . just the way you are."

The Writer looked down at Brute as he turned away from him, rubbing the soreness out of his neck from looking back at The Writer for so long. The last words he heard from Brute made his heart leap, and a tender sensation swept over his whole body. It was as if being told that you were the cause of happiness in the world, that you had changed some aspect of life as nobody else could ever do. The Writer knew of only one man who had that power. He did not wish to feel superior to Him in any way whatsoever. He just let the words of Brute take hold of his heart. That sensation was colliding with how he felt thinking of Joey.

The Writer closed his eyes and envisioned the first time he ever met him. He sniffed and wiped away a tear, remembering in vivid detail how he felt and what he thought upon his first encounter with Joey.

"Where should I start?" he asked.

"The beginning, as usual," Brute said.

And The Writer waddled away . . . to sit next to Brute and tell him all about Joey.

CHAPTER TWENTY-EIGHT

"Okay, all about Joey," The Writer began. He cleared his throat and kept his gaze fixed downward at the blanket. His mind was full of every image he could recollect of the time line of his friendship with Joey, and he told Brute.

"The first time I ever saw Joey was on the very first day of school my senior year. You know nearly every class was mixed with students of each grade level. Well, this class was geography, and I needed an elective, so that class was all I could take for it. It was me with about twenty-five freshmen in the class. I went to my desk as I gradually began to realize that I was gonna feel weird being the only one in there who wasn't a freshman. I sat and watched all the other freshmen kids come in the door, asking if this was the geography class. I looked at all the faces. After the past three years of seeing freshman come and go I was wondering which of these would last the full four years or drop out. I also tried to see which of these would actually try to learn or be big goof-offs. That's when I saw this boy come in with his black hair slicked back and had the most boyish face I'd ever seen. He was skinny and a chatterbox. When he talked he sounded like he had laryngitis, but I soon learned that it was his natural voice. Later that day in the hallway, he just asked me if I knew where his fourth period classroom was. Well, my fourth period class was just next door to his so I just showed him where to go. That was the first time he ever spoke to me. He didn't know my name or anything, but he just randomly asked me where his classroom was.

"About two weeks later, I was standing in the hallway waiting for fourth period class to begin. When the bell rang the hallway flooded with kids and I stood in the corner next to my classroom door, because it was still locked. I stood there and watched as kids come whizzing by not paying any attention to me, not that I cared. Then I felt someone tap me on the shoulder. I turned around and saw Joey standing there. He asked me if I knew about something for another class. My mind wasn't focused at the moment. I had a headache, and I didn't feel like fooling with some clueless freshman's worries, since that was before I really got to know him. I blurted out that I didn't know and stormed off to my classroom. I was also thinking that he was out to make fun of me and I didn't feel like taking it that day.

"Then I think the next day, we were going to our geography class. I was one of the first in the room and went to my desk. I sat in the back row in front of the window. Joey sat in the row over to my left and about three seats up from me. I saw that he was already there so I didn't pay much attention to him. I didn't think he'd have anything to say to me.

"But he did.

"I was getting my book out of my bag when I heard a little raspy voice come out of nowhere. It said, 'Hey Mr. Writer.' I looked up and saw Joey sitting there with his whole upper body turned to me and he was looking at me, waving 'hey' to me and had his eyes wide open. I was surprised that he actually spoke to me so I waved back and sat down. That was the first time we really talked to each other on a friendly basis. I looked at him and remembered him being the kid who was asking me something in the hallway the day before.

"Over the next few days, whenever I walked down the hall during class changes, I would recognize Joey coming in my direction. I'd look at him until he looked at me. Then I'd look away. Every now and then he'd call my name out and give me a high-five. I still wondered why he did that and began to wonder why he was the only freshman who seemed to know of my existence. It puzzled me.

"I would take Tootsie rolls to snack on in classes that the teachers let us snack in. Geography class was one of them. Every morning

before school I'd grab a handful from the jar on the kitchen table
and stuff them in one of my coat pockets. One day I pulled two
out of my pocket. Before I dropped one back in I looked up and
saw Joey talking to the boy in front of him. I saw that the teacher
had his back turned to the class so I aimed to toss the candy over
onto Joey's desk. I threw it and Joey turned around in time to see
who threw it. I quickly made like I was reading the whole time,
but he figured out who it was and said 'thanks.' Then that got to
be a daily ritual. I'd bring him one everyday, and I guess it made
him happy.

"One day I noticed that he didn't look too well. His face was
red and he kept his head down on his desk. I didn't think he'd
want any candy so I didn't bother him with it. The teacher asked
if he needed to go home and he said his mother was on his way to
the school to pick him up. Pretty soon the intercom sounded for
him to come to the front office. I watched him get up and amble
out of the classroom. I looked out the window behind me, which
was where I could see the front entrance where the student drop-
off was. A red car was out there. I saw Joey walk out to it and get
in. When it drove away I went back to work on my assignment.
The next day Joey wasn't in class. I was wondering how I could let
him know of what assignments he had missed. Luckily, as I entered my fourth period class, I passed the trash can and just happened to look in. The teacher had trashed his copy of the list of
students who were either absent or tardy for the day. I picked it up
and saw Joey's name on the list as 'absent.' But the list boasted not
only the students' names, but their school ID number, their parents' names, their grade level, and even their home phone number.
I caught a quick glance at the number and memorized it. That
night I called and asked for Joey. It was him who answered, and I
told him who I was. His voice perked up a little and I told him
what he missed in class. He thanked me and asked if I was one of
those students who were hired to help others. I said I wasn't, because I thought it was obvious that nobody wanted a Jesus freak
holding down any job position of any sort in the public school

system. Before he could say anymore he paused for a moment, then come back on and said that his mother was calling him. We said 'bye' and hung up. That was the first time we spoke on the phone."

"You remember everything don't you Zilla?" Brute asked, amazed at every little detail The Writer put forth in his story. "I could never remember every little thing that happens."

"It's not hard," The Writer said. "I always think back on it when I can. That way the memories are preserved. Nothing is overlooked. Want me to keep going?"

"Of course."

"As time went on I learned that Joey was a star athlete. He played JV football in the fall and would start basketball in the winter. I thought he'd be like all the other athletes at school, become immediate symbols of idolatry and popularity, acting as if nothing in life mattered but sports. The athletes, especially the guys, had a way with getting girls. I thought Joey would be one of them. I don't really know if he had a girlfriend. If he did he never told me. He's not bulky or fat like me, but slim and physically tone. I was so afraid he'd take my heavy size and use it to make fun of me, just like the other athletes would do. But he never did. That kinda surprised me."

The Writer thought of what happened next with Joey. When he thought of it, there came a soft pressing in his chest. His eyes began to sting. He looked down at the lapel pin he was wearing. The memories of that day in December flashed across his mind like a burning lake of fire. It was perhaps the most radiant moment of his life thus far. It was also perhaps the first time ever in his life the sweet touch of happiness pricked his heart the way it did that day.

"Then it got to be a few days before Christmas vacation. It was a Monday I think. I came into our geography class as usual and went to my desk as usual. I wasn't expecting anything, as usual. But when I put my bag down in my chair to get out my book, I saw a slender arm slide something onto my desk. I looked up and saw that it was a small package wrapped in red wrapping paper with a fiery green bow on top of it. The gift tag on it read simply 'To The Writer, From Joey Lowell.' I wondered why he had to be so formal in writing out his full name. I pulled it closer to me and then looked up at Joey. He had gone back to his seat but was turned around facing me. When he saw that I had noticed the present, he got back up and came back to my desk. He told me to open it. I asked him if he meant now, and he nodded. So I carefully peeled off the paper and saw a white box. I lifted the cover off and inside was this gold lapel pin attached to a black plastic backing. It was on top of a small pile of cotton balls. I took it out and looked at it. Then Joey asked me if it was alright. I didn't know what to say or how to act. All I could do was just stand there, holding it, thinking of the thought behind it. I had never been given such a simple gift from someone like Joey. Sure Annie, Lana, Dionne, Elaine, Jackie, Nate, and Blade always did something for me on my birthday and at Christmas and just out of the blue, but there was something totally different about this one. It was like I was holding the most tender ornament of affection ever created on this earth. I was so touched and moved by it I didn't know what to do. Joey asked me if I was going to put it on, so I did. All throughout the day it shined. Annie and the rest of the guys saw it and asked who gave it to me. I told them who it was and when I said it was a freshman they were rather surprised. After that, they got to be friends with Joey and he with them. He was the only freshman friend we had. In fact, he was the only friend we had who was not a senior. He got to know quite a number of the other kids in the upper grades, mostly those who were athletes and some of the popular ones. So now there were nine of us in our little gang. But Joey was so involved with sports and other things he didn't hang around us as much as we did with each other. He had his other friends, those closer to his age . . . and his interests."

He paused for a moment.

"What else is there about Joey?" Brute asked, sensing the sudden silence.

"Well . . . since I didn't go to lunch everyday, I would go out and walk around the track at the football field. I'd walk around once and organize my thoughts, as I called it, trying to figure out what to think and what not to think about. You're not a writer so I guess you wouldn't understand that part. But each year I was in high school I'd go up there and envision my graduation ceremony, try to get an idea of how it would feel and look. Anyway, when second semester started, our classes changed. Joey and I weren't in a class together anymore. His fourth period class was now weight lifting, which was in the field house up next to the football stadium. One day I left the school building to go up for my walk. As soon as I got to the steps that went to the stadium up on the hill over the school, I heard that raspy voice from behind me call out, 'Wait up punk!' I turned and I saw Joey coming, carrying his gym bag. He ran up to me and we walked up together. We went into the field house and he showed me where the football team changed and showered and stuff. I'd stay with him and chat until someone else showed up. That was my cue to leave. Sometimes another guy would come in, slap hands with Joey, and go on to the back of the building. I'd make up some excuse to leave and Joey always took it. But here's how I found out he was my next door neighbor. One Saturday, Rusty made one of his infamous promises to me about going somewhere together. He never showed up. Before I got too upset, I told Mama I was going to a friend's house. I called Joey and told him that someone had just got on my nerves and that I wanted to visit someone. I asked him if I could come see him for a few minutes and he said I could. I asked him how to get to his house and when he said the name of the road he lived on I realized that that was the same road I lived on. Then he described the house. I looked out my window and when he said he lived next to a huge open field next to the house with a blue truck in the front yard, I realized he was describing my house. I later learned that he had lived next to Mama and I ever since we moved there. For nearly 12 years I'd lived just a few hundred feet away from a dear friend and never knew it! I felt so retarded when I found out.

When his mom, Judy, and my mother met, they hit it off right away. Every Saturday morning Judy comes over to the house and she and Mama eat breakfast while they watch the morning fashion show on QVC. One would think they were sisters. I guess so because Mama never had any brothers or sisters growing up. Judy is a free-spirit. She can always make you laugh and be happy. Now they can't stand to be away from each other for long periods of time."

"When did you first take Joey bowling?" Brute asked.

The Writer looked up at the sky and the memories of the first time he ever took him bowling flashed through his mind. He remembered it very well.

"The first time I ever took him was on a Saturday this past spring. I went to his house in Mama's truck and picked him up. We went straight to the bowling alley and bowled five games. When it's just two people it doesn't take as long to bowl. Joey scored higher than me in the last game and when he saw his score, he jumped up and down yelling 'I beat The Writer! I beat The Writer!' He even had the scores printed out. He gave me the copies of the games I won, the ones he won, and when he got to the one where we tied, he tore it in half and gave me one part and he kept the other. But when he got to the one where he beat me by about fifty points he waved it around and said he was gonna put it in a gold frame on his dresser, which he did, only the frame came from a five-and-dime store.

"I told Mama I'd be home later that evening, so by the time we were through bowling we had lots of time to spare. I took him out to eat after we bowled. We took it to this park on the outskirts of town where there were only a few people walking around on the trail next to the river. We then went to Wal-Mart and looked around for a bit, then headed home. I took him back to his house and I visited for about a minute, then left. He kept saying he had a good time, and I hoped he did."

The Writer took a deep breath and sighed. He'd said all he was going to about Joey. His mind was full of Joey, full of Joey's face, voice, nature, and spirit. Everything was Joey. He had to change his thinking or else he'd slump into a pit of miserable depression worrying over what Joey really thought of him.

"Is that all you want to tell me?" Brute asked. The Writer nodded and said he was ready for Brute's story.

"Fine. Let's go to Asheville."

"ASHEVILLE?!" The Writer said shocked. "Brute, do you have any idea how far that is from here?! It's over two hours!"

"So? You can drive that far."

"Oh, so you're from Asheville. Well, that tells me everything. Lovely city in the daytime. I've never been there at night when the thugs and prostitutes come out of their hiding places."

Brute looked at him in frustration. You've never been there so how do you know what it's like at night? he thought as he looked at him. I'm gonna show you where I came from and what I lived with.

"Zilla, just drive over there and I'll show you where to go."

"But I've never been over there this late in the afternoon, and it'll be getting dark by the time we get there. And it'll be real late when we get back to the house and . . . "

"Zilla, please, for once in your life, LIVE A LITTLE! Go crazy for a change my friend! Haven't you ever just gone out and done something wild and outrageous without thinking about it?"

"Well now let me think . . . " The Writer said, looking up at the sky. Brute already knew the answer.

"No you haven't Zilla. C'mon, let's go. I wanna show you what's over there."

"But we'll be late getting home," The Writer protested, trying to his best at the last minute to spit out a good excuse to Brute, but nothing seemed to work. "Besides, I know what's over there, the malls, Wal-Mart stores galore, restaurants, loony teenage drivers who haven't got a lick of sense on Saturday night . . . and besides I . . . I've . . . I've never gotten home later than seven on a Saturday night."

"What time?!" Brute asked in surprise. "Seven! Are you serious?!

For real?! Man, you haven't lived! Eighteen years old and you've never lived! Man, you *are* amazing to me!"

The Writer didn't know what to think or say or do. He'd never been in this situation before. He looked at his watch and saw that it was nearly four-thirty. If they left for home now they'd be there by around six or seven at the latest, and he knew that if he had his way he'd go on up to his bedroom and work on his stories and journal or just sit and listen to his stereo while in his rocker. He'd get his own supper later so Mama wouldn't have to cook. Then Mama would ask him how his day went, where they went, what they saw and did, and if he found out anymore about Brute.

What would I tell Mama, he thought as he debated whether or not to take Brute out to Asheville. What would I say to her when we come in the door after midnight or God knows how late? What do I tell her when I know nothing more about where Brute came from? What will she do to him then? I don't know. I've never 'lived' as he puts it. I don't know how to go crazy. I've never done it before. It's crazy enough not being crazy. Well, I guess it wouldn't hurt for him to just show me. At least I'll have something to tell Mama when I get back. If I go through Canton and avoid the interstate, maybe I can get there a bit faster. Then come that way back home. Okay, I'll do that then. Oh God I hope you know what I'm doing because I sure don't.

"Are we going Zilla?" Brute asked, standing over him. "I'm ready to go."

The Writer nodded, got up, and folded the blanket. Brute took it from him and headed for the car.

"Asheville, here we come!" he kept yelling.

The Writer looked to the sky for a moment.

Then he waddled away . . . back to the car to take Brute to Asheville.

CHAPTER TWENTY-NINE

Somewhere along the outskirts of Asheville, The Writer pulled into a Hot Spot gas station. He paid for the gas and came back to the car. When he did, he saw the card Judy had given him that morning lying between his seat and Brute's. He picked it up as he got back in. Then he noticed the anniversary card Joey had given him, which was lying next to the one Judy had given him. Neither one had been opened.

"When we get to wherever it is you're taking me to in Asheville," The Writer said as he opened Joey's card first, "remember that I don't have enough money to do a lot of crazy stuff, but . . ."

He stopped.

Brute looked at him and then at the card. A twenty dollar bill had floated out of it and into The Writer's lap. The Writer picked it up and read the little message Joey had written inside the card . . .

I know it ain't much, but I hope
you can have fun with it.
Happy Anniversary
Your friend, Joey

"Do I see Mr. Jackson's face?" Brute asked sarcastically. "He can buy us our supper now."

"Don't tell me you're hungry again!" The Writer asked. "Goodness, you eat more than a famished hippo." He then opened Judy's card. In it was a simple graduation card and a smaller white envelope. The Writer tore it open and when he saw what was inside his eyes widened and his mouth became a gaping hole in his face. He pulled the envelope open wider and began counting the slips of paper inside with the face of General Grant on them. He counted seven fifty-dollar bills and the eighth slip of paper was a note from

Judy. With trembling hands mixed with excitement and anxiety at
what all he had just unveiled, he opened the note and Judy's all-
too-familiar right-slanted handwriting appeared before his eyes . . .

Dear Sir,
For everything you've done for Joey, and for what you mean
to us as our friend, you deserve everything in this envelope.
Enjoy it since you deserve it for your graduation and for
being who you are.

Don't worry about trying to repay us for anything.

Love,
Judy

Again he fanned through the collection of crisp money, amazed at
how much was in it, over $350 total with what Joey gave him.
Brute was eyeballing what was inside.

"Oooh, I see money," he said. Then he saw the note Judy
wrote. "Why does everyone call you 'sir' Zilla?"

"Because everyone thinks that being a writer is important," he
replied, glaring at the money. "It's as if nobody in the world can
be one but me."

"You're the only writer I know," Brute said.

"Whatever. Everybody's a writer in some way. It ain't a sacred
talent you know."

"Yes, but you're the only one who actually does it. Others can
yap all day and not say anything. You can write and say more than
anyone else can."

A horn beeped.

The Writer looked in the rearview mirror and saw an angry-
looking lady in a red Explorer drumming her taloned fingernails
on her steering wheel. He realized that they were still sitting at the
gas pump island so he quickly put the money away, revved up the
engine, and headed for the road. The Explorer then roared up to

the pump where he was at. When Brute heard the door slam shut, he whirled around in his seat.

"Hey lady!" he hollered.

She looked.

Brute ran his tongue out at her and waved his hands next to his face. The woman's mouth dropped open and the pump in her hand slipped out of her grasp. It landed on her feet, spilling out some of the gasoline she had just pumped before letting it go. It splattered all over her skirt. Before she could throw one of her high-heeled shoes at the white convertible, it was already out of sight.

The signs on this hidden back road to the great city of Asheville displayed how far they were from the heart of the city. It was no further than if they were driving on I-40, which was congested with the annual summer migration of tourists to the mountains. This road was less crowded and less known than the interstate. As long as it was kept secret it would stay this way.

What else can happen before this day is over? The Writer thought as he came closer to Asheville.

"Hey Zilla, watch for signs for that downtown block party," Brute said. "That's where I want to go."

"To a block party?" The Writer asked.

"Goodness Zilla are you deaf?! Yes a block party! Did you think I meant some English tea party or something?! Step on it!"

Before long he saw big banners and posters promoting a spectacular downtown event draped over the four-lane that took you into the heart of the city. He took the exit off the four-lane and drove up the hill to one of the designated parking lots for the party. It was really just a deserted lot for a business building that had folded some years earlier. Other partygoers took advantage of its vacancy, left their cars there, and walked to the party, which is what The Writer and Brute did.

"Wow! Looks like half of the state is here," Brute said when they looked at the massive crowd that had flooded into the blocked off section of the city. People were streaming in from all sides and vendors, rides, stands, and stages could be seen scattered all over the place. There was the usual bustle of people yakking away, babies screaming, little kids begging mommy for more candy, teens romping around without respect as to who they bumped into, and of course pastel colored balloons floating lifelessly into the sky. With each one there was a crying child to accompany it.

"There are so many people here," The Writer said in a long breath, as if he'd never seen so many before in all his life. "It's crowded."

"That's how downtown parties usually are," Brute said, pulling him down into the crowds that were headed for the stands. Reluctantly The Writer followed him. "Let's see what we can get into!"

An announcer's voice was booming over a loudspeaker that was piped up to all areas of the party.

"WELCOME TO THE LARGEST DOWNTOWN BLOCK PARTY IN THE SOUTH! TONIGHT AT 8, DON'T MISS OUR SPECIAL DANCE AND SINGING CONTEST AT THE SQUARE! ALSO, LIVE ENTERTAINMENT FROM LOCAL TALENT STARTING IN JUST A FEW MINUTES AND MEET THE CREW OF YOUR LOCAL TELEVISION STATION AT THE . . ."

"Let's go over there," Brute said, pointing to a long chain of tents that were lined up along one of the sidewalks. They seemed to reach forever up the street and around the corner in the far distance. Each tent was a vendor, mostly local merchants selling handmade goods and other small trinkets. Some had face painting, served snacks, t-shirts, caps, souvenirs, and other things of the such. The Writer and Brute came to the first one and looked around at the stunning gallery of homemade jewelry in glass displays. The next vendor was selling airbrushed t-shirts and he had a long line of customers. Several girls were fussing over what they wanted on their shirts. Some wanted a butterfly and another wanted a tiger. Some asked for bulldogs, ladybugs, dolphins, and other animals. A few vendors up Brute saw foot-long hot dogs being sold at two for a dollar. The Writer yanked him away up to another one where laser pointers were being sold like crazy.

"I can run the cats crazy with one of these things," he said as he bought one that hooked onto his keys. He and Brute then went up to the next merchant where a middle-aged couple was selling wooden puppets on strings. They had attracted a lot of little kids and several annoyed parents. On up was a vendor selling pictures and paintings of all sorts. The Writer stepped inside the tent to look around and Brute began tugging at his shirt.

"Zilla, I'm gonna be next door for a minute. I'll be back." He then disappeared into the next tent while The Writer continued to look around. He came upon a holographic framed picture of a tiger racing across an open field. He laid his hand down on it and saw that the 3D effect made his hand look as if it were lying down inside the picture just above the tiger.

He flipped it over to see how much it was.

$25.00

He quickly put it back and stepped out to see where Brute went to. He didn't think he went too far but scoured the crowd as best he could. There was no sign of him. Maybe he went up ahead to another vendor, he thought as he proceeded. He kept looking out at the seething crowds in the streets and heard someone making a hissing sound. He turned and saw where it was coming from. From inside one of the vendor windows he saw Brute's face peering out at him. The Writer walked up to see what he was up to now.

"I'm getting a tattoo on my leg."

"You're what?"

"A tattoo. See, looks just like that cross we saw this morning." The Writer couldn't see it from where he stood. His face turned sallow at the very thought of him getting a cross tattooed on his leg. Brute saw the look in his face and reached a hand out the window for him. "Just wait Zilla. I'll show it to you for real what it is." The Writer just turned away and looked at the crowd, waiting for Brute to get finished, which wasn't too long.

"Hey look Zilla," he said, bouncing out of the tent. He was pointing down at his leg. The Writer looked and saw a tattoo in the shape of a cross on a hillside. His eyes widened and he immediately began to recall the story behind tattoos and pagan worship. He looked up towards Brute's face. He just laughed and patted The Writer's head.

"Don't worry Zilla. It's not real. It's fake. See, you just wet it on the skin. I saw it and it looked like that cross we saw on the hilltop this morning. Cool huh?"

The Writer breathed a deep sigh of relief. Fake tattoos he had no problem with. He even wore them sometimes.

"Mister, that's $1.49 please."

Both Brute and The Writer turned around to see a blonde haired girl of about fifteen standing next to Brute with her hand held out. The Writer opened his waist bag, pulled two dollars out of his wallet and placed them in the girl's hand. After she gave him the change, they went away from the vendors.

"Brute, if you want something tell me so I can give you the money," The Writer explained.

"Sorry."

"I thought you were gonna show me where you were from. All we've done so far is look like tourists around here."

"Okay Zilla, after it gets dark, I'll show you where I'm from. Is that cool?"

"Why after dark?"

"Because it'll look more real to you, you know, like the first time you ever saw the beach. Being told about it and actually seeing it are different things."

The Writer looked away at the sky. It was getting darker and darker. The clock on the side of the bank building near the festivities glared in big green digits that it was now 7:37 p.m. and the temperature was 75 degrees. He started walking towards the square where a contest was soon to start. Brute followed.

"What's wrong Zilla? Aren't you having fun, or would you rather be back at your mommy's house?"

He shook his head. That wasn't what was bothering him. It was the illustration Brute had used to make his point.

"I've never been to the beach." His voice was faint and quivery.

"WHAT?!" Brute's jaw dropped. He grabbed The Writer by the shoulder and whirled him around.

"Zilla, you're joking right? Please say you are. You've been to the beach . . . haven't you?"

He closed his eyes and shook his head. "In fact, I've never even been out of North Carolina."

Brute grabbed a clenching hold of his shoulders and jerked his head up and eyes open. The Writer looked again to the skies. Brute waved his hand in front of his face but it did no good.

"Zilla, I can't believe this. You've never been to the beach. Not in your whole life?"

He shook his head again.

"Oh golly Zilla, what am I going to do with you? Every writer has to see the beach before they die. We should go sometime. How about that man? Just you and me. The beach. Zilla and Brute. The coolest guys in the country. Wouldn't that be great man?"

"Yes it would," The Writer said forlornly. He knew it would probably never happen. A gut feeling suddenly took hold of his stomach. This was something very hard for him to ever see happening. When he heard it he detected an empty feeling somewhere. There was something missing from this idea. What it was he couldn't figure out. As much as he'd love to go with Brute to the beach, the very idea did not have that genuine feel to it. "I'd . . . uh . . . I'd like to go . . . I just don't know when."

"Ask your mom," Brute said, already getting excited. "Maybe she'll let us go tomorrow! You think she would Zilla?! Do you?"

Before he could answer, a loudspeaker suddenly crackled and a voice announced that it was almost time for the song and dance contest to begin near the square. Before The Writer could react, Brute was already pulling him over to it. Rather than try to fight him, he just let himself get dragged over there, wondering what Brute was up to now.

By now a crowd was gathering at the staging area, ready for the first series of songs and then the dancing and singing contest. The band let everyone know that it was time to begin with a minute long prologue of loud music from their instruments. As soon as it came to a finish there was an explosion of applause as the lead singer came out onto the stage and went to the far end, which was like a peninsula sticking out into an ocean of people. She waved her hat to the fans and welcomed the crowd.

"Welcome everybody to our little country/rock concert! My name's Janine and I'm here to entertain and sing for you all tonight along with my favorite little band who came up here all the way from the heart of Alabama, just to play for you all tonight!"

She needs to rewrite her opening speech, The Writer thought amidst the screaming cheers.

Janine then introduced the members of the band and then immediately went into the first song, which was a lively tune originally recorded by Reba McEntire called *Why Haven't I Heard From You?* As soon as she the band started playing the crowd in front of the stage parted away into a huge circle to let the dancers come in and show what they had. One teen couple got in the circle first, followed by more couples until it was filled with about thirty people dancing. The surrounding audience began to sing along with Janine, clapping their hands in the air. Brute clapped to the tune of the song. The Writer simply watched from Brute's side. The words of the song Janine was in full throated voice with made him think.

Yea Rusty, why haven't I heard from you? I think I know why after this morning. I don't need your lame excuses anymore. I know all about you now. You are no longer part of my life and I wish I could let the whole world know it. I'd tell the world that I pitched you out of my life and things are already getting better for me. I don't need some horny oversexed beast making a shambles of my life. I'm glad you're gone. And I hope you stay gone.

The more he thought about it, the more it felt so real and so fervent in his heart and mind. Gone was that knifing strain of worry in his mind about where Rusty was, what he was doing, and who he was with. Gone was the notion to call and ask where he was. Gone was the worry of him remembering to call The Writer or to go see him. Gone were the thwarted string of visits to his house only to be told he wasn't home. And gone was all the pain of just having Rusty in his life. He never knew of how great an atrocity Rusty was on his heart. A million tons of fret, worry, and despair had been smashed away from off his back. He was here, on his anniversary, with Brute, having fun, enjoying himself, enjoying life.

Don't think, The Writer thought. Do as Brute says and don't think. Nobody else around here is. Let your mind go. Let it rest for a while. Don't think. Just do it!

He had no idea he had just put his fingers in his mouth the way Brute showed him earlier.

" W E E E E E E E E E E E E E E WHEEEEEEEWWWWWWWWWWW!"

Brute looked at The Writer and saw where the loudest whistle he had ever heard came from.

"Did you whistle Zilla?" Brute asked. "Did you? Was that you?"

He nodded.

"YES! THE WRITER CAN WHISTLE!" He started jumping and clapping. "I have taught The Writer well!"

The song was over and Janine came back to the edge of the stage.

"Alright gang, that was just the beginning. It is now time for the dance contest. Everyone grab a partner and come out into the circle. The couple who keeps moving the whole time without messing up once will be our winner. These next songs are sung end-on-end with no breaks in them. C'mon, get your partner and get out here!"

Couples of all ages started making their way into the circle. It was mostly teenage boys and girls. There were a few in their twenties and thirties, some middle-aged, and nobody over that. A group of four boys went out there and Janine told them to split into two pairs. Those who just wanted to watch made the circle bigger by moving further back.

"Hey Zilla, you and me out there! C'mon!" Brute started yanking at The Writer.

"I can't dance," he protested, trying to keep in his spot. "I've never danced before. I'll look like a retard out there."

"Well those geeks out there are doing it for fun," Brute said, pointing to the dance crowd. "We'll look retarded together. C'mon!"

He kept pulling him but only succeeded in crashing on his rear end. "Come on Zilla. Writers love to dance!" He kept struggling to make him move.

"Not this one," The Writer said, keeping still and stiff. "I'll just watch. I love a dance marathon, and besides, they shoot horses don't they?"

It was The Writer's allusion to a novel he'd read some time ago about a dance marathon during the depression era of the 30's that turned ugly and tragic.

"They do what?" Brute asked stupefied.

"Horses get shot when they're injured and in pain. If we dance till we hurt something and we're in blistering torture then . . ."

"Zilla, this isn't the time for a lesson in human affairs!" Brute hollered, pulling him harder. "Get out here and dance! You'll love it! Just move around like you've lost your mind!"

The Writer tried to hold back but felt himself moving. He looked down and his shoes were rubbing across the pavement for the wooden dance floor that had been built in front of the stage. Brute was pulling him as hard as he could. The Writer tried to hold back but was powerless against Brute. When he got to the floor, Brute gave one final yank and tossed The Writer clear out into the floor. He rolled over on his side and saw Brute coming up to him. He helped him back up on his feet and readjusted his cap.

"Brute, this is so . . ."

"Cool I know," he cut in. "I'm gonna teach you to dance Zilla, then when you meet that girl, you can show her a good time!" He then turned to see if the rest of the dance crowd was getting ready.

The sky was now getting darker and the lights all over the city were coming on. Several spotlights were coming on around the staging area.

"What girl?" The Writer asked.

Brute heaved and rolled his eyes. Teaching The Writer was not as easy as he thought it would be.

"Just shut up and do as I do Zilla."

The lights on stage went down, except for the dim ones the band needed to play by. A spotlight fell on Janine and the band took off into a tune by Lorrie Morgan. The dance crowd immediately scattered in all directions moving and gyrating all over the place in quick slick moves. Some held hands, others danced separately but close together. They had smiles on their faces, laughing, singing, enjoying their youth.

The Writer stood still for a few minutes as Brute suddenly cut loose into a series of erratic movements that resembled the scarecrow in *The Wizard of Oz*. He then grabbed his hands and started swinging them back and forth.

"Zilla you're not moving," he said. "You're like this girl I took out some months ago. She never moved."

He looked at him with a death glare.

"I don't mean that you're like her. I mean . . . oh never mind. Just move! C'mon Zilla! Do this for your ol' buddy Brute. Loosen up and I do mean loosen!"

The Writer remained standing still. He glanced all around him and saw the spectators around the dance circle clapping and moving to the song Janine was in full-powered voice with. Some glanced at him and Brute, others look beyond them. The other dancers made sure they didn't bump into them and moved every which way around them. The lights of the city block were in full beam now, making it look as if this whole section of the city were inside some colossal dome feverishly adorned with lavish decorations. One would take it as the world's biggest Christmas party on New Year's Eve. The stars that appeared overhead in the darkening sky added to the festivities. It was getting cooler, and The Writer was consciously aware of what was going on around him both naturally and physically. He was surrounded by the elusive power of the emotion of happiness. It was in the air, on people's faces, in the music, the weather, the lights, the bustle of the crowd, in his heart . . . all this, and then some, penetrated his mortal spirit as a human but was casting an alluring spell over his immortal spirit as a writer.

He looked at Janine and listened to the words of the song she was singing. It was in the first-person singular and was about someone who had spent days at home sitting and waiting for a friend to come. The friend never shows up, so the one who's waiting walks around the house, still waiting. When that someone gets tired of it, they just tell the friend to not ever come back around again, to walk out that door, don't look back, and that one who was waiting walks the other way, not looking back at the friend who couldn't keep a promise.

I've done that many times, The Writer thought. I've waited for Rusty and he never shows up. He'd better not ever come around the house. If he does I'll slam the door on his ugly face and walk away. Then he'll have to walk away because I've had enough of him.

As soon as he pieced this implication together in his mind, he felt a surge arise within him. He turned his head towards Brute, let a smile melt across his face, grabbed his hands, and started moving slow at first, then faster, and faster. Pretty soon he was kicking his feet up in the air around Brute and swinging his arms with his.

"That's it Zilla!" Brute said, moving along with him. "Just move to the music."

His swift movements in the circle were working out the feelings inside him. Janine's voice became his, unleashing everything inside that had yet to come out about his frustration and abhorrence of Rusty. It was as if the cage of anguish, rage, doubt, and fear that he had allowed Rusty to trap himself in for years had finally been opened and destroyed. Rusty no longer had him in the position to be assaulted by his lies and endless string of deceit. He'd have to find someone else to hurt and abuse.

The second song in the contest resulted in about four couples messing up and becoming disqualified when they crashed onto the floor. The Writer and Brute separated and danced their own movements while watching each other. One went clear across the floor from the other and would watch then come back close. The spectators were clapping and cheering. At one sudden instance Janine gave the order for everyone to hold their partner's hand and go around the dance area in a circle. It was what she called 'the derby,' to see who had the strength to keep going around and around nonstop. Both The Writer and Brute held both hands and they charged around in a mad haste, being careful not to fall down and become disqualified. The song that Janine was singing was more pop than country, had a fast beat, and lots of rhythm. She was walking all around the stage singing and waving her arms out over the crowd. She'd jump now and then and go into a series of movements to complement the beat of the song.

When she ordered that the derby was over, the remaining contestants in the circle split. Some were stumbling around from going around the dance area several times and were dizzy. The Writer and Brute let loose of each other as if it were nothing. The next song came up. By now some of the dancers had collapsed from exhaustion and were out. One by one they crawled out of the circle and back into the crowd of spectators. Brute and The Writer were still standing, ready to go again.

This tune was country, and the words of it talked about going out on the town after a long hard day and going wild. Brute looked at The Writer and smiled. The song was the perfect capper for their day together.

"This song's for us Zilla!" Brute hollered as he clapped his hands in midair. He came up to The Writer, held his hands and twisted him out into the middle of the circle. His coat spun all around his legs and wrapped itself around his front, and before it could unfurl itself, he was already into the beat of this song. Dancers were falling like dead birds all over the floor. Some had to be dragged away. Others got up and ran out of the way of The Writer and Brute. By now it was just a series of erratic compulsive moves that had no rhythm or arrangement. A spotlight that changed colors every few seconds beamed down on them beyond their knowledge.

By now only The Writer and Brute remained on the floor.

Brute came back up to The Writer and he put his hands on Brute's hands and spun him around, lifting him off his feet into the air about three inches off the ground. Brute saw The Writer's huge feet make fast turns and twists. The lights and the faces of the spectators were a blur. When he slowed down he let go of Brute and had him turning around in a daze. He quickly regained control and rejoined The Writer. The song came to its final stanza of lyrics. Before it did, there was a brief moment of nothing but music. During this Brute saw something.

The Writer unknotted his coat, took off the money belt, and tossed them all off to the side. He even turned his cap backwards. The crowd went wild and cameras started flashing from all directions. The lyrics came back into the song and Brute's flabbergasted expression at seeing The Writer quite literally let free of himself remained frozen on his face until The Writer jerked him aside and twisted him around, let him go, and then they were both back into the spirit of things.

The music was building up to its grand finale and Janine's lyrics had run out. She clearly saw who the winner of the dance contest was and ran offstage to get the trophy.

When the music came to a halt, both The Writer and Brute slowed down and stopped, soaked in sweat, heavy breathing, and slumping over. The crowd had lost its composure, screaming and yelling as if some major rock star had just appeared on stage. Lights and cameras were flashing like crazy. The Writer and Brute looked at each other in total confusion. Was it over already? Had all the songs been sung? Where were the other dancers? It took a few minutes for their minds to clear up and grasp the reality of this moment. Brute was heaving and puffing as sweat dripped off his forehead. He leaned over and put his hands on his kneecaps until his breathing returned to normal. The Writer wiped the sweat from his forehead and looked to the darkened sky with the stars glistening from millions of miles away. With his legs quivery, he staggered his way to Brute and put his hand on his wet back. Neither one paid attention to the roaring ovation that thundered from the crowd on all sides of the circle. The band was on their feet clapping and cheering.

Janine jumped down from the stage and walked up to The Writer. With a huge smile on her red face she handed him the winner's trophy, which was two feet high and had blue and black pillars holding up a gold star. The Writer saw it and nudged Brute harder. He looked up and saw what Janine had in her hands. He then leapt up in the air and grabbed The Writer in the tightest hug he'd ever been in. The Writer pushed him off when the stench of his sweat got to be more than he could handle. Janine finally got the trophy into their hands and had them pose for a picture. The crowd was still going nuts and Janine showed The Writer and Brute a spot out of the circle where they could rest and cool off.

The Writer handed the trophy to Brute to carry.

He then looked around at the screaming crowd of onlookers. All of them had their eyes on him.

They're looking at me, he thought. Brute and me. We've done something they like. What else can I do that they'll like? God, please show me what else I can do . . .

And he waddled away . . . to sit with Brute under a tent out of the dance circle.

CHAPTER THIRTY

The Writer placed the trophy on the table that he and Brute were seated at and he rested his head on the table. Brute was still slinging sweat off his head like a dog that just came out of the creek on a hot summer afternoon. The creek would feel good right now, The Writer thought as he felt his strength gradually build back up. Janine had made an announcement that there was going to be a brief intermission before the singing contest got underway. The band left their equipment on the stage and went back behind the tent to the little trailer they had hauled with them all the way from Alabama.

"So Zilla, I bet you've never done this before," Brute said, looking at him.

"You mean dance?" he asked with his forehead resting on the edge of the table.

"Uh huh. Now you have something else to write about. You can write a book on dance lessons. Teach them the Godzilla "PunchWalk" or the Writer's Sling Dance, all those crazy moves you were doing out there."

"Uh huh," he said tiredly. He sat back up with his eyes closed. He opened them up and saw the crowd still anxious for the singing contest to begin. He and Brute were in the shadows under the tent and hardly anyone could see them. They had been given towels and water to cool off with and had a huge fan blowing on them. Someone returned The Writer's coat and waist bag to him. Brute splashed his water in his face and had some more brought to him to pour down his head. The Writer just let the fan cool him down and sipped his water little by little.

I'm gonna be stinking by tonight, he thought. When I get home I'm hitting the shower.

Brute looked at The Writer, his face finally dry from the sweat and water he'd been soaked in.

"You were great," he said.

The Writer looked towards him.

"Whoever told you that you couldn't do anything is a jerk."

"So nearly everyone who knows me is a jerk?" The Writer asked. "If that's what you mean, you're right."

"Well everybody but your friends, and your mother."

He nodded to him and closed his eyes again. "I wish everyone from that lousy high school could've seen me out there." He opened his eyes. "Then they'll think twice about me being too dim-witted to do anything." He turned his cap back around, put his money belt and coat back on around his waist, and looked at the trophy. "So what are we gonna do now?" he asked.

"We're gonna watch these guys try to sing," he said, scooting his seat back to The Writer. "I betcha none of them can sing like Tim McGraw or Faith Hill."

"Or can't sing at all," The Writer added. "Wasn't some pop group busted for lip synching their whole concert?"

"I don't know Zilla. I don't read tabloids."

Janine's voice suddenly boomed out. "Alright now it's time for the singing contest! Get up here and sing your favorite song and have a chance at winning our second trophy of the evening!"

"Another trophy?" Brute asked in amazement. "Really?" He looked out at the crowd that was gathering at the stage. "Well Zilla, guess what?" He had a huge devilish smile on his face. "Wanna make it a clean sweep?"

"Brute . . ."

"Aw yeah Zilla, you wanna sing now don't 'cha? You sang this morning going to Murphy. I heard you now. Don't try to get out of it." Brute ran up to tell her that he and The Writer were gonna do it, but he found out he was act number twelve. Eleven others had beaten him to the stage. He came back and sat down next to The Writer.

"I'll make it easier for you," Brute said. "You either get up there and sing with me, or I break your fingers so you can't write again." He started cracking his knuckles.

"Can't we compromise?" The Writer asked sheepishly.

Brute got closer and grunted. "I'm gonna compromise you unless you get your little Godzilla butt up there and sing with me."

"Okay, I'll sing," he blurted.

"That's what I thought," Brute said, leaning back in his chair as the first act got up to sing. The Writer looked down on all sides of his seat and then up at Brute.

"And my Godzilla butt isn't little."

Act eleven got off the stage to a reception of general applause and cheers of courtesy from the crowd. Everyone knew that a guy trying to sound like Reba McEntire was a croak. The band members looked at each other with glazed expressions and rolled their eyes at the last act. Janine was in her chair offstage yawning. None of the acts so far looked appealing, except for the one guy who got up there and started singing an uncensored version of a song by Rage Against the Machine. When Brute heard it he started moving around in his chair and singing along with the vocalist. He stopped when he realized that there were a few words in the song that he knew The Writer did not like. The guy was escorted off the stage by one of the guitar players and the drummer.

Janine went up to present the last performers of the evening. As soon as she mentioned them being the winners of the dance contest earlier, the crowd broke out into blaring screams and jubilation.

"C'mon Zilla! That's us!" Brute hollered, yanking The Writer up out of his seat.

"But what do we sing?" The Writer asked frigidly. "I . . . I don't know what . . ."

"Don't worry Zilla. I know the perfect song for us to sing. It just fits you. C'mon!" He started pulling him out to the stage.

Dear Lord you better be up there with me, he thought as he let Brute pull him.

Brute whispered to Janine what they were gonna sing. When

she heard it she laughed, told the boys what tune to play, and when they heard what the request was the biggest smiles to ever come over their faces soon elevated into laughs and high fives. The Writer saw this and it only raised his worry level up several notches.

"I can't do this," he told Brute as they waited for their cue to come out on stage. "I can't sing. I'll look ridiculous. You go without me." He whirled around and tried to dash down the steps but Brute caught him by his coattail.

"Come back here you tiger!" he said, pulling him. "You're not chickening out on me now boy! Don't be a wuss. You're gonna love the song we're gonna sing."

"What is it?"

"Wait and see."

The Writer looked at his watch and as soon as three seconds went by he tried to get away again. Brute caught him and started shoving him out into the spotlights that were shooting all over the stage and on the eager crowd. The Writer stiffened up and Brute got behind him, wrapped his hands around his wrists, and started walking him out to the stage just as Janine was about to call them out there.

"Don't get rough with me Zilla," Brute said through clenched teeth as he kept walking him out. "You may be . . . bigger than me . . . but I can . . . still . . . take you. Get out there . . . and . . . just think . . . about . . . RUSTY!"

He gave him one final shove that sent him stumbling out into a barrage of bellowing screams, cheers, and whooping. Like a frightened cat The Writer looked out at everyone as if they were big game hunters having trapped the greatest find of their lives. Janine tossed him a hand mike and winked at him. The band gestured with a simple nod of the head. The leader tipped his hat to The Writer then saluted him. He had no idea what to do. His heart began pounding like crazy and the lights from the rest of the festivities were so bright and colorful it looked as if he were inside some swanky nightclub.

Think about Rusty, he thought when he remembered the last

thing Brute told him to do. Why would I want to think about that horrid beast at a time like this?

Brute stepped out with a hand mike and the band immediately took off into the opening notes of a song The Writer remembered hearing several times on the radio. He had seen the single sell out like crazy in the entertainment department of Wal-Mart and the music video to it was wild.

Brute sang the first few words to the song, and after he did, he came up to The Writer and turned him around to face the crowd. The tune of the song dropped down for a second, then suddenly propelled up into full blast rhythm. The audience went hysterical and began shouting louder than ever.

"Think of that nasty Rusty character," Brute whispered to The Writer. After he did he backed away, sang the opening lyrics of the song, and The Writer immediately got the idea.

The song dealt with someone planning to tell his friend that tonight was it for them and that they were through with each other forever. Brute's part dealt with there probably going to be a fight between them, that the other one was never there for the other one, and that it was time to go on in life alone. The Writer picked up on what Brute was trying to tell him. He smiled big and started his dance movements. Amidst cheers from the crowd, he moved up near Brute and joined in with the rest of the song, which he knew by heart because of the endless number of times he'd heard it from just about anywhere, at school, in stores, car radios, wherever. It had planted itself in his mind and was playing out through his mouth without hardly any effort. It was so natural that he didn't even think about what he was doing. He let himself become controlled by the music, the lyrics, watching Brute, and the crowd going nuts over their act. Girls were waving and screaming, boys clapped, and the dance floor opened up to those who couldn't contain themselves. It began to fill up little by little as dozens of spectators fell victim to the dance urge. Janine joined some guy in a cowboy hat in front of the audience and they clapped and cheered together.

The more he thought of Rusty, the more powerful his voice became. His dance moves soon became as frenzied as those of Brute's. They moved all over the stage, passed each other, walked up to the outstretched portion together, appeared to slap their hands in the air as if they were smacking someone's face, then back up to the band. Each time they did that they imagined they were slapping Rusty across the face. Brute would do it twice, one for Rusty, the other for the girl he was with that morning.

When the lyrics mentioned that life would be better once that "friend" was gone, The Writer spun around, ran up behind Brute as he bent over, and leapt clear over him. The crowd went even more out of control when they saw that. Brute got up and looked in amazement at what The Writer just did. Janine and her friend had gaping jaws and cameras started flashing from all directions. The band, which was singing backup for The Writer and Brute, paused for a second after they saw The Writer's amazing stunt. More of the song mentioned getting tired of being the fool, not going to be the loser, and leaving the "friend" behind. This only fueled The Writer and Brute even more. They made like they shoved each other away and continued at different ends of the stage. With long strides they met back in the center of the stage.

By now the song was supposed to stop abruptly, but the leader of the band was so pumped over what was going on he signaled to his boys to repeat the chorus one more time. When the crowd noticed this the spotlights transformed colors and began turning blue, green, red, purple, orange, white, and then back to blue.

More and more The Writer felt pain and misery leave his soul as he let himself go in the song. Strength took their place, giving him the ability to sing and dance all over the stage. Guts replaced fear. Worry was no longer part of life. Opinions were worthless. A new life had taken sole possession of The Writer tonight. It had pitched out that frightened introverted boy who couldn't bear to be out late on Saturday night and replaced him with a guy who had the guts to look public opinion in the face and spit. He saw the lights and the faces in the crowd, all on him. He saw Brute watching him, the band was in full swing with them, and Janine and her friend were cheering him on. A new creature had blossomed inside The Writer. It was coming out to take over. Anybody from that high school who saw him on the stage would not recognize him. He would be a total stranger to them. Mama would not claim him as her son. Judy and Joey would not call him their friend. Annie, Lana, Dionne, Jackie, Nate, Elaine, and Blade would faint from jolting shock at what they would've seen. Rusty's mind would turn comatose.

The Writer had been reborn, on the night of his baptismal anniversary.

The song ended and he and Brute turned to the crowd and waved. Janine hurried behind stage, grabbed the other trophy, and ran out to them. She had both of them grab hold of it and more pictures were taken. The screams were deafening now. Janine ushered The Writer and Brute back offstage to cool off and she made her closing remarks, thanked the crowd for coming, and had the band stand up, take a bow, and then they left. The crowd began to disperse after the cheering stopped, and pretty soon the rest of the party resumed downtown.

Backstage the band members congratulated The Writer and Brute as they headed for their trailer. The leader again saluted The Writer as he passed him. Brute laughed at him and Janine explained that the leader thinks a writer is as important as a navy captain. Her friend came back to where they were and put an arm around her.

"You ready to go honey?" he asked.

She nodded and turned to the boys. "Well guys, it's been fun. I hope to see you all again soon."

"Where you going?" The Writer asked.

"My friend and I are going out now, away from this block party as they call it. We need our alone time. But, take care of that trophy and send me a copy of your first book when it comes out, okay?" She shook their hands and walked away.

Brute said he was going to the bathroom. The Writer nodded,

still clutching the trophy, and watched Janine get into a huge white truck parked nearby with her friend and pretty soon it took off into the night.

A few moments passed.

The Writer stood there alone in the dark. Brute hadn't come back yet, the crowd had completely deserted the staging area, the band was nowhere in sight, and the lights around the stage were being cut off one by one. In the distance he saw people walking around to the vendors and exhibits, just as if nothing had ever happened. There were a few shouts, kids crying, and the rumbling of the rides.

He decided to head on home.

I'll get Brute, take the trophies to the car, and go home. I'm tired and it's been a long day and a long night for both of us. I can't even think about singing and dancing now.

He was gonna have a lot to tell his mother the next day, and he wondered how much of it she'd believe. He had never done this much or anything like this on his anniversary. This was the smash hit of all of them. In just one day he had collected two more trophies to add to the mantle in the living room. By tomorrow morning his mother would walk down the steps and see four shimmering trophies gleaming back at her, and she'll know that they all represent something her son can do when the world didn't think so, and it wouldn't all be just for writing. Those trophies would shatter any doubts about what he could do in life that involved skill and guts.

He picked them up, went around the corner to see where Brute went to and saw a green portable toilet booth. The sign on the latch handle read "occupied" so he stepped up to it and called into the door crack.

"Brute?"

"Yeah man?"

"I'm gonna put these trophies in the car and come back and get you, and then we're going home. Is that alright?"

"Yeah. I'm tired. Go ahead."

The Writer carried one trophy in each hand and made his way up to the parking lot where it was just Judy's convertible and about four other cars parked in a scattered manner all over the lot. None of the other people he passed on his way to the car seemed to care about what the trophies were for or how he got them. All that mattered to him was that he won them and they were going up on the mantle next to his bowling and writing trophies. He unlocked the trunk, put them in, and closed it. He then headed back for the spot where the booth was and expected to see Brute standing outside around it somewhere, but he didn't see him.

Is he still in there, he wondered. I bet all that singing and dancing and eating all day finally made him sick.

He walked up closer to the door and saw that it was not occupied. He looked all around and saw nobody else but the people walking to and from the festivities about thirty feet away. This booth was off to itself just beyond the beam of a streetlight as well as any other signs of life. Puzzled, he opened the door. The stench knocked him back for a moment, then he made himself take a look.

No Brute.

He looked on the floor.

There were several blobs of a splattered liquid of some sort on the metal flooring. Some of it had been smeared all over. He knelt down and saw that some splotches had marks in them.

They were shoe marks. One foot looked as if to have been facing out the door and another looked as if it were facing inwards, therefore indicating how whoever it was inside here was standing, or sitting for that matter. But there were too many prints here for it to have been just one person in here. The booth was too small for one as it was.

The stench became so powerful he stepped out. Then he noticed the door latch. It had been kicked from the outside and the lock had been busted loose. It all looked bent inwards, as if someone had tried to force their way into the booth. He studied it then looked down at the pavement.

There was a trail. Red spots. Big splotches of thick red liquid.

Blood.

He then realized that the splotches inside the booth was blood as well. It had dribbled down out of the booth, onto the pavement, and turned into a trail of red spots that went around the booth and down into a dark alley behind the booth. The Writer walked a few steps past the booth and saw that the trail went far into the pitch blackness of the alley.

Somebody's got Brute, he thought with horror. Somebody has him. They've cut him and took him away! He could be dead! Oh no! What if he is? What will I tell Mama when I come home tonight without him? That I turned my back for a few minutes to put away some silly trophy and when I turned around I saw blood all over the street? She will freak out.

He stopped himself. He grabbed hold of his forehead and banished all the horrid thoughts of what may have happened. It was possible that none of them could be certain. He didn't know. He was just making random guesses. There was nobody else around here now. The band was gone. Janine was gone. The crowd had long gone their separate ways in the party. And now Brute was gone. So it was obvious that there would be no witnesses to the incident.

I have to find him, he thought. I've got to find him and bring him home. I don't care what's out there Lord. Help me find Brute!

He took a few more steps away from the booth and looked into the blackness of the alley. There were no signs of life. The blood indicated that some living thing had been taken in there, and he had to find it and retrieve it. Dead or alive, he was taking him home. He was not going to leave Brute out here alone. All he had for weapons were his pen and car keys with the laser attached to the ring.

"Help me find him," he said over and over with each step he took. "Keep me safe. Make me strong. Guard me from whatever demons are out tonight. Please bring Brute back to me. Please . . . please . . . please."

And he quickly waddled away . . . into the night to search for Brute.

CHAPTER THIRTY-ONE

His footsteps echoed into the night as he hurriedly walked down the deserted alley. The only light came from the streetlights at either end of the alley and from the full moon above. He looked up and saw no signs of life. The walls on both sides appeared dead and lifeless. Everything was outlined in a dim silvery gleam from the moon, just like how things looked around Joey's house the night he went to see him. He stopped and looked all around.

There was the usual dumpster overflowing with trash. There were beer bottles all around it. Some had been smashed and others were just lying around. White and black garbage bags had been thrown up against it. The Writer walked up a few more feet to see if anything was around that may look like Brute. Instead he saw a fat rat climb out of the muck and scurry away into the dark. He proceeded on ahead, trying to follow the blood as best he could in this dim light. All he could see was the soft reflection from the moon in the tiny puddles of it. He followed it clear to the other end of the alley. There it stopped.

Oh gosh what now! he thought in despair. Just then a car come rumbling down the road. The Writer waved his hands, hoping it was someone who may have seen something. As it got into closer view, he could see that it was dingy, dirty, and had been banged all over in front. It was a four-door car from the 80's which practically screamed for a new paint job. The blue paint was flaking off like nobody's business. There were four people inside it. A man was driving. The Writer got up on the sidewalk and motioned for it to come over to him. It slowed down and everyone inside it gave him the finger.

These guys are no help, The Writer thought as he waved for

them to go on. One girl in the back was licking the window at him and another was ramming her middle finger up in the air at him.

It was nothing unusual for him to see. He'd seen it nearly everyday for four years in high school. He recalled the time he went into one of the halls during lunch when no classes were in session and in one of the exit halls were a boy and girl getting it on while on the floor. They did their best to keep their clothes on though. The only difference here was that it was more explicit. The girls didn't look like they were dressed. The Writer turned away as the car sped on down the road, taking with it the vain laughter that bellowed from inside it.

Keep looking Writer, he thought. Don't give up. Remember who you asked to watch over you. Those freaks didn't hurt you . . .

He walked on down the sidewalk, upset that the blood had come to a dead halt. Maybe he was carried. Or maybe his wound was bandaged up. Or what else? I won't know until I keep looking, he thought.

Then he saw someone standing on the corner, smoking a cigarette. Whoever it was looked slender, almost anorexic. The legs were like weak plant stems, so it could not have been Brute. Maybe he or she or whatever it is knows something, he thought as he hurried up to the corner.

He saw that it was a woman. He tapped her on the shoulder.

"What do you want?" she asked coldly. She took a long hard look at The Writer and sneered. "No boy. Not you. Not tonight. I'd rather wake up stoned than flattened. Go down the street. There's more down there. Maybe one of them will fall for you, and besides, I get thirty bucks an hour. I'm hard to get."

The Writer ignored her slut remarks. "No, but have you seen a guy about as tall as I am, black hair, has a tattoo that says 'Brute' on his arm, and . . ."

"Oh, you know Brute?" she asked. The Writer's eyes lit up with high hopes. "Since when did he turn gay on me? Last time I had him he had to go to the bathroom. He whined that I worked too much out of him. He was good at first, boy, so if he ever gets on you don't let him . . ."

"HAVE YOU SEEN HIM?!?!"

"Boy calm down. I know you need it but go ask one of my co-workers down there. I'm sure one of them will feel sorry for you and . . ."

"THANK YOU . . . slut," he said as he turned around and started down the street. The woman was right. Further down was a whole army of prostitutes waiting to be picked up. They were up against the walls of buildings smoking cigarettes, pot, and exchanging small plastic packets of some sort. Some stood on the sidewalk in pairs, laughing and making jokes of their wild nights with strange guys.

The Writer stopped dead in his tracks. Should I go on or what, he wondered. God, I know I shouldn't be here. I know it probably makes you sad to see me here, but I'm only looking for Brute. That's all. Nothing else. I didn't come here to be a part of their lifestyle. I just want Brute, so please lead me to him somehow . . . please . . . please . . . please . . . lead me through this Sodom and Gomorrah of the night for the one I love . . .

"Lost young man?"

The Writer spun around and was face to face with a black guy wearing a black cap and black gloves. "Come back here. We'll show you a good time."

He bolted up the walk as fast as he could go. Before he knew it he was headed straight for the other hookers. One of them whistled at him as he flew past her. Another stepped out in front of him. He saw her and slowed down, ready to head back in the other direction.

"Well look ladies," she said in her husky voice as smoke oozed out of her mouth. "Looks like we got ourselves a big fish to fry tonight."

"HAVE YOU SEEN A GUY NAMED BRUTE?!" he asked loudly, feeling that it was obvious that if one of them knew him, the rest would.

"Brute? Oh you mean that big bear who showed me how to . . ." one of them was saying lustfully.

"YES! Have you seen him?"

"Not in about a week," another one said, stepping up to The Writer with a cigarette in her hand. "But why bother? You're kinda cute too. Just like Brute. He taught me a few tricks. Want me to show 'em to you?"

The Writer backed away. "No. Where can I find him? Any of you know?"

"Who cares?" another one said, slinking up to him. "How much you got on you? The more you have, the better it'll be baby . . ."

The Writer turned and headed across the barren street for the other alley. There were a few more hookers over on the other sidewalk but they didn't bother him as he shot into the alley and slammed himself up against the wall. He quickly regained his breathing and started up the alley, looking in vain on both sides. All he saw was trash in a flooded receptacle, this time being more household waste. He passed it without a care.

Then a shadow stepped out of it . . .

Find Brute, find Brute, find Brute. The thought played over and over in his mind like a broken record. Each time he thought it he felt some part of him become stronger. He walked faster and turned his head every which way with sharp moves. He was thankful more than ever now for his peripheral vision. It would help him should he have to look straight ahead at something and there be something else off to the side that he'd have to keep a watch on.

Too bad he didn't have eyes in the back of his head. They would have seen the black figure striding up behind him in silent catwalk stealth . . .

The Writer walked up to where another alley branched out from the one he was already in. Had he went straight ahead he'd come out onto the sidewalk where the hookers were. He decided to go down this new route he discovered.

And so did the black phantom figure . . .

At the end of this alley was a white light, not like the light he'd heard of several times from people who claim to have had an out-of-body experience. This light was not as bright, but dimmer, and more luring than the one alleged to be at the end of one's life. It was just bright enough to allow him to look on the brick walls that loomed on either side of him as he hurriedly walked down the alley. He could see a mess of words and images spray painted on the brick structures, suggesting sexual acts and advertising profanity as if it were the one common thing among people in America. These images scurried past him in a fuzzy blur as he made his way for the end of the alley. He kept his eyes peeled wide open for any signs of life and there had been none since the prostitutes.

Brute where are you, he kept wondering. Tell me where you are. I'm not leaving this place without you. Dead or alive I'll find . . .

He was savagely yanked backward onto the ground. He saw the street in front of him at the end of the alley suddenly loom up into the air out of sight and it was replaced by the dingy, whisker-ridden face of a dope head. His mouth was slightly open and he was oozing a steady stream of drool down on The Writer. He turned his head away but the thug grabbed hold of his head and jerked it back around.

This feels so familiar, he thought, recalling what Brute did to him earlier that week in the bedroom. He knew how to handle him this time, even though it wasn't Brute. He could tell this guy was not as sturdy or as physically powerful as Brute was. He was smaller, skinnier, and more wimpy.

He started going through The Writer's pockets, searching in vain for his wallet. His shorts pockets were very deep, and he could feel the bony hands digging all around his waist. Then he saw the waist bag poking out from under his coat. He tore open the zipper, yanked out the wallet and dozens of crisp bills bloomed out of it like a spring flower.

Take it, The Writer thought. Take all of it. Brute's worth more than any amount of money in the world.

And the thug did. He yanked it all out, threw the empty wallet down on The Writer, and took off into the night. The Writer lay still for a few moments, waiting to make sure he was gone. He slowly got up on his feet and looked all around. He was alone. He picked up his empty wallet and stuffed it back into his bag.

I've been mugged, he thought. I can't believe it. I actually got mugged. The thought slowly took root in his mind, embedding itself into his memory of experiences to forever remember. Oh well, it could've been worse, he thought. It's just money.

He took off back down the alley, still looking, searching, trying to find Brute. He walked faster now than before. He wasn't about to let such a dreadful experience with a mugger wreck his desire to find Brute. Maybe if I move faster I'll find him sooner, he thought. He's still here on earth somewhere. I just have to find him. That's all. What's so hard about that?

The thought struck his mind.

Okay, it's harder than I thought.

He came closer to the end of the alley. He saw cars shooting past the alley and the sounds of people talking and making all sorts of racket got louder as he neared the end of it. To him, it meant that there was life after all at the end of this dismal alley, but what kind of life he didn't know. It made him think of all those stories he'd heard on TV where people claim to have been to the other side and seen the white light at the end of a tunnel, as well as some who claim to have been to the edge of Gehenna and seen the lake of fire prepared for Satan and his angels. He already doubted finding a slice of heaven here, and his doubts were soon confirmed.

He stopped at the end of the alley and peered his head around the corner. As far as the eye could see there was nothing but drunks, bums, addicts, and just plain losers in life, all congregated here in one place, as if to support each other in sinking deeper into the failures of life. They were spread all over the sidewalk, lying on the side of the street, in benches, slouched up against the walls of the buildings. Some had their heads covered with blankets and coats. Others were moping around griping and cursing at each other about how much crack and dope they needed to feel "whole" again. Some were up stumbling around in each other's arms. He could see a bunch of teens on the steps to other buildings across the street, drinking beer and making foul remarks to each other about their lives and doings. The street itself was rotting into deterioration. Streetlights were smashed, cars were broken into, graffiti was on the sides of buildings and on the walk, thugs were raiding trash bins, some even taking out the remains of food that others had thrown away.

Mama would have a hissy fit if I brought all these home with me, he thought.

Very cautiously The Writer stepped out onto the walk and looked up and down each direction. It was a toss-up as to which way to go first. Either way was a grueling excursion into the heart of human decadence and spiritual blindness. He felt his feet aiming to go to the right, so he did. He walked quickly so he wouldn't look like a potential victim. He kept his eyes focused on all things as best he could, being more thankful than ever to have peripheral vision. He could see bums lying all around as he passed them. He looked across the street for hopeful signs of Brute's sturdy figure. None of them looked like him in the slightest. They were either too short or too flimsy. But they did look back at him, shouted profane gestures, and gave him the finger several times. In his haste The Writer rammed into a guy who was considerably larger than he was, knocking him back into trash cans. He helped him up and then continued on his way, ignoring the man as he yelled and screamed after him. But there was still no sign of Brute, and he didn't dare ask anyone on the street if they'd heard of him. If they had they probably wouldn't even tell him.

Dear God lead me to him, he thought as he prayed. Where am I to go?

Then it loomed out of nowhere at him. A huge gaping hole of darkness to the right that seemed to summon The Writer to come into it. He dashed into it and looked all around. It was a dead end alley. There was just enough moonlight from above for him to see what little there was in here. Two buildings on either side that looked just as lifeless as everything else he'd seen thus far made this alley one of the darkest and tightest he'd ever seen. There were two trash cans lying around and old tires. A fence made of wooden boards was put up in the center of the alley. It looked as if it'd been there for years, perhaps even decades. It was rotting apart and didn't look very strong.

Someone didn't use water seal, The Writer thought as he caressed his hand over the wood, trying to see just why he came in here in the first place. Brute was not here of course but an eerie sensation was. It was so intense it caused a knot to swell in his stomach. The Writer felt there was someone else in here besides him. If it was another mugger he was out of luck because all his money was gone. He looked up and only saw the black edges of the top of the two buildings where they reached up to the night sky. A warm summer night wind gusted into the alley, just like what he felt sitting in front of his bedroom window in the early evening when the sun casts its orange glory across the skies. This breeze seemed to shoot straight through him. It caused him to close his eyes and the sensation took hold of him. He felt his coat blowing back behind him from the waist. His hands stretched out as the wind swirled its strands of threaded breeze. He let the sensation draw him back against the wall and when he hit it, he opened his eyes and was greeted with a gentle rustling sound.

He turned his head to the left and saw what was making the noise. It was parched, but he could tell that at one time it was white, frilly, and silky. Even in this moonlight he could see that it was the remnants of a huge bow, now droopy and near its end. What was a bow doing in here? he thought as he lifted it up. When he did, he saw why it was there.

Under it was a wooden plaque with a metal plate, tightly mounted onto the fence. He got closer to read what was on it . . .

In memory of
Officer Thomas Jacobs,
for serving and protecting his community and fellow citizens.
This marker erected by his fellow peers and his wife

Linda and unnamed child on
April 14th, 1980

The Writer read the words etched into the metal plate several times, each time letting it sink deeper into his mind and heart. He brushed his hand over it, letting the etching of the words on the plaque scratch his flesh. He looked out in front of him and envisioned how it might have happened eighteen years ago. He chased Mama's rapist into this alley. There was a struggle. The rapist knocked the officer up against the fence and shot him, then the officer shot and killed him as well. He looked down at the pavement under the bow. He bent down and rubbed his hand over the spot where the officer would've fallen. He could feel the sensation stronger than ever. This was the closest he'd ever been to the man who would've assumed the role of his father. It was as if he'd stepped foot onto sacred ground, a place where no man ever dared to tread. Even though his fingers only felt the harsh roughness of the corroding pavement, his heart was feeling the spirit of the one man his mother ever truly loved.

The wind picked up again. The Writer stood back up and looked to the sky. It appeared to be brighter than it was just a few moments ago. His thoughts were focused on the man he'd never met but felt so close to at this moment. I wonder if he knows what I've turned out to be, he wondered. Would he be proud, or ashamed? A real father would know what his son needs and wants in life, what means the world to him, what makes him happy. I know God does that. He knows what is best for us, and for me. He would've known what Brute means to me. God knows that too.

He leaned his face into the fence. So what am I to do about Brute, he wondered. I haven't found him. I can find where my father was shot but not Brute. Why God? Is it best that I find where he was shot rather than where my friend is? Is it?

As he kept his face pressed into the crack of the fence he heard voices that became louder and more shrill. It was accompanied by scraping and jerking of feet against concrete. He opened his eyes and looked at the opening of the alley, thinking a rowdy gang was headed this way. Instead the sounds came from behind him. He found a hole in the fence and looked through it. He could see another street at the end of the other half of the alley brightly lit and there were cars whizzing by every few seconds. He strained to see what the noises were. Pretty soon, there appeared coming down the street a gang of about fifteen guys leading another guy beyond his will. He appeared to be struggling to get away but had no luck. The other guys were telling him to shut up, keep moving, and when someone said 'Zilla' The Writer's heartbeat shot into overdrive. He strained even harder to see just who was being led away. When he saw who it was, he almost wet on himself.

"BRUTE!" he screamed. He looked around for an easy way over the fence but nothing was there, not even a ladder. He searched around in vain before losing sight of Brute. He grabbed the two tires and stacked them up at the edge of the fence. It was almost too perfect, because he easily climbed up and over the fence and jumped down on the other side. He saw that they were still leading Brute away down the street and he took off after them.

"Oh thank you God! Thank you daddy!" he kept saying over and over as he sprinted down the alley at top speed. He dashed out onto the walk and saw that Brute was still being taken away beyond his will by the other guys, all dressed in black and wearing chains that dangled from their waists. He appeared to be struggling but they were stronger. The Writer ran down the sidewalk across the street from them, hoping Brute would see him. When he didn't, The Writer heaved deeply.

"BRUTE!"

All the guys stopped and looked at him. Brute peered around one of their heads and saw The Writer standing on the walkway across the street.

"ZILLA!" He yelled so loud some of the other guys flinched and let loose of him for a split second. That was more than enough time for him to make a mad escape. He knocked two of the men down as he shot across the street in front of other cars. The Writer started across as well and when they met Brute swept him up in his arms in a huge bear hug that only lasted a second, because then he grabbed hold of his wrist and started to run with him. The Writer looked back and saw that the whole gang was charging across the street after them.

This time The Writer couldn't waddle away . . . he ran with Brute.

CHAPTER THIRTY-TWO

The Writer felt the tips of his feet bounce up and off the pavement as Brute pulled him. Everything in front of him was jangled out of focus. Streetlights and cars were blurred images of warped colors and shapes. The walkway in front appeared to jerk all over the road in one piece. He was breathing deeply and heavily through his nose to avoid an asthma attack. To have one now would've been a crisis. He could hear Brute begin to pant and heave as they neared the end of the walkway at the corner.

"Come on!" he yelled, yanking him out into the road. There were a few cars coming down the road that slammed on the brakes and blew their horns for several seconds as The Writer and Brute got across. When the mob reached the corner they were at a standstill because there was an endless stream of cars coming down at the time. Brute pulled The Writer farther up the street where it was dark. Once there they glanced around in all directions, looking for a way to escape safely and get back to the car. By now The Writer had no idea what part of town he was in, but Brute knew it like the back of his hand. He yanked The Writer across another deserted street and down another sidewalk. He kept looking back every few seconds to see if they had lost the mob, and when he thought they had he pulled The Writer into another dark alley.

"Are you alright man?" Brute asked out of breath. The Writer nodded as he kept looking up and down the street. Brute jerked him back in and slammed him up against the brick wall. "Stay out of sight!" he hissed. He then lifted up his leg to The Writer and showed him something. "Look what those clods did to me man!" The Writer bent down and saw that a huge portion of the skin had been scraped off with knives. It was bloody and beginning to swell.

It clearly explained the trail of blood he found going down the alley. "They knifed off my cross! See! Makes me mad!" The Writer reached over to touch it but Brute jerked it away. "No man. It still hurts. I gotta get it covered up." At that moment The Writer gestured for him to take off the white shirt he was wearing. Reluctantly Brute slipped it off and handed it to him. The Writer folded it in half and carefully wrapped it around his leg, tying the arms together into a sturdy knot on the side of the leg.

"That should hold till we get home," he said.

"Man you're a genius. Now let's get going!" Brute dashed out into the street then nearly fell trying to get back into the alley. "NO! GO BACK! GO BACK! HURRY MAN! RUN! THEY'RE COMING!" He ran up behind The Writer and pushed him hard up into the alley. The Writer took the hint and started to run. "GO MAN GO! GO! GO!" Brute was just a few feet behind him. He glanced back and saw the mob start turning into the alley. The Writer ran as fast as he could but it was so dark here he couldn't see the fence he smashed head on into. It wasn't the one he was at earlier. This one had thicker boards and felt to be fairly new. He stumbled backwards into Brute, who drew back and kicked one of the boards off its nails at the bottom. It jerked loose and he swung it open for The Writer to squeeze through. Brute looked up and saw the leader of the mob getting closer. He got down on his knees, pushed The Writer the rest of the way through, and he slipped through. As soon as he was on the other side he saw that The Writer was holding it open for him. He let it go and the leader of the mob poked his head into the opening, and wasn't ready for the board to come swinging back down and bash his head on the side.

Brute lead The Writer out of the alley and up another street. Ahead there was a bridge that stretched over a spillway, which was where rainwater poured into from the drainage holes all over the city. The Writer started across the bridge but Brute stopped him.

"This way man!" He was pointing down into the bottom of the spillway and across to the other side. "It takes too long to go that way! They can see us on the bridge! Your car's just over there! We can get across here, go up the other side, and be right at the car in a few minutes! Hurry!" The Writer looked down and saw that this side of the spillway's concrete embankment was a slope down into the darkness. He came over to where Brute was and they started down, but Brute's ankle twisted on him. He fell onto The Writer and they both rolled down the embankment. The Writer kept his eyes closed, afraid of what they might crash into. He grabbed hold of his cap as soon as he felt Brute bump into him, afraid of losing it here in this dreaded part of the city. When they hit the water they were relieved, but then almost panicked when they felt it carrying them away!

"BRUTE!"

"ZILLA!"

They called out into the darkness. Although the water wasn't very deep, it was moving so fast it was difficult to get up. The sudden surge of liquid coldness stunned both of them. Neither one was ready for it.

The Writer looked up ahead and saw that there was a streetlight at the top of the embankment that had a white beam that shot down into the spillway. He could see a long grill up ahead that stretched across the bottom of the spillway. It was used to keep trash from going farther down and getting to the rivers. The Writer simply let the water roll him down into it. His pudginess softened the collision a bit and then he felt Brute's body slam into his. They held onto the grill as they stood up and saw that the water was barely three feet deep, but still strong enough to carry them away.

"Oh gosh it's cold!" Brute hollered as he waded towards the embankment, following The Writer. "But it feels good!"

They made their way up the embankment and fell onto the soft grass at the top. They looked down and saw that just a few hundred feet past the grill was a steep drop into a small reservoir. The sides to it were vertical, therefore impossible to get out of.

After making sure they were both alright, they got up and

headed for the car. They could see it parked on the hill just ahead. The Writer dug around in his soaked waist bag and pulled out the keys. They came to another street and there was no sign of anyone, not even of the mob. They could hear their shoes squishing all over and leaving prints up the sidewalk. The Writer had his wet face fixed on the car. Brute was walking next to him, then wrapped a wet arm around him as they walked in silence, with the exception of their shoes making smooching sounds with each of their steps.

When they got in the car they sat for a few moments, still in silence. The Writer had put the key in the ignition but never turned it. He kept his hands in his lap and was looking dead ahead at the night sky. Brute was studying his wrapped leg and drumming his fingers on his right knee. He turned to The Writer.

"So, did you have fun today Zilla?"

He blinked at the question. He rolled his eyes towards Brute and slowly let a grin melt across his wet face. Brute returned the gesture.

The Writer turned the key and looked at Brute.

"Let's go home."

Mama was sitting in the house in front of the window alone, watching and waiting for her son and Brute to come back home. In her hand was a letter she'd received in the mail that day from the courthouse, news that she was eager to tell her son. Judy had just left and was already back at her house across the field. They had spent the last several hours discussing their shopping trip, what they bought, and how much they spent. Judy had just assured her not to worry about her son being out so late, considering what he'd seen that morning. During her visit Mama got a call from the preacher's wife, asking her and Judy to come in earlier than usual to church the next morning to discuss plans for the Vacation Bible School for later in the summer. She was not going to bed until she knew her son was back in the house.

Her wait wasn't long after Judy left. She saw the glad sight of two headlights coming up the driveway to the house. Behind them were two boys, wet and tired, but both looked quite happy. She watched her son park the car and get out. She also saw something she never thought she'd ever see her son do.

He was smiling.

And as if that weren't enough, he was also laughing. She could not believe her eyes, so she headed out onto the porch to greet them.

"You know Brute," The Writer was saying as he tried to dry his shirt off, "when I write my first book, I'm dedicating it to you."

Brute was stretching when he heard the announcement. "You're what?"

"My first book. When I write it, and if it gets published, I'm dedicating it to you."

Brute looked at him. "Really? Wow. That's cool. I've never had a book dedicated to me. Wait till I tell . . . never mind." He had seen Mama coming down the porch steps. The Writer quickly lost the sudden surge of elation that had overcome him and his face returned to its normal state of deadness.

"So guys, how was your day?"

"Pretty good," The Writer said wryly.

"Listen at him," Brute said. "Just pretty good! Zilla, show your mom what we have in the trunk."

The Writer looked at him as he headed for the steps to the house. He was tired, and didn't feel like having Mama buttering him up with her overly sweet show of being proud of her little boy. It's just a bunch of trophies, he thought. Anybody can win a trophy. But nevertheless Brute had spilled the beans, and Mama was ready and waiting for him to reveal to her what they had.

Brute held one up and The Writer the other one. Both glimmered in the light from the porch and bore a gold outline. Mama's eyes widened with awe as she gazed at them.

"Oh my," she said. "You two sang and danced tonight? Those will look great on the mantle next to the others. Put them in there son. These we gotta keep."

After Mama spent several minutes telling them what arrangement looked best along with the writing trophy and the bowling trophy on the mantle, she took a picture of all four of them. It resembled a mighty golden temple from certain angles. The bowling trophy was the tallest, and the writing trophy the smallest. She spent even longer standing in the middle of the living room looking at them while The Writer and Brute tried to dry themselves off as best they could. Not even the wind from the down car top could dry them out completely.

"Well boys, I'm going up to bed. It's after one," she said, turning off her camera. "By the way son, I have to leave early in the morning for the church so can you get your breakfast before you leave?"

He nodded. As she headed up the stairs she stopped and came back down.

"Oh, I almost forgot to show you this son." She pulled out the envelope from her pocket, took out a letter, and showed it to The Writer. He read it and saw that it was a request for him and her to show up in court on a set date in July to confront the nefarious Mrs. Moran, for the alleged document to have him sent to an institution. Below it was the real signature of their friend Judy, who had also enclosed a special note to Mama. She had already took it out though. Judy would have to be there as well since it was her name that was forged. The Writer felt a beam of joy inside as he read it and saw that Mrs. Moran would finally get what she deserved for trying to have him committed. Nate might also be there, he thought. He works at the courthouse.

Mama told them 'goodnight' and not to stay up too late. After she went to her bedroom they soon went up to Brute's room where he got out of his wet clothes and got ready to go to bed. The Writer was about to leave him when he asked him to turn out the light and come back to him.

"Why?" he asked. "I'm going to bed."

"Zilla, I know you still wanna talk, so come over here. I wanna talk to you."

The Writer walked over to the bed in the dark and looked down at Brute, who gestured for him to sit on the edge of the bed.

His clothes were still wet, and Brute tossed a towel around him.

"Do you know what I saw today?" he asked. "I saw you happy. I've never seen you look so happy."

The Writer looked towards him with the usual glare. "Why do we have to discuss this now?" he asked. "Can't this wait till morning?"

"No because I want to talk to you now."

"About what?"

"Us. Do you know what's happened? We've been changed. I know I have. You have too. Don't deny it Zilla. You know you've never felt like this before in your life."

"Felt like what? Happy? Well, I guess because . . ."

"No guessing Zilla. I know what's kept you from being happy. People like this Rusty. I saw what he did to you this morning. I saw you crying. I saw the tears. And today I saw it in your eyes that you've never been so happy in your life. Please tell me the truth Zilla, aren't you happy?"

The Writer looked away into the darkness and out the window. A breeze came into the room along with the moonlight. It was just enough for him to see Brute's face and bare shoulders as he lay in the bed looking up at The Writer. Am I happy? Yes, I am happy. I just don't show it. I can't. I never knew how to until today.

"Yes, I am," he said. "But that doesn't mean that I never was before."

"Not as much as you were today Zilla. Do you know what the happiest part of my day was today? Hearing you call my name when those guys were trying to get me to join their gang again. That's who I used to hang around with. We'd steal cars, wait for little old ladies on the street, hit on hookers, we were wild man. They used me for bait to get all these babes to come to us. Sometimes we'd get about four or five a night to do. Anyway, they bust in on me in the john, cut off the cross on my leg, and drug me down the alley. I was afraid I'd never see you again Zilla. I cried your name, but they stuffed a sock in my mouth. When they took me down those alleys I knew I did not want to be a part of that life anymore. I did not want to go back to robbing, stealing, and doing every girl I saw. Some part of me began to feel rotten once I saw those guys again. When I saw you standing across the road I knew that I had been saved and saw a way to escape. I had found something else in life that I never found anywhere else, and anybody who finds what I did has got to be the luckiest guy in the world."

"What did you find?" The Writer asked.

"Someone like you."

"I've never heard you talk like this," he said. "Why now?"

"Because if I don't now I may never get to, and you need to hear it Zilla. You need to know it. And I'm jealous of your friend Joey."

"Why?"

Brute sat up in bed and got closer to The Writer. "Because he's always had you in his life. I never did. I never had someone like you to help me and be with me like you are to Joey. I saw you and him at that bowling tournament thing and I could tell that he thinks the world of you Zilla. Someone like you deserves someone like Joey, and he deserves to have someone like you. And if I ever have to see you wasting your time with some rotten trash like Rusty I think I'd kill you."

The Writer flinched. He began to inch away but Brute's hand was already gripping his left shoulder with great strength. He was pulling him closer to him.

"Do you hear me Zilla? I'd rather see you dead than with anyone who would dare hurt you the way Rusty did. Anyone who does has got to be the most horrible idiot on this earth. Seeing you dead would mean that nobody like that could ever hurt you, but also means that nobody would be lucky to have you for a friend. See what I mean? Joey would not want to lose you, and neither would your mother or your other friends. I know I don't."

The Writer grabbed hold of Brute's hand and swiped it off. "Don't talk to me about death. I'm not gonna die. I don't need to be told this by anyone else and especially by you. I know what he really is now, and I will never ever be with another jerk like Rusty. You don't have to worry."

"I wish I didn't," he said. "But I do. You don't know how to be cruel and hateful like most other people do. All you know is how to be good and how to love. People who love evil hate good and they'll hate you. They'll try to get rid of good because they're afraid of it. Rusty hates you Zilla. What he did to you was evil. I've seen evil and I know what it is, and jerks like him are nothing but evil."

The Writer was taking in all the words Brute was saying to him, words that he never dreamt would ever break from his lips. He sat and looked into the darkness, letting it all sink into his soul. He felt a strong surge of warmth swarm up from his stomach. Is he answering me about Joey in all this, he wondered. God, are you talking to me through Brute? He closed his eyes and felt it overtake his mind. Then he felt another pull.

"Just always be my friend. That's all I want."

"Would that make you happy?" he asked. "Because I am."

"Yes." Brute let loose of him and laid back in the bed. "Go to sleep now. Good night."

The Writer went back to his bedroom and after several minutes of aimless wandering he found himself going outside for a walk to meditate on what he just heard from Brute. The night was mild with a breeze every few minutes. He looked to the sky and saw thin clouds boiling up in the far distant heavens over the mountains. The moon was bright and everything was beaming. So much had been lifted off his mind. The truth about Rusty. Where Brute came from and how he lived. The idea that just maybe Joey wasn't pretending after all. How did I ever get that idea, he thought as he walked around. Rusty I guess. He corroded my mind of everything.

He looked up and saw Joey's house. All the lights were off but he found himself walking across the field towards it, looking at the window to Joey's bedroom. The wind blew his coat back around him and the field of tall grass became a silky ocean of rustling waves around him. He stopped in the field and said a prayer of thanks for Joey, his other friends, and for sending Brute into his life. He also prayed for Brute to get to stay as long as he could, and was thankful for Rusty being out of his life. He kept looking at the window and envisioned Joey standing up there, waving to him, even though he really wasn't. The Writer pretended he was and waved back. After a few minutes he started back to the house, his eyes focused on the skies above.

Lord, I know you're up there, he thought. Thank you for taking Rusty away from me. I leave him in your hands. I hope I never have to see him again.

And he waddled away . . . back to his house to go to bed.

CHAPTER THIRTY-THREE

The Writer awoke the next morning earlier than usual. The deep rumbling of a motor in his dream had somehow broken his sleep. When the sound stopped his eyes shot open. He felt as if he had just slipped out of a huge slithery cocoon because he saw that he had not changed out of his clothes from the night before. And during the night he had sweated profusely. He got up and went to the window. The sky was overcast with a few open slits here and there. The air felt dry and his throat was ragged. He went to the bathroom, got a drink of water, and looked up at the mirror. He saw himself again, only this time it looked darker and more hideous than yesterday when the truth about Rusty was made manifest before his eyes. The curves on his face looked deeper and longer, the shadows stretching further than they normally would in the morning.

He walked out into the hall and looked around. Everything looked the same but the overall feel was sinister and creepy. He peeped in Mama's bedroom and saw that she had already left for the church meeting. He turned and looked back down the hall. Again the appearance looked sinister. Darkness was stronger that it normally was when the only light was from outside the windows, even if the sky was overcast. He went downstairs. He could tell that before he even reached the last step that the feeling was also in the living room, with the same grave darkness lurking all around. What little light there was made the room appear sleepy, as if someone just died in there. The silence was screaming in his ears as he walked to the kitchen. It too, had the same feel. The walls, stove, sink, counters, flowers, everything, seemed to say "Don't touch us. We're sick. We'll kill you."

The Writer went back into the living room. The same sickening feel had overtook it. Nothing looked normal. It looked ill and pale. He went to the front door and out onto the porch. Even out here it looked sour and puckish. A strange shade of dim yellow had settled over everything. The fields were faded of their lush green color and the trees that bordered the main road were droopy and soggy.

All this after I see where my father died, he thought. I can't believe this. This must've been how Hamlet felt after he saw his father's ghost appear to him. I bet he saw a sickening glaze over Ophelia's face after that and his castle in Elsinore became a huge tomb in his eyes. I don't think my father was trying to give me a message . . . was he?

The Writer looked around the porch and saw the cats and dogs all sitting around, glaring in every direction. At one point the dogs swung their heads in the direction of the driveway. The Writer called them to come to him but instead they whined and went down the steps. The cats, even the kittens, had lost their playful urge this morning. Blue was sitting on the railing, his back to The Writer, and appeared to be studying the fields for something. His tail was swishing like crazy.

"Blue," The Writer said. "Here kitty." He made his usual tongue-clicking sound that always got his attention.

It didn't work this morning. Blue never flinched.

"I can't believe this," he said. "I'm being ignored by a cat. I must be somebody."

All the cats ignored him. One of them slinked across the top of the steps to the other side and looked as if he were hiding behind a railing board. The kittens huddled together under the swing, their mother standing guard over them as she watched the top of the steps. The Writer began to go down the steps to see what was going on. The dogs saw him coming and immediately backed away, turned around, and sat down, watching the fields.

What is going on, he thought. This is too eerie. I feel so dry, so mild all over. My skin feels clammy. My heart is beating like crazy.

My stomach feels flat. I feel worse now than when I got mugged last night. He still hadn't told his mother about that incident. The more he thought about it, the more he felt that she was better off not knowing anything about it. If she had then her panic spasms would go so haywire they'd shoot off the charts. She'd forbid him to ever set foot out of the house again.

He looked down and saw where Mama had taken Judy's car with her to church. The tire tracks were fresh. Apparently Judy had been called to go in early too, so they both must be together, he assumed. And Joey must be with them. Judy never lets him stay home by himself. And it's Judy's car anyway. I forgot to drive it back over to her last night.

He wandered a few feet down the driveway and saw nothing unusual, except for the faded colors of the day and the unnerving sour spell that had taken a grisly hold of everything. He felt the crackling crunch of gravel under his feet with each slow step he took. He turned and went back to the porch. All the animals kept watching. He tried to pick up Blue but he slipped out of his hold and kept a firm eye on the fields. The other cats were the same way. None of them responded to his attention. One of them was sharpening her claws on a railing post. Another was washing his face. A few were twitching their tails.

Okay this is too creepy, he thought as he looked all around. God, what's going on? Is this the day you return to earth? Or has Mama and Judy and Joey all been raptured and you've left me behind to warn others? Is that it? What? Lord, this is freaking me out. I can't take this on a Sunday morning. Or am I just being overly dramatic, still aroused by all that happened to me yesterday? Yeah, I guess that's it. Rusty's out of my life and I have so much freedom from worry and wonder I don't know what to do with it. Everything's being reborn to me is it? How I saw the world, my possessions, my pets, everything. Is that it Lord? Have you also restored my writing talent, because the writing's been pretty dead lately. Nothing flowed out of me until now. I guess Rusty even clogged up my inner lines to the heart of life.

He went back inside, leaving the animals as they were. He hoped it was just the weather. After all, wasn't there a storm coming in from somewhere? Then he remembered that animals tend to behave oddly just moments before an earthquake. The thought stunned him. Could that be it . . . any moment now I'm gonna be shook to death and have the house fall on me? Nah, we'd been warned ahead of time . . . wouldn't we? I mean, weren't there just like 50,000 killed in some foreign country when a quake struck them?

He dropped the idea and started back up the stairs to the bedroom. This morning he had no appetite for breakfast. It was dead with everything else. I'd better get ready for church, he thought. I can't let this simple disturbance of nature keep me from going. He got a glance at the wall clock and saw that it was barely a quarter after seven. The Sunday school classes didn't start until ten. Must've been a big meeting Mama had to go to, he thought. He then concluded that Mrs. Graham must have wanted them to eat breakfast with her first. She was a splendid cook and possessed great skill with fixing old-fashioned mountain dishes such as fatback, sausage gravy, cornbread, and so on. I better stop, he thought. I'm making myself hungry.

He got to the fourth step, stopped, and looked up. That menacing sensation of pestilence had taken hold of the stairs. They were darker than usual and looked to be a stairway to the portals of Gehenna, only it was going upwards and not downwards. The top didn't look very inviting and there was hardly any light from the outside coming in through the upstairs windows. Any light that did was grayish.

Lord, what am I to do until time to go, he thought. Just stand around here and let this mental phenomenon crush my conscience? After all, it's all in my mind isn't it? There's really nothing wrong. It's just a cloudy day today, and I woke up earlier than usual. Maybe I can use this setting for a future novel of some sort . . . describe these deathly colors that beckon forthcoming tragedy for its main character. Tell how sour it feels right now, how my stomach is twisted into a choking knot, how I feel I'm gonna have to run for the toilet any minute . . . and how it feels to reawaken to the world when your life is freshly disposed of the feces of a deceitful and heartless friend.

By now he could feel the soreness building up in his legs from running and dancing last night in Asheville. With each step he took it slowed him down, and it soon escalated into pain.

For my novel about the dance marathon, I can simply look back at what happened last night, he thought. I saw all those people fall and collapse and get dizzy. I know how it feels afterward now. It's like you've had your limbs yanked out of their sockets and rammed back into them. Could one classify misery as an art form?

He forced himself up the steps and he made it to the top. Once there he headed for his room when he heard it.

A crash.

Downstairs.

Or was it outside?

Maybe the cats knocked something down, he thought as he began to walk back down the steps. Now it seemed darker going down than it did going up. He looked around the living room and saw nothing and nobody. He went to the front door and looked out. All the cats were still there and the dogs were standing guard at the top of the steps. All of them had the same pose . . . their heads were craned to their right, and their eyes were wide open. The Writer went out onto the porch and peeped around the side of the house. He didn't see anything but was sure the animals had seen something. Animals don't lie, he thought. I guess they're the only creatures that don't know how to lie.

He started to walk around the house. When he did the dogs started to whine and some of the cats leapt up onto the railing and looked at him. Blue was among them and he let out a faint 'meow'. The Writer looked at them and studied the lost look on their furry faces. He then looked at the ground and saw something.

A deep footprint in Mama's flower bed. Mama hated it when

people stepped in her flower dirt. It must've been me, he thought. He quickly rubbed it out and started to go on to the back of the house. The animals watched intently. Then he noticed something else. Under the front porch Mama kept the gardening tools and there was a wooden gate that closed it off. It had a metal lock on it as well as a metal spring that automatically caused it to swing shut.

The lock was lying in the flower bed. It looked as if it had been torn off with powerful hands. He peeped inside and couldn't tell if anything was missing. It was too dark to see all the way in.

He stood back up and looked at the animals again. They were still looking at him. He looked to the sky. It was still just as dismal, with no hope for any sunlight today. The silence of the moment began to howl in his ear. He stood still for a few minutes.

And he waddled away . . . on around the house.

CHAPTER THIRTY-FOUR

Rusty's ugly face, scorched with sideburns and a demonic flaring glare in his eyes, loomed into The Writer's face, shocking him so bad he slammed himself into the side of the house. The Writer let out a faint scream. He stumbled and fell backwards into Mama's flowers. Rusty slithered out from around the corner and took a huge step over on top of The Writer's body. In his hands was an oar, the one Mama told Joey he could put under their porch for safekeeping. The Writer saw it and the look in Rusty's face. He scrambled to his feet and made a mad dash for the front porch. Rusty took a powerful swing at him but instead smashed a crack into the house.

The Writer ran around to the steps and instead crashed head-on into Kelly, who stood at the bottom of the steps with a shovel in her hands. He knocked her backwards and the shovel fell out of her hands. The Writer ran up the steps and screamed for his dogs to sick them. Both of them leapt up onto Rusty and began clawing and trying to bite him. The cats all gathered into a small furry army, arched their backs, and stood sideways, their fur pointy and claws ready. The Writer ran into the house and grabbed the phone that was in the living room. Before he could hit the speed dial button, he heard another crash. He turned and looked and to his horror saw that Rusty had shattered the living room window with the oar and was crawling in. Kelly was beating the lock off the door with the shovel. The Writer fled for the stairs, hoping he could beat Kelly but was too late. As soon as he got up to the sixth step he felt a deafening blow explode from his feet. Kelly was trying to knock him down with the shovel but hit the steps instead. He lost his balance and fell. He inched around and saw her coming up on top of him. The look of hatred and fury in her eyes made her all the more horrendous to look at. As if it were a reflex reaction, The Writer kicked her in the groin and sent her falling down the steps, crashing into Rusty. He then scrambled on up the steps.

Rusty crawled out from under Kelly and dashed up the steps, cursing and swearing, his feet skipping every two steps as he chased The Writer with the oar. He saw The Writer run into his bedroom and slam the door. Rusty smashed the handle off and kicked it open. He went in and looked around.

There was no sign of The Writer. He bellowed his name out and demanded that he show his ugly face to him but to no avail.

When he felt the glass break against his skull he knew he'd been tricked. The Writer had hidden behind the door after Rusty kicked it in. In his hand was a picture of a tiger in a frame. It shattered so easily against Rusty's head it made him dizzy for a minute. The Writer shoved him out of the way and started back down the stairs. Out of the darkness of it emerged Kelly, holding the shovel in one hand and her other hand over the area between her legs. She was moaning profane insults at The Writer as she approached him. He ducked as she swung it, slamming it into the wall over his head by barely two feet. He then ran into her again and made her fall face forward. Down the steps he went, hoping and praying to God that he could get to the phone. He saw the dogs come running in through the shattered window as well as the cats. The Writer told them to sick Rusty and Kelly again. They ran up the stairs after them.

The Writer heard them holler in pain and saw that Rusty had thrown both dogs down the stairs. They landed at the bottom, whining and moaning in pain. He felt a surge of hatred and anger boil up in his stomach and in his heart, unable to fathom what cruelty could ever flow in one's heart to be so sadistic to an innocent creature. The adrenaline inside him began pumping like crazy. He saw Rusty come down the stairs and lifted the oar to hit the dogs.

The Writer charged head-on into him and smashed him against

the wall with all his weight. Rusty let out a wail of pain and dropped the oar. The Writer dug his hands into Rusty's back and knocked him down onto his knees.

"GET OUT YOU BASTARD! GET OUT AND TAKE THAT BITCH WITH YOU!" he screamed. Rusty got up and pushed him back, but it didn't work. The Writer kicked him in the stomach and rammed his forehead with his palm. He fell backwards on down the steps and The Writer picked up the oar. Kelly came down the steps and with one swing of a shovel, knocked the oar out of his hands.

"WHAT DID YOU CALL ME?!" she demanded. The Writer flared one of his death stares at her and blurted out what he said. He then made like he saw something behind her. She turned to see and that's when he lunged up at her and punched her in the face. He grabbed the shovel and as much as he wanted to hack her to death with it, he didn't. He dropped it and the handle hit Rusty's head. He got up and was about to reach for the oar but instead saw The Writer knock him down onto the floor next to the dogs.

Kelly rose up again and lunged for The Writer. He instead grabbed hold of her long hair as she stumbled past him. She screamed in agony as The Writer held her head up by it and bashed it on the steps. This is what Godzilla did to Ghidrah, he thought. He then put one foot down on her hair and raised his other up over her throat. She started flinging her legs and arms up at him. With one leg The Writer pinned one arm down and with his free arms he simply smacked each leg as it was flung up at him. With each slap Kelly hollered to the point where tears came out of her eyes.

Rusty lunged up, grabbed hold of The Writer's shoulders, and flung him against the wall. The Writer reached for Rusty's eyes but instead went for the face. He wanted so much to tear it off his skull and jam it with the poker from the fireplace. He spat in his face and even sneezed into it. Rusty cursed as he let him loose to wipe his face. The Writer ran for the front door again, hoping that if someone out there would see what was happening they'd come to his aid.

It was raining now. The Writer looked to the heavens and saw that the storm he'd heard so much about all week was finally here. He ran down the steps and saw that the only way he could get anyone was to run for the main road. But the rain had made the grass slick. To add to it his legs were hurting so much from the soreness he tried to run but fell. He looked up and saw Rusty come barreling out with the oar in his hands and his face even more savage than before. The whites of his eyes beamed as he saw The Writer in a very gullible position that could easily make him his prey. He tried to crawl away but his legs hurt so bad along with fear it all began to make him weaker. He couldn't even feel the cold rain on his body. He dug his fingers into the dirt and tried in vain to drag himself away from this monster but it was no use. He collapsed in agony and looked up like an injured cat that had just been in the throes of a mad dog.

He saw Rusty's black, beastly image against the white sky looming over him. Then the oar went up, and the last thing he saw was it come plummeting down full force onto his head . . .

Then total blackness . . .

Kelly came running out with the shovel and saw what Rusty had done. The oar was heavily stained with dripping blood.

"Finish him Rusty!" she hollered. "Do it so we can get out of here! He's still alive!"

"You want the shovel or the oar?" he asked. "The shovel would do better!" Kelly handed it to him and he raised it into the air. But once he lifted it over his head it wouldn't budge.

"RUSTY!"

He heard Kelly scream and he felt himself lifted off the ground and slammed back down onto it. He looked up into the mad fury of Brute's eyes as he lifted him up by the neck and began to violently wring it.

"Let go of him!" Kelly screamed and ran up to him with the oar. Before she could swing it Brute dropped Rusty, grabbed a ferocious hold of her and flung her off to the side. He then grabbed the oar and stabbed it into the ground next to her head. Rusty got up and leapt onto his back. Brute hollered and swung his whole body around, tossing him off. Rusty drew back and began to throw punches at Brute, who swung around and lashed a swift kick at him between the legs. Kelly got back up and jumped onto Brute's back, trying to dig her taloned finger nails into his eyes. Instead he let himself fall backwards and slammed her onto the ground again, pinning her underneath. She screamed when her head hit the handle of the shovel. Rusty got back up and went for his neck. Brute rolled back and with one blow punched his feet into his face and sent him falling backwards into a mud puddle. He got off Kelly, went over to Rusty who was flopping around in the puddle, and placed a foot on the back of his head, ramming his face further down into the water. He then placed it on his back and pushed down harder and harder. Rusty began to holler in pain and begged Brute to let him go. Instead Brute took his foot off, bent down to Rusty, and angrily lifted his head up by his hair and put it next to his face.

"Don't ever mess with my friend again buddy! Do you hear me?! Because if you do, he's gonna tear you apart someday if I don't do it first, so I'd be scared if I were you. Now get out of here and take that nasty little bitch with you before I kill you!"

He let him go and Rusty stumbled over to Kelly, lifted her up, and helped her over to the other side of Mama's truck. Thinking they were gonna try to drive off in it before his eyes, Brute inched towards them. Instead Rusty rolled out a red motorcycle, helped Kelly on it, gave Brute the finger, and revved it up.

Brute immediately remembered where he had seen it before, which was the day before when The Writer took him to that place in Murphy, and he now knew who had chased them. He picked up the oar and began to run after them with it. Before he could swing at them they were down the driveway and Brute watched them speed up the main road and out of sight. He dropped the oar on the ground and saw the blood that was all over it. He looked over at The Writer's bruised and bloodied body lying in a lifeless heap a few feet from the porch steps. Some of the cats were crowding around him and sniffing. Blue was poking his foot on The Writer's hand.

Brute went over and knelt down next to him, fearing what Rusty had done. He carefully nudged him and slowly turned him over to see that the whole left side of The Writer's face was soaked in thick red blood. It streamed from his ear, nose, mouth, and had seeped into his eyes. He was still breathing. He looked down his arms and saw bruises begin to develop all over. All the cats looked at Brute as if he were the last sign of salvation for their owner. The dogs inside were still whining.

"C'mon Zilla," he said, trying to revive him. "Don't die on me. Don't let Rusty kill you."

But it was no use. He was out. Brute wrapped his arms around his bloody body, trying to keep from having a breakdown. "God don't take him now please," he said. "Bring him back to me. I can't lose this guy who took me in. Please God."

With that he remembered what The Writer had done for him exactly a week ago.

He waddled away . . . carrying The Writer in his arms to the house.

CHAPTER THIRTY-FIVE

Brute carried the bloodied body of The Writer up to his bedroom and laid him on the bed. The blood had dripped all over Brute's bare chest, ran down the whole side of his body, and left a trail of red from the porch steps clear up to the bedroom. The Writer was unconscious and soaked in rain and blood. Brute looked all around the room for something to put around his mutilated head. Instead he ran across the hall to the bathroom, grabbed a towel, and tucked it all around The Writer's head. Seeing that the blood had not stopped, he ran down to the kitchen, wrapped a bunch of ice in a towel, and took it up to the bedroom. He carefully placed it on the whole side of the head, and remembered the dogs. They were still lying in pain at the bottom of the stairs. After making sure The Writer would be okay for a few minutes, he went back down and carried each one to the couch. They were still whining and moaning and they looked as if their legs were broken.

If they were horses I'd have to shoot them, he thought, remembering what The Writer said the night before at the dance competition, comparing dancers to horses. The rain was getting stronger now and it rattled the roof of the house and hit the windows. It set off a calm and soothing ease throughout the whole house. It lulled the dogs to sleep. Some of the cats that had run in during the struggle were cuddling up in the chairs and in corners, also going to sleep. Not wanting to fall under its drowsy spell himself, Brute ran back up to The Writer, totally stumped at what to do for him next.

He knelt down on the floor and looked at the maimed human that lay on the bed in front of him. Bruises were beginning to form all over his arms and legs. Cuts and scrapes started to swell.

Brute placed his hand on The Writer's forehead and felt that it was a tad warm. He was so thankful to see his chest slowly heave up and down. With each rise of the chest came a painfully high-pitched wheezing sound. It made Brute cringe each time he heard it, but it was also a happy sound. It meant that The Writer was still here with him.

Please Zilla, don't die, he thought as he looked at him. You can't die on me. I won't let you. He looked around the room again for something that would help him. He didn't care what it was, as long as it meant help for The Writer. His eyes shot all over the darkened room and when they cast over The Writer's desk next to the window they saw a heavenly sight.

The telephone.

Brute got up and ran to it, smashed in the button that was marked '911', and waited nervously.

"911 Emergency?"

"Yeah, there's a guy here who's hurt real bad. He's bleeding all over . . . and won't wake up." He tried to keep calm. He could hear the operator madly racing her fingers all over her keyboard on the other end.

"Do you know what happened sir?"

"He got hit with an oar."

"An oar sir?"

"Yeah. An oar."

"Do you know who did it?" Before he could answer, the operator suddenly began talking to someone in the background. Brute could hear her say something about an oar. When she came back on she told him that they were sending an ambulance and the police to investigate.

"He just got hit with an oar!" Brute said loudly. "Why are you sending the police?!"

"Sir, we had a report earlier from two subjects who say they saw what happened and were also attacked. We have the address here on our monitor. The police need to investigate the scene so please don't touch anything until they get there. Do you understand sir?"

Also attacked, he thought. What bull! Zilla's the only one who got hurt! What idiot would . . .

"Tell them to hurry!" he yelled and hung up on her. He dropped the phone down on the desk, went back over to The Writer, and sat with his knees on the floor.

"They're coming Zilla," he whispered, wiping sweat off his forehead and adjusting the towels. "Hang in there." He again re-adjusted the towels and rubbed his forehead. It was sweaty and the blood was beginning to cake on it. "The police are coming. I don't care what they do to me Zilla, just as long as they take care of you."

After a few moments a startling realization seized hold of his mind. It was so sharp it sent a heated wave of fear and anguish over his body. His heart began pounding harder and faster and he took a huge gulp. He began to clench The Writer's left hand tighter and tighter. Images of bars and gray floors flashed through his mind. He could hear the voices spewing vulgar remarks and mak-ing nasty gestures. There was the shattering clang of gates and doors slamming shut.

"It's over," he said quietly. "I'm finished. I've run long enough."

He looked back at The Writer and saw the face. Then he re-membered the first time he saw it, in the darkened bedroom. All he could see was one side of it, the eyes gleaming, and his mon-strous figure. And now all he could see was that same side blood-ied up. Brute got closer and rested his head on The Writer's chest, still gripping his hand, afraid of having a total breakdown right then and there. Soon he lifted his head and looked at The Writer's face.

"Zilla, I don't know if you can hear me, but if you can, prom-ise me you won't give up. Even after all that's happened to you, don't you dare ever quit doing what you're doing. Nobody's gonna tear you down anymore Zilla. You're the bravest, strongest, most loving man I know, next to this guy called Jesus. There'll never be another one like you. And you're not going to die, not now, not here with me. I won't let you. Nobody can kill Godzilla. I'm so proud of what you are, more than I'll ever be. This one you call God needs you here, alive, doing whatever it is you do that everyone else hates you for . . . and I'll never forget you Zilla. I'll always remember you. It's hard to forget something you love."

Brute closed his eyes. "Take care of him God," he said. "Look after him after I'm gone."

At that moment he heard voices coming from downstairs. Then footsteps, several of them, charging up to the bedroom. He heard doors knocked open, and they came to this bedroom. An officer kicked it in.

This is it, he thought.

Brute's eyes met his as he stood up.

"FREEZE!" he yelled, pointing a gun, and ordering him to step away from the bed and to come quietly to him. Brute let out a deep sigh of aggravation as he calmly came to the officer. He looked all around the room for what he felt would be the last time. More officers came into the room along with the paramedics who immediately began tending to The Writer. Brute could overhear them talking about this being Linda Jacobs's boy and about how her late husband once worked with them.

"Don't hurt him," Brute said as his wrists were being cuffed.

"Shut your mouth Brute," the officer said. "Just come with us and let them do their job." As the officer led him out of the room he turned for a final look at The Writer. He barely saw part of his forehead. The medics were all around the bed. He could only whisper to him . . .

"Goodbye Zilla."

CHAPTER THIRTY-SIX

The Writer was brought home the following evening with a stitched up face and still groggy from the stuff the doctors gave him at the hospital. There was nothing that could be done for the horrid cuts and splotches of black and blue marks that were all over his body. Those would have to heal in time, just like everything else that had happened. Mama and Joey had to help him up the stairs to his bedroom and put him to bed. Judy was in the kitchen fixing coffee for the preacher and his wife, who were expected to drop by any minute for a short visit. Outside it was still cloudy and there was a slight drizzle. The weatherman had predicted another thunderstorm to hit the area either tomorrow or the next day. It just added to the dismal mood that had overtaken the entire house since the moment The Writer awoke Sunday morning. Happiness was dormant. When it would return nobody knew.

It was quiet in the living room. The windows that were busted out were now covered up with boards until they could be replaced. Mama was thankful that the chief of police ordered his men to get their stuff cleared out by today so she could bring her son home to rest. The order included that they help clean up everything, especially the blood. The only light in the room came from the lamp next to Mama's rocker where she was sitting. Joey sat on the couch as Judy brought the coffee in.

The atmosphere in the room made Mama edgy and her mind kept racing back to the moment she was called to get to the hospital and find her son half-bludgeoned to death. She grabbed the remote off the coffee table and switched on the TV.

"I don't care what's on," she said, flipping through channels. "It's too quiet in here." She found a nature show about tigers and left it there, the volume not too high. "My son loves cats and tigers," she said. After the coffee was brought out she remembered that Joey didn't drink coffee. She told him there were cokes in the fridge if he wanted one. After he disappeared into the kitchen Mama produced a copy of the police report from her purse. She started to unfold it and read it again for what looked to be the millionth time. Judy sat down next to her and gently tried to pull it out of her hands. It was full of details of what the cops found at the scene, from the bloody oar to the injured dogs right down to the deceptive discovery of Brute's fingerprints on the oar handle. What was even more graphic was the description of The Writer's face when the paramedics examined it.

But the one thing in it that made Mama wonder even more was that "two anonymous young subjects were at the scene at the time of the incident." As much as Mama tried to make the cops tell her who it was they refused to oblige, saying they did not have the authorization to release such information to anyone at the time. All she could do was have them contact her if anybody came in with more information.

"Just let me have it Linda," Judy said. "You don't need to be getting yourself anymore upset over it."

Mama eventually let loose of it and Judy stuck it under the Bible on the table. Mama grabbed a tissue off the table and began wiping her eyes. Judy gave her a cup of coffee and tried to think of some way to get her mind off what had happened. Joey came in with a coke and sat on the couch.

Just then the doorbell rang. Mama flinched when she heard it and had Judy answer it. As she finished wiping her face she saw the preacher's wife coming to her with her arms out for a hug. The preacher walked in, took off his hat, and shook hands with Judy and Joey. Mama had them sit on the couch and started serving them coffee. Before they started the preacher suggested they open up with a prayer. Everyone held hands as the preacher spoke in his usual, low rugged voice that was always full of sincerity and truthfulness. He asked for strength, wisdom, and understanding for what happened, and that everyone would be able to go on in life and not have to dwell on this forever. When he finished the phone rang. Joey answered it since he was closest to it. On the other end was the shrill voice of the one and only Annie Morgan.

"Howdy. Is it okay if me and the gang came to visit for a few minutes this evening? We have nothing else to do."

Joey asked Mama and he told her it was alright. She felt that the more friends she had right now the more she could handle the strain of everything.

"Oh goodness, all these people coming and nothing to feed them," Mama said, getting up and heading for the kitchen.

"Hold it right there dear," Mrs. Graham called out. "You're not setting foot in that kitchen. I'm gonna run out and pick up something right quick. Dear, give me the keys to the van. What would you all like?"

"Oh really," Mama began to protest as Mr. Graham handed his wife the keys. "I don't need you running out just for . . ."

"Don't mention it. I can tell you haven't had a hearty meal in two days. I'm just gonna run to that little place in the plaza."

"I'll come with you," Judy said, putting her jacket on. "I'll help you get it. Joey, help Linda arrange things will you please? We'll be back shortly."

Mama told Joey just to get out the paper plates and paper cups. After that he and Mr. Graham set out the fold-up table and placed it in the living room for the food. That way everyone would be in one room together all the time. Mr. Graham put the coffee pot and cups on it and Joey got out the tea from the fridge. When they finished arranging it the doorbell rang and in came The Writer's friends. Lana and Dionne had a cake, Jackie and Elaine each had a tin full of cookies, Annie had a pie, and Nate and Blade brought bottles of fruit juices. Mama had all of them placed on the table.

"This looks like a party," Mama said as she looked at everything. "I didn't plan it to be."

"Of course it's a party," Annie said. "We're celebrating that The Writer is still with us."

For the first time in days Mama smiled. She felt herself begin to relax and when she thought about it, she was more concerned with what had happened to her son rather than the fact he was still alive, upstairs asleep, and not six feet under.

Pretty soon the room was abuzz with conversation, ranging from what happened to how the weather looked. Mama didn't care what they talked about. She was just glad she wasn't by herself right now and had plenty of support around her. Nate was talking to the preacher about a letter of recommendation for the community college. Lana and Dionne were flipping through a fashion magazine Mama had received in the mail and were comparing looks on each other. Jackie and Elaine were playing with Blue and the other cats that were in the house. She heard Blade and Annie getting into a hilarious tiff about the bowling tournament as they examined the trophy on the mantle. When they saw the other trophies that The Writer and Brute won, they asked Mama what they were for. When she told them, they were astonished at what The Writer did to win them. They had never seen him dance or heard him sing. These trophies were proof enough of what latent abilities someone like The Writer possessed.

"That's more than Annie's ever done in her life," Blade cracked. Annie smacked him on the back and told him to accidentally on purpose drop a bowling ball on his foot. "I hope the next time you go through a metal detector they find a Swiss army knife stuck up your butt!" she said.

"Annie!" Lana said, choked up with laughter. Dionne made a face when she pictured the scene. Even Mama started to laugh. When she did she turned away from the crowd to keep herself from having a laughing fit.

That's when Mama heard Judy and the preacher's wife returning with the food. "Oh good the food's here," she said, running to the front door. She then turned to the crowd and said, "Alright please no more butt talk!"

As they finished eating everyone started talking about the one thing that brought them all together tonight. As calmly as she could, Mama explained everything she knew about what happened, and all The Writer's friends confirmed that they were not at the house when the attack took place. She told them about the dogs being at the vets' for a few more days, the bloody oar, the fingerprints that sent Brute to jail, and the report from the police.

"I know Brute didn't do it," she said. "He loved my son. All my son has to do is just tell me what parts of that report are true. But if he says that Brute did attack him with the oar and tried to kill him, then that means Brute will be charged with attempted murder and cruelty to animals. Oh I hope this makes that Mrs. Moran happy, that is if she knows what happened to my son. I just know she wanted something like this to happen to him."

"Do you think she did it?" Lana asked.

"No, she's in jail waiting for her court date for forging my name on a fake document," Judy said. "Linda, tomorrow morning, I'll tell the chief not to do anything else to Brute until The Writer tells us his side of things. I mean just one thing against Brute can send him to the state correctional facility in no time. We can't let that happen."

There was a heavy thud from overhead. Everyone looked up at the ceiling. Mama raced out of her rocker, up the stairs, and into The Writer's bedroom.

He wasn't in his bed. The room was a darkened bluish shade.

He was at the window, looking out at the rain, his hand up on the glass.

Mama came in the room, touched the lamp on next to his bed, and put an arm around him.

"Son, are you alright? How do you feel?" He never answered. He kept glaring out at the darkened sky as the rain hit the window. "We're eating downstairs. Can I bring you something? Are you hungry?" She carefully brought him back to the bed and had him sit on the edge. She put his bed shoes on his feet and felt his forehead. When she touched it he flinched. He was still sore from the blow and the stitches were still clearly visible up the side of his face. Judy came up along with Joey, who had the police report in his hand. Joey saw him and ran up to hug him, but stopped when he saw the look in The Writer's face.

"He's still sore," Mama said. "Judy, get me the Tylenol from the bathroom and some water please."

"My head hurts," he mumbled, closing his eyes. Mama told him she was getting him something for it and not to worry about anything. She gave him the medicine and told him it would help him rest better. He looked around the room and tried to get back up. He was still weak and had to hold on to Mama and Joey. They sat him down in his rocker next to the window and Judy set up a folding table next to him for his food.

"What day is it?" he asked.

"Monday evening," Mama said. "Don't worry. You don't have school anymore. Look, Judy and Joey's here, the preacher and his wife, and all your friends are downstairs. If you need anything we can get it."

"Where's Brute?"

Mama's gleaming smile quickly melted away when she heard her son's frail, weakling voice ask for his friend. She felt a surge of sobbing start to build up inside. Right now Brute was the one thing she could not give to her son, even at a time like this. Judy and Joey looked at each other as she placed a hand on his shoulder. Joey slowly handed the report to Mama for her to decide what to do with. She kept it out of sight from The Writer for a few minutes.

"Mama, where's Brute?" he asked again faintly. "Is he asleep?"

"Son, just eat your supper when it comes, okay?" she said, trying to get his mind off Brute, but she knew it wouldn't work.

"But where's Brute?" he asked again, a bit louder and in a more cracked voice. He turned and looked around the room. No sign of him. He stood up and looked for some hope in Judy and Joey's faces. He went to Joey and placed his hands on him. Joey warmly took hold of him as if to hug him, but could see the look in his eyes. He didn't know what to say to him. Instead he just rested his head on his shoulder with his arms wrapped around him.

"Joey, tell me, where's Brute? Please tell me."

"I . . . I don't know," he said. The Writer drew back and glared at his face.

"You don't know. Why not? Judy, where is he? Why won't any of you tell me? Why . . . why does my face feel so tight and heavy? Why is everyone here? Why is . . . " He started to fall and all three of them caught him and put him back on the bed. Mama felt her eyes begin to fill with tears again as she saw the pending hurt take hold of her son's mutilated face. All he wanted was his friend. It seemed like such an innocent, simple request, but it was something she felt so powerless to do for him. She saw the report lying on the floor next to the rocker. She grabbed it and unfolded it, hoping in some way she could get Brute back if her son could tell for sure what really happened Sunday morning.

"Son, I want you to read this. Just take your time and read over it. And when you're done, tell me what really happened."

"Happened? When?"

"Just read it first, please."

Judy and Joey watched as Mama looked down at the floor. As he read the scrawled handwriting on the report his eyes started widening and his hand began shaking. Pretty soon tears streamed down his face and he looked up with a vengeful look of hatred in his reddened eyes.

"No . . . no . . . IT WASN'T BRUTE! IT WAS RUSTY AND THAT BITCH OF HIS!" he said, almost tearing it up. Mama grabbed it before he could destroy it and held on to him tighter. "Oh God no! Why?" He buried his face in his hands and almost tore open one of the stitches. He loomed up off the bed and went for the window. All he could see was rain and wind. He turned around. He knocked the table down and almost fell himself. Mama grabbed him and tried to calm him down but he was so overwrought he fought her off. "Rusty . . . swung that thing at me, tried to kill me, had his girlfriend try to kill me, and tried to kill our dogs! And you all let them take off Brute instead! He never hit me! It wasn't Brute! It was Rusty!" He tried to run for the door, crying that he had to get Brute, but Joey caught hold of him and tried to push him back into the room. He stopped struggling and fell to his knees, clutching his chest, then came the bitter sounds of an asthma attack. Mama grabbed the inhaler off his night stand and put it in his mouth. After she got him to stop he calmed down and slowly started drifting off to sleep again. It took Mama, Judy, and Joey to get him back into bed. He was asleep again in no time, his face soaked with tears.

Afterward, Mama called the police station to tell them what her son said. They told her they were sending an officer out immediately to get a direct statement and to keep him quiet. Then she asked about Brute.

After she hung up she was in tears, afraid to tell The Writer what the operator said . . .

CHAPTER THIRTY-SEVEN

"They sent him back," Mama said. Judy and Joey looked at her in shock. "Here's what that lady told me—he ran away from home about two months ago in his parents' car. He apparently wrecked the car, and has been living on the streets ever since, that is until my son found him. How he got here I have no idea. He was waiting for a ride back to Asheville after he got dropped off here in town by some gang he was a part of, then some truck came down the road and knocked him down. That's when my son found him. His parents have been searching for him ever since and today was the first word they'd heard of him so they arranged to have Brute sent back home . . . apparently he got in trouble for something. I don't know. She didn't tell me."

"So he's not cleared up huh?" Joey asked.

"He will be," Mama said, "after they talk to my son. It turns out Brute has no criminal record. He's clean. They'll relay everything my son says back to wherever he came from and Brute will have nothing to worry about. But he's gone now. I have no idea where he's being sent back to. They wouldn't tell me. That's the bad thing about all this, and they confirmed that it was Rusty and his girlfriend out here yesterday morning. They did a check on his girlfriend. She tells people she's eighteen, but she's really fourteen. They lied to the police, which doesn't surprise me, so there is now a warrant out for their arrest. They just can't find them anywhere now. An officer will be out here in a minute."

Everyone in the living room listened while Mama explained it all to Judy and Joey in the kitchen. When they came back into the living room, Jackie asked Mama what Rusty and Kelly would be charged with.

"Just attempted murder and cruelty to animals. If I had my way I'd have their heads."

While everyone started discussing the new revelation of events, Joey crept back upstairs to The Writer's bedroom. The bustle of everyone talking was just enough cover for him to sneak away and go look at The Writer. He carefully inched his way to the bedroom door, which was barely open a crack. He got up to it and peeped inside.

He could see The Writer lying in bed on his back, his face still wet from sweat and tears.

He looked at him for a long time before wandering in. The room was shaded in a dark blue and only the heavy sounds of The Writer breathing could be heard. Joey left the door open a crack and went and sat on the edge of the bed next to The Writer. He could barely see his face, which he was glad of because every time he saw those stitches it reminded him of what Rusty did to him. He carefully placed his hand inside The Writer's, which was on his chest. He tightened his grip on it and looked out the window.

"Do you know the first time I ever saw you sir?" he said quietly. "It was on the first day of high school for me, and the first day of your senior year. It was just before lunchtime was over and fourth period was about to start. I was outside the main entrance waiting for my friends to come and so we could go look for our fourth period class together. I just happened to look up the hill where the football stadium is and on the very top of the visitor's side I saw you. You were standing still, looking out into the sky, with a deep look on your face. The wind was blowing and you just looked as if you had some special power of some sort. I stood there looking at you for a long time and then my friends finally showed up. They saw me looking at you and they told to me to forget about you because they didn't think that you and I could ever have anything to do with each other because we were so different. I told them to hush and when I looked back up there you were gone. I was left to find my fourth period class on my own. Then I saw you in the hallway a few minutes later and I asked you where it was. You took me right to it."

He stopped and looked down at The Writer's face. There was no visible signs of any reaction or expression. Joey gripped his hand tighter and rubbed his other hand over it.

"I just wanted to say that because...well...even then, I knew you were different from everyone else, from the moment I first saw you. I knew there was something special about you that made you so different from everybody else. I felt that I could come to you whenever I needed to, just because I could tell you were different. I know you probably can't hear me, but I had to tell you that, just in case, I don't ever get another chance to..."

The Writer slept all of Monday night and almost all of Tuesday. When he woke up Tuesday evening, he saw that the sky was still dismal looking but not raining. His mind shot back to the fatal words written on the report that Brute was arrested and taken away, then to the disillusioning words from the officer who talked to him last night about Brute being sent back to wherever he came from. To The Writer, it was almost as if someone told him Brute was some disoriented alien from outer space and was shot back out there in a ship. Where he wound up nobody seemed to care. His heart plunged into his stomach and all emotion and care inside him was drained out. There's no reason to get out of bed, he thought. I wake up hoping to see Brute again, but he's long gone, to a place I may never lay eyes on. I wish this were all a dream, which I'll wake up from any moment now and Brute will be in his bedroom down the hall. But no, I'm stuck in this bleak realm of reality. Brute's gone. Taken away. I'm left with an ugly cavity in life, missing the filling of someone I love.

He got out of bed and went downstairs. He saw Mama asleep in her rocker with the lamp still on. Blue was on the couch in a tight ball next to Sampson and Bunny. He didn't wake her up and decided to go back upstairs to his bedroom. He looked at his desk and the journal he had not touched since he couldn't remember how long. I haven't written *anything* these last few days, he thought.

What kind of writer am I when I don't even write? I don't know what to write about. Me? This weekend? Brute, wherever he is? God takes away Brute instead of Rusty. How is that fair? He picked a pen up off his desk and held it, as if it could restore life to his crushed spirit. He sat back on the bed, feeling his eyes well up with tears again and his face feeling sore yet. He closed his eyes and saw Brute's face. He opened them and powerfully envisioned him sitting on the floor next to him.

But it wasn't real.

He was gone.

He's gone you freak, he thought. Get over it. That's what you get for taking up with someone like Rusty, you lose more than you try to gain. God's punishing you now for not listening to your mother or to Annie in the first place, and you deserve every bit of what He dishes out to you.

"Bring it on God," he said. "I deserve it."

He got back on his feet and went to the window. He could see the driveway leading to the house and a drizzle had started. The Writer could not remember it raining so much. Surely the earth has enough water to quench its thirst, he thought. Let the earthworms be at peace, and let the fishermen find them plentiful so they can use them to catch fish.

Joey's house was just out of range from his window. He couldn't tell if he was home or what. If he wants me he'll come here, he thought. I'm not gonna call and bother him just to ask him to come visit for a minute. He's probably sick of seeing me so upset now and has better things to do. My other friends have lives so why shouldn't Joey?

He rested his head on the glass and let the tears run again. When he looked out the figure coming up the road he presumed was just another mental trick his mind was playing on him. But when it got darker, closer, and more focused, he knew he wasn't out of it. He strained to get a better look at whoever it was.

Rusty.

In his hand was a knife.

On his face was a cringing death look.

The Writer backed away into the darkness of the room. His heart began pounding and sweat oozed out from all over his body. He backed into the desk and his hand groped around on what he soon realized was the phone. He grabbed it, slammed in the speed dial button for '911', and tried to control his breathing.

"911 Emergency?"

"Yes ... uh ... there's a man approaching my house. He has a knife."

"Where is he now sir?"

The Writer looked out the window and saw Rusty standing under the tree in the driveway, looking all around as he put on his gloves and cleaned his knife. "He's in the front yard, wiping his knife and looking all around. I ... I don't know if he's alone or what ... " He could have Kelly hiding around here somewhere, he thought with mounting horror. He kept watching Rusty as he wiped a fresh shine onto his appointed murder weapon. Wanting to get a better look at him, he went downstairs to the front door and looked out the peephole.

He was met with the revolting face of Rusty now at the front door! He was looking straight into the hole but he couldn't see The Writer looking at him. "He's on the front porch now!" he gasped into the phone.

"Just keep calm," the lady said. "We have the police on their way. Just stay on the line with me."

He slowly backed away and then saw the handle slowly turn. Someone forgot to lock it back. He looked over at Mama and saw that she was still sound asleep. He wants me, not Mama, he thought, so he'll come straight for me. He hurried quietly but quickly up the stairs. He got where he could see down the steps and where he could get to his room if he had to. Oh I wish Brute was here, he thought. He could take him out easily, but no, I have to do it myself now. He heard the door open and saw a shadow make its way for the stairs. Then a foot appeared out of the dark, followed by the spine tingling gleam of a blade. He made a dash for his room, but stopped.

God, I can do this, he thought. I can't run from this monster. I have to face up to him and let him know what he's done. I've run long enough. God help me. He turned around, told the lady on the phone to listen to him, and he put it down on the floor next to his bedroom door. He walked out to the top of the stairs.

Rusty looked up at him and shuddered. There was this huge black figure standing at the top of the stairs, facing down at him, his arms up at his chest, not moving. In a haste he tried to hide the knife but The Writer had already seen it.

"What do you want?" he asked Rusty in a firm voice.

"Aw now man," he said in his pathetic friendly tone. "Don't be so rude. I just came to visit you."

"No, you didn't."

"Why man?"

"You know what you came here for."

"What in the world are you talking about man?" he asked, taking one step up. The Writer took one step down. "I didn't come here to do anything. I came to see how you were after I heard some guy hit you with an oar. Golly man, can't even pay a friendly visit to anyone anymore without getting pissed off now."

"You've pissed me off long enough now," he said. "This is it. No more. Take your knife and leave."

"Maybe I don't wanna leave," he said. "Maybe I wanna stay a while."

"We don't want you here. Get out."

"I'll leave when I'm ready. I came here to see how you were doing and if there was anything else I could do."

"Anything *else*?"

"I mean . . . was there anything I can do for you?"

"No, you mean what else you could do to make sure I won't tell people what you did, and that you're shacking up with a four-teen-year old prostitute, and that you're the most sickening sight I've ever had to lay my eyes on. God knows what you really are. You can't hide anything from Him. He'll tear your walls down and make everyone see just how rotten you are inside."

"Man you've gone nuts. I wish you'd get off my back about what I do. There's nothing wrong with it. I'm not hurting anyone and as long as nobody's getting hurt then it's alright. I don't need to hear your religious bullcrap about what God says is right. Keep that for your little band of gullible followers."

"It hurts me Rusty," The Writer said. "I thought you were my friend and that you had better sense about those things. I had hoped you would know that it's not right. I was hoping I could help you before . . ."

"Help me?! Man, I don't need your help for anything! There's nothing wrong with me! I'm fine just like everyone else! YOU'RE the one who needs help, going around with this zombie face all the time, trying to convert everyone to follow what you believe in. No wonder you were sent to that shrink at the hospital. Maybe if you were sent to the state asylum you wouldn't be like this."

"You're right. They'd tell me how crazy I am for believing in God and Jesus and for trying to do what the Bible says. I try to do what I can, and I tried to help you but you wouldn't listen to me. I shook the dust of your house off my feet."

Rusty looked down at the steps, went up one, and slipped a hand into one of his deep pockets. The Writer could see the shape of the knife moving through the cloth.

"Man, you're crazy. I tried to be your friend, but you . . ."

"You were never my friend," The Writer said a bit louder, taking another step down. "I was just some weakling creature you could use to get what you wanted. You knew I was a Christian and would be willing to do anything, and you used that against me. I was just a pawn in your life to serve your nasty deeds, someone you could have the shrill joy of hurting and making an idol of pain out of. You never kept a single promise to me Rusty. I've waited on you and for you long enough. I wish I'd listened to Annie long ago about you."

"Annie, that spoiled brat? Don't tell me you're with her man?! You are beyond crazy if you go that far with some addlebrained hoe like her."

The Writer took two steps down and was about four feet from Rusty. "She's my friend, more than you ever were. She knows all about you, and she made me see what a disgusting one-eyed snake you are."

"Man you're plumb out of it. That hit on the head must've knocked a screw loose in your noggin."

The Writer inched his head slightly to where he could see the phone on the floor. He raised his voice a tad.

"No, it made me see what a terrible mistake I made trying to be friends with you you dirty nympho. You are the most revolting piece of trash I've ever seen. You make me sick and I wish I had never met you. I don't know what's real or not anymore because of all the lies you've told me. You've made my life a living hell for the last four years, you caused my friend to get sent away, you tried to kill me, you tried to kill Brute when you had that truck, you tried to kill our dogs, and you've made my mother get upset more than she's ever been in her life, you've messed up my mind, my heart, and my whole life. I hope I never see you again you filthy bastard!"

"That can be arranged," Rusty said, drawing out the knife and taking a swing at The Writer. He jerked to the side and Rusty fell face forward. The Writer stumbled and fell back on his rear end. With his legs his kicked the knife out of Rusty's hand and rammed a foot into his stomach. Rusty stumbled up the steps and was about to grab The Writer's throat as he fell forward when something happened . . .

His face deadlocked and his eyes widened into frozen horror. The Writer felt something wet on his hand. He pulled it out from under Rusty and saw it was covered in blood. Rusty slowly inched up away from him and The Writer saw the ghastly sight of what just happened.

Rusty had fallen onto his hand which, beyond The Writer's knowledge, still had the pen in it. It had rammed itself up in the fold above his left leg and right under the pit of his stomach. Any farther down it would've pierced into his crotch.

The Writer lay gasping and panting, watching Rusty. He got

up and fell backwards down the steps and crashed into the arms of four cops who had been standing there, watching the whole thing on the steps.

Touchdown, The Writer thought when he saw what happened. He got a better look and saw Mama come racing up the steps to him, Judy and Joey standing on the porch, and a total of seven cops waiting to take Rusty away. They hurriedly clanged handcuffs on him and stood him up. One of them ordered the doctors to be ready at the hospital.

"That was really strong Writer," one of the cops said. "Even we don't get that brave with someone who has a butcher knife." They got Rusty on his feet and faced him towards The Writer. "Either one of you have something to say?" one of the cops asked.

"You saw that?! He tried to kill me! You've got the wrong guy!"

"Sorry nympho. The pen was mightier than the sword in this case. You're coming with us, and rest assured the pants we'll give you have no zipper in them."

"And your friend is in a juvenile detention center for girls," another cop was saying as he filled out a paper. "I don't think either one of you will be getting any . . . never mind."

You never know with nymphos, The Writer thought. He slowly came down the steps with his mother beside him. His clothes were stained with blood. The light from the lamp slowly illuminated on him bit by bit. When it hit his face, everyone saw what Rusty did to him. All the cops looked in horror and Rusty's face turned ashen. One of the cops, a woman, saw enough of The Writer's face. "Get that son of a bitch out of here!" she ordered, carrying the knife in a plastic bag. They hauled Rusty out and put him in one of the cars, groaning in pain. The Writer walked out onto the porch to watch him be taken away, for what he hoped would be for a long time now.

"Go, go, leave," he said quietly. Mama came up to him and put an arm around him.

"He's going now son," she said. "He can't hurt you anymore."

"First Brute and now Rusty," he said. "I can't keep anyone. I

lost Brute because of him," he said in sobs, starting to rub the side
of his face with the stitches. "I've lost so much."

The cops who were still there helped Mama get him back up
to bed. They offered to get a doctor but Mama told them he was
just tired and upset. After they all left Judy helped her change his
clothes and put him in bed. They stayed in the room and talked to
him for a little while about everything. The Writer insisted that he
was alright and that he just wanted to be alone right now. Mama
and Judy each gave him a hug and left him alone with the light on
next to his bed.

The Writer heard them talking as they headed downstairs. He
could tell Judy was trying to get Mama to stop worrying and he
could hear her trying to control her sobs. This house has never
seen or heard so much crying, he thought as his own eyes welled
up and spilled over again as he thought about Brute. He wished
he could wrap his arms around his huge sturdy frame and tell him
how much he loved him. But the more he thought of how
impossible it was now he kept erupting painful sobs.

He turned and looked at his night stand. On it was his necklace with the pen on it. With his shaky hand his lifted it up to his
face and read the gold inscription Joey had put on it. It still had its
shimmering gleam and looked good as new. He rubbed his finger
over the words and pictured Joey's face in his mind. He was thankful that this was not the pen that stabbed Rusty, although the
results would've been more painful.

He remembered the times he took Joey bowling in Mama's
old truck and the times he went to his house. Then he remembered
the book of poems he gave him for graduation, which seemed so
long ago now. It was on the night stand as was the eagle pendant.
He picked it up and opened it to the page his finger had slipped
into. On the left side was a watercolor painting of a boy standing
under a tree on top of a hill. In the background was a setting sun.
On the right side of the book was a poem entitled 'Don't Quit.' Off
to the side, in his familiar scrawl, Joey had written,

   This poem made me think of you.

It is also my favorite.

He read it about halfway through but his eyes were so thick with tears he couldn't see the words. He felt his sobs still coming out and his mind was growing foggy. God, get me out of this, somehow, tonight, please, he thought. This is killing me. I can't do this . . .

He rolled over onto his side, dropped the book on the floor, and laid his head down on the pillow. His face was hurting but he was too weak to ask for anything. He was sniffing and trying to keep his sobs from being heard. He raised his hand up to touch the lamp to turn it off. He could only reach the brass base of it and touched it once, then again, and finally, with one strong hit with his knuckles, the light went out.

In the dark, his sniffles and pending sobs was all that could be heard.

CHAPTER THIRTY-EIGHT

The Writer woke up sweaty.

It was still dark outside. He found that he'd been hugging his pillow, thinking it was Brute who had come back, but it was only a dream. He tossed it off to one side and sat up. He looked at the digital clock and saw that he'd only been asleep for no more than two hours. His face was caked with dried tears and his nose was snotty. His throat was dry and he could feel the strain left behind in his chest from sobbing.

Only in my dreams can I see him, he thought with mounting pain and anguish. He went to the window and looked out at the world shrouded in darkness. He could hear the slight tapping of rain against the window and felt the coolness of it mash against his forehead.

What will I do, he thought. What can I do? There's nothing out there for me. All I've done is make Mama upset and had Judy and Joey come wait on us hand and foot. I don't have Brute anymore. I can't write feeling like this. I don't know what to think anymore. What can I do about it?

He closed his eyes and when he did, he remembered seeing the knife Rusty had. Its blinding gleam shot out at his eyes and he jerked his head up. Oh no, he thought. Is that it? If I was gone, Mama wouldn't have to worry about me, Joey wouldn't have to put up with me, and I wouldn't have to fear this thing happening again. Nobody today wants to read what a Christian writer writes. How do I know I'll survive out there with this so-called talent of mine? Doomed to failure I suppose, just like my algebra teacher told me. What've I done right? Anything worthy . . . I don't know. I can't write anything that hasn't been written already in some form or another. Who wants to see what a fat kid from North Carolina can do? He's done nothing but make his mother worry and get upset. His friends think they have to be his friend out of pity and just because. Joey is just too good to be true, isn't he God? How do I know he loves me if he does? He never tells me anything like that. How do I know that when I go to his house he doesn't start condemning my presence there? How do I know he doesn't just go out with me just to please me? What can a guy like that see in a fat homely guy like me? I don't know. I've failed you God. I couldn't even bring Rusty to you. I haven't done as you want me to. I tried and failed, I know I have. I haven't used this talent you gave me. I shouldn't even be here should I? That's it. I'm an error of nature. An illegitimate bastard child, just like that counselor said I was. An accident just put up with in life for eighteen years.

He carefully studied how it looked outside. It was dark and still raining. They couldn't find me out there, he thought. The dogs would lose my scent. My footprints would vanish in all the water. They couldn't see me if I wore all black. Tonight I come to God. He'll do with me as He pleases. He knows what is to be done with things He makes . . . and He'll know what is to be done with me . . .

CHAPTER THIRTY-NINE

The knocking on the door stirred Mama out of her sleep in the rocker. She jolted wide awake and looked at the clock. Seeing the time it was she approached the door with careful apprehension after all that had happened the last few days.

"Who is it?" she called out.

"Joey."

She opened it and discovered it had been left unlocked again. Not wanting to worry about it now she let Joey come in, soaked.

"Mom sent me over here. She said she saw your living room lamp still on and thought you needed something."

"Oh I must've dozed off again," she said, taking his jacket off. "Did you need something?"

"No. We thought you did."

Mama thought long about it but nothing sprang to mind. She rubbed the crank out of her neck from where she slept slumped in the rocker. "No, I'll be fine. I'll just go to bed right now. But tell Judy to come over tomorrow if she wants to, okay?"

Joey nodded. "Now, uh, can I see him, I mean, just look in on him?"

"Of course. I don't mind a bit. He should be asleep, but you can go look." As he went up the stairs she took her cup of coffee into the kitchen, put fresh water in the bowl for the cats, and when she heard the heavy thunder of feet charging down the steps she came back into the living room.

"He's gone!" Joey cried.

"What?!"

"He's gone! His bed is empty!!!"

Within an hour of the discovery, Mama had all of her son's

friends at the house along with Judy, the preacher, his wife, Lucille from the store, and members of the church. Joey had already looked around the house and up on the hill behind the house and saw no sign of him. From there he got a good view of the area and saw that The Writer would probably head towards the town first because the main road lead directly into it.

"What about the police will go after a hardened criminal the moment he escapes, but they wait a freakin' 24 hours before they'll help me find my son!" Mama said when she hung up the phone after calling the cops for the fifth time. Judy calmed her down as best she could and told her to decide who should be in charge.

"Nate, I want you to organize this search thing please," she said. "You and Blade."

Blade did a quick count of how many people were at the house and there was close to about thirty. Nate ran out to his car to get a map of the general area around town where The Writer might have wandered off to. He also got a box full of flares ready to be used. He didn't care if it was raining. Anything that would help find The Writer was needed.

Nate then ordered everyone to call their friends and have them come help. "I don't care if they're asleep or watching the late show! Tell them to get out here NOW! Annie, Lana, Dionne, call your parents, tell them to call their friends and to get over here themselves!"

But there was only one phone line to the house, and a church member was using it. A few had a cell phone they were using. Nate told everyone to share the phones as quickly as possible. Joey ran to his house and got all the flashlights he could find. Mama ran to the basement and found a few.

"Are we going out into the woods?" someone asked Blade. He didn't think about that. The Writer could wander off anywhere, not wanting to be seen. The woods on a rainy night was the perfect place for it. He knew that in the woods in this area, there were briars and weeds like crazy. Only a knife or a strong pole could tear through them.

"Blade, do you have any spare knives in your car?" Lana asked. "No why?"

"Because if we have to go out in the woods, we'll need something to cut through the briars with, and you have hundreds of knives Blade." Several stopped and turned to him. Yes, he thought, I have enough knives to go around, but most of them are collector's sets and have a very rare . . . no wait . . . this is The Writer we're searching for! He jumped up on a chair to make an announcement.

"Listen everyone! I'm gonna run to my house and get every knife I can grab to fight the briars and weeds with! If you can, find a strong stick of some sort to beat your way through because it looks like we may have to go into the woods to find him."

"I have some in the kitchen," Mama said, going in to get them out. When she pulled out the butcher knife from the drawer half the women in there with her gasped and jerked back. "This one's mine," she declared, holding it up to her face. Blade ran up to the wall where the plaque was that he gave The Writer for his graduation present and yanked it off, giving a knife to Jackie, Annie, Lana, Elaine, Dionne, and Nate. He then took off out the door for his house. Mama and Judy passed out flashlights and fresh battery packs. People were still calling everyone they could find and there were a few more pulling into the yard. Some of the men brought their dogs. Outside came a blast of thunder and the lights in the house blinked. Everyone took it as a sign to hurry up.

Once Blade returned with boxes and bags full of knives he handed everyone else one and told them to be careful and not to hurt anyone. He and Nate then gathered the whole clan together outside in the rain in the front yard and saw they now had close to fifty people helping out. Blade told them to scatter all over the area and if they did not find anything within the hour to meet at the old car lot on highway nineteen, which was at the base of a mountain where the woods started.

Then there was a procession of cars tearing out of the driveway a few minutes later, slinging mud and water all over the place as engines roared and brakes were jerked into drive. The procession went down the main road and came into town, splitting into every direction possible. Some turned back for the back road that went behind the town and those with jeeps took the off-road route. It was after one in the morning and the town was a dead hamlet. Only sheets of rain covered the area and the streetlights gave the only signs of life. Very carefully everyone shined their lights at the stores, buildings, and wherever it looked dark. Those who were on the back road put their lights on high beams and shined their flashlights all over the place. Wherever they saw movement they tracked it down, even if it was just the wind playing tricks on them. Jackie and Elaine took off together downtown, flashing their lights everywhere and flagging down whoever was out. The few who stopped they asked, and all of them said they hadn't seen The Writer.

Lana, Dionne, and Annie got out of their cars and ran down the street with their lights, calling his name out into the rain. Mama and Judy were across the street doing the same thing. Nate was scouring all the dark spots along the road honking his horn while Blade flashed his light down steep embankments. He was thankful not to have found him lying down there on the rocks but also not thankful because there was still no sign of The Writer.

"Did something happen to him?" Judy asked Mama. "I mean did someone say something to him?"

"I don't think so," Mama said, walking faster. "I was asleep. If he got out I wouldn't have heard it. I feel like all this is my fault. I couldn't stay awake to be there if he needed me. Only God knows what's going through his mind right now."

Here's the river, he thought as he looked at it. If I follow it this way, it'll take me into town, but if I go down this way, it'll take me to the dam at the edge of town . . . and the road across the dam isn't closed off now. It's open for the season. Nobody should see me over there. They'll find what's left of me tomorrow . . .

The river flowed straight through the town, and it went all around a little island that was made into a picnic spot for tourists.

It was now swarming with flashlights and people calling for The Writer left and right. They looked in the bathroom stalls, under the walkway bridge, and some feared that he may have fallen into the river.

Mr. and Mrs. Graham had Lucille with them. She suggested they look at her little store in the plaza. Thinking that any idea was worth a shot, they went by there. She got out of their van and went to the front door. She looked down and saw a familiar sight. Wet fresh footprints of a huge shoe size that went up from the parking lot, to the window, and then lead down the walkway back out into the rain. She knew nobody in town had a shoe size like his. She went to the end of the walkway and looked out into the rain. There was no sign of him but since the footprints were still wet it meant he was just here a few minutes ago!

Other members of the search party saw the van in the rain at the plaza and came in to see what was up. Lucille told them what she found and everyone headed out in that direction. Ironically the lot lead straight out onto highway nineteen and the base of the mountain started no more than fifty feet from the back of the plaza. "He loves his sandwiches," she said as she joined the rest of the party in the deserted car lot.

As the hour wore away the lot began to fill up with cars and trucks and jeeps. Everyone piled out and crowded around Blade and Nate. Behind them loomed the shuddering darkness of the mountain, and a beaten down road eaten away with grass that lead up into it. Blade told everyone to stay as close together as possible and as they got higher up they'd spread out, but once they were turned loose they charged up the road. When the road felt as if it leveled off some they got off and headed up the side of the mountain. Everywhere people were calling his name. Beams of white light shot into all directions. The dogs were itching to be let loose to go after him. Everywhere there was a jangled mix of rain falling and voices calling out all over. Men were going off on their own while the women took their time in groups looking around.

One woman fell on the wet grass. Mama got down beside her

and begged her not to give up on her. "This is my son," she said over and over. "Don't give up on him just for your ankle, please!" The woman grabbed hold of her shoulders, got up, and began calling The Writer's name louder than before.

From somewhere on the mountain Nate lit a flare and shot up into the night sky. It exploded, but burned out within a few seconds because of the rain. Every time one exploded the light from it gave everyone an idea of just how far apart they were and what was around them. It also told them just how much higher the mountain was.

Somebody must be shooting off fireworks, he thought when he saw the reflection of the white light in the water near the dam. The Fourth of July isn't until next month . . .

As soon as they stumbled upon the weeds and briars everyone got out their knives and sticks and started beating them to pieces. Men took strong swipes with the knives and crushed the briars and thorns that stood in their way. The women found sticks and used them to tear up what was left. Any animals that were in their path made the sudden dash to get out of the way of these humans searching for another one. The lights and heavy mushy sound of feet against wet earth gave them enough notice. Even the birds took to the rainy sky.

Joey was one of the first to get up on the mountain. When he heard Nate shoot off another flare he looked at the ground and saw something glimmer for only a mere second. He shined his light on it and there, in the muddy remains of a huge footprint, was the pendant he gave to The Writer for Christmas last year. He picked it up and saw that the backing on it for the needle to go through had broken apart. All that was left was just the eagle with the verse from Isaiah still clearly visible under it. He shined his light in front of him and saw what looked like some huge beast had trampled through . . .

"I DON'T CARE! I'M BUSTING IT DOWN!" Annie screamed to Lana. She was trying to lift a huge branch off the ground and ram it into the side of what appeared to be a worn-down wooden shed long forgotten by the real world. "This shack is a part of Rusty, and I'm tearing it down with or without your help!" Even in this faint light Lana could see the look of deadly vengeance flaring in Annie's tender eyes. She realized that this was the spot she had heard Annie make mention of at The Writer's house the night of graduation. It was where all the high school kids brought their dates to "score," and it was where Rusty loved to take his women on first dates. Seeing the horridly disgustful purpose behind it, she told Annie to wait.

"Hey guys! Over here! Help us tear this nympho shack down!" Lana shouted to the men who were nearby. About five of them came running. Seeing it as just an old shed, they asked why it had to be torn down now. "BECAUSE I SAID SO! I'M SICK OF BE-ING A SWEET GIRL TO EVERY GUY I SEE NOW TEAR THIS WHOREHOUSE DOWN!" The men immediately grabbed hold of the branch and saw that it was too small to even penetrate the wall. One of the men went to get others members of the search party to come help and pretty soon, there were about twenty men, plus Mama, Judy, and some other women there helping lift a huge log up to it. Annie threw herself in front and led them up to it. Lana and Dionne got behind her. Jackie and Elaine threw them-selves into it as well, their hair matted down on all sides of their faces. Annie pulled and when they got in front of what looked like the front door they heaved back.

"Ready?! One . . . two . . . THREE!" The piercing screech of Annie's voice fueled everyone's adrenaline and one powerful heave busted out the whole side of the shack. Pretty soon there came a loud cracking sound and it slowly eased away from them. The roof fell in first then the entire structure collapsed into the rain. The main beam inside it fell towards the crowd and ran to get away from it. It crashed just a few inches from Annie who refused to budge an inch. She trudged up into what was left with a knife and stick, hitting and slashing things apart. She looked down and saw that she was standing on an old mattress that had been used quite a bit. Pieces of the structure had crashed down all over it. Annie took the knife Blade gave her and slashed it open as best she could.

Dionne knocked open a rusty old chest and out poured dozens of clear plastic packages containing rubbery looking articles along with suppositories, tubes, pills, boxes, and small whips. She kicked these out into the water puddles that were forming all around and stomped on them. Lana took her knife and stabbed them to pieces. "We'll come back when it's not raining and burn what's left," Annie said as she proceeded on, kicking things out of her way. Everyone else followed and shook their heads in disgust at what the teenagers were obsessed with nowadays. Mama covered her face when she walked past it. Another flare was shot up. It reminded everyone of why they were out here and they continued to trudge on, remembering Mama's direct orders that they were not quitting until they found her son, dead or alive.

He had fallen along the edge of the river. When the flare exploded he lifted his head up and he grazed it against a tree that was next to him. His face was smudged with dirt and sweat mixed with the rain. He looked to the sky and saw it flicker out. Oh God get me there please, he thought as he dragged himself along the shore. If I can just get to the road, and get to the dam . . . then God, I'm all yours . . . please take me as I am . . .

Joey tucked the pin into his pocket and saw that most of the search party had suddenly bunched up for some reason about a hundred feet away from him. He got a better look and saw that they had now disbanded again and were still looking around. He didn't call to them because he knew they would never hear him. I want to find him, he thought. God let me find him please. I don't know what he's done or what he thinks, but God, please get me to him before it's too late. He then walked faster up the way he hoped and prayed his friend had trudged through not too long ago. He flashed his light down and sure enough, those huge footprints were going straight ahead in front of him. To Joey, it was like being one of those scientists in those old Godzilla movies, where they follow the tracks of the monster until they find him.

He's no different God, he thought as he followed the tracks. Both The Writer and Godzilla are huge creatures just misunderstood by those who aren't willing to understand them. Only those who love them understand them, and I love both of them.

Joey followed the tracks clear up to the top of the mountain. He looked down and saw the reservoir far below that had been dammed up. He flashed his light around and the tracks did indeed go on down the mountainside. He looked back and saw that he was far ahead of the rest of the search party. Rather than wait for them to catch up he went on. He found that it was much easier going down that it was going up, especially in the rain.

I gotta get to him God. I gotta get there quick . . .

When he felt that he had gone about halfway down his foot stepped on a slab of mud and he fell on his rear end. Before he knew it, he was on a huge muddy slide down the mountainside, hitting branches and knocking them out of his way, and before he knew it he landed into a ditch full of muddy water. His flashlight rolled in after him and plopped into the water. When he got it out he saw that it had burned out on him. He dropped it back in the water, got out of the ditch, and saw that he was on the road that went across the dam. He was thankful for the lights that were on the edge of the reservoir behind the dam and it was just enough light for him to see the road. He ran down it as fast as he could, hoping he would see some sign of The Writer nearby. He ran across the road to the edge of the lake and didn't see anything but tall grass that looked as if someone or something had crawled its way through them. That was enough for him to go by. He got up on the road and ran down towards the dam. As he got closer he could hear a steady gushing sound. He realized it was the dam with its floodgates open to let out the excess water the storm had produced the last few days. By now he could see the bridge. And he saw something else over there.

It was standing on the side of it, its clothes wet and muddy. Its big feet were not on the road itself, but on the railing . . . on the side of where the spillway was.

"OH GOD NO! WHAT ARE YOU DOING?!" Joey screamed as he took off for the bridge . . .

CHAPTER FORTY

He looked down at the thick waters falling into the dark riverbed about seventy feet down. The last time he was here he saw that at the bottom of the spillway was a slight curve upwards about three feet from the river bottom. Below the curve was a mess of sharp jagged rocks and rough concrete. Anything that fell besides the water would slam into the spillway, then plummet helplessly to the shallow waters below, possibly busting open or even shattering the skull if aimed just right. The waters were so strong they could move the body farther down the river, making it days to find anything that remained.

The Writer climbed up on the railing, looking down, his face cold and wet from the rain and endless stream of tears. His cap was soaked through, his clothes dirty, caked in mud, and the soreness from what happened Sunday morning was worse than ever. His muscles ached all over, slowing him down greatly as he climbed up. He kept his eyes focused on the sky, his coat blowing back with the rain that hit against him, as if trying to keep him up on the bridge. His stomach slithered with anxiety and deep rumbling within his intestines. His kidneys had already caused his bladder to deceive him, and he didn't know how much muddy water he'd swallowed.

"Forgive me God, for what I am about to do. I have caused so much misery for so many being how I am, not like other people in this world, always told to be sent away somewhere, making my mother worry all the time, and being a burden for Joey to put up with. I've made a mess of myself Lord, I can't do anymore here for you. I always seem to mess up. I can't write anymore, I don't know what to write. If you have taken my talent away from me I probably deserve it. I probably deserve all that has happened to me. I must've done something terrible somewhere that you see fit to take Brute away from me, and I finally see what Rusty really is, and now I can't tell if Joey or my other friends are true or not. How do I know? I don't know. What does Joey see in me? He won't say. He just puts up with my being around. I can't even keep a simple pendant he gives me much less a friendship with anyone. He deserves better, someone just like him, not what I am. I really thought I could serve you, but I can't like this. I'm not fit for you. I have used my tongue to lash out at my enemy. I said words I should not have said. Please forgive me, for all I've done wrong in your sight, things I know and that I may not know I've done. I couldn't even bring Rusty to you. I failed at bringing just one to you. What good am I if I can't do that? So please God, now, take me as I am. Look after my friends for me, take care of them, no matter what they really think of me. Take care of my mom, look after her as she did to me for the last eighteen years."

By now his sobs were out of control. He was about to raise another foot up on the railing.

"And Joey . . . dear God, take care of him please. I love him so much, even though he may not say so to me . . . I wish I knew if he really did . . ."

He closed his eyes as the tears poured out. The rain splashed into his face and he felt the eerie fathoms of what was below. The loud gush of the water filled his ears. The wind got a bit stronger, hitting his face, causing bumpy sounds in the air around him. The sounds got louder bit by bit. The incessant sound of the rushing waters below him seemed to blend in with the wind, and it became one voice in his mind. His eyes were closed, yet through his eyelids there appeared a blurred image of some sort, its face slowly fading out of the darkness. By now the wind was beating into his ears, its sounds almost like a muffled human voice . . .

"Don't . . . don't give up . . . Zilla . . . don't you dare ever quit what you're doing . . . you're the strongest, bravest, most loving man I've ever known . . . next to . . . Jesus . . . you're not going to die now . . . not now . . . not here with me . . . I won't let you . . . I'm so proud . . . of what you are . . . God needs you here . . . alive . . . I'll always remember you . . . it's hard to forget something you love . . . don't give up . . . don't . . . give . . . up . . ."

In the instant he opened his eyes he felt something strong across his chest, pushing in, holding him away from the edge. He looked and saw nothing there but the wind blowing at him. The pulling got a tad stronger and he was unable to move. Whatever had him was far stronger than he was, and it was warm. The sensation spread through his whole body. He could feel something being pulled out of his body. Whatever it was left him feeling lighter and stronger. His sobs were muffled and he looked above his head. The force left him. There was a lone faint cloud spiraling up into the sky, twisting and fading away. He was still on the railing but nowhere near over the top of it as he was a few minutes earlier. He then looked out in front of him and saw, in the far distance, the sun's dim rays of dawn beaming into the heavens.

He slowly inched a foot down off the rail and when he turned around, there stood Joey, looking up at him. His face was dripping wet from the rain, his eyes red, and he had been crying.

For the longest time he and The Writer looked into each other's eyes, for the first time ever. Joey didn't know what to think when he saw those deep hazel eyes set upon him. Even from where he stood he could see his own reflection in those eyes full of pain and loss.

He took one step closer to him and The Writer stumbled down off the rail. He went for the pavement but Joey broke his fall. He held onto him as he went down, ashamed of what he was about to do. As he tried to get back up on his feet despite the agonizing soreness in his legs, he realized who was holding on to him tightly. Joey helped him up and started walking him back to the end of the bridge. They never said a word to each other. All the time he kept one arm around The Writer and watched his face. The Writer never looked at him again until they reached the end of the road.

The Writer collapsed on the side. Joey got down to him and asked him if he was hurting.

"I'm sore . . . I can't walk . . . it hurts."

Joey wiped his eyes and looked around. The search party had not even gotten halfway down the mountain yet. They were taking their time because of the rain, which was slacking off right now. Nate fired up another flare which stayed lit a bit longer now. Maybe if they know he's here and alive they'll come quicker, Joey thought.

"Listen, will you be alright here if I run and tell them I found you?"

He nodded.

"I'll be back, alright man? Or do you want me to stay with you?"

He shook his head and turned away from him. With that Joey took off down the road but came back a few seconds later. He got down to The Writer and hugged his neck, almost choking him. In one quick breath he gasped "I love you" and started running back up the road.

The Writer sat still for a moment as the words from Joey's lips sank into his heart and mind. He slowly laid down on the wet grass, waiting for his friend to return.

"He's down there!" Joey hollered as he ran to the first men he saw. "He lying down there next to the road. He's alive, thank God!" Immediately the men called back to the others what Joey said, and he ran to find Mama and Judy. The moment he told his mother she dropped her flashlight and started running. Judy took off after her and Lana and Dionne followed. Word spread like wildfire among everyone and it gave a surge to their adrenaline. The women in the group saw no need to stick in bundles so they scattered. Some cheered, others sighed in relief. Dozens took a moment to say 'Thank God' and took off. They were hollering and screaming to one another the glad news. Others kept asking where he was, but took the hint to just follow the crowd as it charged down the mountainside.

But the one thing nobody planned on was the mountainside getting steeper as it reached the road to the dam, as Joey found out earlier. Men started falling one by one. Women began to scream as they felt their feet slide out from under them. Everyone told each other to hold hands or find something to hang onto as they went down. Mama fell and rolled down into a fallen log. Judy got to her and helped her up but the drive to get to her only child made her body numb and immune to any injury she had. Lucille, the preacher, and his wife tried to make it down but Nate ordered them to follow him back to the road they first started out on that ended somewhere near the top of the mountain. He would have a jeep come up and take them down around the mountain to The Writer.

By now everyone was stumbling and falling. Some clung to branches for dear life and others, mostly men, just slid down as far as they could on their rear ends. Everywhere came hollering and shouting about where The Writer was and how steep the mountain had become. Men stopped to help the women down as best they could. Joey got to the road before any of them and looked all around him. In all the haste of discovering where The Writer was, they had taken a sharp turn coming down the mountain and Joey saw that when they finally got down to the road, everyone would be further away from the dam than he was when he got to The Writer earlier. He looked up towards the bridge and could see the lights on it. It looked to be about a thousand yards away by now. He would wait as long as he could for the first few to get down to the road so he could point them in the right direction.

The Writer lay still on his back, in the wet grass, the last droplets of the rainstorm falling innocently upon his sore body. One arm was on his chest and other lay out next to him. His eyes were still full of tears but the sobbing had stopped for now. He was looking at the heavens as they cleared, the stars slowly breaking out of the haze before the sun would outdo their gentle light. The last clouds were carried away by the wind as they broke up into weak threads. His mind was still centered on what he almost did, and the powerful grasp that was around him. His breathing was full of loose strands of wheezing. I wish I could sleep here, he thought. I'll sleep for days after this.

Another flare went up, this time shot into the air by Blade. When it exploded its white beam fell across his face. He inched his head around to see what it was and he saw a beautiful sight. There were dozens of white and yellow lights wobbling down the side of the mountain in the not-too-far distance. With them came voices. Whatever they were saying was inaudible, but it meant that there was some other form of life out here besides him and Joey.

He closed his eyes and lifted his hand to the sky, as if to touch the stars. In his mind, he was reaching for wherever Brute was right now, as if to pull him back, but he knew it wasn't possible. At least I can dream, he thought as he lowered it down. I love Joey, he thought, and he loves me. Oh God, he really said it. He loves me back! God, he actually said it . . . and he meant it!

The sudden joy of it made his eyes spill over again, this time for sheer happiness. He turned his head to the lights and saw that they were bunching up in a pile way up the road. They're too far away, he thought. I'm over here.

"Here, over here," he said, but it came out as no more than a whiney whisper. He rolled over onto his stomach as best he could but he could not raise his voice. How do I get them over here, he wondered. Then it hit him. He remembered what Brute taught him that day at the lake when they were discussing how to talk to a girl. The Writer, aching and hurting all over, drug himself up to the edge of the road where there was an old stump. He grabbed hold of it, propped himself up, rammed two fingers into his mouth, and let out the loudest whistle ever heard. It got the attention of those on the road and one by one they started coming down towards him. Men began hollering about the whistling and followed it.

The Writer kept whistling as best he could, tears streaming down his dirty face, watching them come one by one, with Joey in front.

CHAPTER FORTY-ONE

The sun was setting, and the sky flamed bright orange as Mama and Judy sat on the swing on the front porch.

"My son got a letter today," Mama said. "It's from the director of admissions at a college in Alabama. He's asking us to come visit sometime this summer."

"Really? Is it a Christian school?"

"Uh-huh. Pretty small campus. Everyone knows each other, and the letter raved about this social club called Zeta Eta Theta and its sister club called Alpha Alpha Alpha. Ironically their colors are orange and black and they have tigers and butterflies as their mascots."

"Mind if Joey and I tag along?"

"I was hoping you would. He says he heard about my son through some band that was on tour here in North Carolina a few weeks ago. They say they saw him dancing with Brute and won a trophy. Must've been a recruit of some sort."

Judy looked off down the road, watching for The Writer's friends to arrive at any moment. "I never knew The Writer had such skill. Seems he can master more than just a pen."

Mama looked down the road with Judy and clasped her hands together. "You know, for eighteen years I wondered, what would've happened if I hadn't taken that walk home alone from the store. When you think about it, none of this would've happened had I not done that. I wouldn't have what I have now had I not done that so long ago. Looks like God knew what He was doing even then."

"He always does," Judy said.

The Writer waddled calmly up the hillside to his spot under

the tree. The wind was sending waves across the tall grass, making it look as if he were walking through a golden brown ocean of water. His black coat whipped back behind him and his pen dangled at his chest. He came to the tree and leaned against it, looking off into the distance at the small town, and beyond it the mountains. He looked at them in deep wonder, thinking back at who created them millions of years ago with His own hands. A sense of peace settled over the entire region, a sensation he had not felt since he could not remember when.

He closed his eyes and let the feel of the moment overtake him. When he did, a memory shot into his mind. He recalled the moment he walked into the class he had with Joey and saw on his desk a small white box wrapped in red paper. He remembered looking at the gift tag on it and seeing Joey's scrawl on it. He looked up and saw Joey sitting at his desk, watching The Writer, wanting him to open it. After he did, he heard Joey's innocent response, "Is that alright?"

He opened his eyes and a tear ran down his face. The moment sent a surge of warmness through his whole body. He looked down at his shirt, thinking the pin was there, but it wasn't.

Oh no! I lost it! I lost the one thing that started our friendship! It's missing! He sat down on the stool and tried to think where he lost it. I hope Joey won't get mad when he sees it's not on me, he thought. He looked up and saw a bald eagle flying around the valley. Maybe that eagle has seen it, he thought. They have good eyes.

Back at the house, all of The Writer's friends had shown up to go bowling. It was the first time they'd been since the tournament and they were eager to polish up their skills. Mama had them come into the living room and see how it was redone after the attack incident. It was hard to imagine that just a little over a week ago, the windows were smashed and blood was all over the floor. It looked like a whole new room and Mama was relieved to see her house back the way it should be. The dogs were in a corner, happily munching away on the food Mama put down for them before they left for the bowling alley. There was a white cloth wrapped around their bodies and they would be taken off in a few weeks. All the cats were on the porch, waiting for Judy to feed them as well.

When Joey and Judy finally arrived it was time to go. Everyone piled out of the house and headed for the driveway. Joey was looking around for The Writer.

"I think he's up on the hill," Mama said. "Why don't you go get him down here?"

"Sure, I have something for him anyway." Mama let him out the backdoor in the kitchen and locked it. She watched him start up the hill for a moment then came away from the screen door. She locked the wooden one behind it and went into the living room. All was quiet now with everyone waiting in the yard to go. Judy, Elaine, and Jackie were discussing the sales that were going on at all the big stores and planning when to go. She could hear Annie and Blade having another silly argument and Lana and Dionne going off on each other's makeup. Nate just petted the cats, listening and giggling to what was being said all around him.

She walked into the living room and looked at the mantle, all aglow in orange light from outside. The trophies were sparkling with radiance as they always did. She got a closer look at each one and saw her son's name on each of them. A smile greeted each one as she looked at it, then seeing Brute's name she stopped and gently touched a finger over his name engraved in gold. Someday she would let her son go find him, but how and when she did not know just yet. So much had to be taken care of first, from the court date with Mrs. Moran to seeing what was to be done with Rusty and Kelly.

Then she came to the picture she took of The Writer and Joey in his bedroom the night before graduation. When she saw it she stopped and paused for a moment. There was something about it that made her pick it up, something unusual, something she never thought she'd ever see.

It was on her son.

On his face.

A smile.

She then remembered that the sunlight coming in the window that evening was so bright it blinded her, and she just hit the 'flash' button to get the picture taken. During that split second her son smiled, and she knew why.

All she had to do was look at who was standing next to him in the picture.

Anyone could see that Joey was one true thing in life for The Writer, as were his other friends, as well as the one they all simply knew as Brute.

But as for right now she was going bowling, with her best friend, and with her son's friends. She went out the front door, locked it, and waited for her son and his friend to come down from the hill.

The Writer watched the eagle soar through the sky without a care in the world. It looked so calm and serene with no worries, and he wondered if God wanted all of us to be like eagles, soaring without any worries that keep us grounded. He watched it soar off to the left, then make a sudden veer for the right. He watched it and turned his head to see where it was going. When he did he saw Joey coming up to him, with his right hand tightly clenched around something. The Writer walked up to him and Joey nearly ran towards him. He put his hand up to his face and opened it.

In it was the pin he'd lost. It had a new and stronger backing and looked good as new. The Writer carefully took it out of his hand and started to put it on. Instead, Joey took it from him and put it on his shirt himself.

"We're ready to go sir," he said, wrapping an arm around him and motioning for him to go ahead first down the hill. "We can't win without our captain."

The Writer took one last look at the eagle and saw that it was soaring away into the far distance out of sight.

And he waddled away . . . with his friend to go bowling.